Heart *of the*
COUNTRY

Also by Tricia Stringer

Queen of the Road
Right as Rain
Riverboat Point
Between the Vines
A Chance Of Stormy Weather

THE FLINDERS RANGES SERIES

Heart of the Country
Dust on the Horizon

Heart *of the*
COUNTRY

TRICIA STRINGER

First Published 2015
Fourth Australian Paperback Edition 2016
ISBN 9 781489228 284

HEART OF THE COUNTRY
© 2015 by Tricia Stringer
Australian Copyright 2015
New Zealand Copyright 2015

Published by
Harlequin Mira
An imprint of Harlequin Enterprises (Australia) Pty Ltd.
Level 13, 201 Elizabeth Street
SYDNEY NSW 2000
AUSTRALIA

Printed and bound in Australia by McPherson's Printing Group

MIX
Paper from
responsible sources
FSC® C001695

About the Author

Tricia Stringer grew up on a farm in country South Australia. A mother of three wonderful grown-up children and Nanna to two boys, Tricia now lives in the beautiful Copper Coast region with her husband, Daryl.

Most of Tricia's life so far has been spent in rural communities, as owner of a post office and bookshop, as a teacher and librarian, and now as a full-time writer. She loves travelling and exploring Australia's diverse communities and landscapes, and shares this passion for the country and its people through her stories. One of Tricia's rural romances, *Queen of the Road*, won the Romance Writers of Australia's Romantic Book of the Year award in 2013.

Heart of the Country is Tricia's fourth book with Harlequin.

www.triciastringer.com
www.facebook.com/triciastringerauthor
@tricia_stringer

For Daryl

Prologue

The ancient rock shimmered in the afternoon sun, absorbing and reflecting the heat as it had done for thousands of years. Above it, the sheer cliffs were dotted with the twisted forms of straggling gums and adorned with the stories of ancient humanity. Below it, the dark pool of permanent water rippled, hiding in its depths the primordial stones washed there from another time.

In the hollows and ledges around the edge of the pool, several men rested, their dark skins blending with the shadows created by overhanging rocks and towering gum trees. The group were conserving their energy for the final stage of their journey home.

Only one man moved: their leader, Yardu. He was high in a red gum, braced in the fork of the tree, and the stiff rush gripped firmly between his teeth was already threaded with several of the delicious fat grubs he relished. He inserted his barbed stick carefully into the last of the little tunnels then began to wiggle the fat delicacy out of its burrow. This one would be for his wife.

A loud crack echoed across the valley, followed by a scream. Yardu jerked and the grub slipped from the hook and bounced away down the smooth trunk. He grabbed at the tree. The cry had sounded like his wife's, but he was still a long walk from home.

He pushed his back hard against the branch behind him and listened. Perhaps his longing for her had conjured up her voice.

The cry came again, shouting rather than calling, then a scream he didn't recognise. It rippled down his spine. Perhaps an animal, though not one he'd heard before.

Yardu slipped his barbed hook safely into the pouch hanging from the band around his waist and, still gripping the rush between his teeth, he stretched his toes to find the first notch below him. A distant bang reverberated through the trees and this time the men below him must have heard it. They called to each other and to him uneasily. It had been a sharp crack, like a gum branch makes when it suddenly drops after long periods of dry, but this sound was too loud for that, and had echoed to his ears from a distance.

Yardu slipped and slithered down the tree. Before his feet reached the ground his brothers and uncles began talking at once. He held up a hand. He wasn't the oldest of the group but he had earned their respect; they stopped. None of them spoke as he stowed the grubs in his bag. They would eat them later.

"We must go," he said. He walked away from the waterhole, around the edge of the ridge and into the valley towards home. Down in the bush no more strange noises reached his ears, but the silence didn't ease the dread in Yardu's chest.

One

1846

The biting wind tugged at Thomas Baker's hat as he turned the corner. He pressed it tightly to his head with his hand and bent into the wind. Another miserable day in Adelaide but he would not be deterred from his purpose. He kept to the wooden palings that served as a footpath in front of the assorted stone buildings that made up Hindley Street. Most were single storey, and on this part of the street there were no verandahs. The few people brave enough to be out huddled against the cold with bowed heads and moved quickly. Horses and carts churned along the muddy street. Thomas hunched his shoulders and pulled his coat tighter against the chill, thankful at least that he wasn't wielding a shovel trying to keep the road passable.

He came to a stop in front of a white picket fence and peered up at the sign suspended from a wooden post. The Black Bull Hotel was written in bold lettering and beside it someone had painted a picture of a serene-looking bull. This was the place. He pushed open the gate. Below the name of the hotel there were more words in smaller print.

The bull is tame, so fear him not, so long as you can pay your shot.
When money's gone and credit's bad, that's what makes the bull
go mad.

The warning in the words fitted the brooding appearance of
the grey stone establishment. A short sharp shower of rain propelled him forward. He shook the drops from his coat and ducked
his head through the door.

Inside the hotel, he stopped and peered through the smoky air
and was pleased to see a fire flickering in the grate. A bar ran the
length of the large rectangular room and several rough tables and
chairs were scattered along the opposite wall. Most of the occupants
stood, crowding the space in front of the bar. They were a rough-
looking lot; from their dress they were mainly sailors and bushmen.

Raucous laughter and a jaunty female voice drew his gaze to
the bar. A barmaid was flirting with the men in front of her as
she set down their drinks. She glanced in his direction, but he
looked away. He had no intention of buying a drink. With any
luck he could conduct his business and be on his way quickly. He
sought one man in particular but he could see no-one who met
the basic description he'd been given. He squeezed behind two
sailors arguing about whose turn it was to buy the next drink.
One of them swayed and someone knocked hard against him.
Men complained around him. He collided with a chair.

"Steady up."

"Beg your pardon, sir." Thomas dipped his head to the seated man
he'd almost fallen over. Even though his clothes were unlike any
Thomas had seen a gentleman wear, the tone of the man's voice and
his stature put him a cut above the rest of the patrons. The man gave
him a good look then went back to eating the food in front of him.

Thomas edged into the corner. The sight of the gentleman's
steaming bowl reminded him he'd eaten nothing since the pitiful

porridge he'd been given at his lodgings that morning. He eased off his damp outer garment and hooked it over the back of the chair. At least from here he could better inspect those at the bar and he would see anyone who came in the door.

Slowly the warmth of the room thawed him. So far the fourteen grey, damp days he'd passed in Adelaide had done little but remind him of the miserable cold of England. They had shown no signs of producing the fresh start his father had predicted. But today would be different. The fledgling hope that had been with him as he stepped ashore all those weeks back, and which had gradually ebbed away, was strong in his chest again. Today was the start of something new.

A pot of ale hit the table in front of him with a thud. He lifted his eyes to those of the barmaid. She leaned in. He pulled his head back from the smell of sour beer and sweat.

"If you're going to sit here you have to buy a drink."

The lilt of her Irish voice reminded him of the girl who'd been the cook's assistant back home, but the barmaid was nothing like Bernadette, who'd made his face heat with her flirting. There were deep lines around this woman's eyes and mouth and her cheeks were ruddy. From across the room it had looked like a youthful glow but now he could see the skin was rough and the glow probably the product of her employer's slops.

"No, thank you." He frowned at her. "I don't want it."

"This is a pub. Everyone wants it." She rolled her eyes and pushed her barely covered bosom closer. "Especially a good-looking feller like you."

Thomas started to rise but the barmaid put a hand on his chest and pushed him back.

"Sure, you've enough for one drink."

He looked over her shoulder through a gap in the crowd to the bar, where the bartender was watching them intently. The woman was right: if he was going to sit here any longer he needed a drink or he'd draw more attention to himself than he wanted.

He slipped a hand into his pocket for his money pouch. The pocket was empty. He patted his pants and reached for his jacket. No pouch there either. He must have left it in his trunk when he repacked it that morning. "I don't have my pouch."

"Cut the games." The barmaid fixed him with her small round eyes. "Pay for your ale or leave."

Thomas hesitated. He recalled the menacing words painted on the sign outside. He had notes concealed inside his shirt but he was reluctant to reveal them here.

A large hand appeared between them and slapped some coins on the rough wooden surface. Thomas looked up into the eyes of the gentleman from the next table. In spite of his clean-shaven face he had a rugged appearance, but none of that changed Thomas's earlier impression that he had the air of a gentleman.

"I'll shout the gentleman; and one more for me thank you, Mary," the man said.

Before Thomas could protest Mary had scooped up the coins. "Thank you, Mr Browne." She did a small bob and was gone, weaving skilfully through the crowd to the bar.

Thomas studied the man who'd come to his aid. "You're Mr Browne?" he said.

The man's sharp gaze locked on Thomas. "That's me. Who are you?"

"Thomas Baker. I've come about the job. I'm sorry I didn't recognise you. I was told you had long hair and a beard."

Mr Browne gave a hearty laugh. "I did until this morning. I've been out of town a long time with only sheep for company. I've just come from the barber shop." He studied Thomas. "You're early, and not what I was expecting."

"I can work as hard as any man." Thomas pulled back his shoulders and lifted his head as the older man looked him over. This was not how he'd intended to approach his prospective employer.

"Well, Thomas, since we're sharing a drink, is it all right if I move myself to your table?"

Before he could answer, Mr Browne took up his bowl and moved it across, then shifted his large frame into the chair alongside. The smell of some kind of stew reached Thomas's nostrils. His mouth watered and his eyes were drawn to the bowl.

Another pot of ale appeared at the table.

"Mary, bring us another bowl of whatever this is." Mr Browne waved his hand over his food and dropped more coins on the table.

"It's Irish stew, Mr Browne, me old mam's recipe."

"Whatever it is, we'll have another for my new friend."

Once again Thomas began to protest but Mary had taken the coins and gone.

"You look like you could do with a good feed."

"It's very kind of you, Mr Browne, but –"

"The name's Andrew James Browne. People call me AJ." He reached out and gripped Thomas's hand in a firm shake. His face crinkled into a smile then he pointed to his bowl. "You'll be hard pressed to find much mutton in the stew. Mostly potatoes and onion, but it's tasty all the same."

"Thank you. I'm not sure how I can repay your kindness."

"It's not necessary."

Thomas sat back quickly as Mary plonked a bowl of stew in front of him. His stomach rumbled in anticipation.

"Eat your fill." A deep chuckle gurgled from AJ's throat and he ate from his own bowl.

Thomas did the same, and by the time he'd swallowed the last mouthful the stew had warmed his insides and the ale had warmed his blood.

AJ sat back and folded his arms across his broad chest. "So Thomas Baker. What brings you to the new colony of South Australia?"

"It was my father's idea originally." Thomas paused, not sure how much of his story he should tell his prospective employer. "He worked back in England managing a farm. After my mother died he decided we should make a new start."

"I'm sorry for you loss. What kind of work are you and your father looking for or has he already found employment?"

Thomas hesitated. "My father died aboard ship on the way here."

The sharp gaze that studied Thomas softened. "Once more, I am sorry," AJ said.

Thomas clenched his jaw. The promise of a new start had been the only thing to brighten their days since his mother's death. They'd heard Australia was a wonderful new land with plenty of work and money to be made. His father had taken their meagre savings and accepted cheap passage to South Australia but he had not taken to ship life, succumbing to constant sea sickness which had finally killed him just before they'd reached Adelaide. For a moment, Thomas was transported to his father's burial and the memory of the weighted shroud as it slid from the board and plunged into the rough ocean below. The mournful tolling of the bell marked the moment, as Thomas braced himself against the railing, gusts of wind ripping at his coat and wailing through the rigging. The waves had swallowed his father's body, and slammed against the wooden hull.

He took a deep breath. Their employers, the Dowlings, had made a mockery of his father's decision, called them both fools as they'd left and warned them not to come crawling back looking for handouts. Perhaps the Dowlings had been right ... Now there was only Thomas, the last of their money hidden inside his shirt, and the two trunks of basic items they'd brought with them.

"Have you worked before with animals?" AJ's question cut into Thomas's thoughts.

He swallowed his grief once more and gave his full attention to the man opposite. "Yes. The farm I worked on had sheep and there were cows to be milked. We also helped with the horses."

AJ studied him closely. "You're not quite what I was expecting."

Thomas felt as if his deception was written all over his face. His job at the Dowlings had been footman. He'd only assisted his father in his rare moments of spare time.

"In what way?"

"I was hoping for someone more robust."

"I was very sea sick on the trip out," Thomas said quickly. "I've lost weight but I'm strong." He hoped the good Lord would forgive him his lies but he needed this job and after the labouring work of the last few weeks he had certainly built up some strength. The rain that had fallen on his arrival in South Australia had hardly let up and the streets of Adelaide had turned to slush. He'd been given rough lodgings in Emigration Square and in return he'd been sent to work with a few other men. No sooner had they shovelled and scraped the roads into a traversable surface than it rained again and a fresh lot of horses and drays passed by, causing the ruts and pot holes to return.

AJ pursed his lips and drew a watch from his top pocket. He opened it, peered at the face, then snapped it shut. "I'm sorry for all that's befallen you, Thomas, but I don't know if you're suited to my needs."

Thomas drew himself up. "I am quite used to hard work if that's what bothers you."

"Rest assured," AJ reached across and gave him a firm pat on the shoulder, "I didn't take you as a man not prepared to work for his living. I was hoping for someone with a little more experience. There were a couple of men interested."

Thomas held AJ's gaze. He could see the older man was weighing something up.

"Whatever the work is, I am sure I am up to it," Thomas said.

AJ studied him a moment longer then his face relaxed into a smile. "You remind me of myself ten years ago. I came to Australia in similar circumstances, although not orphaned, I had only the clothes on my back and little money. I learned as I went. Hard work has stood me well." He leaned forward and the smile dropped from his face. "I'll tell you what I need, Thomas Baker. You may well change your mind once you've heard me out."

Thomas recalled his father had used nearly the same words before he'd told of his plan to leave England. He needed to do this, not only for himself but for his father. He pulled back his shoulders and clasped his hands firmly together.

"I don't believe I will, Mr Browne."

"Very well. There's plenty to be made from this land if you are prepared to work. I have property in the north and I've stocked it with three thousand sheep. It's rugged country. Water's not so abundant and it's no place for the faint hearted. There are wild dogs up there and there's also been trouble with the natives. In spite of that the sheep don't need shepherding as you would know it in England." AJ leaned closer. "I have other land to see to and I need an overseer."

The word hung in the air between them.

Finally Thomas spoke. "So you would want me to be your overseer?"

"I need someone reliable. It's no easy job. I've left one shepherd up there, a redheaded Scot with a quick temper. McKenzie's his name but he's little more than useless when left to his own devices. He needs a master."

Thomas held Mr Browne's look across the table. He was a footman. What did he know about shepherding in the bush of South Australia?

"So now you know," AJ said. "I need a man I can trust. I am in a hurry but I can wait for the others." He paused. "Unless you believe you could be that man."

Thomas swallowed his doubts. "Will there be some guidance?" he asked.

"You seem a bright enough fellow to me. McKenzie knows sheep; you'll learn from him. He's just not what I call reliable." AJ lowered his voice. "I'll pay you sixty pounds a year."

Thomas's reply died in his throat. That was a decent sum of money. It would come with a lot of hard work but he had nothing to lose and he needed the experience a job like this would give him.

AJ was watching him closely. "I'll loan you the money to buy a horse and saddle. If you do well, I'll increase your salary each year."

Thomas's mind raced as he calculated the income. Maybe he could make enough to get his own place one day. His father would have been proud. "It's a good offer, Mr Browne."

"Call me AJ." The older man reached his hand across the space between them. "Do we have a deal?"

Thomas hesitated then thrust his own into the firm grip of his new employer. With not much to lose and a lot to gain, he felt a surge of optimism.

"Well done, Thomas. It's a good opportunity I'm offering you. It won't be a ride in your English countryside but I'm sure you're up to it. Come on." AJ rose to his feet. "No need to wait around here any longer. There's a lot to organise. We might as well make a start."

Thomas reached for his jacket. No longer would he have to wield a shovel in the endless job of keeping Adelaide's streets passable. He would still be working for someone else but for a good wage and AJ was already proving to be a most agreeable employer. Outside, the heavy clouds had lifted and broken apart. Sunlight reached his patch of the street. Thomas was happy to take that as a sign his life was improving. He pushed his battered hat firmly onto his head and strode purposefully after Mr Browne.

Two

Septimus Wiltshire crawled out from under his wagon. He stretched his arms high then wide, extending his tall frame after a night in the cramped hollow. The damp mist clung to him and shrouded the surrounding bush in its veil. He stood still and listened. The soft snort of Clover, his horse, tethered beyond the wagon, was the only sound. Not even any birds yet. He swept a dark lock of hair from his face and peered into the shadows of the pre-dawn gloom. Nothing. He shrugged his shoulders then stretched again. Maybe it was the cold that had woken him rather than a noise.

Hoofbeats echoed behind him then stopped. He turned on silent feet, keeping his back to his wagon. The place he'd chosen for his overnight camp wasn't far from the road that ran from Adelaide to the port. He knew well enough the types who might be afoot at this hour. He eased down, picked up a thick branch and gripped it with both hands.

Clover gave another snort. A short whicker echoed in return. The hoofbeats came closer and a large shape loomed out of the mist. Septimus lowered his weapon. The horse was riderless. It had a bridle with a short piece of frayed rope hanging from it but no saddle. Clover snorted and shifted behind the wagon.

"Easy." Septimus hoped to reassure both beasts. The newcomer pricked its ears and lifted its head.

"Are you lost, my beauty?" He kept his tone low and took a tentative step, offering his upturned palm.

The horse eyeballed his hand then gave a small toss of its head.

"Where's your master?"

Septimus cast a look over the horse then behind it. Whoever had lost this magnificent animal would surely be searching for it. He took another step and reached forward. The horse watched him closely but didn't shift. Septimus gripped the rope.

"There you are my beauty, safe now."

The elegant creature lifted its head but didn't pull away as he stroked its neck.

"You were lost but now you're found. Septimus will look after you."

He ran his hand down the horse's shoulder then along its back to its flank. It was a fine creature. He was already imagining how much he could get for it. More money than he made in a month of selling his lotions and potions. He led the horse to the wagon and secured it with another piece of rope then hurried to his campfire.

The small fire he'd made to boil his billy the night before was cold. He scraped bark and leaves from the dry area under the wagon and soon had flames flickering. His stomach rumbled and he went in search of the last of his bread. He'd scrounged a loaf from a baker in exchange for a couple of hair-restorer pills. The baker had very little hair left on his head but Septimus was hopeful the two pills and his convincing talk would be enough to encourage the man to buy a whole bottle today.

While he was at the food bag he dug out the last shrivelled carrot, pilfered from a garden, and broke it in two. He gave the smallest piece to his faithful Clover and the rest to the prize beauty tethered to the back of the wagon. The urge to run his hand over the animal's fine rump was too great to resist. In the sunlight just beginning to filter through the trees, he could see no distinctive markings. It would be easy to find a buyer for this fine beast.

"Perhaps I should name you Treasure," he murmured and patted its neck again. "With the profits from your sale, I can buy a range of wares."

Septimus left the horse and returned to his fire, his mind racing with possibilities. South Australia was the land of opportunity and Septimus was an opportunist. There were many settlers spreading out into the country beyond Adelaide. They were isolated and in need of supplies. He would have to move swiftly; find someone to buy the horse, stock his wagon and move on.

He warmed his hands over the flames and contemplated the money the horse would bring.

"Steady up, Septimus," he muttered. "You need a strong plan." It might not be his usual form of theft but this mission was tinged with danger all the same. He squatted down to think it through.

Just a few hours later he hovered outside the Horse Bazaar. He'd dressed in his only set of fine clothes for the occasion. Under his long black jacket he wore a green patterned waistcoat over a white shirt. A neatly tied cravat sat around his neck and a broad-brimmed black hat sat atop his head. Not only did he want to give the impression he was indeed the owner of the horse, he wouldn't be easily recognised by the young girl who lived in the whore house nearby.

He'd bedded Harriet several times in the stables at the back of the Horse Bazaar before discovering that she was younger than she appeared. She wasn't worth losing his newly gained freedom over. He'd served out his time in New South Wales and now he was a free man with a fresh start in South Australia. No one here knew his history or anything about him and that's the way he planned to keep it. He liked his women unsullied and Harriet had been a virgin. A pity to give up the pleasures of her body but he didn't want some young whore, nor the old madam who kept her, tripping him up.

He glanced around. It was early yet – the auctions weren't due to start for another hour. He'd tethered Treasure a way off in the bush as he certainly couldn't sell her in the bazaar itself. There was plenty of activity around him: there were men bringing in horses and other men inspecting them, their deep voices mingled with the gentler tones of the few women who had braved the early hour to accompany them. He was looking for someone more gullible.

"Oy! Watch it."

Septimus twisted at the loud shout. His eyes widened. He dipped his head and tugged down the brim of his hat. The lad who'd shouted was leading a horse with each hand. A man had been in his way … a young man Septimus summed up immediately as a new chum, wet behind the ears. From below the brim of his hat he watched as the younger man stepped over a pile of horse dung still steaming in the cool air, adjusted his grip on the new saddle he carried and walked further into the bazaar. Septimus followed a short distance behind.

"Take a look at this one, sir." A man beckoned. "He only needs a bit of feed and he'll do you proud."

Septimus watched as his target looked from the man to the poor bag of bones he was tending and shook his head. At least the new chum seemed capable of recognising sorry horseflesh. After wandering a little further into the bazaar the fellow suddenly hefted the saddle higher and turned back. Septimus dodged out of the way between two horses then followed his mark at a safe distance.

In a clearing at the end of a lane, the fellow stopped beside a loaded bullock dray. Septimus watched from the corner of a building. He wasn't comfortable here, so close to the madam and her young trap, Harriet. If he hadn't been certain he'd found the buyer for his horse, he'd be on his way.

The fellow lowered the saddle to the ground next to a large trunk. He lifted the lid and peered inside. He reached into the trunk and lifted out a silver hairbrush, turned it over in his hands and stared at it a moment, then suddenly dropped it back into the trunk and lowered the lid.

He stood back and straightened his shoulders. He was dressed in the same brown trousers, white shirt and brown coat as you would see on half the men around; there was nothing special about him, though he was tall and Septimus conceded he emanated a look of strength. He was perhaps in his early twenties, so a good ten years younger. The sound of the bazaar grew louder as the auction began. A look of determination spread across the fellow's face as he turned to look in that direction. He took a deep breath, squared his shoulders and stepped away from the dray.

Perhaps he wouldn't be so easily fooled but it was now or never. Septimus moved directly into his path and was struck by the new chum's shoulder. "Careful there," he groaned. The collision hadn't been forceful but he staggered back against a fence as if it had.

"I beg your pardon, sir." The younger man reached out a hand to steady him. "I wasn't watching where I was going."

Septimus remained doubled over. "Knocked the breath out of me, that's all," he wheezed.

"Would you like to sit?" The man cast a hand towards the trunk beside the dray.

"That's very kind."

Septimus hobbled forward, leaning slightly on the offered arm, and sat himself down.

"Will you be all right?"

"Just need to get my breath back," Septimus gasped.

"I should have taken more care."

"No harm done." He brushed at the arm of his jacket and made sure his hat was pulled low on his head, casting a shadow over his face.

"Thank you for your generosity."

"It was an accident. No need for people to be unsociable on such a fine day." Septimus turned his lips up in a smile and ran a finger along his pencil-thin moustache. He glanced into the deep brown eyes studying him carefully.

"Since we've run into each other perhaps we should introduce ourselves. My name is Seth Whitby." It slipped off his tongue easily. He'd needed an alias several times before this. He had spent a lot of time perfecting the fine manners and speech patterns of a gentleman.

"Thomas Baker." He shook Septimus's hand in a firm grip. "If you're sure you are well, I must be on my way, Mr Whitby. Once again I must apologise for my clumsiness. I'm afraid my mind was on other matters."

Septimus continued to grip his hand. "It must be important business that has you in such a rush."

"I have a new job." He slipped his hand out of the grip. "I require a good horse."

"Then you are in the right place," Septimus said and stood up.

"Yes." Thomas nodded in the direction of the bazaar. "I've looked at a couple of fine animals here. It is my hope to secure one of them at a good price."

Septimus flung out his hands. "Well, Thomas, isn't that amazing? We are not only moving in opposite directions but have opposite duties today."

Thomas hesitated. "What do you mean?"

"Only that I am about to head out bush and I must get my horse ready for sale." Septimus put one hand to his chest. "Reluctantly, of course, but it is surplus to my needs. I am in a hurry to be gone and it appears I am too late to put my fine animal into today's auction."

"And I have held you up." Once again Thomas started to leave.

"But perhaps …" Septimus laid a hand on his arm. Thomas was slightly taller but Septimus stared directly into his eyes. A frown crinkled the other man's forehead. Septimus slid his gaze away.

"Yes?" Thomas asked.

"Well it's just that – maybe our accidental meeting could be of benefit to both of us."

"How so?" Thomas turned slightly at the loud call of the auction beginning.

Septimus leaned in closer. "We are both anxious to be on our way. You need a good horse and I have one to sell. If I wait for the next bazaar I will be held up from my departure by a few days and time is money."

"I'm not sure I …"

Septimus could see Thomas was torn between the proposition and the sound of the auction starting without him.

"Hear me out. You have my word as a gentleman. The horse is an excellent animal. As good if not better than anything on auction today, and he's used to the bush. I need to be on my way so I am prepared to sell him below the price I could have got at the bazaar."

Thomas hesitated.

"I have him tethered nearby. And as I'm a desperate man and you seem like a genuine fellow," Septimus lowered his voice, "you could take him off my hands for, let's say, fifteen pounds."

He tipped his face so the brim of his hat kept the shadow across his face, but his eyes held Thomas's gaze.

"I'm not sure." Thomas said. "I'd need to see the horse."

"Of course. He's not far from here." Septimus placed his hand on Thomas's shoulder. "Come with me now and if you like him he will be yours immediately."

The younger man looked back at his dray attached to the bullocks.

"We won't be long," Septimus said.

"It's the trunk. I was going to find somewhere to store it. The things inside will be no use to me on the road."

Septimus eyed the trunk. No doubt half of what it contained was worthless but he had seen the silver hairbrush. "I may be able to help you there as well," he said, once more smoothing his moustache with the tip of his finger. "Like you, I have things I don't need on the road. There's a woman lives quite near here, my landlady, looks after a few items for me. I could add your trunk to mine."

Septimus ran a caressing hand over the trunk. Landlady was a generous name for Mabel, though of course he wouldn't be taking Mr Baker's trunk anywhere near the brothel and its trouble-some inmates. "She charges." He smiled. "But if you add another pound to the purchase of the horse I am sure I can cover it. You'll be gone a year or more, I am assuming?"

"To tell the truth I don't know when I'll be back."

"That's settled then," Seth said. "I'll come back for it once we've dealt with the horse."

Thomas kept looking at the trunk. Once more there was hesitation.

"We'd better move quickly now. There's a lot to do and I want to be on my way by midday, as I'm sure you do too." Seth put a guiding hand on the younger man's shoulder and pointed towards the street. "The horse is out along this way. Bring your saddle."

He strode off. A quick glance over his shoulder saw Thomas following him. Septimus felt the familiar warmth of success spread through his body. He had hooked his man, and now it was simply a matter of concluding their business, coming back for the trunk and leaving Adelaide for the bush.

Three

Harriet crawled out from under the dray and sat on the trunk watching the place where the two men had disappeared into the bush. For a moment there she had thought the good-looking stranger must have seen her. He kept staring towards her hiding place, but now she realised it was the trunk that had his attention.

Septimus hadn't seen her either. She had been feeding the chickens when she'd seen him pass by. He was walking strangely; dodging along fences, peering round corners, so she decided to follow him. When she realised he was watching the tall stranger, she'd edged her way around behind and under the dray to see what held his interest.

She hadn't seen Septimus for weeks but for a while he'd been her lover. He used to have an old trunk stored in Mabel's stable and he came across Harriet there one day. She saw he was a chance at escape from the whoring life she knew was laid out in front of her. Harriet knew Mabel was saving her for the right well-paying gentleman; someone who wanted a young, untouched woman. It was nearly her birthday, so it wouldn't be much longer. She decided to make her own destiny.

She'd learned a lot from observing the other women at their work. She recognised the lust in Septimus's eyes when he realised she was a virgin. He was aroused by the fact he was her first and only lover. He had been gentle with her and even paid her a few coins. Then he became a regular, secret visitor. Harriet got to know his body and what he liked done to it. He was much older than her and so handsome with his thick dark hair and piercing grey eyes that mesmerised her. She grew besotted with him. Then one day she let slip her true age. She was only thirteen, soon to be fourteen. She had a body that was developed beyond its years and Septimus had made the most of it, but since he'd discovered her age he hadn't come back.

That had been a few weeks earlier and she hadn't seen him again until this morning. He'd been in such a hurry and with the new coat and the hat pulled down over his head, she'd nearly not recognised him.

Now she was puzzled by what she'd heard. Was he Septimus or Seth? She didn't know all his business but she was pretty sure the only horse he had was the stock horse that pulled his wagon. The way he'd been speaking it was as if he'd owned this other horse a long time.

She'd also seen the crash between the two men. Septimus had sidestepped into Thomas whoever he was, she hadn't caught his last name, and yet he had let the fellow believe the accident had been his fault.

Harriet leaned her head back against the dray. The trunk beneath her was warm. She closed her eyes, loosened her shawl and wiggled her bare toes in the grass. She turned her face to the sun and inhaled deeply. The air was so much fresher away from the stinking house, where the harlots' cajoling and the men's gratification filled her ears. Wet weather had kept them all inside for so long it was a joy to escape.

Harriet shuddered and pulled her dirty shawl back around her breasts. Thankfully she was young; that and Mabel's promise to

Harriet's dying mother meant she hadn't been put to work in the bedrooms yet, but it was only a matter of time. Of course Mabel didn't know about Harriet's liaisons with Septimus – the red-cheeked madam would carry on like a headless chook if she were to find out. Harriet kept quiet and earned her keep, cleaning up after the other women and helping in the kitchen.

"Can you see me now, Mother?" she murmured. "What must you think?"

She felt a pang of loss for her mother. Harriet's childhood had been a happy one. She'd been well fed and loved by both her parents, even though her handsome father had been rarely at home. Their little cottage on the edge of the bush near Port Phillip had been filled with laughter and happiness and even more so when he was with them. It had naturally all fallen apart when her father's real wife had arrived from England. Harriet discovered her mother was her father's mistress and, as the result of their union, she was a bastard. Her father had been forced to send them away or lose the money his wife's family had given him to set up a new life in Australia. He was otherwise penniless.

They had travelled to Adelaide but his promise to follow was never kept, forcing them to take refuge at Mabel's when Harriet's mother, with poor sight from failing eyes, was unable to find other work. The meagre purse of money they had left with was soon gone. They had been at Mabel's little time at all when she had taken sick and died. It took another year for Harriet's hope that her father would come for her to be totally destroyed. Mabel and her whores were her only family now.

A wave of longing for the cossetted life she had lost swept over her. No point in that. She swallowed hard and wrapped her arms around herself. Somehow she had to make a change. Now that she knew Septimus was still around she would work out some way to lure him back. He was her ticket out of her predicament and besides, she missed him and what he did to her body. She knew Mabel would soon expect a greater return for her charity.

"That's not for me," Harriet muttered. "I'm not going to live my days flat on my back in a whore house."

She was startled from her reverie by a sudden movement beside her. She didn't have a chance to turn before rough hands grabbed her, one on her breast and one on her mouth. She gasped in some air through the dirty fingers and tasted mud. She struggled but someone had her firmly in his grip. Bile rose in her throat as she sniffed in a breath and the overwhelming smell of pigs engulfed her. Both her arms were pinned to her sides. She kicked with her feet as the man dragged her backwards, behind the dray. She wriggled and twisted. The arm around her body gripped tighter, squeezing the air from her lungs, forcing her to inhale another sickening breath.

The sound of pigs grew louder. Harriet realised she was being dragged behind the animal yards. The man pulled her through a low door into the dark. She almost choked on the stench. Squeals erupted around them. She cringed in disgust. They were in a pig shed and she was being held by the great oaf who tended the pigs. He was a giant of a man though barely out of his teens. 'Pig Boy' they called him. He never spoke even when the whores made lewd remarks implying that the thing in his pants didn't match the size of the rest of him. No amount of goading extracted a sound from his lips. He would just look at them through blank hooded eyes.

She prised her lips apart and tried to bite his fingers. He let go the arm that was wrapped around her and smacked her across the side of her head. For a moment she saw stars and the sound of the pigs was replaced by a ringing in her ears.

He dropped the hand from her mouth and pushed her back against the wall. Her head hit the wooden beam. Once again she almost lost consciousness.

Her attacker muttered some words, the sounds thick and guttural. Harriet registered vague surprise.

"You my woman," he garbled and this time she understood.

"No, I'm only a girl." Her voice came out as a whimper, lost in the sounds of the pigs.

The shawl was dragged from her shoulders. His face loomed closer, contorted into a terrifying leer. "Big diddleys."

Once more Harriet understood the guttural sounds. Her heart hammered in her chest. She watched a dribble of saliva slip from the corner of his mouth and pool on his chin. The filthy oaf grabbed her breasts. A jolt of pain forced a shriek from her throat. He pressed his body hard against her. His erection left her in no doubt that what was in his pants was indeed in proportion to the rest of his giant body.

Tears rolled down her cheeks. This couldn't be happening. She'd seen all too closely the results of a customer's violent abuse of one of Mabel's whores. The girl hadn't been able to walk for a week, let alone work. Harriet shuddered. Her young body had only known Septimus's lusty but careful attention.

Pig Boy eased away from her and put a hand to his belt. This couldn't happen. Not to her. Harriet was sure she was destined for better things. She stiffened and pushed with all her might, but he flung her aside. Her scream was lost in the cacophony of noise made by the pigs and cut short as her head banged on the muck-covered ground.

Four

Thomas finished strapping the saddle and ran a hand over the glossy hair on the horse's neck. Pride swelled inside him.

"You and I are going to get along fine, Treasure," he murmured into the gelding's ear.

That was what Seth had called the horse and Thomas saw no need to change the name. Treasure suited the fine animal and a treasure he was, much better than Thomas had expected he'd be able to get and at a very reasonable price.

Yesterday his new employer had explained the job and the journey that would take Thomas to the northern property called Penakie. The bullock dray was loaded with provisions and all that was needed today was for Thomas to buy a horse and his own kit. Once again AJ had generously offered a small loan towards these expenses and this morning had directed Thomas to the Horse Bazaar.

The enormity of the decision had overwhelmed him as he moved among the animals about to be auctioned. There were several mounts he believed would serve him well but they were likely to go for a decent penny.

It had been most fortuitous to literally bump into Seth Whitby. Thomas noted straight away the sharpness of his grey eyes and the neatness of his moustache. There was also the strong smell of something spicy. Seth was clearly a gentleman already making his mark on the business life of Adelaide.

The offer Seth made was a good one. Thomas had thought he would have to pay as much as twenty pounds to get the kind of horse he would need. They'd done the deal quickly and agreed to meet in an hour back at Thomas's dray to take the trunk to Seth's landlady.

Thomas mounted the horse and wove through the trees to the road, where he tried to avoid the deep ruts made by wagons. He smiled. At least it would no longer be his job to try to keep the streets passable. The traffic both on horse and on foot grew thicker. Most of Adelaide was out making the best of the sunshine. Ladies carried parasols, children jumped the last of the muddy puddles and a dog chased a bird across the road in front of him but Treasure didn't falter.

Thomas felt a building sense of anticipation. A new job and a new horse! As he drew level with the low verandah of the general store he pulled up and dismounted. He had an idea he'd buy himself a broad-brimmed hat like AJ's. His boots echoed on the wooden floor. The storekeeper turned from the two ladies he was helping and looked Thomas up and down.

"I'll be with you in a moment, sir," the man said.

Thomas studied a shelf of hats. Behind him the two women were discussing the qualities of the fabrics spread on the counter before them. He selected a hat with a broad brim and put it on his head. It felt stiff and awkward. Thomas imagined it would blow off at the first puff of wind.

"What purpose do you require the hat for, sir?"

The shopkeeper had left the women to their inspecting and had come to stand beside him.

"I'm going to work in the bush." Thomas returned the hat to its place. "An overseer on a sheep property."

"In that case may I suggest this one, sir?" The storekeeper selected a light brown hat and offered it to Thomas. "It's made of a softer felt, so it moulds to your head, and the wide brim will give you protection from the sun and the weather. Most suited to a man of your profession."

The hat fit snuggly and was comfortable. He glimpsed the younger of the two women studying him. He noted her pink cheeks, fair hair and nipped-in waist. He was both uncomfortable and intrigued by her scrutiny. The women aboard ship had been married and he'd had little chance to make the acquaintance of any young ladies since his arrival. Where he was going there'd be even less chance. There would be plenty of work to keep him busy.

"I'll take it," he said.

The hat helped give him confidence to follow his new occupation but he really didn't have time to waste. He conducted his business swiftly, aware of the continued gaze of the young woman.

Thomas bid the shopkeeper farewell and left the shop, in a hurry to be on his way.

He shoved the new hat firmly back on his head and took Treasure's reins.

Suddenly a voice shouted across the crowded street. "That's my horse."

Like those around him, Thomas looked in the direction of the voice but a buggy bounced past and there was no one to be seen. Thomas turned back to Treasure.

"I said that's my horse, you thief."

Thomas looked around again as a man in a top hat and a green velvet coat strode across the now clear street towards him. There were no other horses nearby. Thomas looked at Treasure then back at the red-faced man as he came to a stop and crossed his arms over his rounded stomach.

Thomas frowned. "Are you speaking to me, sir?"

"You are the one with my horse," the man growled and pro-ceeded to run his hand down Treasure's flank.

"This is my horse."

"Your horse be damned. I'm Charles Bayne and I've had this horse for three years. I know my own animal."

The horse lifted his head and snickered.

"There, there, Gideon," the man soothed. "You're safe now."

"There must be some mistake." Thomas glared down at his accuser, who was a good head shorter. "I have just paid good money for this horse."

A group of people began to gather.

"Need help, Mr Bayne?" One of the bystanders stepped forward and grabbed Thomas by the arm.

"Thanks, Jim."

Thomas wrenched his arm from Jim's tight grip and his new hat was knocked from his head in the scuffle.

"I bought this horse this morning," he said and bent to pick up his hat.

"Who did you buy it from?" Bayne sneered.

"Where's your bill of sale?" Jim's fingers poked Thomas in the chest.

He thought back over the deal he'd done with Seth. The money had been counted out and handed over but Seth had been in such a hurry to get on, Thomas hadn't thought beyond saddling the horse and setting off on his own journey.

"I don't have one but I am meeting the previous owner of this horse back at my dray." Thomas pushed Jim's stabbing hand away and turned back to Bayne. "You can ask him yourself."

"What's going on here, Mr Bayne?" A constable made his way through the crowd of eager onlookers.

"Arrest this horse thief," Bayne said and waved an arm at Thomas.

The constable pushed back his round peaked hat, revealing shrewd brown eyes that looked Thomas up and down.

"I am not a thief." Thomas met the constable's look. "I bought this horse earlier today from an acquaintance."

"Piffle!" Mr Bayne spat. "Just look at him: he's no gentleman. I certainly didn't sell my prize horse to him. It was stolen."

The crowd began to mutter and push closer.

"I know this is Mr Bayne's horse," Jim said with a firm nod of his head.

"All right, thank you everybody. I can handle this from here," the constable said. "Move along now, please."

The crowd muttered and mumbled. Thomas caught a glimpse of a blue and brown patterned skirt. He didn't look up. He knew it would be the pretty young woman from the shop. Somehow her seeing him caught up in this made it even worse. Those gathered began to disperse except for Jim, who remained close to Thomas, ready to pounce at any moment.

The constable drew himself up. "I said move along."

"It's all right, Jim," Bayne said. "I am sure the constable will deal with this thief now he's been caught red-handed."

Thomas opened his mouth to protest but the constable put a hand up in front of him and continued to glare at Jim, who slowly backed away. Finally it was just the three of them and the horse.

The constable lowered his hand and spoke to Thomas. "What's your name and where are you from?"

"Thomas Baker, recently arrived from England."

A snort came from Mr Bayne and the constable turned his attention to him.

"Now, Mr Bayne, if this is your horse as you say, how did you …" the constable paused "… misplace it?"

Bayne puffed himself up and went red in the face again. "I didn't misplace it. My horse was stolen by this Baker fellow." He stabbed the air in front of Thomas.

Thomas glared back.

"How and where did he steal the horse?"

Bayne looked at the constable. "I was on my way back to Adelaide, after some late business at the port. It started to rain and I was tired. I found a place to shelter so I tethered my horse and I must have dozed off. When I woke up this morning my horse was gone. This young thief stole it in the night."

"I did not!" Thomas was fed up. This Mr Bayne was obviously a man of some standing around Adelaide but it didn't mean he could falsely accuse people. Thomas was also aware that even though the crowd had moved away, some were still watching from further along the street.

"Tell me then, Mr Baker," the constable said, "how did you come to be in possession of this horse?"

"My horse," Bayne snapped.

The constable ignored him and kept his shrewd eyes on Thomas. "Your turn, Mr Baker."

Thomas spoke evenly. "I stayed last night at the accommodation of my new employer, Mr AJ Browne. This morning I rose early to go to the Horse Bazaar. Mr Browne suggested I go there to purchase a mount to suit my new role as overseer of his property. I met a man outside the bazaar who had a horse surplus to his needs and wanted a quick sale."

Bayne snorted again. Thomas ignored him.

"He took me to see the horse in the bush – along the road to the port ..." His voice trailed off as he realised how dubious his story sounded.

"A likely story," Bayne said.

The constable ignored him again. "And you bought the horse for how much?"

"Fifteen pounds."

"He's a liar," Bayne shouted. "The horse is worth twice that much."

"What was the man's name?" the constable said.

"Seth W–" Thomas frowned. "Whitby, I think he said."

"Is it on the bill of sale?"

"I don't have one." Thomas began to lower his head then lifted it again with a jerk. "But I am supposed to meet Seth again at my dray. He's organising storage of a trunk for me. He's probably waiting for me now. He'll sort this out."

"Very well," the constable said, "lead us to your dray, Mr Baker."

"You surely don't believe his preposterous story." Bayne had one hand on the horse and pointed a finger at Thomas with the other.

"I need to gather all the facts, Mr Bayne."

"I'm a busy man."

"I'm sure you are, but if Mr Baker thinks he's bought this horse we need to sort it out." The constable untethered the reins and looked at Thomas. His expression gave nothing away and Thomas began to realise how precarious his position was.

"Lead on, Mr Baker."

Thomas moved off along the street, past the staring eyes of the remaining onlookers, followed by the constable with the horse and a muttering Mr Bayne. He hoped with all his might Seth would be at the dray waiting for him.

Five

"I would like to have spent more time in the dispensary." Lizzie looked wistfully over her shoulder as the little hut that marked the edge of Adelaide disappeared from sight. Thick bush closed in around them. The wagon, pulled by six bullocks and loaded high with their purchases, lurched beneath her as the wheels rolled down and up through a deep rut in the road. Lizzie gripped the rough wooden seat with one hand and held the brim of her hat with the other. Even though her mother had made some padding for the seat out of bags stuffed with wool offcuts, it was still hard beneath her skirts.

Beside her sat her mother and her father. Isaac, the youngest of her four brothers, rode his mare alongside. Tethered to the back of the wagon was a new horse for her oldest brother, Edmund. The occasional squawk could be heard from the new rooster in his wooden cage perched on top of the load.

"We achieved quite a lot in the short time we had," her mother said.

"You do well enough with your home-made medicines, Lizzie girl," her father said.

"We suffer enough already," Isaac teased. "You don't need to be poisoning us with any new potions."

Lizzie poked her tongue out at him.

"That's a fine look," he said. "I'm sure all the gentlemen in Adelaide were delighted by it."

"We had no time to meet anyone, let alone any gentlemen – and I certainly don't see any here." Lizzie glared at him. There was so little opportunity to meet other people in the isolated part of the country where they lived, let alone a suitable husband.

Isaac poked his tongue back at her and crossed his eyes. "No one could compare to your handsome brother, at any rate," he said.

She chuckled. A good-looking young man of twenty, he was two years younger than Lizzie and her favourite brother. When they'd arrived in New South Wales their father had managed a property and their mother had been kept busy with their three older siblings and the work of managing a home and garden and feeding them all. Lizzie had happily looked after her baby brother for as long as she could remember. Not that he took too kindly to her ministrations these days.

"We did come across a bit of a fuss in the street before we left," her mother said.

Her father glanced across at them. "What happened?"

"A gentleman was accusing a young man of stealing his horse."

"It was a lot of nonsense about nothing," Lizzie said.

"It drew a large crowd," her mother replied. "At least until the constable came and moved everyone on."

"Horse thieving," her father shook his head, "is a hanging offence."

Lizzie frowned at the thought of the handsome young man at the centre of the disagreement being stretched by his neck. It wasn't a pleasant picture.

Lizzie's mother tut-tutted. "I hope it won't come to that, George."

"The accuser looked like he was a heavy drinker," Lizzie said.

"How can you know that?" her mother asked.

"His ruddy cheeks. He looked just like Mr Duff from next door."

Lizzie saw her parents exchange looks. "He probably lost his horse and thought the one the young man had was his," she continued. "I'm sure the accused was too well mannered to be a horse thief."

"You seem to know a lot about this chap," Isaac said. "I thought you didn't meet any gentleman in Adelaide."

"We didn't meet," Lizzie snapped. "I just noticed his good manners in the shop where he was purchasing a hat."

The wagon gave another sharp lurch, tilting them forward on their seat. Lizzie and her mother both cried out and held on as best they could.

"Damnation!"

"George," his wife admonished.

"Well it's enough to drive a man mad, Anne. It's barely two days since we passed this way and the road is even worse than when we came in," George complained. "Ride ahead, Isaac. See what we're in for. I remember there was a creek crossing all churned up. We might be better to camp this side of it for the night and make the crossing in the morning."

Isaac urged his horse forward into a trot.

Lizzie watched him dodge skilfully under a branch and disappear around a bend in the road. How she wished she were on a horse, free to ride beside her brother. Her behind was already aching from the unforgiving seat beneath her. Her father had resourcefully made a bench seat across the front of the large wagon to give them somewhere to sit. It was a practical innovation but offered no comfort save her mother's cushions.

"Pity we didn't have another saddle," she said. "I could have ridden Edmund's horse."

"That horse is far too spirited yet," her father said.

Lizzie sighed. "Can I walk for a while?" she asked.

"At the rate we're moving you may as well." Her father brought the wagon to a halt and she climbed down. She stepped back away from the wheels then fell into step beside as he urged the bullocks on.

The late afternoon sun shone weakly through the clouds building on the horizon. She was happy to be returning home to their place in the bush. She found the landscape always changing and full of surprises. At this time of year the creeks were flowing with water and the bush dotted with the brilliant yellow of the wattle in full bloom.

Their run was nearly the furthest from civilisation but its isolation didn't bother her. It was seven years since they'd made the tedious journey by ship to Australia; the excitement of their grand adventure had been tainted by the barely tolerable conditions aboard and her mother's disposition to sea sickness. After several years in New South Wales, her father had put money aside and had moved them to South Australia for the prospect of owning their own property. He had secured land in the country to the north of the colony. It had been hard work and they'd never looked back but now, as she approached another birthday, she did wonder how she would meet a suitable partner. She didn't want a man who stuck to the town. She loved the bush life but they were surrounded by properties overseen by shepherds who were either already married or older, and with bad habits.

Time aboard ship had given her the chance to read and she had been taken with the grand adventure of Mr James Fenimore Cooper's *The Last of the Mohicans* and the forthright main character of Miss Jane Austen's *Emma*. Lizzie wasn't prepared to settle for a quiet life keeping house for some pale office-working husband. That was not her intention at all.

"We have to look for more land."

She lifted her head at her father's voice. It had that tone he used when he and Mother were discussing things by the fire after she went to bed. They always thought she couldn't hear them, which was quite ridiculous since her bed was in the main room of their small home. She took a few extra steps so she was a little closer to the seat of the wagon.

"With four sons we need to look beyond the land we've got now," he continued.

"George." Lizzie could hear the placating tone in her mother's voice. "We've just started to make ends meet."

"We can't rest there," George said. "Once we've enough money put aside we've got to expand. The country beyond us will be next to open up. We have to be ready." Suddenly her father stood up on the board and peered forward. "What's that in the shadows? Looks like another deep rut. Hang on, Anne."

He climbed down from the slowly moving wagon. Lizzie hastened her steps. Just as her father drew level with the lead bullock she could see there was indeed a deep gouge in the track in front of it. The bullock stepped down and as it did, its solid body lurched sideways and slammed her father into the trunk of a large gum tree.

"Father!" Lizzie ignored her mother's scream and ran to him. "Are you hurt?"

He leaned against the tree clutching his arm to his chest.

"George!" Anne cried.

"The wagon," George groaned and pushed himself away from the tree. Lizzie turned to see her mother slide along the seat as the wagon rolled down through the cutaway. The horse tethered behind pranced and whinnied and the rooster carried on with a series of strangled squawks.

At that moment Isaac rode up on his horse. Instantly he was out of the saddle and beside the bullocks bringing the whole parade to a stop.

Lizzie watched him help their mother down then turned her attention back to her father. His face was ashen and his breaths came in shallow gasps.

"Zac," she called. "Come and help."

"George, are you hurt?"

Lizzie was surprised by the wobble in her mother's voice. With five children there had been many accidents over the years. She was normally stoic in the face of adversity.

"I'm all right," he wheezed. "Just knocked the stuffing out of me for a moment. What about you, my love?"

"I was frightened, that's all."

Lizzie could see her mother was holding one arm stiffly, cradling the elbow with her other hand.

George sucked in a ragged breath. Lizzie thought him in more urgent need of attention.

"Let's sit you down, Father," she said. "Isaac, take his other arm."

Together they eased him to the ground with his back to the tree.

"Where are you hurt?" Lizzie asked.

He moved his legs up and down and stretched his left arm out. "Nothing broken."

She eyed his other arm, still pressed to his chest.

"Isaac, can you get to the calico we bought? It's somewhere in the wagon. Father might need some support for his arm."

"Perhaps we should go back for the doctor, George."

"It's not broken, Anne. Don't fuss. We don't need a doctor when we have our Lizzie." He managed a smile and Lizzie's heart swelled at the trust he placed in her.

"Where in the wagon?" Isaac was already moving away.

"I'll come with you," his mother said. "I know where it is. We don't need everything turned upside down."

Once they'd moved away, Lizzie reached for her father's arm.

"How is it really?" she asked.

He lifted the limb in question and his face creased in pain. "A bit sore, Lizzie girl, but I'll live."

"Can you wiggle your fingers?"

She watched as he did then gently prodded and probed. He had movement, albeit with significant pain. It was his chest she was worried about. He could easily have broken ribs.

"Here we are." Anne had returned with some large strips of calico. "Isaac is going to look around for a place for us to camp the night. It's best we all rest and start afresh in the morning."

Lizzie was pleased to hear her mother's usual good sense had returned.

"I think Father's right," Lizzie said. "Nothing broken." She cupped his face with her hands. He was still pale but his breathing had returned to normal. "I'll bandage this arm so it's supported. It will help while you give the damage time to heal."

Lizzie set to her task. She'd realised long ago they were so far from anywhere that there was no hope of medical help and had taken it open herself to learn the basics. She'd already patched her brothers up on several occasions and dealt with a variety of ailments.

"There." She sat back and admired her handiwork. "Is that comfortable?"

"Much better." Her father managed a smile. "Thank you, Lizzie." He turned his eyes to his wife. "What about you, Anne? I see blood on your sleeve."

"I'm fine." Anne brushed gently at her sleeve. "Just a graze."

"I'll get some water," Lizzie said.

Her mother stopped her with a brief hug. "You've done a fine job once more. Thank you."

Lizzie brushed at her skirts. Anne wasn't often one to make a fuss.

"What would we do without you, Lizzie." The colour was returning to her father's face.

She felt her cheeks warm as she glanced from one parent to the other. She smiled, enjoying their praise and relieved at their escape from real harm. She put her hands to her hips. "I'm not a doctor but I think you'll both live."

"That's good enough for me." George beamed at her and reached for his wife's hand.

Lizzie made her way to the wagon. Isaac had untethered the flighty horse and led him away. Thank goodness no greater damage had been done to man or beast. There were still many miles ahead of them, and it would not be a comfortable journey for her father. She pushed the bolt of calico back under the cover and ladled some water into a tin mug. She turned to see her mother sitting beside her father, her head on his good shoulder. Lizzie paused. It was so rare to see them like that. They made very little public show of affection and yet she was in no doubt of their love for each other. Lizzie wanted that kind of love. But where would she find it out here?

"I've chosen a suitable camp to settle in for the night." Isaac strode up beside her. His smile split his face from ear to ear. "And I've got dinner." He hoisted a small furry animal into the air.

The rooster picked that moment to let out a hearty crow.

Lizzie sighed. "You make the fire and I'll prepare it," she said.

Six

"Get ready."

Yardu glanced across at the bright eyes of his cousin, Gulda. His own eyes opened wide at the thrum of many feet and an unfamiliar bleating. He tensed. With a snap the bush parted and the strange creatures Gulda called sheep skipped and bounded through the narrow gap in the scrub. Gulda leaped forward and threw his arms around one of the animals, yelling at Yardu to help him. Yardu grabbed at a kicking back leg but it slipped out of his hand. He looked down to see tiny streaks of blood on his palm from the prickles in its fur.

The two younger cousins who had herded the animals through the gap ran to help Gulda wrestle the sheep. Yardu picked up his spear but one of the men hit the animal on the head with his waddy and it collapsed. Gulda gave its neck a sharp twist.

"Hurry," he said.

Yardu picked up the young sapling branch he'd prepared. With practised dexterity, they tied the sheep to it. The two cousins hoisted the branch to their shoulders as a loud crack echoed down the valley.

"Go, quick!" Gulda said and gestured to the bush behind.

A shout rang out but Yardu didn't understand the strange dialect. The sounds were nothing like he'd ever heard but there was no mistaking the threat in them. Loud drumming reached his ears. He remained rooted to the spot. A huge beast appeared through a gap in the trees, a white-skinned man on its back.

His cousins were already weaving through the thick bush, headed for the narrow ridges where they would disappear into a cave, but Yardu remained, mesmerised by the shouts of the white man and the heavy thudding of the animal he rode. A horse, Gulda had told him. The hat blew from the man's head revealing a pale, hairless scalp as he pulled the beast to a stop. It made loud screeching calls and danced in circles.

Yardu kept perfectly still. These sounds had echoed in his head for many cycles of the seasons, ever since he'd first heard them much earlier, in his own country further up the ranges. The noise had terrified his wife so much she'd slipped down the rugged cliff she'd been climbing and fallen to her death, their unborn child dying with her. He had come to visit his cousins to bring her bones back to her country. This was her heart country, where she was born.

Yardu drew himself up, sucked in a breath and began to chant, hoping the spirits from his country would join the spirits from this country and give him strength to avenge his wife's death. He could see his wife walking towards him through the trees. He smiled at her, knowing they were both invisible to this white stranger.

The horse and rider stopped and the man leaned forward, scanning the bush. With a final culmination of the chant, Yardu called to his wife. The white man lifted a large stick and pointed it in his direction. Yardu rushed forward and flung his spear. The white man's stick lurched up. A loud bang reverberated around the bush.

Gulda's hands gripped Yardu from behind and dragged him into the shadows. "Go," he urged. "We must go."

Yardu glanced back to see the horse once again dancing in circles. The white man was no longer on its back. Instead he lay spread out on the ground like a kangaroo skin stretched for curing. Yardu lifted his eyes to the sky. He shouted his gratitude. His wife and child had been avenged at last. Yardu gave one last look at the figure on the ground then spun on silent feet and followed his cousin into the bush.

Seven

Thomas shifted in the saddle. The pain that shot up his back made him wish he hadn't. The poor horse beneath him was barely more than a bag of bones but it was all he could afford. Beside him the bullocks pulling the dray came to a stop. Ahead of him was the first of the inns that would pepper his journey north. AJ had marked it on his map as a place to feed and water the stock and get a meal.

The rough-built establishment was barely bigger than a hut. A small verandah was propped up at its front with lengths of tree branches. Smoke billowed from the small chimney just above its thatched roof. In front and around were several teamsters from the copper mines, already arrived with their assorted drays, carts and wagons.

Thomas would see to his animals but his own food would be some bread and pickles from his supplies. He was down to his last coins thanks to Seth Whitby's deception and he wasn't planning on parting with them any time soon.

He eased himself down from the saddle. He'd only been on the road a short time yet every muscle and joint screeched in protest.

He lifted his head at the thud of hooves. A horse skidded to a stop in front of the inn and the rider slid from its back with a shout. The man was gesturing wildly.

Men went to him, and raised voices carried across the clearing. He watched for a moment as the men milled about the newcomer, until he heard someone call out, "Constable!" That was sufficient incentive for Thomas to mind his own business. He'd had enough of the law for one day. Anger burned in his chest again as he recalled the way he'd been duped.

He'd taken the constable and Mr Bayne to his dray, but his hopes of a reasonable explanation diminished with every minute that passed with no sign of Seth.

The constable had asked Mr Bayne to send for his stable master. When he verified the horse was Gideon and owned by Charles Bayne, Thomas had finally conceded he had been well and truly tricked and was in real danger of being arrested.

It had been then that a dishevelled man had rushed at the constable, grabbed him by the arm and tried to drag him away, babbling something about a dead woman. It had taken some effort to calm the fellow down, partly due to his mad ranting and partly due to the overwhelming stench keeping them at bay. He obviously worked with pigs – and lived with them, if the smell of him was any indication.

The constable had decided he should investigate and that took precedence over the discrepancy with the horse. He'd sent Bayne grumbling on his way and warned Thomas to be more careful about his future purchases, before hurrying off with the pathetic gibbering man in search of a corpse. Thomas had felt both relief and guilt. Some poor woman had lost her life but at least it had taken the constable's attention from him.

Once he was alone, both emotions were short lived as he realised the trunk he'd left sitting on the ground was also missing.

He harboured little hope Seth had put it with the landlady for storage. The man was obviously a liar and a thief.

With the last of his money, Thomas had gone back to the bazaar. There had been few horses left to select from. The animal he'd purchased was all he could afford, having spent Mr Browne's money on Treasure.

"Treasure indeed," he muttered. "It certainly cost me." He looked at the pathetic creature he had now and the aches in his body gave him cause to lament his foolishness yet again.

He removed the saddle and allowed the horse to eat and drink while he looked after the bullocks. The huge animals would have none of his urging. At the rate they travelled, he'd be lucky to reach the property in a month rather than the three weeks AJ had advised it would take.

It was nearly dark by the time Thomas had tended the animals. The poor light didn't help his temper as he fiddled with the harness. He was trying to work out some way he could attach a rope to tug on and so urge the bullocks forward at a faster pace, instead of the stop-starting ramble they'd had today.

"Where you headed?"

He turned to see a man leaning against a tree. His face under a broad hat was almost completely hidden by a thick grey moustache and long woolly beard. His shirt was brown with grime and his black baggy pants were held up with a piece of rope. Thomas glanced past him to a group of teamsters sitting around a fire. He assumed that's where the man had come from.

"North," Thomas said.

"North takes in a lot of country. You going far?"

"Several weeks' journey. My employer has a sheep run. A place called Penakie." Thomas turned back to the rope. He hoped the fellow would go away. He was in no mood to trust another stranger, not to mention the rope needed to be fixed before he lost the light. He wanted to be ready for an early start in the morning and he still had to prepare himself something to eat.

"Can't say I've heard of it," the fellow persisted. "Your employer own these animals?"

"Yes," Thomas said quickly followed by, "No … At least, the bullocks are his. The horse is mine."

"I'm not a horse man myself. You worked with bullocks before?"

Thomas glanced at the rough face. He couldn't see the man's expression but the question sounded genuine. "No."

"Would you accept some advice from someone who has?"

Thomas hesitated. He was tired and hungry and his confidence in humanity had recently taken a beating.

"These bullocks are trained to walk beside you," the man continued as he came closer. "They won't be dragged."

Thomas let go of the rope in his hands and felt an ache across his shoulders. When he had agreed to be AJ's overseer he hadn't realised quite how hard it would be just to get to the property.

"My name's Bert Hawson." The man thrust his hand out.

Thomas hesitated a few seconds then put out his own hand and accepted the rough grip. "Thomas Baker."

"We've got a fire going, some food and stories to share." Bert flicked a look back over his shoulder. "You could be a long time on the road. It's good to seek company when you can get it."

Thomas hesitated. The smell of roasting meat wafted around him. He accepted Bert's offer and walked beside him to the fire. Thomas reminded himself he was only sharing a campfire, not looking to buy anything.

"We're all headed to the mine at Burra," Bert said. "We spend a lot of time together so it's always good to meet someone new. This is Tom Baker," he announced to the group.

Thomas smiled at the shortened version of his name. No-one had ever called him Tom before.

Those grouped around the fire looked up. They were all older men with wrinkled faces and ruddy skin. They welcomed him then fell silent. Thomas's stomach growled loudly. Bert began to laugh and his friends joined in. One man thrust some meat sandwiched in damper into Thomas's hands and another shuffled along the log so he could sit.

They let him take the first mouthful before they began with their questions – where had he come from? Where he was going? He felt obliged to tell his story between mouthfuls of the delicious meat. They offered condolences at the loss of his father though there was no pity in their words.

"You'll make a go of it here in South Australia, Tom," Bert said. "We've all come from different beginnings to this country but we wouldn't trade the life, would we, mates?"

A chorus of voices agreed with Bert.

Then the stories began, each man giving an account of where he'd been and what he'd been doing since they'd last met. Some stories sounded rather embellished to Thomas but they made him laugh and he was glad of it. They passed a jug of some kind of liquor between them, and when it got to Thomas he hesitated then took the offered drink. His eyes opened wide as the liquid burned its way down to his stomach. The man next to him grinned and slapped his back. There was laughter all round and they continued their story telling.

Thomas was enjoying their easy company but he could feel his eyes getting heavy. He wasn't as adept at life on the road as these men appeared to be. He waited until the next story was finished and the jug was going around again, then stood up.

"Thanks for your hospitality," he said. "I'd best turn in."

Bert stood. "We'll be doing the same soon." He shook Thomas's hand. "Always happy to help a new chum."

Thomas nodded farewell and made his way back to his own temporary camp. He dragged a blanket and pillow from the dray

and crawled underneath. The murmur of voices and the shuffling
of animal hooves were the only sounds in the cool night.

Before he knew it, the movement of men and animals around
him told him it was morning. He didn't remember shutting his
eyes. Thomas scrabbled from the rough bed he'd made for himself
and groaned as the aches and pains from yesterday returned, only
strengthened by his dreamless sleep on the hard ground. In the
dim light of early dawn, he saddled his horse and harnessed the
bullocks. The sounds of other men doing the same renewed his
enthusiasm for the adventure ahead.

"Ready to go, Tom?"

Bert was beside him, the broad hat on his head. Thomas
wondered if he slept in it and looked around for his own hat.

"I reckon so," he said.

"This might come in handy," Bert said.

Thomas peered at the stick Bert pressed into his hands. It was
about six feet long and smooth, with an even longer plaited leather
strip attached to it.

"It's a whip."

"Thank you." Thomas accepted the gift, still not sure what he
was to do with it.

"I'll give you a quick lesson before I head out."

Thomas had planned to boil a billy and have some bread and
a mug of tea before he left but he could see some of the bullock
drivers were already urging their teams away; some headed along
the road to the mines at Burra and some back towards Adelaide.

Bert gave a quick demonstration then urged Thomas to try.
The long tail of the whip wrapped around him several times
before he managed to get the end to go where he wanted it.

"Keep practising," Bert said. "Remember it's not meant as a
weapon. These bullocks are well trained. The whip helps you to

give them a reminder from a distance. They're fine animals your boss has supplied. My advice is get to know them. Learn their names. They'll respond to your voice."

Thomas looked at the bullocks. The two leaders came as high as his shoulders and had long, twisted horns. He hadn't thought of them as anything but beasts to do the work of pulling the wagon.

"You got a firearm?"

Thomas turned back to Bert. "Yes."

It was somewhere in the dray. AJ had given him brief instruction in its use. He wasn't sure he would remember how to fire it.

"A shepherd rode in last night looking for the constable. Says blackfellas have been stealing their sheep and one of them threw a spear at him. Evidently it's near that Penakie place where you're headed."

Thomas stopped flicking the whip. AJ had suggested he watch out for natives pilfering sheep but he hadn't said they were dangerous.

"Perhaps you'll accept some more advice from an old man before you go." Bert didn't wait for a reply. "Reading and writing is one thing, but out there," he stabbed a finger in the direction Thomas was headed, "out there, you need common sense and patience to survive."

Thomas found himself staring into the bush. Bert's words sounded more like a warning than advice.

"You're a good man. You listen and learn and you'll be right." Bert thrust his hand out. "You take care."

"Thanks Bert." Thomas accepted the strong grip.

"On your horse, Tom."

Bert tugged the whip from his hand so Thomas could climb into the saddle. Suddenly there was a loud crack and the bullocks moved forward. He clutched at the reins as his horse turned in a circle.

"The horse will get used to it." Bert grinned and tossed the whip up to Thomas. "Good luck," he said as Thomas gained control of his mount and moved away beside his steadily plodding bullocks.

He looked back to see Bert lift a hand in a wave then stride off to his own team. Thomas turned again to the track leading away through the bush; his rear end ached already at being back in the saddle but his spirits, high with anticipation for what lay ahead.

Eight

Septimus pulled his wagon into the shade of some large gums. He was pleased to see water in the bottom of the stream below. In the last few hours the breeze that had helped cool him had dropped right out and the late afternoon sun had beat down with more ferocity than he expected for early spring.

He stretched and looked around. This patch of trees and thick bush was off the track and afforded him protection from the sight of anyone following the road north. He'd kept moving steadily for two days since leaving Adelaide, avoiding the busy inns along the way and only making a basic camp each night, not even lighting a fire for his billy. He knew his wagon was distinctive and that it was best to remain cautious. He wasn't yet confident he'd put enough space between himself and any trouble that might have come if the real owner of the horse he'd sold to the gullible Baker should make a fuss. At least Baker had never seen the wagon.

Tonight Septimus would set up a better camp, maybe catch something to roast over a fire and – he wrinkled his nose as he inhaled a breath. He'd have to go through his wagon and work out what that terrible smell was. He'd noticed it briefly the previous night then again once the breeze dropped out a few hours before. Perhaps one of his potions had leaked or, worse still, some of his bottles had broken. He couldn't think what else among his things could make such a stink, unless of course there was something in the trunk.

A smile spread across his face. It had given him great pleasure getting Baker to buy the horse: a touch of delight from the good old days in England. He'd made a good living from trading behind his employer's back until he'd slipped up and been caught red-handed. That had resulted in his transportation to New South Wales. He'd survived that and now he was set to make a good living from the unsuspecting folk of South Australia.

Septimus tutted to himself and climbed down from the dray. Of course, tricking someone so wet behind the ears was almost too easy. The money from the sale of the horse had enabled him to purchase an assortment of goods to sell and taking the trunk had been icing on the cake. At a quick glance he knew there were several items he could peddle on his travels. Serve the man right for being so green.

The sun was dropping quickly. Septimus rubbed at the seat of his pants, stretched his arms back then reached under the wagon to retrieve his animal trap. The small cage had served him well in the bush before. He'd become quite adept at snaring a small furry creature, snapping its neck and roasting it. Now he had some provisions he could make damper to go with it.

He busied himself finding a grazing spot for Clover, setting the trap and preparing a fire. Just as he neared the wagon again to locate his flour and tea, he stopped short and listened. Birds chirped from the nearby bush and Clover ripped at some grass and munched, but Septimus could swear he'd heard a moan. He tugged the new hunting knife from inside his trouser leg, wishing he'd spent some of his cash on a firearm as well, then he heard it again. Groaning, coming from his wagon.

Septimus undid the straps that held the cover in place and care-fully lifted the canvas. There was very little space in the wagon. He had packed a lot of supplies around his potion shelves and the large trunk he'd stashed in the back. Then right in front of him, in the middle of the wagon, the pile of new men's shirts and trousers moved. Some kind of animal had buried itself in his goods. He reached across and began lifting the clothing away, then lurched back as an apparition in human form began to rise from underneath.

He covered his nose and mouth with his hand. The smell was unbearable and the being so ugly he would have thought he'd trapped a ghoul if he believed in such nonsense.

"Help me." The voice was feeble.

Septimus didn't move. He couldn't comprehend how this female – he could see more of her now – had got into his wagon, or when. The head was a mass of matted hair, caked in mud and possibly blood, if the congealed stains down the side of the face were any indication. The eyes were swollen slits, the nose was at an odd angle and the mouth was a mangled mess.

He winced and watched in horror as a filthy hand reached towards him. "Septimus," she croaked.

He gasped. How did this creature know his name?

"Help me, please. It's ... Harriet."

Septimus gasped again. "Harriet?"

But as he spoke she slowly sank back into the pile of clothing.

"No," Septimus bellowed. Those clothes were part of his new money-making venture. He didn't want the filthy creature spoil-ing them. He pulled on her arm but she didn't move.

"Harriet." He tugged more fiercely and then gagged as the smell enveloped him again. It was a mix of human and animal, putrid and overpowering.

He flung back the good clean clothes she'd burrowed under. Her dress was torn and caked in mud. He picked up one of the hessian bags he kept for carrying animals he trapped and used it to grip Harriet and lift her from the wagon. She didn't move or murmur as he laid her at his feet. He poked her with the toe of his boot but there was no response. Someone had done her over good and proper from the look of her and somehow she'd got into his wagon.

Septimus looked around. He was a long way from anywhere but he suddenly felt vulnerable. There was no way he was going to take the rap for the little slut's death. He took the bag and wrapped it around her then lifted her up. She felt barely heavier than one of the sacks of flour he had stashed in the wagon. He walked towards the stream then thought better of dumping her close to where he was camped. Further along, the water trickled and disappeared into large flat rocks. He jumped from one to the other then the stream dropped away and he looked down into the large pool of water that had formed below: the perfect spot. He stretched out his arms and let the body roll off the bag. There was a satisfying splash as it hit the water. In the dim light, Septimus turned and retraced his steps.

Close to his camp he heard the sounds of something scrabbling in his trap.

Good, he thought. There'd be something to roast for his evening meal while he cleaned up his wagon.

A small furry creature with a long tail ran around in the cage. Perhaps a stew would be better, possum stew. There'd be plenty of time for it to cook. He would probably have to wash some of the shirts and trousers and rearrange the wagon. Septimus wrapped the animal in the bag, slit its throat then set about preparing his meal and cleaning out the wagon. He decided to leave washing the clothes till morning, seeing as it took till full dark just to move boxes and barrels around and scrub the filth from the boards. He gave no further thought to Harriet.

A crackling sound penetrated his sleep. Septimus was instantly awake. He lay perfectly still in the cosy bedroll he had created for himself, but opened one eye a slit. The fire was flaming gently in the hollow he had created last night. His brain registered the flames, which should be coals now, not fingering skywards with a steaming billy beside. There was a movement to the edge of his vision. He slid his hand down for the knife he'd tucked under the canvas and jumped up, ready to lunge.

"Septimus, it's me, Harriet."

He froze and gaped at the small figure in front of him. The clothes were those of a man but there was no mistaking the soft voice and battered face belonged to Harriet.

"But …"

"You must have thought I was dead." Harriet placed a steaming mug of tea in front of him and stepped back. "Is that how I got in the water? I don't think I could have crawled there myself."

Septimus didn't speak. Harriet moved away around the fire. He noticed her steps were careful and deliberate. He kept the knife in his hand at his side and watched her like he would a snake in his camp.

She picked up another mug and stood gazing into the fire. "I sure wished I was dead." Then she looked directly at him through swollen lids. "I don't know how you got me here but that dousing in the water saved my life."

Septimus still didn't move. The water had cleaned her up. All the mud and blood was gone; just the bruising remained. She might be lucky and not have permanent damage although the nose would never be straight again. Dressed in the men's trousers and shirt she looked as if she could blow away in a breeze. He looked down at the tea by his feet then snapped his head up.

"They're my clothes," he snarled. "I was going to sell them."

"They were out on the ground in a pile. I'm sorry about the filth, I …" Harriet's voice trembled. "I've washed some and aired the rest." She nodded to the trees behind the wagon where he could see the various shirts and trousers draped about.

"You can't be here."

"I might be able to repair my dress if you have needle and thread."

"You can keep the clothes but you can't stay." He'd give up the shirt and trousers just to be rid of her.

"Where will I go?"

"I don't care where you go. Head back that way." He indicated the track his wagon wheels had made in the gaps between the large gums. "I'm not getting into trouble over you."

Harriet sighed and bent to the fire. She poked at something on the edge and the delicious smell of hot bread reached his nose.

"Nobody knows I'm here," she said. "Like you, they thought I was dead."

Septimus scowled at her. There was no way he wanted this piece of damaged goods anywhere near him.

"I could help you," she said.

He snorted. "I work alone."

She walked towards him, each step placed carefully. She pressed a chunk of the hot bread into his hand. "I'm fourteen now." Her tattered lips tugged up into a smile. "Today's my birthday."

He took a bite of the bread. It was good.

"Besides," she said, "now we're both running away from things we don't want others to know about, aren't we, *Seth*?"

He dropped the bread and was on her in an instant. He twisted her in front of him, bringing the knife up to her throat.

"I could just as easy slit your throat and drop you back in that pool," he snarled in her ear. "If everyone thinks you're already dead they won't be looking for you."

She went limp in his arms. "Killing me could be the best thing for both of us."

Septimus held her a moment then thrust her away. She stumbled and moaned as she fell in the dirt. He picked up the bread
and shoved the rest of it into his mouth, then sat down again. He
chewed and kept one eye on her. The dough was soft and sweet,
like Harriet had once been, far better than the damper he made
himself. She slowly picked herself up. He took a slurp of the tea.
It was strong and black, just the way he liked it.

"I can cook and keep things clean while you do your work."

Her voice was soft but not weak. Whatever had happened to
her she wasn't giving in, despite her talk.

"I can be your woman like I was before."

He shuddered. "Don't talk," he snapped. Bits of bread flew
from his mouth.

Harriet gathered herself up and went back to the fire. She
began to pack up the pots and utensils she'd used, along with his
from the night before.

He watched her as she worked. Someone had done her over and
there was no way he wanted to share his bed with her any more. He
never wanted a woman who'd been used by other men again. He'd
had no choice in the past and now it sickened him to think of women
who'd bedded any other man, willingly or not. In spite of that, an
idea was forming in his head. Maybe Harriet could be useful for a
while. He could set up camp and leave her there while he went off
selling his wares. She would heal with time and no one would see
her. When the time was right he might be able to trade her at some
isolated shepherd's hut.

"As long as you cook and clean you can come with me."

She turned her head towards him and opened her mouth but
his glare silenced her.

"Never call me Seth again and don't speak unless you're asked.
I don't want anything else from you." He stood up and flung the

last of his tea at the fire. "Now get those things washed up. We need to get on the road."

She watched him a moment through one puffy eye. Then she gave a slight nod and headed to the stream.

"Happy birthday, Harriet," he said as he watched her pick her way to the water.

Nine

Thomas studied the rough structure in front of him. Last night he had finally made Penakie just as the light was leaving the sky. During his journey he'd got used to the bedroll, spread out in some soft soil or sandy ground, but he had been looking forward to the comforts of a proper bed and a roof over his head. A quick glance inside the homestead made him decide to stay with the bedroll one more night. Homestead was indeed a grand name for the hovel that was to be his home. The hope he'd held that a day-light inspection would reveal improvements he hadn't been able to see in the moonlight was slipping away.

The roof was thatched with some kind of thin vegetation, not thoroughly by the look of it, and he could see no sign of a chimney. The walls were pine trunks barely taller than he was. They were ranged upright and in the daylight he could see gaps partly filled with mud.

He stooped through the space that served as an entrance. There was no actual door. After a minute his eyes adjusted to the gloom. The only furniture was a rough table, one chair and a long wooden shelf. Thomas assumed that was to be his bed. In the wall opposite the entrance was some kind of shutter. He pushed it out and sunlight poured in, revealing the motes of dust swirling in the air.

"Home, sweet home." Thomas's words hung in the air with the dust. He would have to do a lot of work on this place to turn it into a serviceable structure, let alone a home. He slumped to the hard wooden shelf, tipped his head against the wall and closed his eyes. He'd made it to Penakie, but now what? Overseer was a grand word but what did it mean? And where was the shepherd AJ had mentioned?

His eyes flew open at the bleating of sheep. He was getting to understand the ways of bullocks and had made some connection with his poor excuse for a horse but sheep were a new proposition. He jumped up from the plank and strode outside. There was work to be done. He'd come all this way and he had three thousand sheep to look after. Thomas couldn't imagine that many all in one place. Nor could he imagine how AJ thought two men could manage such a flock. Still, his boss had been determined it could be done and Thomas was determined that he be the one to accomplish it.

By the end of the day, his behind once again aching from being jolted along by his horse, his earlier enthusiasm had ebbed away as he came to the full realisation of what he had taken on. The three thousand sheep might be there somewhere but they were not all in one place. The property was vast and everywhere he went there were small flocks. There was no sign of the shepherd, McKenzie. Thomas would need his help to keep the sheep together or there would be no hope of managing such large numbers. If he were to succeed he would need some kind of strategy.

He rode out each day, gradually his body accustoming itself to the saddle and the horse to him. Thomas had named the animal 'Derriere' in wry deference to his mother, who had always used the French word for buttocks. He didn't think his derriere would ever recover from the experience, so he thought the name fitting.

He treated the animal well and talked to it constantly, there being no one else but the sheep for company. The horse had no trouble with the rough terrain and was responsive to working with sheep. Thomas only hoped the animal could be restored to the good workhorse the auctioneer had said it had once been.

Each night he'd light a fire wherever he was, and dine on damper and the dried meat from his provisions. A rough map, scribbled with AJ's notes and landmarks, was his bible as he explored each part of Penakie. One particular morning he studied the landmarks on the map and deduced he was quite close to McKenzie's hut, though there'd still been no sign of AJ's shepherd. Today Thomas planned to visit the hut. Their employer had said the man was unreliable. Perhaps he was doing nothing while he thought there was no one to check on him.

Thomas had barely been in the saddle an hour when he saw a horse ahead of him. It was in the shade of a tree, head down. It was saddled but there was no sign of a rider. Thomas dismounted, tethered his own horse nearby and approached on foot. The horse lifted its head and shifted uneasily.

"Steady," Thomas soothed.

The horse shook its head and stomped its foot. Thomas could see its reins tethered in the low branches of the tree.

The buzz of bush flies grew louder as Thomas got closer. He reached for the reins and ran his hand down the horse's neck. It threw its head up and shifted its feet but appeared unable to move very far. A cloud of flies rose from its other side. Thomas ducked down to see what was holding the horse in place, then reeled back. No wonder the poor horse was agitated. There was a man lying on the ground, his leg tangled in the stirrup. Thomas had seen enough to know he was dead.

The horse shook its head again. Thomas pulled his collar up over his mouth and nose.

"Take it easy, boy," he said.

He took the reins, which he could now see were tangled rather than tethered, and eased his way around the horse to a point where he could reach the stirrup. The horse tried to move away, shifting the body on the ground. Flies rose up then settled on the flesh. Thomas's stomach turned. What a ghastly business. It took him some effort to get the foot out of the stirrup, but finally it fell to the ground. Thomas turned his back on the man a moment and led the horse away, talking to it as he went. He'd come through a small creek a short distance back, so he took the horse there and let it drink before tethering it. It had a bed-roll, and saddlebags with food and a firearm packaged around the saddle. The rider had obviously been setting out somewhere. Thomas left the horse and went back to face the gruesome task of dealing with the body.

The man's eyes bulged and his open mouth, a yawning gap in his thick beard, showed lips and tongue swollen and crawling with flies. There was a wound across his forehead and congealed blood matted his orange hair. The leg that Thomas had extricated from the stirrup was twisted almost back to front. The horse had dragged the man a distance by the look of the tracks. Thomas followed them across open ground to some thicker trees. There the tracks stopped. Not far above his head a thick branch jutted out. He could only assume the rider had connected with that and been knocked from his horse to be dragged to where Thomas had found him.

By the colour of his hair and the greasy clothes, Thomas was guessing he was AJ's shepherd, McKenzie. Whoever he was, he needed to be buried without delay. He was already starting to smell. Thomas mounted Derriere and went on to find the shepherd's hut.

He passed through the trees and around the dangerous bough and continued along a low ridge until he found the hut on a flat area a hundred feet or so beyond. A gust of wind swirled the ash from the dead fire into his eyes as he climbed down from his horse. The hut looked even rougher than his own; it was hardly more than a box with a sloped roof of bush and sticks. He poked his head in the open space that passed as a door. As he had expected there was no one-there. He found a shovel by the fire and headed back to McKenzie.

It took him half a day to dig a hole he deemed deep enough. He covered the body and marked the grave with three large rocks. He had no idea if McKenzie had family or anyone who would mourn his loss. Thomas looked down at his work and said a prayer. The sun was getting low in the sky by the time he'd tidied up around the hut. He collected the few items of food that he had room to carry. The rest would have to wait. McKenzie appeared to have had few personal effects. Thomas would have to get word to AJ to see what should be done.

Two days later, with the sun once again low in the sky, he reached his homestead. It hadn't improved any with his absence. Thomas was tired and hungry, and more than that, McKenzie's death weighed heavily on him. Nevertheless he dismounted and took stock: there was no help for it but to keep going.

First he dealt with the horses. McKenzie's had been useful to carry extras. Earlier in the day Thomas had found a young sheep trapped in a waterless stream bed, tangled in a clump of tree roots. Its leg had been broken so he'd put it out of its misery. He'd made sure he recorded it in the little book he kept so that he could report everything to AJ.

Now he made a fire in the crude stone setting at the back of the hut. He dragged the table out and cut up the sheep. While the meat roasted he pondered his predicament. How was he to manage without a shepherd? AJ had an enormous flock, though by Thomas's count they were a few short. He was determined not to lose any more.

He studied the map in the light from the fire and re-read the notes he'd added. What he'd noticed about Penakie was that, even though it was a vast area, there were stretches of land with low vegetation bounded by the long arms of ridges rolling down from a band of hills. It was in these natural paddocks, not far from the trickles of water that flowed in the streams, that he'd found larger numbers of sheep gathered. The sheep were a mix of old and young, some in better condition than others.

The first thing he needed to do was sort them. If he could break them into three flocks it would be a start. On the flat between the house and the stream was a small yard built from roughly hacked timber. He put the horses in there at night. It was the only other structure here besides the hut and far too small for what he had in mind. He needed a large drafting yard for this many sheep.

With a belly full of meat and a plan forming in his head, Thomas crawled into his bedroll and let sleep claim him.

The next morning, Thomas woke refreshed and keen to map out his plan for a yard. The sight of his camp in the early light made him stop. He had another problem: his stores and water. He hadn't unpacked many provisions from the dray because there was nowhere to put them. There was plenty of water in the stream but it was quite a walk from the hut, and AJ had warned him the pleasant spring weather would quickly turn to heat. In the gentle light of the morning, with a breeze almost cold across his shoulders, Thomas took a gulp of tea and tried to imagine the heat AJ had alluded to. Thomas hadn't experienced summer in Australia but his employer had. It would be prudent to heed his advice and be prepared.

A bird warbled loudly from a nearby tree and another answered. The breeze swirled and blew ash from his fire into the open barrel he used to store water. Thomas rose from his squat, looked around again at his crude home and made a decision. The sheep work would have to wait a few days. If he didn't make good his living conditions there'd be no one to look after the animals anyway.

The thought made him hesitate. He'd felt a pang of loneliness the night after he left Bert and the other teamsters. He'd enjoyed sitting around the fire listening to their yarns. On the track to Penakie he'd come across a couple more small eating houses and had spoken to people there, but he'd been in his new home a week and not once had he felt lonely. Now the thought of his isolation engulfed him. This property was supposed to be the furthest from Adelaide of any in the colony. He hadn't even seen any sign of the natives who were supposed to inhabit the place. McKenzie's death weighed heavily on him. What if Thomas took sick? He could die out here like the shepherd and no one would know until AJ checked up on him in a year.

The bird warbled again and the sun, rising quickly now, was warm on his back. Thomas turned to the hut. His survival and that of the sheep depended on him alone. There was no time to be idle. He pushed the melancholy thoughts from his head and set to work.

Ten

Several days later, as he trimmed the last of the meat from the sheep carcass for a stew, Thomas pondered his progress. The hut was filled with his provisions stacked on shelves or hung on hooks. Coming back from the stream one morning he had discovered a small furry animal with a long tail hovering on the threshold. He had immediately set too and made a door that would close and hopefully keep such creatures out.

Down at the stream he had made a rough apparatus to enable him to fill multiple water barrels, rather than the one bucket at a time he'd been carrying up to the hut. A fork-like structure sat in the stream, which supported the barrel on its side to capture the water. A rope thrown over the bough of a tree and wrapped around the barrel levered it up enough for him to fix its lid in place. Once the barrels were full he rolled them up to the dray, using the natural slope of the bank, some saplings and more rope. Then he transported them to the hut, where he stored them outside against a wall with their lids still on to keep out the dirt.

He'd even built a proper fireplace with a chimney, found a large tree trunk to use as a preparation block rather than the table, and dragged a log close to form a rough bench. Over in the trees, a little way from where he'd hung the sheep carcass, he'd created a hammock for his bedroll like those he'd seen on the boat journey. He hadn't left himself much room inside the hut and found he'd got used to sleeping outside, although he wasn't sure how much protection the trees would give if it rained. They had strange trunks with lots of rough bark that changed colour from grey to deep orange depending on the light. The leaves were thick at the top and gave good shade but how well they'd repel water, he'd yet to find out.

He looked up at the vivid blue sky. He still had no idea what to expect of the weather. The sky since he'd arrived at Penakie had been clear with only the occasional clump of white cloud but he'd noticed heavy clouds forming over the distant ranges that morning. They looked quite dark now though still a long way off.

He scraped a last sliver of raw meat from the bone and threw it off to the side, then watched as the black and white bird that had been lingering nearby made several quick hops, snapped up the meat and flew to a nearby tree. As Thomas had toiled around the hut over the last few days, he had discovered it was the bird that made the warbling sounds. He'd also found it liked meat. Yesterday it had hopped closer and closer until it dived on a scrap he'd dropped.

Thomas chuckled out loud and the bird warbled as if in response. The week before he'd had only a horse, some bullocks and a few thousand sheep as friends. Now he could add the black and white bird to his circle of associates.

He looked across at the two horses grazing the low vegetation under the trees. McKenzie's horse had proved to be on a par with his own but at least he had two of them now. With little to do this last week, and plenty to eat, they were both visibly filling out. When he rode out again to check the sheep, Thomas hoped the ride wouldn't be as jarring on his own derriere.

Suddenly both horses lifted their heads, ears pricked. Thomas put the lid on the pot of stew and listened. He heard a couple of soft clumps and then to his utter surprise he saw a horse, complete with rider, coming around the side of the hut.

"G'day, mate."

Thomas stared at the man climbing down from the saddle.

"Looks like you got yourself well set up here." He pulled off his hat to reveal a balding scalp and stepped across the open ground towards Thomas with his hand stretched out. "I'm Frederic Duff but everyone calls me Duffy."

Thomas took in sharp eyes that were more red than white, and a wrinkled face half covered by beard and whiskers. He moved his hand forward and the visitor shook it vigorously.

"Don't get many callers out here, do ya?" Duffy grinned at him and Thomas realised he still hadn't said a word.

"I'm Thomas Baker – Penakie overseer."

Duffy dropped his hand. "Thought that'd be who you was. Mr Browne told me he'd be sending someone. I'm a shepherd for the Gwynn brothers. Their place is that way." He jerked his thumb in the direction of the stream. "My hut's a day's ride other side of that creek but thought I'd better come and check on ya."

Thomas found himself having to listen carefully as the other man spoke. He dropped a lot of sounds from the ends of his words and it made him difficult to understand. The man was scanning the site, taking in the outside kitchen, the hammock bed and the improvements around the hut.

"Is that McKenzie's horse? Where is the lazy devil? Still sleepin'?"

"You knew McKenzie?"

Duffy turned his red eyes to Thomas. A frown wrinkled the tough skin of his forehead. "Course. We were sent out on the same ship."

"I'm sorry to have to tell you Mr McKenzie is dead."

"Dead?"

"I found him not far from his hut."

"He was as tough as nails. What killed him?" Duffy's eyes darkened. "Bloody blackfellas."

Thomas shook his head. "It was an accident. It looked to me as if he'd hit his head on the bough of a tree and been dragged by his horse. There was nothing I could do but bury him."

"Well I never." Duffy's shoulders slumped as if the wind had gone out of him.

"Can I offer you some tea?"

"That'll do for starters." Duffy patted his coat pocket. "I've got something here to keep us warm later."

Thomas went to the fire, where the kettle was still hot.

"You sure been busy making this place fancy," Duffy said from behind him. "I live on my horse most of the time. Don't get much opportunity to tidy up my hut."

"I don't imagine I'll be here much either," Thomas said. "But I had to make sure the provisions would be safe; and I've made an apparatus so I can fill the barrels down at the stream." He was rather proud of what he'd done there.

"Well listen to you with your talk of streams like there's a constant flow of running water." Duffy laughed. The sound came out in short brittle jabs. "That there's a creek, mate. It might be swollen with raging water one day and then for months hardly a drop. Can't rely on it."

Thomas thought of the pool of water further downstream where he could barely touch the bottom when he bathed in it and the constant trickle that flowed around the rocks and reeds where he filled the barrels. Maybe Duffy's streams weren't like this one.

Duffy sat himself on the log bench. His eyes darted about, taking in everything. The man could be a thief rather than a shepherd, although he certainly had the smell of sheep about him. He accepted the mug of tea Thomas offered and grinned. There were several teeth missing from his mouth.

"I'd have been to see ya sooner but I had some trouble." He looked over his shoulder. "You seen any of those thieving blackfellas yet?"

"You're the first person I've met since I left the last eating house, way back."

Duffy snorted into his tea. "They're not people, mate. Those blackfellas aren't no more'n animals. They've been stealing sheep. While ago I caught them red-handed, the thieving buggers. Then one of them up and threw a spear at me. Frightened my horse and I got tipped off. Knocked me right out for a moment. I could've been killed. I was lucky he didn't stick a spear in me while I was out to it. But the blackfellas and the sheep were gone when I came to. I rode straight for the constable. He's off looking for the culprits now."

Thomas recalled Bert's warning weeks earlier at the watering place. "I heard there'd been some trouble as I travelled here."

"Trouble's what those thieving mongrels are. You watch out for them. The way they move about and take what they like, you'd reckon they owned the place." Duffy's sharp laugh punctuated the air. "We'll see what the magistrate has to say once the constable catches up with them. Reckon nothing short of a hanging."

Thomas stirred the stew but made no comment.

The visitor fixed his eyes on the pot and spat. "That's smelling good."

"It's just a stew. I found a sheep with a broken leg."

Duffy gave another of his sharp laughs. Thomas was coming to realise there was no mirth in the sound.

"That happens. Between that and blackfellas and wild dogs it's a wonder we got any sheep left. How about you show me round? Is there somewhere I can put my bedroll? No point in rushing off now that I come all this way."

Thomas hadn't taken to Duffy with his prying eyes, mocking laugh and dislike of the natives but beggars couldn't be choosers. Like him or not, Duffy was human company. Thomas showed him the improvements he'd made.

When they reached the stream, Duffy laughed long and loud at the barrel-filling device. When he finally drew breath he pointed to the dark clouds way off in the distance. "We'll see if it's still here in a few days," he said.

Thomas was perplexed. Firstly by the connection between those distant clouds and his stream and secondly by his visitor's intimation that he would still be with Thomas in a few days. Company was one thing but he had to get back to work. He'd spent more time than he should have improving his living arrangements and it was time to earn his keep, looking after the sheep.

"You might want a bit of help once you start building things," Duffy said when Thomas mentioned the need for a yard and shearing shed. "We've had some hut builders our way that did a good job. Cost the boss eight shillings a week but it was worth it."

Thomas thought about that. He would need yards and other sheds to store the wool. "Where are they now?"

"Think they were headed across to the Smiths but I could get word to them."

Thomas said he'd think on it.

By the time they'd had a good look around and Duffy had opted for the bench in the cramped hut to lay out his bed, rather than by the fire or in the trees like Thomas, the stew was ready to eat. Duffy ate a small portion then pulled a bottle of some pale liquid from his pocket. He raised it in the air. "To McKenzie," he said. "Rest easy, mate."

He took a swig, wiped the back of his hand across his mouth, then offered the bottle to Thomas. "Get some of that in to ya, Tom me boy."

As he put the bottle to his mouth, Thomas could smell the liquor. He took a small sip, which took his breath away and then burned a path down his gullet. He gasped. It was even rougher than the liquor the teamsters had passed around on his first night on the road.

This time Duffy's laugh had the sound of merriment to it as he took back the bottle. "I can see you're not much of a drinker," he said when he finally caught his breath. Then he turned his red beady eyes to Thomas and there was no longer any humour in them. "You need to get a taste for it. Unless you got a woman there's nothing else to do out here once you've done with the sheep for the day."

Thomas watched as Duffy took another deep swig from his bottle and continued to talk. He went on about the natives again. Thomas gave the occasional murmur or nod when it appeared a response was required. As pleased as he had been to have another man to talk to, he was tired and wanted his bed. Duffy's talk became more and more fanciful, blaming the natives for everything from the sore on his leg to the lack of spring rain. Finally the drink took its toll and Duffy's ranting came out in shorter bursts until he suddenly started to snore. Thomas left him there and went to his bed in the trees.

When he awoke next morning there was no sign of Duffy by the fire; he had moved to his bed, judging by the snores echoing from the hut. Thomas hoped the man would move off quickly so he could pack up and be away himself.

That day he planned to look at the lay of the land close to the hut again. He needed to sort the sheep into separate flocks and to do that he'd need to build drafting yards. It would take him some time but he remembered a clear patch of land in a hollow nearby, where the vegetation was thick on one side and a small cutaway made a boundary on another. He might be able to make use of the natural features to lessen the task, but he'd still need help.

Duffy finally stumbled from the hut and disappeared towards the stream. When he came back his head was dripping and his skin glowed under the facial hair.

"Nothing like a dip in the creek to wash away the cobwebs," he said and slurped down some tea. Thomas noticed the shake of his hands as he clutched the tin mug and knew by the smell of him it was only Duffy's head that had got wet.

"Would you like some damper?" Thomas offered. There was work to be done and he was pondering how long his visitor would stay.

"No thanks. That stuff sits too heavy in your guts when you're in a saddle all day. I've got what I need." Again he patted his pocket and gave his trademark laugh. "Thanks for your hospitality, Tom. I'd best be off."

Duffy made his way to his horse and Thomas followed.

"I would appreciate some help from those hut builders if you can get word to them," he said. "Mr Browne has given me his authority to make improvements."

"I'll see what I can do."

Duffy leaned down from his saddle and gripped Thomas's hand.

"Thanks for giving McKenzie a proper burial," he said. "Mr Gwynn's going to Adelaide soon. He can get word to Mr Browne." He sat up straight in the saddle. "Come my way whenever you need some company. I want to know how your water structure survives in the *stream*."

Duffy turned his horse and rode away. The echo of his sharp laugh punctuated the air, gradually fading until Thomas was left with only the sounds of the birds and the rustle of the trees in the stiffening breeze.

Eleven

Harriet lifted her head from her sewing and listened. The sounds of the bush and the crackle of the fire continued but there was no sound of a horse or wagon. Since her beating, her left ear didn't hear so well, making it difficult to tell the direction of sounds. And sometimes, out here all alone in the bush, her mind played tricks on her, inventing noises that weren't there and putting her on edge.

Today she was feeling especially jumpy but she couldn't put her finger on why. Maybe it was the dress she had been plying with her needle. Harriet tossed her sewing aside and rose to stir the pot. She inhaled the delicious smell and replaced the lid. It was only soup made from the last bones of a sheep but she'd added an assortment of vegetables and the small bunch of parsley Septimus had brought back yesterday.

She had been travelling with him for several weeks now and he regularly left her alone wherever they camped while he visited nearby homesteads with his wagon full of goods to sell. Barely a day went by when he didn't return with some extra food for her to cook. His eyes would gleam as he handed the supplies over. Harriet always responded demurely, careful not to mistake his enthusiasm for interest in her.

The dress she'd been mending lay across the log where she'd left it. Only a few final stitches were required and it would be wearable again. She hated the sight of it even though she'd made a good job of cleaning and mending it. It reminded her of the time she'd last worn it. Harriet shivered and looked down at her clothes. She had become used to the men's trousers and shirt and, as no one but Septimus ever saw her, she preferred them.

That morning he had spoken to her directly. He had told her to finish mending the dress and he had made it quite clear she was to be wearing it by the time he returned. She had accepted his order with only a nod of her head even though her eyes had searched his face, looking for a clue as to why he suddenly cared about what she wore.

She glanced around the camp. The two trunks were stacked under a tree, the bedding folded on top, and the food and utensils, except those she was using, were packed away. They had been in this place for several days. Usually they kept on the move, only making camp overnight and sometimes staying an extra day, but this time they were close to the new mine at Burra and Septimus travelled into the town each day. He'd even unfurled his Royal Remedies sign. From the little he told her, he was doing a good trade in lotions and potions.

She worked hard in his absence, adapting quickly to their life in the bush. Harriet had many skills for her young years, not all of them learned in a whorehouse. Her mother had been a seamstress and before her eyesight had deteriorated, she had taught Harriet how to sew and to read and write. Growing up in their cottage on the edge of the bush, Harriet had spent a lot of time with the woman who had been employed as their cook. She had been happy to teach Harriet all about food and tending the little garden, growing whatever she could to augment their food supply.

Harriet sighed. There was no point in dwelling on the past. She had to survive the here and now. There was nothing but the sewing left for her to do and still hours before Septimus was due back. Too restless to stay in the camp, she wound her way through the trees to the creek. He always managed to find a creek to camp by. Sometimes they had water in them and sometimes they didn't but this one was flowing well. The day was warm. If she had to wear the dreaded dress perhaps she would wash herself and her clothes. It had been weeks since the night of her dunking and she'd only given herself quick washes since. It would be wonderful to wash her hair. Maybe if the trousers and shirt were clean she would be allowed to wear them again.

Harriet stopped at the edge of the thick bush and looked around. The ground sloped gradually to the creek from there and the main vegetation comprised huge trees dotted along its sides. That was the reason they were camped so far away. Septimus chose a spot that was concealed and away from the usual roads and tracks. Harriet had thought his purpose was to keep her hidden but the more they travelled the more she realised secrecy was his habit.

A large gum tree spread its thick branches across the creek just where the water pooled in a natural hollow. Harriet crossed the open space quickly. She climbed over fallen logs until she sat on the branch that hung over the water. She pressed her back to the huge trunk behind her and closed her eyes. The warmth of the tree was comforting.

She flung her eyes open again at a rustling sound in the low branches behind her. Relaxing was how she'd got into trouble the last time. She looked carefully around either side of the trunk. A large lizard waddled away from the pile of leaves and logs beside it. Harriet exhaled the breath she'd been holding.

She could have died after being violated by the pig boy. The experience had left her always on alert. After his attack she'd come too in the patch of bush behind the pig shed. Fearful he would return, she'd crawled away to the river. She'd tried to reach the water but her shawl had become snared among the reeds. She'd heard people nearby calling her name but she hadn't wanted to be found. Somehow she managed to make it to the relative safety of the lane beside Mabel's stables.

Her goal had been to get to the stable and nurse her wounds. She knew if Mabel found her, there was a good chance she'd evict her. Pain radiated from between her legs and her body ached all over, she'd been badly used, and she was sure her good looks had been permanently damaged. If she was no longer a pretty virgin, Mabel would lose any return on the years she'd invested in her.

Septimus's horse and wagon had still been in the lane and Harriet had climbed in and burrowed to the centre, and remembered little else until the cold water of the creek had shocked her awake. Septimus must have thrown her in, even though he'd never admitted it. In fact, they hadn't spoken again about why she was in his wagon or how he'd come to have it loaded to the hilt with new goods for sale. The past was left behind. Harriet was determined this was to be her new future. Septimus would come around eventually, and although she wasn't looking for his physical attention yet, she planned to be his wife in every way.

She looked down at the creek flowing beneath her then edged from the branch and lowered herself into the freezing water. She pursed her lips to stop her squeal of shock. The overhanging branch helped conceal her from anyone who might pass. She smiled. In all the time she'd been on her own she'd never seen another soul. Septimus had warned her to be on the lookout for the natives, who were known to steal things. She'd never seen any of them either.

The water was deep in this little patch, enough for her to sink below the surface and remove her clothes. She hadn't thought to bring soap or anything to dry herself but it was too late to worry about that now. She revelled in the freedom of no clothing.

Harriet worked quickly. She washed herself then scrubbed her clothes with little sound to give away her position. The coldness of the water soon forced her back to the branch, where she spread out her garments. Once again she pushed her back to the warmth of the trunk. The sun soon dried her skin but it would take a while to work on the clothes.

She inspected her nakedness, something she'd not done for a long time. Her breasts were well rounded and firm, the nipples pointed out now after her swim. The rest of her body was smooth and the bruising was all but faded. She wasn't sure about her left leg: there were still yellow patches high near her hip, and when she bent her knee up to her chest, she felt the twinge of pain that had eased but not completely left her since her beating. Maybe she would always have it, along with the damage to her face, a permanent reminder of her ordeal.

She shivered and looked around. How stupid she was for not thinking ahead. She was stuck there until her clothes dried. There was no way she would walk back to camp naked. She rearranged the garments on the branch to get the best of the sun. As she sat back, a movement from across the creek caught her eye. She pulled behind a leafy branch and stared. She could see nothing but two other large gums opposite her and yet she was sure there'd been something, a shadow of movement.

Maybe it was one of those black people Septimus had warned her about. Harriet's heart thumped so fast in her chest she felt it would burst. Her mind scrabbled over ways to escape but there were none. The stretch of sparsely vegetated ground was the only route to reach the bush behind her. She sucked in a breath and forced herself to remain still. Her eyes searched the opposite bank. There, in the mosaic of light and dark within the shadows, she saw a figure standing tall. It was a kangaroo. He was on his hind legs, pulled up to his full height. If he had been beside her he could have looked her in the eye. His ears pulled back. He stared in her direction.

Harriet exhaled. One of the kangaroo's ears twitched. He lowered his head a little. Then she noticed the others at his feet. They were various sizes stretched out in the shade. Harriet eased back into the sun. The largest kangaroo lifted his head then lowered it again. He knew she was there and had decided she wasn't a threat.

She smiled. She wasn't any good at killing things but Septimus had recently traded some potions for a firearm. With the last of the sheep gone they needed more meat. Kangaroo would make a good stew. If the animals camped there regularly Septimus might be able to shoot one for her.

Septimus stopped the wagon in his usual spot and unhitched Clover without a word to the woman tending the fire. He'd nodded in her direction as he'd arrived then kept his eyes diverted. He knew the time had been right for her to wear a dress again instead of the dirty men's clothes she hid beneath. The real Harriet emerged in that dress. If he went closer he would see the bump in her nose and the jagged scar on the side of her face but from this distance she was an attractive woman. Besides, he had a man lined up who wouldn't care what she looked like. He wanted a woman to keep him warm at night and cook whatever he brought home. Harriet was capable on both counts. If her attack had left her less willing in bed, he'd be long gone before her new husband found out.

Septimus whistled as he went about tending the horse and repacking his wagon. The people of the new Burra mine had been eager for his Royal Remedies. After today's sales his stock was all but gone. It was time to make the trek back to Adelaide to restock. He stopped sorting the small bottles and pots. Harriet remained by the fire but she was standing still, watching him.

"Something wrong, Harriet?"

"No, I wondered –"

He dismissed her with a glare and turned his back on her but he could feel her stare. A tiny part of him wanted to talk to her, to hold her in his arms even. Wearing that dress, she looked so like the sweet little Harriet he had bedded when he'd first arrived in Adelaide. If only she hadn't been attacked he might have been tempted to … Septimus shrugged his shoulders and got back to sorting the last of his bottles. She was nothing to him now but a saleable item. He would make good money to add to the stack he had already then go back to Adelaide for more goods – alone.

That night, while he swallowed her appetising soup, Septimus once again studied Harriet. She sat on the other side of the fire, her head bowed over her own bowl of soup. Now that he actually looked at her carefully there was definitely something different about her besides the clean dress. Then he took in her hair. It shone in the firelight, falling in thick bunches around her face and flowing over her bare shoulders, left exposed by the low-cut bodice.

"Did you bathe today, Harriet?"

She lifted her head. He noted the gleam in her eyes but her face remained expressionless.

"Yes." She went back to her soup.

"I have a brush in my trunk. It was my mother's." The lie rolled off his tongue so easily he could almost believe the trunk and contents were his own. "You can use it if you'd like."

Harriet didn't look up. She put her bowl down and reached her hands towards the fire. "Thank you," she said.

"I think there's a shawl in there as well." He took a branch from the fire, strode over and stuck it in the ground to throw some light on the trunks. He opened the larger one. He'd removed from it anything he'd thought he could sell in the bush but there were a few things he'd kept. The shawl was soft, made of deep green wool in a large triangular shape. Clean and serviceable, it still smelt a little of the rose petals that had been in its folds when he first unpacked it. Harriet was still sitting with her hands stretched to the flames.

"Here," he said. "You can keep them."

She stood up, took the shawl and, with great care, drew it around her shoulders, leaving him to stand still holding the brush. The shawl covered her pale shoulders and the paisley dress. Harriet was not tall but she stood straight, shoulders back. She looked so much older than her years. Septimus tossed the brush beside the log she'd vacated and spun away. He returned to his side of the fire, where he drew out a recently acquired pocket knife and began to whittle at a stick.

In between the sounds of the knife on the wood he heard the soft rustle of her clothes.

"I saw a mob of kangaroos today."

Septimus lifted his eyes. She had kept to the bargain and not spoken but to answer his questions. This was the first sentence he'd heard her speak since their uneasy alliance began. She was watching him as she pulled the brush through her hair. He went back to his whittling.

"We don't have any meat left," she said. "I thought you might be able to shoot one."

He threw the stick into the fire and rose to his feet. "Don't mistake my generosity for anything else, Harriet," he growled. "Keep your trap shut."

She pursed her lips but held his gaze, still using long, slow strokes to tug the brush through her hair.

Her apparent lack of fear was infuriating and her silence, even though he demanded it, exasperated him. He covered the space to where she stood in a quick movement, grabbed a handful of her hair with one hand, yanked back her head and laid the knife across her exposed neck with the other.

"I could still do you in," he snarled.

"Yes," she whispered and he saw the tremble of her pulse just below the surface of her pale skin. Perhaps she wasn't as tough as she made out. That gave him some satisfaction, although really it no longer mattered. The next afternoon he'd be rid of her.

He pushed her away. She stumbled close to the fire.

"Go to bed, Harriet," he said. "Tomorrow you can brush your hair again, tidy yourself up and put on your best face. I'm taking you to meet some people."

Twelve

Thomas slithered from the saddle. The throbbing pain in his backside eased, only to return with each step he took towards the hut. He'd been away for five days and most of that daylight time had been spent in the saddle. Derriere had gained in strength and was proving to be a steady worker, but the pain in Thomas's left buttock had increased.

This morning he had gingerly tested the area with his fingers and found a large lump that throbbed at his touch. He suspected it might be a boil. Some of the men he had shared quarters with back in Adelaide had suffered with the large pus-filled sores on their arms and legs and Duffy had pulled up a trouser leg to reveal one when they'd sat by the fire.

Thomas hobbled from the trees towards his hut then pulled up, gritting his teeth as the pain radiated further. His fire, which should have been cold, was sending up puffs of smoke. He cast his eyes around the camp but there was no other sign of movement or change. Carefully he stepped forward again. The fire had been burning long enough to make coals, over which his pot was steaming.

He pushed back his hat and scratched his head. Maybe Duffy had come back and was sleeping off his drink in the hut. No tell-tale snores reached Thomas's ears as he slowly made his way around to the door at the front. It was closed. The hinge creaked as he opened it. A quick glance showed nobody inside. He looked towards the stream but could see nothing. He didn't want the pain of walking that far.

His thoughts were on the coals and the pocket knife he carried. If he could heat the tip of the knife he might be able to cut open the boil. Back at the fire he threw fresh twigs and wood on the coals to make flames then lay his knife on the stone beside the pot. He undid his belt and buttons, lowered his trousers and twisted to try to see the cause of his pain.

A footfall and gasp made him spin. Beside his hut stood a young woman carrying a small bag and an armload of sticks. It was, God help him, the very same young woman he'd seen in the shop when buying his hat. He staggered and tried to pull up his trousers but tripped and fell to the ground, landing with full force on his bottom; the pain knifed up his body and he let out a yelp.

The woman dropped her load and rushed toward him. "Are you hurt?" she said, her face lined with concern.

Thomas pushed one hand towards her to stop her coming any closer. Besides the merciless pain he was aware that his garments were still tangled around his legs and he was sitting in his drawers. "I'm all right," he gasped.

"You don't look all right. Can I help?"

Thomas scrabbled backwards and cried out as he put his hand too close to the coals of his fire.

She took another step forward. "It looks like you need —"

"Stay back," he gasped.

She held him in a piercing gaze. A puzzled look crossed her face as if she was trying to remember something, then it was gone.

"All right," she said, "but I have four brothers who have had all kinds of injuries and ailments. I am quite used to the male form, from helping Mother mend them."

"Please, Miss …"

"Elizabeth Smith." She nodded her head. "But as we're neighbours, you can call me Lizzie."

She spoke so fast Thomas thought his head would spin, and oh *dear,* she looked like she was going to step forward again. "Please, Miss Smith, can you turn away?"

"Men," she huffed. "Too much pride." She spun on her heel and walked back to where she'd dropped her things.

Thomas got to his feet as quickly as he could, eased his trousers back around his waist, did himself up and inspected his hand. A red mark was forming. He must have put it on a coal. All the while the woman continued to speak about the weakness of male vanity. Finally he interrupted her.

"Miss Smith."

She spun around, a big grin lit up her face. "It's Lizzie."

Now that he was dressed, Thomas had time to study her. She looked to be his age, and was short in stature, with fair hair parted straight down the middle and swept into a knot at the back of her head. Her lips were pink and full, below a button nose and her eyes – He drew in a breath. They sparkled back at him.

He cleared the lump in his throat. "Where have you come from?" he asked.

"We are your neighbours over that way." She pointed in the opposite direction from the way Duffy had come. "We heard Mr Browne had employed an overseer. Father had to take the wagon with supplies to the men camped not far from here, building some yards. He dropped me off to say hello and leave you a welcome pie. You've made some good improvements around here already. I put it inside on a shelf," she said.

Thomas frowned. It was hard to keep up.

"The pie that is." She continued to talk at speed. "I made it myself from the delicious little red fruits that are ripening now.

We call them wild peach. That's why I wasn't here when you returned. I was checking to see if you've got any of the trees nearby and you have. Only one but it's loaded with fruit. I've picked some." She raised the bag she held in one hand. "You can dry them. They keep well."

She spoke so fast and the pain of his burned hand along with the throbbing boil was making it hard for Thomas to concentrate. "Your father left you here, alone?" he said.

She pulled herself up. "You're alone. Women are often alone when the men are all working. It's the way it is in the bush. No point in putting on airs and graces out here. Although names are helpful."

"I'm sorry; I'm Thomas Baker, from England, and more recently Adelaide and now here."

"Pleased to meet you, Thomas Baker," Lizzie said.

The smile on her face took his breath away. She was the prettiest woman he'd seen in a long time. Then he couldn't help but smile at the thought she was the only woman he'd seen in a long time.

She strode forward.

Thomas stepped back. The movement made him wince.

"Oh, *what's* the matter? Please let me help you, Thomas. I can see something is bothering you." She put down her bag, dropped the bundle of sticks close to the fire and brushed off her hands.

He turned over the hand that he'd touched on the coals. "It's a bit of a burn."

She took his hand gently in hers. His looked like a meat cleaver in her small grasp. She bent her head over it and inspected the red welt on his palm. "You're right, it's not too bad and the best thing for it is cool water."

"Shouldn't it be butter?" Thomas said, remembering a similar burn from his childhood.

"If you have some I'd be happy to apply it for you."

Thomas watched the sparkle in her eyes grow brighter until her face burst into a grin again.

He couldn't help responding with a small smile of his own. He hadn't had any butter since the meagre scrapings they had sometimes put on their bread at the Square. "Water will be fine," he said. He didn't mind what she did as long as she didn't remember the original pain site was his rear end.

"Sit yourself down and I'll have that seen to in two shakes of a lamb's tail."

"I'll stand," Thomas said.

"Suit yourself." Lizzie hurried away to the keg beside the hut and brought back a dipper of water and an empty pot. "Hold out your hand."

He obeyed. She trickled the water over his palm to the pot below. The cool water gave immediate relief from the sting of the burn.

"How did you know this would help?"

"I stumbled too close to a campfire once myself. I burned my leg but there's hardly a scar there now."

Thomas was appalled to see her put down the dipper and reach for her skirt. He bent to the pot, which was now full of the water, and submerged his hand.

"You can reuse the water. It's a good idea to keep your hand in it. Luckily my father did that for me. It was when we first came here. There was no hut and our fire was a hole in the ground. I was in my shift preparing for bed and somehow fell on the edge of the flames. My hem caught fire. It was my good fortune we were beside the creek. My father threw me in. Over the days that followed I discovered the cold water of the creek was the only thing to bring me relief from the pain. We didn't have any butter either."

Lizzie paused and smiled at him. This time Thomas smiled straight back. She was certainly a chatterbox but there was warmth in her words that lifted his spirits, and those *eyes*. They were the blue of cornflowers and mesmerising.

"I spent a lot of time in that creek," she said. "The leg blistered but by the time the blisters came off, I had new skin growing underneath. A miracle really." She poked at the fire. "The coals are ready. I was going to make you a kangaroo stew. Father will be ages yet. You keep dipping that hand in the water while I set to work."

Thomas did as he was told and watched as she carried food from his hut, including kangaroo meat that she must have brought with her. He leaned one hip against the side of his makeshift table while she worked. She dropped the meat in a pot with seasonings and vegetables, some of which he'd never seen before. She talked the whole time. He stopped cooling his hand and shifted himself to a different position. The pain in his backside was growing stronger.

"Whatever else it is that's bothering you, you should let me help."

Thomas looked up. Lizzie had finished rearranging the coals and settled her pot among them. Now she stood with her hands on her hips, studying him closely.

"It's probably only a boil," he said and straightened up. "I'll be all right."

"Samuel had a patch of them on his back a while ago. I had to deal with them. There was no way he could reach them." She paused then her lips turned up in a gentle smile. "I'm guessing from the way you were nearly twisted inside out when I appeared that your pain is in a … delicate spot."

Thomas could feel heat rising in his cheeks. "It's only a lump; I'll manage," he said.

Her gaze softened. "It could get very nasty and you've no one to help you. I'll go into the hut and finish putting away my things. You get yourself organised so the 'lump' is exposed but all else covered and I'll come back and take a look."

"Miss Smith …"

"Lizzie." She smiled again. "Now come, Father wouldn't forgive me if I let our neighbour take so ill that he died before we all had the chance to become acquainted."

Thomas frowned at her. "Died?"

"People have died from a nasty case of boils, you know." Once again her smile sparkled with kindness. "But no one in my care. Now you give me a call when you're ready."

Thomas watched as she disappeared around the corner of his hut. He scratched his head and looked around. He couldn't reach the troublesome lump on his own. What was he to do? The boils he'd seen on others were certainly nasty-looking things but they surely wouldn't kill a person – would they?

"Are you ready?"

"No, not yet," he called and hobbled over to his horse, where his bedroll was still hooked to the saddle. He brought it back by the fire and with a series of manoeuvres, he managed to uncover the troublesome area without too much of the rest of him being exposed for Lizzie's eyes. Finally when he was stretched out on his belly, he called out and tucked his head back into his arms under his hat. He felt a movement as she settled on the ground beside him.

"Oh, poor Thomas. However did you stay on your horse?" she said. "That's a nasty boil but I am sure I can bring you some relief."

Thomas heard the rustle of her movements as she busied herself at the fire.

"I'll need to bathe it in very hot water. It might be a bit painful but I'm sure it will improve once the poison is released."

He pressed his head further into his arms, not sure which was worse, his extreme embarrassment or his alarm at the treatment.

"Now this will be hot." He felt her kneel beside him again. "It looks ready to explode so you should have relief in two shakes of a lamb's tail."

He gritted his teeth as the first press of heat was applied. Lizzie chattered away as she worked and after a while he forgot about the pain and listened to the soothing tones of her voice. Finally there was a sharp sting and then the throbbing pressure eased.

"There you are," Lizzie said. He could hear the satisfaction in her voice. "I'll bathe all the poison away and it should clear up. I am wondering though, Thomas, if you have more drawers."

Thomas kept his head buried, suddenly remembering he was stretched out with his rear end partially exposed to a young woman he had barely met. How was he to extricate himself from this position?

"It would be a good idea if you went down to the creek and had a wash," Lizzie said. "If you don't have clean trousers I could wash these for you and –"

"I can manage now." Thomas twisted his head sideways. "If you could give me some privacy, Miss Smith, I'll go to the stream."

"All right," she said. He watched her bite at her lip to hold her twitching mouth in check, then she stood and turned away.

Thomas scrambled to his feet and pulled up his pants and, with the blanket draped over his shoulders, he made for the stream. What he saw there pushed his mortification aside. There was more water in the stream than before he'd gone bush, but to his dismay, his carefully built barrel-filling structure was nowhere to seen. There were a few pieces of timber scattered on the highest part of the bank – it was obvious that a lot of water had been through the stream while he'd been away although there had been no rain while he had worked the sheep. He looked towards the distant hills and recalled Duffy's sharp laugh. Damnation but perhaps the smug man had been right. The water must have come all that distance and in large volumes, judging by the damage.

Further downstream he lowered himself into the water. He sucked in a breath against the cold. The pool was deep enough for him to submerge himself. The level was much higher than when he'd bathed there previously. He could see the ripples lapping at the bases of trunks that had been well out of the water before. It was late in the afternoon and the sun was low in the sky, taking the warmth of the day with it.

He shivered and climbed out onto the bank, where he tied himself in a knot trying to see the site of the boil. It was impossible, but at least the pain was gone. He wrapped himself in the blanket and gathered up his clothes. They were a reddish brown and now that he'd washed himself he could smell them.

He peered up over the edge of the bank and scanned the open ground between himself and the hut. He prayed that Lizzie had gone but common sense told him that was unlikely. Her father was to collect her and there had been no sound of drays or bullocks. Thomas made it to his hut without encountering the bold young woman and put on his extra set of clean clothes. It was a pity he didn't have the other trunk. His father's clothes would have been useful, even if a little small.

Through the crude opening in the hut wall, Thomas could see Lizzie sitting close to the fire, stirring the pot she'd filled with kangaroo and vegetables. She had wrapped a shawl around her shoulders and removed her hat. The late afternoon sun made her hair glow like gold. There was nothing for it but to join her. He couldn't hide in the hut forever.

As he opened the door he heard a distant call and then the faint rumble of wheels. He walked around the corner of the hut and Lizzie bumped into him coming the other way.

"Sorry." They both spoke at once then Lizzie moved around him.

"That will be Father," she said. "He's late. It will be dark soon."

They watched as two bullocks emerged from the bush pulling a wagon with a man seated on top.

"Hello." She waved.

The man lifted his hand in response then called the bullocks to a halt.

"You've been a long time," Lizzie said. "Is everything all right with the boys? We'll never make it home before dark you know and there's that treacherous stretch of gully."

"Slow down, Lizzie girl," her father said as he climbed from the dray. He slapped his hand on the side of his pants then extended it to Thomas. "I'm George Smith, but I'm sure if you've spent any amount of time with our Lizzie you'll know more about me than I do by now."

The man smiled as they shook hands and Thomas saw the same sparkle that lit Lizzie's eyes.

"Thomas Baker." The hand he held barely gripped his before it dropped away. Mr Smith rubbed at his shoulder.

"Oh, Father," Lizzie said, hurrying forward and poking at his arm. "You've overdone it again, haven't you? Those lazy brothers of mine have had you working."

"I'm fine, Lizzie girl," her father said and gently pushed away her prodding hands. "I injured my arm a while back," he explained to Thomas. "It's not as strong as it used to be."

"Injured!" Lizzie snorted. "You did everything but break a bone. It was a right old mess. It happened a month ago and he still can't use it properly. I'll have to make a new poultice for you when we get home."

"Our Lizzie fancies herself as a nurse, Mr Baker. If you don't watch out she'll be plying you with potions and bandaging or bathing some part of you."

Mr Smith chuckled. Thomas cast a wary glance at Lizzie, who was still fussing over her father. Surely she wouldn't tell him about the boil.

"We should stay the night," Lizzie said. "We can leave at first light and be home for breakfast."

Thomas stared at the back of her fair head. He would enjoy the company but he was sure at any moment Lizzie would tell her father about her earlier ministrations and then, weak arm or no, Thomas was sure Mr Smith would want to kill him.

"Mr Baker may not want visitors, Lizzie." The man was looking over his daughter directly at Thomas.

"Your company is most welcome, Mr Smith, but my camp is very basic –"

"Listen to you two, Mr Baker and Mr Smithing," Lizzie said. "George and Thomas is so much easier, and your arrangements are more than adequate, Thomas. You should see ours: it's no palace, is it, Father?"

"You and your mother have made it a home, Lizzie."

"I haven't been back from my rounds all that long, sir, but Lizzie has been busy cooking in my absence." The wind had dropped to a soft breeze and the delicious aroma of Lizzie's stew wafted around them. "Why don't we eat?"

Thomas led the way to the fire behind the hut. He would have to keep an eye on Lizzie and make sure the conversation was kept far away from ailments. As they ate their meal, he relaxed. The talk was all about the land and managing the sheep. George had lived on the neighbouring run for over two years and had developed a broad knowledge of the conditions.

He agreed with Thomas that AJ's sheep needed to be sorted into groups, mobs he called them, and he offered his sons to help. He was also less harsh than Duffy had been in his talk of the natives, although it was obvious he wasn't fond of them.

They followed the kangaroo stew with a slice of the wild peach pie. It had a tart flavour but was most enjoyable, and very good for them, according to Lizzie. Finally it was Lizzie who urged both men to their bedrolls. Thomas climbed into his hammock and watched her moving around in the firelight. Lizzie Smith was the last person he'd expected to meet out here but he was glad he had. Embarrassed as he'd been over her ministrations, he couldn't help but be taken in by her easy manner and charming smile.

Thomas slept soundly and woke to the vision of Lizzie tending his fire in the predawn gloom. He wondered if she'd even been to bed. They had a mug of tea and a slab of damper and then Lizzie and her father were on their way.

"Come and see us when you are ready for the boys to help with the sheep," George said, and climbed up onto the wagon seat beside Lizzie. "We can repay your hospitality."

"I'm not sure I provided much but a fire to sit around," Thomas said. "Thank you for the food, Lizzie." He gave her a smile and she beamed back at him. He felt his heart skip. She really was the prettiest woman. He would most definitely have to visit the Smith property soon.

"My pleasure, Thomas," she said and tied her hat on her head as her father called the bullocks to move forward.

Thomas stepped away from the wheels. He wondered how George did that without a whip.

Suddenly Lizzie twisted in her seat and called back over her shoulder. "You make sure you keep washing that boil, Thomas Baker. Don't let it get dirty."

Thomas could feel the heat in his cheeks again. In his guilty mind he expected George to stop and ask questions but the older man didn't look back. Thomas returned to the fire and sat with little pain. Silence pressed around him. His feelings of guilt and embarrassment were overtaken by a desire to hear more of Lizzie's cheerful banter. In spite of her forthright ways, he looked forward to seeing her again.

Thirteen

Septimus pushed the last morsel of damper into his mouth and washed it down with sweet tea. He would have to get used to his own cooking again. He sat a moment longer by the fire, sliding his gaze sideways to watch Harriet as she cleaned up the pots. Her hair shone in the morning light, flowing in thick locks down her back. She looked much better than he'd hoped. Her hair hid the scar on the side of her face and, apart from the limp and a slightly bent nose, she had recovered from the beating, as far as he could tell. She'd go to the farmer for good money and Septimus would get on his way back to Adelaide to restock.

Of course he wouldn't return to the area for a trip or two, until she'd settled to her new life, but there were plenty of other farms and little settlements spreading out across the land for him to visit. One day he would come back and Harriet would have a husband and a brood of children. He was doing her a favour really. Better off a farmer's wife than the whore she'd have become under Mabel's tutelage. He stood up and stretched. "Time to go, Harriet."

She washed her hands with the last of the cooled billy water then twisted her hair up into a knot before tying on the bonnet he'd given her. She threw the shawl around her shoulders. Suddenly she was transformed into a modest young woman. Septimus chuckled to himself. Only he knew any different. He helped her up onto the seat of the wagon and climbed up beside her.

"Come on, Clover," he called. The horse moved obediently forward, towing the wagon onto the trail he had worn through the bush to the track that led to Burra.

The sun was struggling to shine from a cloudy sky by the time they reached the outer edge of the community. Septimus noted another hut finished. The mine had only been opened a short time but already little hamlets were appearing close by. He stopped the wagon. There were a couple of women here who had wanted some of his Royal Syrup for the coughs and colds that afflicted their families. He had done a roaring trade with it. Today was pay day at the mine so it was worth stopping.

He told Harriet to stay in the wagon while he unwound his Royal Remedies sign. Before he had even finished setting up his little store, the women were gathering.

"I'll take two bottles of your syrup, Mr Whitby." A small woman had pushed in close, her round face looking from him to the shelves of potions over his shoulder.

"Leave some for the rest of us, Edith," another of the women snapped. She was tall and thin with a face pinched into a scowl.

He opened his hands wide and smiled. "Ladies, ladies, take your time. I assure you there will be enough to go around, but ..." he paused and cast his look over the crowd of women "... I will soon be on my way back to Adelaide, where I hope to restock, so do make the most of my presence today."

That sent them into a buying frenzy. For a time, Septimus was busy dispensing medical advice with every sale. Finally it was down to two women standing near his horse. He was surprised to see one of them was Harriet. He'd forgotten during the dispensing of his Royal Remedies that he'd even brought her with him.

Harriet reached an arm across the other woman's shoulders and gently propelled her towards him. "This is Mrs Kemp, Seth." He noted the stumble in Harriet's voice as she said his name. She drew closer and lowered her voice. "She has been having difficulty … keeping with child. I told her you would have something that would help her."

He looked from her to Mrs Kemp, who appeared hardly any older than Harriet. Worry was forming fine lines across her forehead.

"Rest assured, Mrs Kemp," he soothed and took her hand. Patting it gently, he drew her under the tiny awning and reached for a bottle of pills from the shelves. "These Queen's Own Pills are just what you need." He held the bottle and read out the label. *"Queen's Own Pills as taken by many a female royal personage will surely relieve and cure you. Each pill has a specific soothing, healing and curative effect on all female organs and functions. It relieves headache and backache, stops periodic pains and strengthens the womb during the first two months of pregnancy."*

He took in the look of anticipation spreading across Mrs Kemp's face.

"Now I may not be back in these parts for quite some time and you need to take two pills a day so I am going to let you have this large bottle for the reduced sum of one pound." He saw a flash of hesitation pass over the young woman's face. It was probably her whole housekeeping allowance. "I wager by the time I see you again you will be cuddling a bonny baby in your arms." The words tumbled swiftly from his tongue. He gave the young woman another gentle pat on the hand.

Immediately she dug in her purse and pulled out the money. He slipped it into his bag. She took her pills and hurried away.

"Do you really think they will help her?"

Septimus spun around. Harriet was standing close to the wagon inspecting his rack of pills and potions. He raised his hand. She flinched but stood her ground. He didn't slap her as he would have liked to do, but instead began rolling down the canvas side of his wagon. There were still people about and he didn't want to draw attention to the woman he was about to part company with. Besides, she had lured the young customer in. Mrs Kemp might not have been brave enough to approach him if it had not been for Harriet.

"Trust me," he said. "Those pills have assisted many a woman."

"It's just that she seemed most anxious to have a baby. Her husband wants children and he beats her when he finds she's not pregnant. Those pills are a lot of money; if they don't work he'll probably beat her for that too –"

"Enough, Harriet. You've brought in a customer but I asked you to wait in the wagon. Go there now."

They made two more stops. Each time he was busy with customers but he noticed Harriet out of the corner of his eye. She stood on the edge of the crowd, watching, but when the purchasing was finished, she would be back in the wagon.

By mid-afternoon he had sold the last of his supplies. There was still the trunk of items he'd taken from the Baker fool. He'd got rid of the clothes but some of the other items he thought more valuable. He imagined he'd get a better price for them in more established villages. He'd save them till the time was right. The brush and the shawl would be Harriet's dowry. His lips tugged up into a smile at the thought.

Septimus pulled in close to a roughly built hut that was little more than a room where ale was sold. He knew the man he was seeking would be inside now.

"Is this where we will find the people you want me to meet?" Harriet's gaze switched from the hut to Septimus in quick flicks.

"Stay with the wagon, Harriet," he said. "There's a man who wants me to buy clothes for his wife and, from his description, she's about your size. He'll want to look at you to confirm so that when I go back to Adelaide I can buy the right clothes. He will pay me well to do it. Your job is to smile nicely and *not* speak."

She gave him a slight nod. He climbed down from his seat, feeling her gaze on his back. He stooped through the small door of the hut. Before his eyes adjusted to the gloom, a hand grasped his shoulder. "Have you brought her?" a voice hissed in his ear.

Septimus shrugged from the grip and turned his lips up in a smile. "Of course, Mr Jones." He looked around. There was no one but themselves and the owner in the drinking house at that time of the day. "Let me buy you a drink then, Mr Jones," he said, "and we can finalise our business." He strode to the crude logs that served as a bar. The big man followed him.

The barman poured two drinks then snapped at Septimus, "Do you want some food too?"

Septimus looked from the ruddy-faced man behind the bar to the nearly empty tin plate in front of Jones. A vile-looking grey slosh lay across the bottom with a few small lumps of some kind of greasy meat barely recognisable as food.

"No, thank you," Septimus said. The bartender left them to it, busying himself moving bottles from his store.

"You said I could view her," Jones said.

"Of course you can." Septimus smiled up at the big man. "She's as eager as you to start a new life, although she won't let on to begin with. She's rather shy." He took a swallow of the gut-burning brew.

Jones wrapped his hand around his cup and swallowed half the drink in one gulp. "I'm not spending a lot of money on goods I haven't seen," he said.

Septimus watched him wipe the back of his huge hand across his mouth and tried hard not to recoil as a loud, smelly belch erupted from the big man's mouth. Just for a moment he entertained a pitying thought for Harriet.

"We don't want to involve my dear sweet sister in the financials, do we?" He pulled a concerned look onto his face. "I wouldn't be leaving her here with you if it weren't for her desire to find a husband and settle down in the country, away from Adelaide." He paused, looked down at his drink and lowered his voice. "Times have been so tough for us since we lost both our parents and all our belongings in the fire back in Adelaide. Harriet has only a few possessions but whatever you give me I will spend wisely on goods to help her make your hut into a home. I'll be back as quickly as I can but the journey back to town then here again would only wear my poor sister out and delay your wedding."

Jones tipped the rest of his drink down his neck and once again wiped his mouth with his hand. "Where is she?"

"Sitting in the wagon." Septimus laid a hand on the big man's arm and leaned closer. "She feels very awkward about this. She's eager to marry but she won't show it in public. She's a very proper and modest woman. Once you get her home, she will be happy to be your wife in all ways. For propriety's sake just pretend you are taking a walk in the fresh air. Don't stare at her too much."

Jones went outside and Septimus took another mouthful of his drink to steady his nerves. There was still so much that could go wrong. He really couldn't predict what Harriet would do – whether she would remain silent and not give the game away.

Jones stooped back into the room, silhouetted by the light behind him.

"She's a fine young woman," he said and now that he was close Septimus could see the grin splitting his pudgy face.

"Of course. Even though she's my own sister I know a good-looking woman but," Septimus laced his voice with concern, "you did say you were expecting the priest soon, didn't you?"

"He should be my way during the next few weeks."

"That's good. I would stay but I am out of goods to sell and the sooner I leave the sooner I'll be back with your supplies." Septimus hesitated. "These are unusual circumstances, Mr Jones. You do understand I don't want to leave my sister with you if your intentions aren't to make an honest woman of her."

"I understand but …" Jones's voice trailed off. He looked from Septimus to the door. He lumbered outside again. Septimus thought the game was up, but when he came back through the door, Jones pulled a wad of notes from his pocket. "Here's the money." He pressed the paper into Septimus's hands and gave them a firm squeeze. "Call me Bill. We are to be family now."

"Thank you, Bill." Septimus pushed the money into his coat pocket. He glanced around. The bartender was nowhere to be seen. "No doubt Harriet will be a great companion but may I suggest you don't engage her in lengthy conversation until you've reached your home. She will naturally be a little anxious at our separation; best to leave her to her solitude for a day or so."

"Whatever you think best." Bill dug in his pocket again. "There's a list of items but perhaps your sister should check it. There may be other things she'd prefer. Fabric for clothes perhaps? Please buy some with that."

Septimus looked at the dirty scrap of paper with crude letters scratched across it. "Harriet is not a woman of huge needs, Bill. She will make do and be happy about it."

"She'll have to manage quite a while without these extra things though. My hut's a couple of days' journey from here and I won't be back to Burra until … How long do you think it will take you?"

"Why don't you draw me a map of how to get to your place?" Septimus said. "I'll come on out to you when I get back. I will be anxious to see my sister is doing well, so I will be as quick as I can."

"Very well," Bill said and he drew rough directions on the back of the supply list. He gave it back to Septimus, and they shook hands. Bill let forth with another loud, smelly belch. "Beg pardon," he said and edged to the door. "I've been in town longer than expected so I really must get on my way. My horse and cart are round the back."

"Why don't you go and get organised? I will bring Harriet round to you."

Bill nodded and Septimus stayed at the crude bar, his mind racing over the words he would use to get Harriet to go with Jones without making a fuss. Finally the perfect scenario formed in his head, as he had known it would. He smiled to himself, drained the last of the fiery liquid and stepped outside.

Fourteen

Harriet smiled politely as the big man came out of the hut again. He barely acknowledged her before turning and hurrying away around the side of the little building. She shivered and nestled into the beautiful shawl Septimus had given her. It had taken all her strength to remain calmly in the wagon and smile when the man had first come out and looked at her. He was so tall that his face was nearly level with hers, and the size of him and his silly grin had immediately reminded her of Pig Boy. Thankfully he'd only inspected her for a minute before returning to the hut.

She had no idea if she was the right size to match his wife. Maybe he didn't either, and that's why he'd come out for a second look. She really didn't care but she knew Septimus was prepared to do almost anything to make a sale. The man must have had some money to part with. If Harriet could help by being appraised she would put up with it, but the big man's gaze had left her with an uneasy feeling.

She was relieved when Septimus emerged from the hut. He looked so handsome as he strode towards her with a determined look on his chiselled face. He was a survivor and so was she. One day they'd be a team. Harriet just had to bide her time. He stared at her briefly then moved quickly to her side of the wagon.

"Get down, Harriet," he said.

She did as he bid, having learned the hard lesson of not asking questions out loud, though her head was full of them. She was both surprised and comforted when Septimus took her arm and helped her to the ground. She followed him to the back of the wagon where he tugged out a hessian bag.

"These things are to take with you."

Harriet's heart began to race but she kept her voice calm. "Take where?"

"We are paying Mr Jones and his wife a visit. He has some wool I can sell on his behalf for a commission. His wife is rather poorly and he's anxious to get home to her. I'm going back to camp to rearrange the wagon. I might have to stash some of the trunks and shelves in the bush to make way for the wool."

"But —"

"Harriet, I will follow tomorrow." His voice was low but sharp. "Don't argue with me on this score. There's no need to make the trip longer for you. If you go with Mr Jones now you'll be there ahead of me, and it sounds as though his wife will be pleased for the company. Once I get there we'll stay another night, load up and begin the journey back to Adelaide."

Harriet took the bag he pressed into her hands. She had no desire to be anywhere near the big man let alone share a wagon ride with him.

"Come, Harriet." Septimus offered his arm. Reluctantly she slipped hers into it. "The sooner we all get on our way, the sooner we'll be headed back to Adelaide to earn a fat commission and restock the supplies. Oh, one more thing," Septimus leaned in closer, "Mr Jones isn't one for the prattle of women. No doubt that's why his wife would enjoy your company but it means you should keep your silence until you reach their home."

They rounded the back of the hut, where the big man sat like a giant on a small cart.

"Here we are, Mr Jones," Septimus said. "This is Harriet."

Before Harriet could say a word she was being hoisted up onto the seat next to the huge man. Jones gave a little smile then turned away quickly and belched.

"Beg pardon," he muttered into his hand.

Harriet looked back at Septimus, hoping desperately he'd change his mind and keep her with him.

"Take care, Harriet," Septimus said. "I'll see you soon."

She looked down at his hand patting hers. He had barely touched her except to threaten her but this afternoon he'd been attentive several times. She stared at him, trying to gauge what was going on behind his smooth smile.

Mr Jones urged his horse forward. With a lurch they were on their way. Harriet gripped the side of the seat, trying to stay in place and not bump against the big man, whose smelly body was taking up most of the bench. She risked a glance behind. Septimus had already disappeared from sight. Harriet's heart raced and her mind clouded with fear. Beside her was a man very like the pig boy who had nearly killed her and ahead was thick bush that appeared to stretch on forever. She prayed Septimus wouldn't take too long to collect her.

They hadn't travelled very far when Mr Jones belched again then turned worried eyes in her direction. "Beg pardon, Miss Whitby," he said. "I live alone but I try to be couth when there are ladies present."

"Alone?" Harriet gasped, but Mr Jones didn't seem to notice her alarm.

"I'm feeling very poorly. I promised your brother I'd look after you but …" He belched again and clutched at his stomach.

"My brother?" Harriet's voice came out in a whisper. What story had Septimus spun this time?

"Something I ate is churning in my guts."

Harriet stared at the man. Beads of sweat formed on his brow even though the afternoon was cool.

"It may be a slow trip to your new home but I am sure once we're there I can make you very happy." Mr Jones's words came out in gabble.

Harriet could hear a loud rumble growling somewhere from within his immense body. "My new home?"

"I know I promised your brother I wouldn't speak of it too soon …" Mr Jones moaned and clutched at his stomach with his free hand. "But I will make you a good husband, Miss Whitby, rest assured about that."

"Husband?"

Harriet's feeble gasp was smothered by another loud belch from Mr Jones.

"I'll have to stop," he said. The cart was barely stationary before he scrambled down and disappeared into the bush.

Harriet listened to the sound of him heaving up the contents of his stomach. Her own insides were churning but her turmoil was out of fear not illness. Septimus had given her to this man to be his wife. She sucked in a breath. Not given – she was sure there would have been money in it for Septimus.

The heaving and groaning continued. Harriet felt sorry for Mr Jones, but there was no way she would be his wife. In her mind she already belonged to Septimus. He'd treated her kindly once and he would do again. She was older now and he'd never know she'd been violated. She would stick to her story that Pig Boy had only beaten her. She would help Septimus build his business and they'd have a new life together. Harriet could see their future; she would just have to work out how to get him to see it too.

She looked in the bag he'd given her. It held the men's clothes she'd worn until she fixed her dress, her sewing kit, the small tin she'd used to make sweet damper and the silver hair brush. His parting gift brought a wry smile to her lips. Where would he be now? She looked behind at the rough track back to town. Septimus was planning to go back to Adelaide but he'd left the trunks and their cooking things at the camp. She was fairly sure he'd go back there today and set off early in the morning.

She looked over in the direction Mr Jones had disappeared into the trees. He wasn't visible through the bush but by the sounds he was making, he wouldn't be returning to the cart any time soon.

Harriet climbed down, taking the bag with her. The sun was getting low in the sky. She didn't know how much time she had before it set but if she could survive Pig Boy and all that had happened afterwards, she could survive this. Clutching the bag, she started back along the track towards Burra.

Septimus urged Clover forward. The path wasn't easy to negotiate at this pace but it was getting late. He wanted to pack up the camp and be ready to take the road back to Adelaide at dawn the following morning. He'd done very well from his first trip as a hawker but now he would have to make changes. It would be some time before he would venture back to Burra, which was disappointing. He'd done very well from the miners and their families but it would be best if he kept his distance for a while.

Once he got back to Adelaide he intended to get a bigger wagon. He had very little of the Royal Remedies left and he was sure the man who'd sold them to him wouldn't be easily found. People out in the bush would always need cure-alls, so he had to find a new supplier. "Medicines" would continue to be a good sideline, but what he really wanted to do was stock up on clothing, tools and a few trinkets for the ladies.

There were a few remaining things in the Baker fellow's trunk that would make good sales to the right person. Septimus smiled to himself. Baker was the gift that kept on giving: first handing over money for the horse, then leaving a trunk full of items.

It had been soft to give Harriet the brush and the shawl – even the cooking tin would have been a saleable item. Septimus had never bothered with it but the girl had put it to good use. He smirked. It was his wedding present to her.

The wagon lurched over a large rut in the track. Septimus held the reins tighter and peered ahead. The rays of the setting sun hit him in the eyes, making it difficult to see the track. Regardless of the rough ride, he continued to urge Clover on.

He wondered how far Harriet had got along the track with Jones before her tongue loosened. Septimus hoped the farmer had had the good sense to keep his answers vague until they reached his hut. There was no doubt Harriet could be a wild cat but if she was isolated she would surely accept her situation and make the best of it. She would have a new life and Septimus had done very well out of the deal.

He patted the pocket where he'd stashed the money then threw his hand back to the reins as Clover rounded a bush. A dry creek bed spread out before them. Even though a full moon was rising, Septimus had misjudged their location. He tried desperately to steady the horse, but again the wagon lurched to one side. Clover slowed to negotiate the bank but the tracks they'd made going back and forth to their camp were more to the left. Septimus sensed rather than saw the bank crumble under the weight of the wagon. He slid forward. The wagon lurched and tilted and he cried out as he was thrown from the seat.

He landed across the rutted bank and though the wind left his lungs he somehow managed a guttural shriek when the wheel rolled over his leg. Pain ripped through his body. He welcomed the black oblivion that enveloped him.

Fifteen

Thomas sat very still. He had his back to the wall of his hut and his bottom in the dirt. His arms rested on his raised legs. Not the most comfortable spot, but the shade thrown by the hut gave relief from the late-afternoon heat. He'd been away days in the saddle again checking the sheep. He'd found the remains of a carcass that had been mauled and eaten. He still hadn't seen any wild dogs but it was evidence of their presence.

Duffy had made contact with the hut builders. They were headed his way but Thomas had no idea when to expect them. He'd done what he could to start the drafting yards – each time he was at the hut he cut more wood for the rails – but he needed the expertise and hands of the other men.

Duffy had once again turned up unexpectedly, and again Thomas was relieved he hadn't stayed long. The shepherd had been too full of anger, mostly directed at the magistrate who had dismissed the attempted murder charge Duffy had set in motion against the native who'd thrown a spear at him.

Duffy had obviously been drinking heavily. He had ranted and raved at the magistrate's injustice: accusing him, Duffy, a white man, who had only been protecting his employer's sheep, of being an aggressor. Duffy had gone on about the magistrate, who had said the native was justified in throwing a spear to protect himself from someone riding at him on a horse and discharging a firearm.

Duffy's words still rang in Thomas's head.

"I was the one getting a telling off," he'd yelled then continued to rant and fume, his cheeks growing even ruddier.

The final straw for Duffy had been when the magistrate said he wasn't happy that the native in custody, a man called Gulda, was actually the native who had thrown the spear. Duffy had launched into another tirade about how they all look alike so how could anyone be sure about anything? The strength of his dislike of native people had made Thomas uncomfortable. He had been glad to see the shepherd leave. That had been a few days back. Since then, Thomas awoke each morning hoping the new day would bring the men to build the yards.

Today his shepherding brought him close to his hut again and he was using the opportunity to cook a pie. He smirked to himself. Only he would describe it as a pie. It was the remains of the sheep meat and some potato and onion with a crumpled crust of flour and water. No comparison to Lizzie's wild peach pie, which he'd eked out for days.

The fruit she'd picked had dried well in the sun. He had it spread out on a bag just beyond where he sat and was planning to gather it and store it today. The dried fruit wasn't as sweet as her pie but made a welcome addition to his simple diet. If he had time, perhaps he would seek out the tree she'd picked the crop from and harvest some more.

He glanced in the direction Lizzie had indicated then squinted, peering hard. He was sure he'd seen a movement in the trees, perhaps an animal. Thomas stared for a long time then gradually eased his head back against the hut. The combination of the warm afternoon and sitting still were making him drowsy. As his eyes fluttered, he saw movement in the trees again. He sat perfectly still. A woman emerged from the shadows. He lowered his gaze to the ground, not sure what to do or where to look. Her skin was glossy black and she was naked. Not a stitch of clothing. The natives he had seen in the streets of Adelaide had all worn some kind of covering.

There was more movement; he risked a peek. Now there were three women, all carrying wooden objects and all naked. Thomas looked down again. Once more there was movement. This time they were close enough for him to see from the corner of his eye. He eased himself up to a standing position and risked another look. The women were halfway between the trees and his hut. He studied each of their faces. They looked down but didn't retreat. The wooden objects they carried were shaped like oblong bowls.

"Hello." Thomas spoke quietly.

The smallest of the three women giggled. She was stopped by a muttered command from the oldest woman. She was much older, Thomas thought, if the creping of her skin was any indication. Then he felt the heat in his cheeks as he took in the sagging of her breasts compared to the plumper rounded bosoms of the other two.

The older woman said something to him then watched him expectantly.

"My name is Thomas," he said and took a small step forward, reaching out a hand.

The younger woman screeched and hid behind the other two, who held their ground.

"Thomas," he said again as his hand dropped to his side. What was he doing out there in the middle of nowhere, trying to make conversation with three naked ladies? The thought of it struck him as so funny that laughter erupted from his throat and he was unable to stop it. The cackle echoed around them. He wondered if this was what it was to go mad. He stopped as suddenly as he had started.

Once again the older woman spoke. He couldn't understand her but the tone of her words were like his mother's when she'd rebuked him. No doubt this native woman thought he was mad as well.

"Sorry," he said. "I have no idea what you are saying."

She muttered at him and pointed. He looked down at the fruit drying on the bag.

"Would you like some?" He bent to gather up several of the leathery morsels.

The woman spoke again, much louder. He looked up to see her tipping her bowl forward. It was full of the bright red fruit. The woman beside her indicated her own bowl. They must have been picking from the tree Lizzie had found.

The older woman muttered again and the three of them turned away.

"Wait," Thomas called. He held up his hand. The older two kept walking but the youngest looked back at him and spoke. Her companions stopped and watched him.

"Wait," he said again and rushed into his hut.

He took a small calico bag and scooped some flour into it, and then he picked up the plate with the last piece of Lizzie's pie and went back outside. He was pleased to see the three women still waited. He lifted the pie for them to see then held out the bag with his other hand.

The oldest woman spoke and the middle one moved forward. She looked at the pie and poked it with her finger then she took the bag from his hand and retreated to the other two where they all looked inside.

"It's flour," Thomas said, "to make a pie with your fruit."

The three of them looked from the bag to Thomas. Once again the oldest woman spoke in the tone of a reprimand but this time the youngest woman's lips turned up in a shy smile. For a moment her deep brown eyes held his gaze then she looked down. The three of them turned and walked back into the trees, where they merged with the shadows and disappeared from his sight.

"Nice meeting you," he called, then struggled to stop the laugh that gurgled in his throat. "Perhaps I am going mad," he muttered and proceeded to shovel mouthfuls of the last piece of fruit pie into his mouth.

One thing Thomas felt quite sure about. Duffy was wrong about natives all looking alike. The three women had looked quite different. He suppressed another urge to laugh out loud and strode off to chop more wood.

Three days later, after more time in the saddle checking the sheep, Thomas was returning to his hut in the hope he'd find the men waiting to build the yards. He'd spent his rounds observing the sheep rather than trying to shepherd them and found, without his interference, they maintained a pattern of grazing and rotating back towards the nearest water supply. Thomas was beginning to think AJ was right about not needing to shepherd.

Derriere snorted as they rounded the last of the trees to the clearing where Thomas wanted to build the yards. He reined the horse to a halt. Standing beside the pile of timber for the drafting yards was a black man. In his hands was Thomas's axe.

Thomas felt for the firearm attached to his saddle. He'd fired it to try to kill one of the hopping animals that shared the country with the sheep but he'd had no luck and only managed to scatter the flock. The only hope he'd have of defending himself with it would be to use it as a club.

The black man put the axe down and stepped away from the wood. Thomas was relieved to see he had a small animal skin hanging from some kind of string around his hips to cover his private parts.

"Hello," Thomas said and dismounted.

"Hello."

Thomas lifted his head at the response. "You speak English."

"Little bit." The man moved closer.

Thomas stepped forward himself and extended his hand. "I am Thomas."

The native reached forward and, as he took his hand, Thomas noticed the weeping broken skin around his wrists. He repeated Thomas's name but only the first part was recognisable. They barely gripped before their hands dropped away.

"Gulda," the black man said.

The way he made the sounds was strange but Thomas surmised this was the native Duffy was determined had thrown a spear at him. He glanced around. This man didn't appear to have any weapons, but there could be other natives hiding in the trees. He remembered how easily the three women had blended into the shadows.

"Hut?" Gulda pointed at the lengths of timber.

"No. I am going to make drafting yards and a shed."

Gulda looked from the timber back to Thomas. There was no understanding in his deep brown eyes.

Thomas drew a square with the toe of his boot in the dirt. "For the sheep."

Gulda's head shot up and his face split in a grin. "Sheep. Mr Tom, sheep." He pointed to his chest, which Thomas now noticed was marked with thick scars. "Help."

Gulda turned and went back to the axe. He threw it over his shoulder and moved to the timber still to be split. Straight away Thomas could see the native knew what to do. It didn't seem right to sit down and eat while another worked, although he was tired from three days away and looking forward to eating something other than dried meat. He went to the hut and took another axe. For the next couple of hours the two men worked side by side with no conversation.

Suddenly, Gulda stopped. He placed the axe by the pile of timber he had split and nodded at Thomas. He didn't even look tired.

Gulda pointed at the large orange moon that was rising swiftly over the hills, then traced an arc through the air with his finger. "I come back." He nodded at Thomas and moved away through the trees.

Thomas looked at the pile of timber Gulda had cut and pondered the man's motives. Had he stolen sheep from Duffy's employer? Had he been the one to throw the spear? Thomas shook his head. Weariness seeped through his body.

He made his way to the stone-cold campfire and busied himself lighting it, desperate for a mug of tea. Finally he sat in the dirt. He rested his back against the log bench and chewed some of the dried red fruits. He had no energy to prepare other food. Once again his isolation threatened to envelope him.

He'd been here for several weeks and yet felt he'd achieved very little. Thomas was grateful for Gulda's work, but even with the native's help, the yard was going to take too long to complete. The sheep needed drafting now and many of them would need to be shorn. That was another job Thomas couldn't do alone. Weary and despondent, he dragged himself to his bed.

The sound of chopping woke him the next morning. He listened for a moment. Either there was an echo or both axes were being used. Thomas stepped out from the trees to see Gulda and another native wielding the axes.

When Gulda saw him he stopped and called out, "Cousin," pointing to the man next to him.

Thomas waved and both men lifted their hands to him in a stilted response, then went back to chopping. With both of his axes in use, there was nothing he could do to help so he set about preparing some damper. He was starving and if these men were going to work for him he would need to provide them with food.

Gulda wolfed down the damper. His cousin, who he called Tarka, wasn't so enthusiastic but both men seemed to appreciate the gesture. They drank the sweet tea Thomas made for them then returned to their chopping.

Before he knew it they had settled to some sort of routine. Thomas selected the trees he thought would make the best rails and took short trips to check the sheep. Each day the natives came back and Thomas grew used to their help and their few words. In the mornings they shared damper with him but they were always gone before the sun set and he ate his evening meals alone.

Sitting by his fire one night, he wondered if the natives would be able to help him draft the sheep. Then there was another problem. How was he to pay them? He suspected they had little understanding or use of money. They'd already done so much for him and all he'd given them was a small amount of food in return. He was getting used to Gulda's broken speech and Tarka's silence, but he recalled how both men's eyes lit up whenever he mentioned the sheep. Perhaps that could be their payment. Maybe they would accept a sheep for all their hard work. Thomas didn't think AJ would object to that. He would try to talk to Gulda about it.

But when the next morning came there were no sounds of chopping and no sign of the natives. Thomas picked up the axe again himself and began to work but his heart wasn't in it. Even though they spoke very little, he had enjoyed the presence of other human beings around the homestead. Still, he was not their employer and he'd given them no payment. He couldn't expect them to work for him for no return. Maybe they'd decided to leave him to it.

The pile of timber they had made was large although nowhere near big enough to build the yards that were needed. Thomas decided it was time to measure out and plan the layout. He spent the morning stepping out and driving in marker sticks. Once again the day had become hot very early and by mid-morning the sweat was trickling down his chest and back, inside his shirt.

Thomas lifted his head when a different sound reached his ears. A crack like that made by a whip echoed from beyond the hut. His spirits lifted: maybe George and Lizzie were paying him a visit. He heard the heavy clump of hooves and the sound of male voices. Definitely visitors, although he remembered George didn't use a whip on his bullocks.

"*Coo-ee.*"

The loud call echoed along the creek. Thomas strode around the hut. Coming towards him was a bullock dray and several men on horses.

"G'day, mate." The lead man called. "We hear you want some building done."

Thomas could feel the grin burst across his face and the weight of the work ease from his shoulders.

The man in front stepped down from his horse. He was taller than Thomas, a big solid man with a thick, full beard. He stood straight and surveyed the area. There was no denying he was in charge. His gaze swept back to Thomas and he thrust out his hand.

"Captain's what they call me," he said. He jerked his thumb over his shoulder. "These men don't look like much but they're good workers."

"Thomas Baker," Thomas replied as he accepted Captain's firm grip. "You're welcome. All of you," he called to the assembled group.

Captain kept Thomas's hand in his grip and leaned down. Thomas took in the lines on his brow and the narrowing of his eyes.

"I don't ask where they've come from," he said in a steady voice just loud enough for Thomas to hear. "I expect that they follow my rules and work hard. In return I treat them fair. They get fed and earn a wage and we all get along fine. No need to get too friendly with them." Captain let go of Thomas's hand and slapped him on the back. "Where do you want us to make camp?"

Thomas led him to a clearing in a patch of bush not far from where he hoped the new shearing shed would be built. Captain's manner reminded Thomas of the man who'd captained their ship to Australia. His commanding presence was reassuring. Thomas's spirits lifted. With Captain in charge and so many men, they would get the job done in no time.

Sixteen

Harriet pushed one foot in front of the other. Her darting gaze scoured the bush for the place where she hoped the bright moonlight would illuminate the wheel marks from the wagon. Septimus had made the journey in and out of Burra several times. She knew so many trips would leave a track to follow but she had only been along it once. Perhaps she'd missed the place where he turned off the road. A wave of anguish washed over her. She was so tired. The moon, which had risen over her shoulder, was now low in the sky. She was running out of time.

Every sound she'd heard in her desperate rush back along the track away from Jones had sent her heart racing. She'd imagined the big man chasing her but there'd been no pursuit. She'd made it back to Burra and picked her way around the huts and shelters where she'd heard and smelled the evidence of people eating their evening meal. The damper she'd made for breakfast was a vague memory but she'd kept going. It was best if no one saw her in case Mr Jones did come looking.

Now that Burra was well behind her, she felt safe from pursuit, but she still had to find the camp and hope that Septimus had stayed the night. Harriet knew he wouldn't be pleased, but if she could just get to the wagon before morning she could once again hide inside. By the time he discovered her they would be too far away to return her to Mr Jones.

A small branch dangled from a tree in front. It hung at an angle like a finger pointing. There below it were the tell-tale signs of wheels leaving the road to make their own track through the bush. Harriet's tired feet hurried her forward. This was the path that wound through the trees and across a couple of dry creek beds to the place where they'd camped.

The night was still and, even though the track was well lit, she staggered over the ruts made by the wagon, tripped on rocks and got hooked in the branches that reached out to slow her progress. Finally she paused. She must be getting close to the camp. She'd crossed one dry creek bed and knew there was another soon. Not far beyond that was the creek with water where they'd camped. Septimus had good hearing. She would have to travel much slower and take care if she was to secrete herself in the wagon without him knowing.

She set off again more carefully. The nickering sound of a horse close by pulled her up. She turned her good ear to the track behind her. Surely it couldn't be Mr Jones after all this time. She heard the nicker again: the horse seemed to be ahead of her, but it was too close to be Clover at their camp.

Harriet's frightened mind swirled with the possibilities. Mr Jones had somehow got ahead of her and was waiting to pounce, or one of those men who had taken to robbing people as they travelled through the bush was camped nearby, or maybe Septimus had moved and was ready for an early start.

For a moment Harriet froze. Fear threatened to engulf her. How had she got to this point? From her idyllic bush childhood to her and her mother's exile and still further to Pig Boy's attack and this precarious existence with Septimus, who would rather sell her to a barbarian than love her?

"The only one who can look after you is you, girl." Harriet's whisper was loud in the still night. She put a tentative foot forward. There was no help behind her. The only way was in front of her. She had to face whatever was ahead.

She placed her feet carefully and followed the track again. Each step gave her courage. She continued around the bend, even when the horse snorted quite close. The sight before her drew a gasp from her lips. The dry creek bed was bathed in moonlight and nearly to the other side was a horse and wagon. She glanced around, wondering why Septimus would leave Clover attached to the wagon in a creek.

A moan sent her heart racing. Then she saw the shape of a man stretched out in the sand between her and the wagon.

"Septimus." She scurried down the crumbling bank to his side. "Septimus," she said again. "Where are you hurt?"

He was stretched out face down, as if he'd been trying to reach the wagon. He turned his head slightly to the sound of her voice. Sand and sticks were stuck to his face. He tried to lift himself. A moan gurgled from his throat and he collapsed.

Clover nickered and the wagon shuddered.

Harriet looked from Septimus to the horse. "Septimus!" She shook his shoulders.

This time he opened his eyes. "Harriet?"

"Yes, it's me." She clutched his face between her hands. His skin was cold even though the night was mild. "What happened, Septimus? Where are you hurt?"

Clover snorted and stamped and the wagon lurched away a few feet.

"My leg," Septimus said. "It's broken."

Harriet's heart hammered in her chest. She glanced along his body to his legs spread out behind him. Now she looked she could see the odd angle of his left leg and the drag marks in the sand. He'd crawled some distance.

A hand clutched at her dress. "Help me, Harriet." His voice was barely a whisper.

He must have been lying there for some time. Without help he would probably die. Harriet's mind flashed back over her own agonising injuries. She had a fair idea Septimus had known she was still alive when he threw her in the creek, but his actions had saved her. She was sure their lives were linked and this was proof. He needed her help now. They only had each other.

She brushed the sand from his face with her dress and used the trousers from her bag to make a pillow for his head. All the while her mind raced. She had no idea what to do. Septimus's eyes were shut again but she could hear the rasp of his breathing. Perhaps he had other injuries. The only thing she could think of was to get him to a doctor. She knew there was one in Burra, though there was no way she wanted to go back to that town. Mr Jones could be there waiting to pounce! But she couldn't let Septimus die: he was her future.

She stood up and called reassuringly to Clover. The horse was obviously spooked but he either couldn't run away or had decided to stay near his master. With careful steps she approached the animal, speaking in soothing tones. Clover nickered again in what Harriet hoped was a call of recognition. She reached out and stroked his neck. He turned his head in her direction and gave a throaty call. He shifted his weight on his legs but he didn't move away.

Harriet walked all around him looking for any obvious signs of injury. There were none. The apparatus that attached him to the wagon looked as it should. She reached up and took hold of Clover's bridle, urging him to follow her in a big arc until they stopped beside Septimus. Clover nickered at his master but there was no response.

Harriet looked at the man stretched out in the sand at her feet. He wasn't a fat man but he was taller than her and muscly; there was no way she could get him into the wagon alone.

Suddenly his hand grabbed her skirt. "Harriet."

She dropped down beside him, grateful he was still alive and remembered she was there.

"I've brought the wagon," she said. "But I can't lift you on by myself."

"Splint the leg first." His words came out in stilted rasps. "Then I can stand."

Harriet looked from his ashen face to the broken leg. What could she make a splint with and, even with that, how would he have the energy to stand?

Septimus tugged at her skirt. "Hurry."

Harriet scoured the creek bed. There were logs and sticks but nothing she could use for a splint. She looked in the wagon. It was nearly empty. Septimus hadn't made it back to camp to load the trunks and the rest of his camp-kitchen items. Her eyes rested on the shelves he used to display his Royal Remedies. They would do the job but first she had to break them apart. She pulled at them with her hands but couldn't loosen them. A search of the wagon unearthed a hammer. She wielded it with all her strength and smashed the shelving. Septimus would have to make a new set for his pills and potions.

Harriet carried the two flat shelves back to Septimus. She took her scissors and the shirt from the bag and made long strips of cloth. She'd never splinted a leg before but she'd seen her father's handiwork on the leg of a shepherd. She checked Septimus again. His eyes were closed but when she moved his leg he let out a guttural scream.

Seventeen

The waves of pain were more bearable now that the wagon had stopped. Septimus had lost all track of time but when he flicked his eyelids he could see it was day. Somehow Harriet had splinted his leg and helped him into the wagon and then had begun the next part of the nightmare. Every jolt of the wagon brought fresh waves of pain.

Voices approached, then he heard rather than saw the side of the wagon roll up.

"How're we going to get him out of there?" a rough male voice asked.

"Have to lift him between us," another replied.

Septimus groaned at the thought of disturbing his leg again.

"Surely the doctor has a stretcher." Harriet's voice was demanding.

"Look, Miss –"

"It's Mrs. Mrs Seth Whitby. My husband has been through enough to get here. You're not going to drag him from the wagon without care."

Septimus thought he was dreaming. Had she said Mrs Whitby?

"Nothing else for it, missus. We don't have fancy equipment out here."

"But we can improvise, Ned."

"Dr Nash."

Septimus heard a new and respectful tone in Ned's voice. He squinted in the direction of the talking. Two burly men stood beside him. The doctor and Harriet were out of his line of sight.

"What's happened here?"

"Thank goodness you're here, Doctor," Harriet said. "My husband was thrown from the wagon and broke his leg. I made a splint but it's been a long night getting him here. I'm worried he may have other injuries."

"What's his name?" The doctor's voice was close to Septimus now.

"Seth Whitby."

"Mr Whitby?"

A hand shook his shoulder. Septimus opened his eyes into a squint again.

"You have a broken leg, Mr Whitby. Do you have pain anywhere else?"

Septimus would have hit the doctor if he could. Pained raged through him from every quarter. He tried to speak but all that escaped his lips was a groan.

"I need to get him inside for a proper examination." The doctor's voice receded. "Samuel, get the planks we strapped together for that miner the other day. You can carry him on that."

"Yes, Dr Nash."

"And mind you do it carefully."

Septimus felt a gentle hand on his brow.

"You'll be taken care of soon."

Harriet's voice was soothing but quickly forgotten as the two men returned and began to slide him onto their rough stretcher. Once again he receded into a fog of pain.

★

A terrible smell tugged Septimus from the peace of sleep. He opened his eyes to a gloomy room lit by candlelight. He was lying on a narrow bed. His body ached but the excruciating pain that was his leg had been subdued to a dull throb. The air was close and fetid.

He wrinkled his nose. He must have vomited, judging by the overpowering smell.

"Look who's awake."

Septimus turned his head and frowned. Not two feet from him loomed a familiar face.

"Mr Jones?"

"Yes, it's me."

The big man belched. Septimus felt his own stomach clench at the smell.

"Don't reckon you were expecting to see me again, were you, Whitby? A fine fool you made of me. Selling me that woman then poisoning me so she could escape."

"I didn't poison you," Septimus growled.

"Granted that may have been the muck that bartender fed me but you and that woman … your sister." Jones spat the words then belched again. "Tricked me, the pair of you, with your fancy story. No doubt you had plans to dupe some other poor soul at the next place but looks like justice caught up with you."

"My sister?" Septimus feigned surprise and reached a hand down under the blanket to feel his leg. It was wrapped in some kind of solid casing. He didn't like his chances of a speedy escape.

Jones grabbed his shirt. "Don't think you're going anywhere soon," the big man hissed. "I want my money back."

Septimus had no idea where his jacket was. He'd been wearing it when he drove the wagon but all he had on now was his shirt. He peered around the gloomy room. There was another crude bed across from him where the Jones fellow had obviously been installed. The blanket had been tossed aside and draped to the ground. Between the beds was a crude table with the candles, a bottle of medicine and beside that was a roll of bandage and a pair of scissors.

"Where's my money?" Jones hissed and lowered his face towards Septimus again.

Septimus shot a hand out. He snatched up the scissors and stabbed them into one of the burly arms that clutched him with as much force as he could muster.

Jones yelped and flung his arm back, knocking the candles. His sleeve began to smoulder. They both stared as the shirt erupted into flames. Then Jones began to bat at it. One of the dislodged candles rolled to the floor, where it set light to the discarded blanket.

Another yell brought Septimus's eyes back to Jones. The big fool must have lifted his arm to his head and his hair was now on fire. He was dancing around on the blanket, which was also burning and before long his trousers were alight.

"Help me!" Jones's cry filled the room. Septimus edged away to the end of the bed and tested his feet on the floor. Pain surged up his leg again. The room was full of screaming and the foul smell of burning. Septimus watched Jones clawing at his head and jumping around fanning the flames into life. There was a way to be rid of the unfortunate Mr Jones. Septimus reached for the medicine bottle. He removed the stopper and sniffed the contents. As he had hoped there was alcohol in the mixture. He tugged the blanket from his own bed, poured the liquid over it and tossed it onto the burning blanket. It too quickly caught alight. Then, using the wall to support himself, he hobbled to the door and threw it open.

Behind him the flames leaped higher and Jones bellowed into the night. A voice called out nearby and others joined it. A man put his arm around Septimus and led him away. The night was full of fire and noise. Septimus turned to watch. The men who were trying to reach Jones were held back by the ferocity of the flames. The screams from within stopped.

The hut they'd been in stood alone, behind the doctor's house. He was there as well, standing in his dressing gown. People came from everywhere with buckets. Water was thrown at it. Finally the little hut fell in on itself. The worst of the flames subsided.

Once it was clear the fire was in no danger of spreading, the doctor wrapped Septimus in a blanket and took him into his home, where questions were asked about the fire. Septimus put on a terrified face and told how he woke to the room ablaze. He spoke in a troubled voice, not difficult when his own leg was giving him so much pain. He told those gathered in the doctor's front room how he'd tried to smother Jones with his own blanket but the man had pushed him away. They called him heroic and Septimus shook his head.

"Poor man," he moaned. "I couldn't save him."

The doctor tut-tutted. He inspected Septimus for burns, listened to his chest as he breathed in and out and took another look at the bandaged leg.

"You're lucky you weren't lost in the fire as well," the doctor said. "I should never have left Jones unattended. I didn't realise he was still disoriented."

He tucked Septimus up on a padded couch. "There will be more questions in the morning but I want you to rest until then," the doctor said. "You've had enough ordeals for any man in a short time."

"Who was that man in the hut with me?" Septimus said.

"A farmer from out of the town. He was found passed out near his wagon. I diagnosed some kind of food poisoning. Goodness knows what the fellow had eaten. I put him to bed thinking the worst was over and he'd be too weak to go anywhere for a while." The doctor looked closely at Septimus. "You have no idea what happened?"

"No. As I've already told you, I awoke to the flames."

"He must have wandered and knocked the candle."

"Where is Har– my wife?" Septimus asked, not wanting to be cross-examined by the doctor any further.

"There was nothing she could do for you while I worked on your leg so she said she was going back to pack up your camp. She will return for you in the morning. I told her your leg casing should be strong enough for travel by then. She seemed to think you needed to be back in Adelaide urgently."

"That's right."

"Try to rest then," the doctor said. "Morning will be here soon enough." He nodded and left.

Septimus smiled. Good on Harriet. She could be of some use to him while his leg was mending. Once she got back they'd be on their way from this place, perhaps never to return, in light of all that had happened. It would be a pity to lose such a lucrative market but there were plenty of other opportunities for a smart salesman like himself. In the current circumstances it appeared he was going to need some help. Having Harriet around for a while would be very beneficial.

Septimus nestled back on the doctor's comfortable couch and allowed himself to relax. His smile turned in to a snigger. Twice he'd tried to get rid of the woman and twice she'd come back. Next time he sent Harriet packing the odds would be on his side.

Eighteen

"You fell on your feet here, Mr Baker."

Thomas turned to see one of the men slip from the shadows beyond the fire. When everyone else had retired for the night, Thomas couldn't drag himself away. The flames were mesmerising. He knew he would fall asleep in an instant if he went to his bed. The last two weeks had been constant work from sunrise until dusk. The men had built the yards and now they'd started on the shearing shed. He ranged between checking the sheep, marking out plans, finding the right timber and working alongside the builders.

The man, whose name was Gurr, was a nasty-looking character with a scar under one eye and several teeth missing. Short of stature and with a stooped appearance, he always seemed to be looking over his shoulder. He held his hands to the flames. There could be no mistaking the mockery in his tone when he spoke Thomas's name.

Gurr's equally menacing mate, Platts, appeared beside him. "Nice set up," he murmured.

Thomas ignored both men and threw another large bough on the fire. He did not like or trust either of the men; Platts was as unpleasant as Gurr, if not as brazen. Thomas had noticed their shifty behaviour on the first day but his initial dismay had been put to rest when they kept their heads down and got on with their work. Until now they hadn't spoken to him nor he directly to them but he'd kept his eye on them.

They both sat and Thomas noticed a small flask slip from Platts's hand to Gurr's. They obviously weren't abiding Captain's no-drink rule, though neither did they appear inebriated.

Platts belched. "At least you provide good food here. Better'n the last place. That was terrible tucker, wasn't it Gurr?"

"Bloody kangaroo, the same wherever we go."

Thomas didn't care what they thought of the food but he'd certainly enjoyed it tonight. They'd eaten kangaroo courtesy of Captain's ability with a firearm. The large, hopping animal had been down by the stream. Thomas had mentioned his difficulties managing the weapon and Captain had given him some lessons. Thomas was confident that, once the builders left, he'd be able to shoot a kangaroo for himself. They were in abundance, along with similar-looking smaller creatures. There was no need for a man to live on mutton alone.

"You got any blacks camped near here?"

Gurr's question surprised Thomas. He flicked a look at the man, who was grinning like an idiot. Gurr spat at the fire then took a swig from the flask.

"No." He hadn't given a thought to Gulda and Tarka since Captain and his men had arrived, but he wasn't going to share any information with these two.

"You should find out," Platts said. "Make friends with them."

"Gets very lonely way out here with no female company," Gurr said. He winked at Thomas.

"The women are very obliging," Platts added.

Thomas thought of the three women who had come to pick the red fruit. He felt heat in his cheeks as he recalled their nakedness.

"Nothing like a bit of black —"

"You men get to your beds." Captain's growl came from the gloom beyond the fire.

Gurr and Platts jumped.

"I've warned you before," Captain said. "If you so much as look at a woman while you're working for me I'll pack you off back to Adelaide to fend for yourselves. That's your last chance." His voice was low. There was no doubting the threat.

Gurr and Platts muttered, "Yes, Captain." They both turned away but not before Thomas had seen the hostile look Gurr shot his way.

"My apologies, Thomas," Captain said. "Those two have some bad habits which they've promised me they won't nurture if I keep them on. They're good workers so I've been lenient, but I won't abide interference with local women, black or white."

"Don't worry about it, Captain. I'm sure you've noticed there are no women around here."

"Perhaps not now but there have been natives camped nearby."

"I've not seen a camp."

"I saw their markings on some rocks further up the creek," Captain said. "There's evidence they lived close by, but you're right, they've gone now."

That would explain Gulda's easy appearances and disappearances, Thomas thought. "A couple of the men came and helped me cut the first timber for the yards," he said. "I didn't know where they came from. I've seen no sign of them since you arrived."

"You've got a lot of sheep to manage out there." The big man swung his arm in a wide arc. "In my experience it's best to leave the natives alone. Don't encourage them. I've had no trouble by following that principle. They keep out of my way and I keep out of theirs, including my men. Now if you'll excuse me, I must turn in."

Thomas acknowledged Captain's departure with a nod, then eased himself back down by the fire. There were no clouds in the sky and the night had turned: he was cool in spite of the extra log he'd thrown on. He felt edgy. The thought of Gurr and Platts with native women repelled him. A vision of the three naked women played in his head but always there was Captain's stern face watching him. It made his skin prickle. The man had warned him against working with the natives but Thomas still thought it the sensible thing to do, and he felt guilty he'd not given Gulda and Tarka something in return for their work. Perhaps once the builders left they would come back. One thing was certain, Thomas wouldn't relax now until Gurr and Platts were gone.

The business of building a shearing shed took another week of back-breaking work once the drafting yard was finished but finally it was all done. There had been no more talk from anyone about the natives and their women. Captain had even found time to suggest some additions to Thomas's hut. It now had a verandah across the front and a second room with a fireplace. Thomas would be able to sleep and cook inside during the winter. It was still not a homestead but certainly more useful.

The last night together around the fire was much noisier than usual. Everyone was happy the work had been completed but none more than Thomas, who was now anxious to begin the huge task of drafting the sheep so they could be shorn. The thought of it no longer overwhelmed him. It seemed a lifetime ago rather than a few months since he'd met AJ and taken on the position.

Now that their job was done, Captain supplied some drink for his men. Thomas had taken a sip to be sociable but once again the fiery liquid was not to his taste. He noticed Gurr and Platts drank a big share. Gradually the stories around the fire became bolder and merrier. From time to time he caught Gurr's steely glare but Thomas kept his distance. Platts took no notice, more intent on swallowing as much of the shared grog as he could. Finally he stumbled close to the fire. Captain called it a night at that and urged the men to turn in ready for an early departure. Once again Thomas was the last to leave the warmth of the fire. As he approached his bed a man stepped from the shadows into the faint light of a half moon.

"A word before we leave, Mr Baker."

Gurr, Thomas could see, was drunk and looking for a fight. Thomas felt his body tingle on full alert.

"Types like you think you are special with your fancy job."

"What do you mean?"

Thomas might have been bigger than Gurr but the man was used to fighting. He glanced around. There was no sign of Platts, but plenty of shadows to conceal him.

Gurr moved swiftly and grabbed Thomas by the arm. He pushed his face in close and Thomas wrinkled his nose at the boozy breath.

He wrenched his arm free.

Thomas was thankful Gurr couldn't see the heat that throbbed in his cheeks. But he was also sure now that the despicable man was alone. Thomas eased his shoulders back. The odds were more even now, and he did not like bullies.

Gurr gave him a shove. Thomas was ready for it and pretended to wobble backwards, then lurched forward, swinging his clenched fist. He connected firmly with the side of Gurr's face. He felt the jar through his fist. Gurr gasped. Before he could recover, Thomas stepped around him. He slammed his fist under Gurr's chin, sending the man backwards to the ground.

Thomas snatched the firearm from its position in the tree.

Gurr growled. He struggled to his feet but froze when he saw what Thomas was pointing at him.

"I had no quarrel with you or your friend." Thomas's voice was low and unwavering. "But tomorrow you will leave my land and never come back."

Gurr spat at his feet. "This isn't your land."

"No, but I am in charge of it for now." Thomas gripped the rifle tighter. "Our paths should never cross again, but if they do, you will be the one who is sorry, Gurr."

Gurr looked from the rifle to Thomas. He put a hand to his face and rubbed it slowly. "We'll see, Baker, we'll see." He gave Thomas one last withering look then eased backwards and slipped into the shadows.

Thomas remained rigidly holding the firearm. He listened to the soft tread of Gurr's feet until they were lost in the whispers of the trees. He hoped never to be bothered by the odious man again but, just in case, he would keep the firearm close.

Thomas startled awake the next morning at the sound of voices. Captain was barking orders at his men, getting them packed up and ready to move on to the next job.

Before they left, each of the men shook Thomas's hand, except for Gurr, who was busy tying down a wagon cover. He glanced up just as Thomas looked his way. The black eye he sported gave Thomas some small satisfaction. A strong hand gripped his shoulder. He turned to see Captain's rugged face.

"Take care, Thomas," the other man said, "and I'll be more than happy to work for you in the future. You're a fair and honest man with a good brain. I am sure the day will come when you will be in charge of your own property."

Thomas couldn't imagine life beyond Penakie, but who knew what the future held? He was happy to wave the team goodbye without the regret that the return to isolation would normally have brought. Apart from getting rid of Gurr and Platts there was work to be done. Thomas had a plan. He took a bag of the dried fruit and mounted Derriere. He had to find his way to the Smiths' homestead. George had offered his sons to help with the drafting and Thomas hoped that would still be possible. Once he set off, he realised seeing the forthright Miss Lizzie again wouldn't be a bad thing either. He urged Derriere into a trot.

Nineteen

Lizzie glanced from the front door of the Smith house back to her father. "No sign of Edmund and Zac." She lifted the cutlery she held in her hands. "Should I set places for them?"

"I don't know when they'll be back," George said.

Lizzie's other two brothers, Jacob and Samuel, were seated at the table. They both groaned.

"My stomach thinks my throat has been cut," Jacob said and clutched his middle.

"No need for that kind of talk, Jacob," his mother reprimanded. "Lay the table for those of us here, Lizzie. I'll set some food aside for Edmund and Isaac."

"They were headed west following that dry creek with the big washed rocks. Edmund said he could see tracks." Jacob blew out a breath. "I don't know how."

"With any luck, Edmund will catch the thief this time and we'll put an end to it." Their father sat himself at the head of the table. "I'm fed up with losing sheep to those natives."

Lizzie paused in front of him. "But how will you put an end to it, Father? Even with five of you, you can't be everywhere at once."

"They need to be punished."

"In what way punished?" his wife asked.

A distant "*coo-ee*" echoed from outside and stopped any reply George was going to make. Jacob and Samuel were first to the door. Their father was close behind, Lizzie following him outside. Her mother was busy patting down her hair. It was rare to have visitors.

Lizzie put a hand to her brow. A man on a horse was crossing the yard in front of their house. She grinned. It was their neighbour, Thomas Baker.

"Hello, Thomas," she called and waved vigorously.

Her mother had arrived to stand beside her and tugged gently at her arm. "A little less vigour, Lizzie dear," she murmured.

The visitor's face too was lit in a smile. He waved back.

"You found us all right," George said. "Welcome."

Lizzie watched Thomas climb down from his horse. He was moving freely. No sign of any tender spots. Her grin widened at the thought of their last encounter. He had been so embarrassed, poor man, but he wouldn't have been able to lance that boil without her help.

"This is my wife, Anne."

Thomas raised his hat.

"And you know our Lizzie, of course."

Lizzie felt her mother's restraining hand still on her arm as she went to rush forward. She stayed where she was. "How are you, Thomas?" she asked demurely.

"Well, thank you, Lizzie," he said.

Lizzie studied his face. Had he put extra emphasis on the *thank you*?

"These are my two middle boys, Samuel and Jacob."

"Pleased to meet you all," Thomas said. Lizzie noticed they were all of a similar height and stature though her brothers had a few years on Thomas. She was sure he was looking much fuller of body. "You've certainly developed some muscles since I saw you last and –"

"Lizzie!" her mother reprimanded.

"I was only saying how much healthier he looks. You should have seen him before with his pale skin and skinny –"

"Is this a social call, Thomas, or are you in need of help?" George cut in as Lizzie's mother tapped her on the arm again.

"Both." Thomas turned back to his horse. "I've brought a gift." He unhooked a calico bag from his saddle.

"You may have plenty of these but Miss … Lizzie showed me how to dry them, so I thought I'd bring you some of my first attempt."

"Thank you, Mr Baker." Lizzie's mother took the bag and gave the contents a brief glance, then passed it to Lizzie.

"Oh, you've dried some wild peaches," Lizzie said. "Thank you."

She beamed at Thomas, who stood tall in front of her, clutching his hat in both hands. She was rewarded with an equally broad smile and something inside her did a little flip. He was quite the most handsome man she'd met.

"Won't you join us for something to eat, Mr Baker?" Anne said. "The boys went off without breakfast this morning so we were about to sit down to our midday meal a little earlier than usual."

"Yes, come and join us, Thomas." George threw an arm across Thomas's shoulders and drew him towards the door. "You can tell us what you've been up to and what brings you our way."

Lizzie followed a few steps behind the others. She would much prefer to be the one leading Thomas inside but her mother was always reminding her she was far too forward. At least he was to stay for the meal. It would give her the opportunity to find out more about him, even if she did have to share him with almost her entire family.

Lizzie was curious to know what had happened with that horse back in Adelaide. She hadn't said anything at the time, but she'd recognised him immediately. She didn't know a lot about horses but she was fairly sure neither of the horses he'd had at his hut was the one she'd seen him with in the street outside the general store.

Everyone was seated around the table except Lizzie and her mother, who served plates of mutton pie, pickled cabbage and boiled potatoes. Anne had allowed Lizzie to toss the warm potatoes in a skerrick of butter with chopped parsley.

Once grace had been said, her brothers were quick to begin their meals, though they paused between mouthfuls, taking it in turns to ply Thomas with questions. Before long he had told them about his life in England, the death of his mother back home and then his father on the voyage to Australia, and his meeting with AJ. Lizzie noted nothing was said about the horse. Perhaps one day she would ask him about it, but not now.

"This is an isolated life compared with the way you lived in England," she said. "Don't you get lonely?"

Thomas looked across the table and she held his gaze. He had deep brown eyes that gave her the feeling he was much older than his twenty years. There was something strong and dependable about his look. She felt her heart beating faster.

"Sometimes," he said.

"McKenzie's death was a bad business," George said. "You've got a big job there on your own."

"Do you have much trouble with the natives?" Jacob asked.

"Everyone stop asking Mr Baker questions," Anne said. "The poor man has hardly taken a bite of his food."

"We don't see many visitors, Thomas," George said. "You eat up."

Lizzie watched as Thomas tucked into the food while the talk of her father and brothers flowed around them. Finally, he sat back.

"Thank you, Mrs Smith," he said. "That was the most delicious pie."

"I suspect you don't eat many pies, Mr Baker. In any case, I didn't make it. It's Lizzie you should be thanking."

"It was very good pie." Thomas smiled at Lizzie.

Lizzie basked in his attention. "Mother says my pastry needs a gentler hand."

"She probably talked to it too much," Samuel said.

"Or slapped it too hard," Jacob added with a playful tap on his sister's shoulder.

"That's enough, boys," George said. "If your mother and sister are good enough to put food on the table you'll accept it with good grace."

"Gather the plates please, Lizzie." Her mother stood up. "Would you like a cup of tea, Mr Baker?"

"Yes, please, and won't you call me Thomas, Mrs Smith?"

"Thomas it is," she said, "and you may call me –"

"Mrs Smith," Lizzie and her brothers chorused. Everyone except their mother laughed.

"No." She glanced at each of her children sternly then looked at Thomas with a smile. "I was going to say, Anne."

"You *are* a special visitor," Jacob said. "Everyone but us calls her Mrs Smith."

She left the table to make the tea while Lizzie picked up the plates. Once again her brothers and father began to talk. Lizzie noticed Thomas looking around the room. No doubt he thought their place more homelike than his own; it was certainly a little bigger, although when all six Smiths were home it was a tight squeeze to fit everyone around the table. There were only two bedrooms, one for her parents and the other for her brothers. Lizzie slept on the long low couch under the window.

"So, tell me now, Thomas," George said once the tea had been set in front of them. "What brought you to our door today?"

"I've had the hut builders at Penakie," Thomas said. "They've built drafting yards and a shearing shed. I've come to ask for some of that help you offered."

Before George could answer, a distant shout turned everyone's attention to the door. Samuel and Jacob immediately started pushing at each other to get through the gap first.

"That sounds like Zac." Lizzie stood up.

"Stay here, Anne," George said. "And you, Lizzie," he added as she went to the door. "You'd best come with us, Thomas. You will no doubt have to deal with natives yourself in the future."

Lizzie saw a slight frown cross Thomas's face before he turned to follow her father. She stepped after him. She wanted to spend as much time in his company as she could but her mother put out a restraining hand.

"You heard your father, Lizzie. We must stay here," she said. She looked past Lizzie out the door. "I don't like the sound of this business at all."

Twenty

Unease settled on Thomas as he followed his neighbour outside and across the yard towards a large gum tree away from the house. Already at the tree were three men. Two of them, he could see, were so like Samuel and Jacob they had to be the other two brothers, the only visible difference being Samuel and Jacob were fair like Lizzie and their mother and these other two had dark brown hair like George. Thomas couldn't see the face of the other man but could tell he was a native from the black arms and legs flailing about.

The taller of the two brothers spoke as his father approached. "We've got him."

The other said, "Who's that?" They all turned and looked at Thomas, who was several steps behind. He didn't know what was going on here but he was certain he did not want to be involved.

"Come and join us, Thomas," George called. "You should learn how best to deal with these fellows."

Thomas glanced behind him. Lizzie was at the door, her face full of concern. Anne was looking over her shoulder.

He sucked in a long, slow breath and continued after George. He frowned as Samuel produced a thin branch and held it out for his father. George took it and flicked it on the ground like a lash.

The two brothers who had brought the native had him spread around the trunk of the tree. His bare back glistened in the dappled shade of the giant gum. He was struggling against the arms that pinned him to the tree and yabbering in his native tongue.

Thomas glanced from the scarred wrists to the native's head. Only his side profile was visible but Thomas knew him. The man turned his black face and his fear-filled eyes locked on Thomas.

"Mr Tom," the native cried out and then babbled something Thomas didn't understand.

"Do you know this person?" George said to Thomas.

All eyes were now looking at him.

"He cut some timber for me before the hut builders came."

"He's probably been stealing your sheep. If the truth be known, he'd owe you," George said.

"I have no evidence of that."

"Well, we do." One of the brothers holding Gulda to the tree spat at his feet. "Caught him red-handed this time. You going to give him those lashes, Father?"

"Boys, this is our new neighbour, AJ's overseer, Thomas Baker." George indicated the men to the left and the right of the tree. "That's Isaac and that's Edmund."

Thomas nodded as one man and then the other acknowledged him.

"You're the man Lizzie was prattling on about," Edmund said. He was the one who had spat and, by the look of him, was the oldest of the brothers.

"Thomas will be needing help from you boys to get his sheep in and drafted." George tapped the branch in his hand against his leg.

Thomas looked at each of them in turn. Did none of them think it was strange to be having such a civil conversation while they held a poor native man pinned to a tree? He wished he'd never come.

Suddenly Gulda kicked out with his foot and connected with Edmund's shin. The kick carried enough force to make Edmund yelp and let go his grip.

Quick as a flash Samuel stepped in and grabbed Gulda's free arm. George ignored Edmund's threats to thrash the man himself and stepped in closer. He raised the branch and Gulda called loudly. Once again the only word that made any sense was "Tom". Thomas was appalled at what was about to take place. He forced himself between George and the gibbering native.

"What are you doing?" George glared at him as if he'd gone mad.

"I never paid this man for the work he and his cousin did for me."

Edmund stepped forward to reach for Thomas but George held up a hand. His son stopped but stood his ground and fixed a stony scowl on Thomas.

"As I said, he's probably been stealing your sheep already." George's voice was low and calm as if he was explaining something to a child. "He and his friends have been pilfering ours for a long time but we've never been able to pin him down. The boys set up a trap to catch him in the act and they've done that today."

"I can't let you hurt him, George."

"You don't make the decisions here," Samuel growled.

Thomas sensed movement on his other side and knew Edmund was itching to drag him away.

"Steady, boys." Once again George held up a hand then he turned his serious eyes back to Thomas.

"If you don't punish them for stealing your stock they will get the better of you and you'll never stop them, Thomas. We've caught this man stealing. I could take him to the magistrate but he could end up in chains and I'm not sure that would serve a good purpose. If he receives some punishment from me here today, he will tell his friends that we don't allow thieves. I am happy to trade from time to time but I won't abide theft."

Thomas had no idea what to do but he felt he owed Gulda something. He turned to Edmund. "Did you get your sheep back?"

"Of course." Edmund puffed out his chest. "We set it up so we had him surrounded. He didn't get a chance to escape. We released the animal before this native could kill it."

"So he has nothing of yours in his possession?"

"Well, not now." Edmund spat at Gulda's feet again. "But he would have if we hadn't caught him."

"Enough!" George's voice had lost its patient tone. "Get out of the way, Baker."

Quick as a flash Edmund had him in a grip and started dragging him away. Months of physical work had built up Thomas's strength and Edmund could not shift him far until Jacob joined his brother. Thomas was no match for two of them.

"Let it be," Jacob said softly in his ear.

Thomas stopped struggling as soon as George applied the first lash to Gulda's back. The poor man cried out but Thomas knew there was nothing further he could do. He only hoped his presence might prevent them from going too far and overdoing the punishment.

It was over very quickly. George hit Gulda ten times. Thomas could see welts forming where the lash had struck but there was no blood.

George leaned in close to Gulda's face. "No sheep from my place." He yelled the words slowly. "Don't take my sheep or I will hit you much more." He stood back. "You understand? No sheep."

Gulda stared at something on the ground at George's feet. He'd stopped making any sound.

Samuel shook his shoulder. "You understand? Tell Mr Smith."

Thomas could feel both Jacob's and Edmund's grips had eased. He took the opportunity to wrench himself free. He needed to come up with an idea to get Gulda away. George had seemed a reasonable man but the situation was volatile.

"His English isn't good," Thomas said. "You are only making him more frightened by yelling at him."

"I think we should tie him to the tree," Edmund said. "Make sure he's learned his lesson."

"Let him go," Thomas said.

Edmund's face darkened and his hand curled into a fist.

Thomas turned back to George. "Let me take him with me. Gulda's worked for me before. I owe him. I'll make him understand he can't just take a sheep."

Edmund snorted.

George turned a pitying look on Thomas. "You won't be able to teach him anything he doesn't want to know." He pointed at Gulda, who had been looking up but quickly cast his eyes down. "And he understands plenty English, don't you?"

Thomas tried another tack. "I need help and AJ –"

"Wouldn't want you wasting time and resources on a black man," George cut in.

Thomas met George's look. "AJ has given me the authority to do it my way." He felt indebted to the native. He didn't want to make enemies of his neighbours but he needed to end this violence.

"How will you get him to your place? Drag him behind your horse?" Edmund smirked at him. "Judging by the marks on his wrists, someone has already tried that method."

Thomas hesitated, anger burning in his chest. Edmund might be the delightful Lizzie's brother but there was none of her compassion or laughter in him.

"We could lend him a horse, couldn't we, Father?" Jacob said. "When we go to help yard the stock, we can bring it back."

"I'm not helping people who are native lovers." Edmund spat into the dirt.

Thomas clenched his hand into a fist.

"Let Thomas take the man on a horse, Father."

They all turned as Lizzie stepped forward. She held a bowl in her hands.

"You shouldn't be here, Lizzie girl," George growled but there was no real anger in his voice.

"We don't need to make this man suffer any more than necessary."

"Take your fussing away, Lizzie," Edmund snarled. "You're wasting your time on this black man."

"Mother sent me to tend to him." Lizzie was a lot shorter than her oldest brother but she held his glare.

George shook his head. "Jacob, saddle old Tucker. Baker can take the native with him. We'll get the horse back later." He shook his head again as Lizzie examined Gulda's back. "I haven't harmed him, Lizzie," he said softly, then turned to Thomas. "We're neighbours so you know you can always count on us for help but I can't make my boys work for you. It'll be up to them who comes," he said. He turned and walked back to the hut.

Isaac stayed with Gulda but Samuel and Edmund followed their father. Lizzie stepped back. "Father hasn't hurt him too much. Only his dignity," she said.

Isaac released the native's arm and Gulda looked ready to run.

Thomas held up a hand. "Stay, Gulda," he said. "I will take you to my hut." It saddened him to see fear in the black face that had once looked at him with amity. "Can you ride?" He pointed as Jacob led a horse towards them.

Gulda's eyes widened but he remained still, watching as the horse was brought to him.

"This is Tucker," Jacob said. "He's an old plodder. Won't get up more than a trot and won't stray far." He smiled at Thomas. "He'll always come to you for tucker."

"Get on the horse, Gulda," Thomas said, but when the native still didn't move, Thomas, with the assistance of Jacob, hoisted him onto the horse and demonstrated how to hold the reins.

Isaac brought Thomas's horse and held Tucker's reins while he mounted, then passed them across.

"Zac and I will come over tomorrow," Jacob said. "We're happy to help round up your sheep, aren't we, Zac?"

Isaac nodded.

"Thanks," Thomas said, "but I wouldn't want to cause more trouble."

"All will be well," Jacob said in a voice sounding much older than he looked.

Thomas gave them a grateful smile. Beyond them Lizzie was still standing with her bowl but there were no other Smiths to be seen in the yard or on the verandah. This was not at all how he had thought his first visit to his nearest neighbours would go. He wondered what she thought of him now.

"Goodbye, Lizzie," he said and raised a hand in farewell.

Her face lit in a smile. "Goodbye, Thomas, and good luck," she said.

At least Lizzie didn't seem to have turned against him like the other half of her family. His spirits lifted a little as he turned his horse, and Tucker carrying Gulda, and began the journey home.

Twenty-one

Septimus slapped his leg in frustration. The casing was off now but the leg was weak and he thought it looked crooked. He was afraid to put his full weight on it after hobbling for so long. "That blasted doctor was no more than a charlatan."

Harriet put down her sewing and looked across the small clearing in the bush they had turned into a camp. "Can I do something for you?" she said.

Her patient tone only served to irritate Septimus further. He'd been confined to the wagon and then to this camp for nearly two months, reliant on a slip of a woman to help him with everything. While he had felt he was shrinking away, Harriet had blossomed, even though she was doing the work of a man.

"Not unless you can mend this leg," he snapped.

"The casing only came off this morning. It's bound to feel strange, but it won't be long and you'll be able to do everything you could before."

Her smile was sweet, but it couldn't shift the scowl he knew was set on his face. What a conundrum Harriet was. Where she sat now, the warm afternoon sun slanted through the trees and underneath the canopy they'd erected, shining on her dark hair and making it gleam. She wore the same dress she'd been wearing when he'd found her in his wagon but she filled it out even more than before. She'd grown taller and looked a picture of womanhood and good health, despite their limited diet and rough conditions.

He'd been a tough patient, complaining in spite of all her attentions. For quite a while she'd had to drive the wagon, set up camp each night, feed and care for Clover and find them food. Harriet had been useful to him but he was anxious to get back on the road. Being tethered to the camp and Harriet made him edgy.

"Let me make you some tea." She rose from the log that she'd made into a semi-comfortable seat with some bags for padding.

"I don't want tea," he growled.

"Very well, Septimus, but I won't offer again until after our evening meal."

"Possum again." He spat the words even though he knew Harriet was a marvel at turning whatever animal they trapped into something delicious.

"If you don't like it you can always get your own."

Even now, when he'd goaded her yet again, her tone was neutral. She sat back on her seat and bent her head over the shirt she was mending.

When they'd first set out from Burra he'd been barely able to drag himself from the wagon. He'd taught her what to look for when choosing a site for the trap and how to set it. Harriet was a fast learner and they'd always had something to eat on the journey. Before Harriet, he'd been happy living on dried meat and damper and the odd stew from whatever animal he trapped or shot, but her cooking always made things taste better. He'd become accustomed to it.

Now they were camped close to Adelaide it was a little easier. He'd given her some money and sent her to get supplies. They'd been out of flour and sugar. She'd been nervous to go back but he convinced her she wouldn't be recognised and besides, no one would be looking for her. After all this time with no body found she must be presumed dead or a runaway.

They'd been camped a little way from the nearest road. There was plenty of protection from the late spring sunshine and a source of water nearby. He'd planned to stay there until his leg was healed and the casing was off. He didn't want to appear in Adelaide with any impediment. While he was convinced no one would be looking for Harriet, the same might not be the case with him. Septimus wanted to go into town discreetly. He needed to find out if there were to be any repercussions over Baker and the horse before the task of setting up his wagon properly as a hawker's business could begin.

He stood up, ducked under the canopy and wobbled over to where the fire had just enough coals to keep the billy warm. He had grown so accustomed to the casing on his leg that he felt lop-sided without it. The leg that had been broken was weak. Each step he took was tentative in case it gave out underneath him.

He hobbled away from the fire and then from tree to tree around the edge of their small clearing. When he glanced at Harriet she had her head over her sewing, but he'd felt her eyes watching him. His confidence in the leg grew. He kept walking until it began to ache. The sun was still a way from going down. Harriet had wrapped the possum meat in layers of bark and buried it in the coals, so it would still be some time before they ate. Septimus looked around for something he could do. He'd kept himself busy during his convalescence, whittling creatures from wood, but now he wasn't in the mood for that.

Then he thought of the trunk in the back of the wagon. His was smaller and Harriet could shift it by herself, but Baker's was big and heavy. Septimus wondered how she had managed to get it into the wagon by herself after his accident but he'd never asked her. It was still in the wagon. Now was the time to get it out and go through the contents again. The remaining items would bring better money in Adelaide. He would just have to be cautious in case Baker was still around.

"Come and help me, Harriet," he said as he made his way past her to the back of the wagon. "I want to get the trunk out."

She followed him without a word. He lowered the gate and reached in. "Take one side."

"It's too heavy for me, Septimus, and you're not back to your full strength yet. Your leg will buckle."

He tugged at the trunk. It budged a little but he knew she was right. He wouldn't be able to lift it down even with her help. He slapped the side with his hand.

"Is there something you need from the trunk? I can get it out for you."

"No." He thumped the trunk again. He hated being weak and he hated relying on Harriet. "I want to go through it myself. There are things to get ready for sale."

"I could help you climb into the wagon. You could go through it there."

He glared at her. "I want the trunk out." When he went to Adelaide with the wagon he didn't want the trunk with him, only the contents he was planning to sell.

Harriet looked at the trunk, her hands on her hips. "I could unpack some of it so it's not so heavy, then perhaps we could slide it out in a similar fashion to the way I got it in."

He stayed by the wagon as she picked up the axe and disappeared into the surrounding bush. There was the sound of distant chopping followed by rustling. Finally she emerged dragging two sturdy branches. She strapped the branches to the back of the wagon, adjusting them so that the stumps from the smaller foliage she'd trimmed stayed pointing up.

"It will be easier with both of us and this time we'll be getting it out not in."

Septimus looked from the branches to the trunk still not sure what she intended. She climbed into the wagon. He watched her lift out clothes, books, pots and a wooden tray, then she closed the lid and turned back to him.

"Help me tug the trunk to the edge of the wagon. Then the branches will help us take the weight. The smaller branches will stop it from getting away from us too fast."

Septimus reached for the handle on one side of the trunk as Harriet did the same on the other. He could see how the branches were going to become a slide but he still didn't understand how she could have used this method to get the heavy trunk into the wagon.

Once the weight was over the lip it took all his effort to hold the trunk steady so it didn't slide away of its own accord. He could see Harriet's end was in danger of going then it hit the small branch sticking out on her side and stopped. Together they paused then on her command they lifted and slid the trunk down the next length until the trunk stopped at the second barrier. Once more they lifted and slid until the trunk landed with a thud on the ground.

They both collapsed on top of it, gaining their breath. They sat shoulder to shoulder. He was aware she was puffing softly like he was.

"You know, it was the devil of a job getting that trunk into the wagon by myself." Harriet gave a small chuckle. Septimus looked down at her breasts bulging from the top of the dress that was really too small for her now.

Suddenly he was filled with desire. He hadn't been with a woman since the night in the stable when he'd discovered Harriet's age. He hated the idea that another man had used her but his lust for her overwhelmed him.

He stood up and pulled her to him. He noted her small look of surprise before he pressed her face to his chest and used his free hand to lift her dress. It was awkward with his weak leg threatening to go out from under him but his manhood was bulging against his pants. Somehow he was going to have Harriet whether she wanted him or not.

He paused as he felt her hands at his belt. She managed to manoeuvre him towards the little bed she'd made for herself on the edge of their camp. They crumpled to the ground and he was on top of her, letting out the pent-up frustrations and desires he'd kept at bay for months. She yielded beneath him; the same pure sweet Harriet that he remembered.

Very quickly he was spent. He rolled away, his eyes closed, savouring the release. Today was the most exercise he'd had in a while but he realised Harriet had been right. He would build up his strength again and he had easily proved there was nothing wrong with his manhood. All would be well.

He heard soft rustlings as Harriet moved away beyond the wagon. He closed his eyes but before long she was back beside him. She hadn't said a word while he'd driven into her in his hunger. Now his eyes flew open at the feel of her lips nibbling his ear. She was naked. Her breasts were round and supple, her flesh pink from their activity. The rustling he'd heard must have been Harriet removing the rest of her clothes. Then he took in the bump in her nose and scar on her cheek. They reminded him that someone else had used her. He pushed her away, sickened that his body had overridden his pact to only bed a pure woman, unsullied by other men.

"What is it, Septimus?"

"Your … injuries."

"I am fully recovered."

"Another man …" He turned his head, unable to look at her, angry with himself.

"There has been no one but you."

He looked back at her big round eyes, her sweet lips.

"The beating … Someone violated you."

Her eyes widened and she put a hand to her scar. "It was a beating, that was all. I escaped before anything else happened. I am … as you left me. Yours and yours alone."

Before he could speak she was on top of him, her mouth covering his and her firm body pressing against him. He felt his desire for her return. He reached for her but her mouth was at his ear again.

"Let's take it slowly this time," she whispered. "You're still convalescing. Let me do the work for you."

Septimus opened his mouth to protest but instead let out a groan as her lips and fingers moved down his body.

It was much later when they finally got around to unpacking the remaining items from the trunk. They had dragged it close to the log and Harriet had been like a child, marvelling at the items he pulled from the depths. She had been especially taken with the china tea set, which he'd told her had been his mother's. After all the rough treatment it was a miracle nothing was broken; it had been well wrapped in several pieces of linen. Harriet had said the tea set reminded her of her own mother's kitchen. Her pretty face had looked a little melancholy and in a moment of weakness he'd allowed her to use it. It would still fetch a good price later on.

He watched Harriet now as she bent over the fire, preparing to unwrap the possum meat. Her dress was only loosely laced and he knew she hadn't put her undergarments back on. The thought of it aroused him again and the recollection of their time in her little nest of a bed made him want to drag her back there again but he remained on the seat, watching her. She'd said no one else had used her, but could he believe her?

She put the possum on an old china serving plate that had also been in the trunk then went and fetched his blanket from his bed under the wagon. She draped it over the log and onto the ground, then she placed the plate of food on it and sat down, resting her back against the log. She patted the space on the other side of the plate.

"Rest here, Septimus," she said, "and eat."

He hesitated a moment then did as she asked. Together they ate the food in silence as the sun went down behind them.

Twenty-two

Harriet woke to the cool early morning air on her bare leg. She pulled the blanket her way a little then nestled against the warm body beside her. From the sound of his deep rhythmic breaths, Septimus was still fast asleep. Yesterday had been a big day for him, for both of them, but she knew he would be physically exhausted. He'd taken her to bed as soon as she'd offered to lick the possum grease from his fingers and once again their bodies had joined together. He'd fallen asleep the instant he was spent.

She couldn't see his features in the murky pre-dawn light but she hoped he would still be without the scowl that had permanently lined his face since his accident. Yesterday she had seen the old Septimus. The one who had taken her in the stable at the back of Mabel's and enjoyed her body and her company. The man she loved. His thick wavy hair was in need of a cut but it didn't hide his angular cheekbones and lively eyes.

Harriet slipped from the blanket, pulled on her clothes and made her way down to the creek to wash. The water was freezing but ever since her swim in the waterhole near Burra she'd taken to bathing more often. The cold water invigorated her and made her skin glow.

Back in camp she could hear soft snores. She was glad Septimus was still asleep.

Yesterday had been wonderful, a big step towards the future she knew could be theirs, but she wasn't sure whether he would feel the same in the light of a new day. He had been overcome with lust for her as she had thought would eventually happen. It had been her opportunity to remind him of her abilities. All the same, she knew she'd have to tread carefully. Septimus wasn't a fool, or easily manipulated, but she hoped he would soon see the benefits of keeping her with him.

She had been wise to keep silent about her violation. There was no need for Septimus to know of it. Her body had healed from Pig Boy's assault – in all places. Mercifully she'd been unconscious when he raped her but she'd known about it for weeks afterwards. Yesterday she had served Septimus well, as she would continue to do. If that meant convincing him he was the only man who'd ever entered her then that's what she'd do.

Hands ripped the dress from her body. She gasped. She had been so lost in her own thoughts she hadn't heard his approach. He spun her around. His hands gripped her tight. She shivered and kept her lashes lowered. Had he found out she'd lied? Then suddenly his arms were around her, holding her against his warm body.

"I think it's time I bought you a new dress, Harriet." She felt the chuckle rumble in his chest. "You seem to have outgrown that one. Can't have Mrs Wiltshire, wife of respected hawker, Mr Septimus Wiltshire, looking like a whore can we?" He lowered his voice. "Even if she acts like one in bed."

Her teeth were chattering, whether from the cold or the release of the fear that had coursed through her body when he'd grabbed her, she wasn't sure.

"In the meantime I'd better warm you up," he said and guided her back to the bed in the bush.

*

Septimus wouldn't linger in the bed as Harriet wanted him too.

"I've got too much to do," he said as he buttoned up his pants.

He went to the trunk and came back with some clothing. He tossed a pair of men's trousers and a shirt beside her.

"You can wear those until I return," he said. "I've got many jobs to do in Adelaide and one of them is to buy you a new dress, Harriet." His moustache twitched above his lips. "One that fits."

Harriet smiled back. She knew he would look after her. She dressed in the men's clothing and cooked him damper for breakfast while he scurried around their camp. He almost had a spring in his lopsided step. Before she knew it, he had kissed her goodbye and set off with Clover pulling the wagon.

She listened to the sounds of his departure until she could hear him no more. She shivered. A niggle of doubt wormed its way into her chest but she pushed it away, remembering his smile and his kiss. She reorganised the small stores in the wooden box and packed the pretty tea set back into the trunk. One of the linen tablecloths had a tear in it, so she took out her needle and thread and mended it. Once that was done she thought about food. She broke up the remains of the damper. Supplies were low but there was still possum meat left for their evening meal. There was nothing else to prepare.

In the late afternoon she sat huddled alone by the fire. Her earlier doubt returned to unsettle her. Septimus had been gone a long time. Perhaps his tenderness towards her had all been a ploy to lull her into believing he wanted her to stay with him. She'd been duped before.

She put more wood on the fire and stood warming her hands. Yesterday there had been brilliant sunshine and the promise of a warm summer ahead. Today the sky was murky; a chilly wind had blown up, whirling the ash from the fire into her eyes. Today she'd been glad of the shawl she'd tied around her shoulders.

Harriet glanced around the camp. There was very little left there. Septimus had even taken down the canvas cover and put it back on the wagon. Her gaze skipped over her old dress folded up on top of the trunk, then returned to study the solid chest still beside the log seat where they'd unpacked it last night. A quick surge of excitement raced through her. Surely Septimus would come back for the trunk.

She knew it had belonged to the man called Thomas. It was his goods that Septimus was taking to town to sell off. The rest of the items Septimus said had been his mother's, including the books. He wasn't a reader, so he hadn't thought them very important, but Harriet had pored over them when he'd pulled them from the bottom of the trunk. His mother had written her name inside in tiny flowing letters, *Hester Baker.*

Books had been a part of Harriet's early childhood, but they'd been lost along with her innocence, and there'd been no books at Mabel's. It warmed her heart to think Septimus at least had his own mother's books and that they could also be hers.

Now, with nothing left to do, she settled back and started to read, her ears alert for the sounds of Clover and the wagon.

By the next morning, Harriet had resigned herself to accept he'd gone. Besides the trunk, he'd left little of value at the camp. The cooking pots and few provisions would be easily replaced with the money she knew he'd made. Perhaps he'd decided the trunk wasn't worth the bother of loading up again. Even though he'd been markedly stronger on his leg, it still would have been a struggle for both of them to get the trunk back into the wagon.

Harriet didn't bother to wash but she encouraged the fire into life again. The previous day had been cool and today the clouds were thicker and ranging in colour from light to grey to almost black. It looked like rain.

She folded up her bed with a heavy heart then slumped down at the edge of the fire and gave in to the tears that had been threatening to flow all morning. How could she have ended up like this? She'd survived so much, then found Septimus when he most needed her, got him to the doctor and managed to help him make the long journey back to Adelaide and now, when she thought he'd finally accepted her worth, he'd deserted her again.

This time he had a good head start on her – and she had no idea which direction he'd taken. Every crumb of energy and intuition that had helped her in the past washed out of her with the huge sobs that wracked her body. Harriet had never been one to indulge in self-pity but now she couldn't help herself. She cried until her stomach muscles cramped and she vomited a small amount of liquid onto the dirt beside her. Had she eaten today? She didn't care. She shuddered as another posset of bile trickled from her mouth. When finally her muscles relaxed she curled up in the dirt by the fire and closed her eyes, oblivious to the first drops of rain dotting her body.

Twenty-three

1847

Every one of Thomas's muscles screamed as he bent to haul the next struggling sheep towards him. The air was thick with the oily smell of wool and the astringent pong of urine. Over the clicking of the blades, the bleating was constant, even pervading his sleep at night. Sweat soaked his clothes and dribbled down his brow. He brought one hand up to wipe the trickle from his eyes and the sheep kicked, connecting with his shin. The pain jarred up his leg but he contorted the yelp into a low groan and gathered the animal back. Just one more and he would have to go and help the lad with the fleeces. There was quite a pile for him to sort again.

Along the boards beside him he knew the three men were still clipping the wool faster than he could but each sheep he could shear meant they were one closer to finishing; and it was one less for which he had to pay the shearers.

The three shearers were a rough lot but he'd had no other choice. Over the few weeks of the job they'd revealed little about themselves, camping together in the bush on the other side of the shed at night. Thomas had the distinct impression they were keen to be away from civilisation. He'd learned from the vile Gurr that this type of man could mean trouble but they kept to themselves and didn't come near his hut. Even so, Thomas felt uneasy. After the first night, when he'd heard heated voices and strange yelps from the direction of their camp, he'd taken his bed roll into his hut and slept with his gun.

The lad they'd brought with them helped in the shed and cooked food for them, most of which was supplied by Thomas. This young jack-of-all-trades was a nervy, gangly creature they called Wick. He never walked anywhere but jumped and darted, often startling the sheep, for which he'd receive a clip over the head if he was close enough, or a mouthful of abuse if he wasn't.

Wick was quick around the shed, pushing sheep up, gathering the fleeces and sweeping the boards. If he wasn't doing that it was up to Thomas, or Jacob when he'd been there. Thomas smiled at the thought of the younger Smith brothers, Jacob and Isaac, who he now counted as firm friends. Without them – and Gulda and his cousin – Thomas knew he wouldn't be ready for shearing. He'd still be searching for sheep and drafting them.

Once the shearers had arrived, the natives had disappeared. This time Thomas had given them a sheep and some other provisions for their work. Zac had gone home but Jacob would stay a few days to help shift the sheep and press the wool, then he'd leave as well, returning a few days later to help again. Each time he came back there was some small item of food from Lizzie. That brought a smile to Thomas's lips. He planned to eat a piece of her latest gift, a possum pie, for his lunch today.

A bellow from the man next to him startled Thomas. Wallis was the unofficial leader of the small band of shearers. He was a thick-set man with wide shoulders and his upper body looked out of proportion on his short legs. Of the three shearers, Wallis had the most to say and usually did so with many expletives.

Thomas looked over his shoulder to see bright red blood pouring over the white of Wallis's newly shorn sheep. Wick appeared with the pot of black tar. Thomas watched as it was applied to stop the bleeding. That was just one more thing he didn't like about these men. They were far too rough. He'd lost count of the number of sheep they'd applied the thick black mixture to, and he'd had to slit the throat of one on the first day, its injuries were so bad. He docked money from their tallies for damage but it didn't seem to make them take more care.

Wallis glared at Thomas over Wick's head then shoved the lad out of the way before doing the same with the poor sheep. Thomas watched that Wallis didn't put a mark on the board. There was no way he'd get paid for that one.

"Should have slit its throat. Would have made a good roast for tonight." Wallis twisted his pock-marked face into an ugly sneer. He held Thomas's look a minute longer then slid his gaze sideways and reached into the pen for the next sheep.

Thomas hauled his own sheep to its feet and pushed it through the door behind him with some small satisfaction. They were almost there. By knock-off this afternoon the job should be done: nearly three thousand sheep shorn. He had promised a celebratory meal, not that he felt the shearers deserved it; the celebration for him would be in seeing them off Penakie.

He moved quickly around the last pile of fleeces, pulling off any dags and checking for prickles and marks that could lower the price AJ would get for his wool. Jacob had already helped him load the first of the bags of wool onto the dray. As soon as shearing was finished, Thomas would make the trip back to Port Adelaide with a full load.

Outside, the midday sun belted down with the ferocity that had made the shed so hot, but at least the air was fresh. Thomas sucked in a huge breath and stretched. Behind him he heard Wallis give the shout to down shears. The men would take a break for an hour now, out of the heat of the shed. Wick shot out the door, making for their camp. Thomas once again felt pity for the young lad. There was no rest for him. He would have to be dishing up their food by the time the men reached him.

Thomas crossed to the water barrel and took a long drink before going to his camp kitchen where he had buried kangaroo meat in the coals to cook slowly for tonight's meal. Gulda had shown him how to do it so the meat didn't dry out or toughen. It was tempting to remove the dirt to check the heat of the layer of coals below but Thomas resisted. He knew he had to trust the process and leave it alone.

He wondered where the native and his family were now. Gulda had been a quick learner once he got over his initial fear of the horse and could ride quite well. He was also very good at rounding up the sheep, even without the horse, when he was with his cousins on foot. Thomas wanted Gulda to keep an eye on things while he was away taking the wool to the port.

He pushed his hat firmly onto his head and tracked around the side of his hut to fetch a piece of Lizzie's pie. He had just taken the last mouthful when the sound of a horse and cart rumbled from the creek. His spirits lifted at the sight of not only Jacob on his horse but Isaac driving the cart and, beside him on the seat, Anne Smith and Lizzie. They all raised their arms in greeting. He did the same then saw another rider bringing up the rear. Samuel had come as well.

"Hello," Jacob called. "I thought you'd be about finished."

"Not quite," Thomas said, "but we'll cut the last sheep by knock-off time today."

"You can't have cut out without a party," Isaac said as the cart rumbled closer.

Thomas looked at Lizzie, whose face glowed under her wide hat. All the Smiths were beaming; even Samuel wore a small grin. They'd come to visit and he didn't have anything but a baked kangaroo to feed them.

"What's wrong?" Jacob was off his horse now. "I'd have thought you'd be celebrating. The shearing will be finished and you can see those poor excuses for shearers on their way."

"I wish I'd known you were coming. I would have prepared more food."

The cart came to a stop in front of the hut.

"Don't you worry about food," Isaac said. "Mother and Lizzie have brought enough to feed an army."

"I hope you don't mind us doing that, Thomas," Anne said. "I knew you'd be too busy with the shearing to be thinking about food."

"I've made a pie with the last lot of dried fruit you gave us," Lizzie said as Jacob helped her from the wagon. She stopped in front of Thomas and her sweet smile made his heart thud in his chest.

"There could be extras if Mr Duff arrives in time," Anne said.

"Duffy?" Thomas pushed back his hat and scratched his head.

"I saw him near the boundary yesterday," Samuel said. "I mentioned you were close to cut out and that Mother and Lizzie were planning a feast." He looked at Thomas apologetically.

"You don't mind, do you, Thomas?" Lizzie's gaze met his over the armload of food Isaac had passed to her from the cart.

Once again Thomas scratched his head. Some good company was more than welcome and it seemed that most of the Smith family were happy to talk to him. He glanced back at the track in case George and Edmund should suddenly appear as well.

"I assure you we only mean well by our unannounced arrival," Anne said.

"You're always welcome," Thomas replied.

She patted his arm. "My husband sends his apologies. His shoulder is causing him a lot of pain at the moment and Edmund has stayed back to keep an eye on the place."

They all looked around as a man's bellow was heard, followed by a high-pitched wail that sounded a lot like Wick.

"I'd better go and see what's happening," Thomas said and, with a final glance at Lizzie, he set off for the shed.

He reached it at the same time as Wallis, who stuck his head through the door and bellowed: "You skinny little fool, I'll have your hide. Get out here you little –"

"Wallis." Thomas's sharp call made the man stop his tirade and turn.

"We're still on our break. Don't interfere," Wallis growled.

Thomas stood up straight. He glared at Wallis. "I'm in charge of this shed. What's the problem?"

"That halfwit knocked hot tea over me." Wallis pointed to a stain across one lower leg of his trousers. "I was going to give him a taste of his own medicine. Make him more careful in future."

"I'm sure you've given him enough of a scare to remember." Thomas assumed Wick was hiding in the shed. Wallis still looked as though he was planning to follow. "There's no point in injuring the boy; we're short enough on labour."

Wallis grunted and kicked the step. "You've been lucky this time," he shouted into the shed. "Only I need my rest or I'd still be after you." He turned back to eyeball Thomas and then stalked away to his camp.

Thomas stepped up into the shed. There was plenty of sheep noise but no sign of Wick.

"You'd better make sure everything's ready to start again," he said into the space. "I don't want any delays."

Thomas busied himself packing the last lot of fleeces and didn't turn when the sound of sweeping reached his ears. He knew Wick would have emerged from wherever he'd been hiding and picked up the broom. There was little Thomas could do for the lad. Tomorrow the shearers would be gone and Wick with them. He would have to fend for himself, but at least Thomas took some pleasure in giving him a small reprieve; he detested bullies and injustice.

The afternoon's work was punctuated by Wallis's bad-tempered outbursts. His fellow shearers copped a few foul rants aside from Wick's usual share. The Smith brothers joined them so that at least Thomas was free to sort the fleeces as they were cut and make sure they got packed in the right bags. Finally the last sheep was shorn and they could all escape the heat of the shed.

The shearers and Wick headed to the stream to wash. Thomas was conscious of his own dirty clothes and body – he hadn't expected to have company and certainly not female company. It was difficult to get to his clean clothes, though, as Lizzie and her mother had taken over his hut. When he saw that both the women were tending the food at the fire he took the opportunity to get fresh clothes and slipped away to the stream.

Lizzie was on the little verandah when he returned.

"No more boils that need attention?" she said.

Thomas stopped and looked around. She always had him on edge, and buzzing with a strange kind of anticipation. He was never sure what she might say.

"You walk very well, so I am guessing there's been no reoc-currence of the –"

"I'm quite well." He cut her off and ducked past to deposit his dirty clothes inside the hut. When he came out she was waiting for him. This time he noticed the mischievous lift of her lips and the twinkle in her eye.

"You know I'm good at lots of things. I can even cut hair."

She reached up, her hand brushed his cheek and she tugged at a lock of his wet hair.

Thomas restrained himself from grabbing her hand and pulling her closer, aware that her mother and brothers were on the other side of the hut and could appear at any minute.

"Of course some men prefer their hair longer," Lizzie said. "You have waves in yours so it falls well. When my brothers' hair gets too long, it falls in clumps like bits of rope."

He swept his fingers through his hair and pulled it back from his eyes. "It does need cutting. I hope to be able to do that in Adelaide."

A loud call startled them both. Thomas turned to see Duffy riding towards him and another man with a woman following in a small cart.

"I'm sorry about your last visit to us." Lizzie spoke softly. "Jacob said the native man wasn't harmed too much."

"No."

"Father means well," Lizzie said. Thomas felt the soft pressure of her hand on his arm. "I thought you were so brave to stand up to him and take the native away."

He looked down to find her face turned to his, and that she was looking at him with admiration. He wished they were alone. Her pretty blue eyes were mesmerising. He longed to take her in his arms and kiss her.

"G'day, mate." Duffy's arrival startled Thomas from Lizzie's spell. "And who do we have here but Miss Lizzie Smith herself."

Lizzie stepped forward and nodded.

"Mr Duff," she said then waved to the couple getting down from the cart. "Hello, Mr and Mrs Gibson."

The couple came over to meet Thomas. John Gibson was a shepherd with Duffy, and his wife was an angular, pinch-faced woman whose lips turned down when she spoke, giving her a dour expression. Anne Smith appeared and drew Mrs Gibson away, calling for Lizzie to come and help with the food as she went.

Twenty-four

It was a large group gathered around the outside fire that night. After the heat of the day it was a perfect evening, with just a gentle breeze to stir the air. A few more logs were drawn up for seating and both the Smiths and the Gibsons had brought extra plates to add to Thomas's meagre collection. When he saw the meat being cut up on Mrs Smith's serving plate, he was once again reminded of what he had lost in the trunk Whitby had stolen. Thomas had thought he'd have no need of the items within it but he'd been wrong on several occasions.

When everyone was seated, Thomas gave thanks for the work that was completed and for the food before them. Along with the kangaroo meat there were potatoes and pumpkin, baked to perfection in the coals, and Anne had also made some kind of turnip mash. He'd not eaten so well in a long time. Judging by the comments around the feast, the others all agreed.

Wallis and the other two shearers were there, looking the cleanest Thomas had seen them. Wick seated himself on the opposite side of the fire from Wallis and tucked into his meal as if he'd not eaten for a week. Thomas noticed a red mark down the side of the boy's face that hadn't been there at the last bell of the day.

Apparently Thomas's protection hadn't lasted once Wick had left the shed.

Thomas glanced at the others around the fire. The mood was jovial: all except Wallis and Mrs Gibson had smiles on their faces as they ate and talked. Jacob, Isaac and Samuel sat with their mother and Lizzie had chosen a spot close to Thomas. Duffy on his other side was full of questions about the shearing.

Finally Anne asked her sons to collect the eating utensils and Thomas raised his mug of tea. "To a most delicious meal," he said.

There was a chorus of voices agreeing with his sentiments. He noticed Duffy taking his customary sip from the flask he'd slipped from his pocket.

"It's not over yet," Lizzie said and bounced to her feet. "There's the fruit pie and Mother has made jam roly-poly."

"There's also a small pot of cream from our cow," Anne added.

"I thought it was time for men's business," Wallis grumbled and tugged a pipe from his pocket.

"Sweets first," Lizzie said. "It will be ready in two shakes of a lamb's tail."

There were groans of delight as the women set about serving. Once again they were all soon intent on eating – even Wallis, Thomas noticed. The sweets were delicious.

"When do you leave for Adelaide?" Lizzie's question came just as he scraped the last of the pudding into his mouth.

"Tomorrow, I hope."

"You will be gone a while."

"Yes. I was hoping your brothers might take turns to keep an eye on things but they've already done so much for me."

"I'm sure they won't mind." Lizzie leaned in closer. "We're neighbours." With her hat off, her golden hair shone in the rays of the setting sun and he noticed she wore a pair of dainty drop earrings. There was a velvet ribbon crossed over at her throat and clasped with a small brooch that matched the earrings.

"Time for dancing," Jacob said. Lizzie laughed as her brother pulled her to her feet.

"The shed's the best place for that," John Gibson said, and he pulled a harmonica from his pocket. He ran it across his mouth, producing a merry blast that stirred everyone to movement.

The men helped clear the boards in the shed. They carried in some logs for seating while the women cleaned up the dishes and food. In no time they were all gathered again in the shearing shed.

The breeze had cleared some of the heat and smell. Baskets of wool off-cuts were pushed to the sides and Lizzie draped small branches of flowering eucalypt along the tops of the pens. She and Anne had removed the outer coats they'd worn all day to reveal patterned dresses underneath, adding to the festive look. Lizzie's dress was deep blue, with small white swirls on it. The neckline was cut straight across her shoulders and, while the sleeves puffed out around her wrists, the bodice was tapered to hug her chest and her trim waist. She looked like a princess.

With the light from some lanterns and the music played by Gibson, the atmosphere in the shed became quite celebratory. Duffy danced with Mrs Gibson, and Isaac with his mother. Jacob twirled Lizzie around the floor before stopping in front of Thomas and bowing out. Lizzie's face shone. Dancing with her made him feel carefree and even light on his feet, although he'd never been much of a dancer.

Even the shearers joined in. One of them dragged Wick to the floor. They tied an old sweat rag around his waist like an apron and pulled his hat down with a cord so it resembled a bonnet and whizzed him around. All Wallis's animosity seemed to have evaporated with the music. Thomas suspected it was also something to do with the flask that Duffy was happy to share with him.

Lizzie was swept away by Samuel. Thomas danced with Anne Smith and with the dour Mrs Gibson, who threw herself in to the activity with great enthusiasm and even managed a smile. After several dances, Thomas found himself without a partner for a while. With all the movement, the shed had warmed up again, so he strolled to the door to take in some fresh air. There were no clouds and little moon: a million stars glittered across the velvet sky.

Thomas thought of England and the life he'd lived there. Back then he could never have imagined this. If his parents could see him now, what would they think? It was harder work than they'd done in England. The land here was much harsher than the Dowlings' lush green pastures. Was this what his father had been hoping for when he'd booked their passage? Thomas looked down the sweep of the hill to the glowing coals of the outside fire and the dark silhouette of the rough hut. It all seemed insignificant under the huge sky.

His spirits dipped at the thought of the big trip ahead of him. Then there was the problem of who would look after the place in his absence. AJ hadn't given him any instructions about that.

"You're deep in thought."

Thomas looked down into Lizzie's upturned face. She was puffing slightly and a little bead of sweat glinted across her brow. Behind them the music continued and the laughter got louder.

"There's a lot to do tomorrow," he said and looked back at the night sky.

"You've done a good job so far. I am sure Mr Browne was right to put his faith in you."

"I'll be gone a long time."

"My brothers can take turns checking your sheep."

"I don't like to ask them for help again."

"Why not? That's what neighbours do. I'm sure you'd help us if we needed."

Thomas gave a soft snort. "I can't see that being necessary. Your family is a small army."

"You never know." She leaned forward to look out at the stars and he was surprised by her hand gripping his arm. "Anyway, the good Lord will make it right. Just look at this beautiful night he's provided."

"Yes, it is beautiful," Thomas said, but he was looking at Lizzie. Some wisps of hair had escaped the upwards-sweeping knot at the back of her head and they floated over the pale skin of her neck. The gentle hint of lavender followed her, reminding him of England.

Suddenly there was a bellow from behind them and the music stopped. Thomas spun in time to see Wallis strike Wick a blow with the back of his hand. The lad sprawled to the floor with a yelp. He scrabbled backwards as Wallis went after him.

Thomas strode over and stood between the wild-eyed shearer and the whimpering lad. "That's enough, Wallis," he said.

"The young idiot stomped on my foot and he'll pay," Wallis bellowed.

Thomas was sprayed with spittle and boozy breath. "I think we all need to turn in."

"There's still plenty of music left in Gibbo yet." Duffy's words were slurred and he struggled to get to his feet.

"Everyone has an early start in the morning." Thomas kept his eyes locked on Wallis's brooding face.

"That's right," the shearer said. "We'll be on our way." He leaned forward and peered around Thomas. "Then you won't be able to hide."

Thomas put his hands up as Wallis swayed into him, and got a shove in return.

"Don't touch me," Wallis growled.

Jacob and Samuel moved in either side of Thomas.

"It's been a wonderful night." Anne Smith spoke brightly. "But Thomas is quite right, it's getting late and we ladies will retire. I think the gentlemen should too."

Wallis stepped back and suddenly the shed was alive with movement again as everyone bade their good nights. Duffy continued to suggest they keep dancing but no one took any notice. The women gathered their coats and left to share the small space inside the hut. The men would spread bed rolls by the fire and Thomas had hung his hammock in the trees again.

He remained rigid on the spot and nodded as each of them bid him good night and left the shed. Wallis was the last and didn't speak until he reached the door.

"Come on, Wick. Get back to camp," he said.

"Wick can stay with me a little longer," Thomas said. "I've a couple of jobs still to do here."

Wallis's eyes flared. Then he twisted his mouth in to an ugly smirk. "Don't keep him too long. We want to be gone by sun up."

Finally there was just Thomas and Wick. The lad scrambled to his feet. Now he had a red mark on the right side of his face to match the other.

"What do you want me to do, Mr Baker?"

Thomas was saddened by the eagerness in the lad's voice. He knew Wallis was right. He couldn't protect Wick for much longer.

"Stack those logs by the door and turn out the lanterns," Thomas said. "Then perhaps you can sleep in here tonight. Get a good rest before your journey."

Wick flashed him a grateful smile and Thomas left the shed. He felt an ache in his muscles and the weight of deep tiredness. He was only a few years older than Wick but tonight he felt ancient. He climbed into his bed and gazed at the stars through the branches of the tree over his head. Even though the evening had ended on a sour note, nothing could spoil the memory of his first cut-out party and dancing along the boards with Lizzie in his arms. Very quickly, he drifted off to sleep with a smile on his lips.

Thomas was awakened by a rough shake of his shoulder and the puff of unpleasant breath in his face.

"Where's that young imbecile?"

Thomas felt as if he'd just shut his eyes but beyond the looming figure of Wallis he could see the pink glow of the rising sun.

He rolled out of his bed away from the foul man. "What are you talking about?"

"Wick," Wallis said. "We're ready to go and the young idiot's nowhere to be found." He jabbed a dirty finger towards Thomas. "You've hidden him somewhere."

"I've done no such thing." Thomas pulled on his boots. "I gave the lad permission to sleep in the shearing shed and that's the last I saw of him."

"Wick!" Wallis bellowed.

"Quiet, man," Thomas hissed. "You'll wake everyone up with your noise."

He strode to the shearing shed. Inside, the logs had been stacked and beside them on the floor were the cold lanterns. With Wallis right behind him, they looked in every pen and every corner.

"He's not here," Thomas said.

"I can see that for myself,' Wallis said.

"Perhaps he's asleep somewhere in the bush."

"I've called all around. He's always close by … until your place. You've made him soft."

Over Wallis's shoulder Thomas saw a small movement in the wool swept to one side of the shed. It was a mound of dags, the dung-caked locks trimmed from the backsides of the sheep.

"Perhaps he decided to go his own way," Thomas said and made his way out of the shed. "He could be anywhere by now."

"We can't waste any more time looking for him," Wallis pointed at Thomas again, "but we'll be back this way one day and if he's here —"

"He's a free man to go where he pleases."

Wallis snorted and opened his mouth to speak, then closed it again only to spit at Thomas's feet. He turned and strode away, past the yards with the last of the shorn sheep, to where the other two shearers stood with their meagre possessions over their shoulders. Thomas watched as Wallis gathered up his things, including a collection of pots and pans that clunked together as they moved off.

"I'm not sad to see them go." Jacob's voice startled him.

Thomas turned to see the Smith family; the three men had moved up close behind him with the ladies a little further back.

Anne raised her eyebrows. "You seem to make a habit of helping lame ducks, Mr Baker."

"It shows he has a kind heart, Mother," Lizzie said with a gentle smile.

"Or he's easily duped," Samuel said.

"What's all the noise about?" Duffy stumbled out from under the Gibsons' wagon.

"Time for us all to head home, Mr Duff," Anne said. "Perhaps you'd like some tea and damper before you go?"

"No thanks, missus. Gibbo and I should be on our way. The Gwynns are due any day. Got our own sheep to attend to."

Thomas waved them off and watched as they disappeared through the trees past the stream. The Smith brothers busied themselves with their horses and cart and Lizzie helped her mother with the breakfast. No one was paying him any attention as he headed back to the shed.

"You can come out now, Wick," he said. He watched as the boy slowly emerged from the smelly wool heap.

"I don't want to cause you trouble, Mr Baker." Wick picked at the clumps of wool sticking to his clothes and hair. "But I don't want to travel with them shearers no more."

"I can give you a ride back to Adelaide."

"No thanks," Wick said quickly. "I prefer to keep away from busy places."

"Where then?"

"I could stay here. Keep an eye on things while you're gone."

"This isn't my place." Thomas wished there was some way he could help the lad. "Perhaps the Smiths?" Even as he said it he realised there was no way the Smith family needed any more help.

"You don't need to pay me and I'm good at finding me own food. I just need somewhere to stay for a while."

"You don't think Wallis might come back looking for you? There'd be no one to help you if he did."

"He won't be back." Wick stuck his hands in his pockets and gave a shrug. "Least not for a long time. They keep moving, those blokes. Shearing or whatever they can to earn some money."

"Looks like you've found your help."

Wick jumped at the sound of Lizzie's voice.

"I'm glad to see you're not lost, Wick," she said. "Mr Baker was only saying last night that he needed some help and here you are – the answer to his prayers."

Thomas looked from the smiling Lizzie to the startled face of Wick. The gangly lad was not what he'd imagined the Lord would provide but he decided he had little choice but to give him a try. If he worked out, he may become the replacement shepherd.

Later that morning, his wagon loaded high with wool bales, Thomas began the journey back to Adelaide. The Smiths had suggested they would take turns at visiting Wick, who had promised most solemnly to look after the sheep until Thomas's return. And so it was, with some small degree of excitement, mixed with an element of uncertainty, that he cracked his whip and urged the bullocks forward.

Twenty-five

1848

"I hope your wife isn't encouraging mine to buy frivolous trinkets, Mr Wiltshire. She has no need of such rubbish out here."

Septimus lifted his head from the bag of wool clippings he'd been checking. The rotund man next to him was an ugly figure with small beady eyes, a bulbous nose and a bushy beard. Bull by name and bull by nature. Septimus couldn't imagine how the man had attracted such a young woman as his wife. Then he recalled his own travels with Harriet, and decided anything was possible in this isolated Australian bush.

He looked over at the two women seated beside the wagon. They were drinking tea from dainty china cups, deep in conversation. He knew he could leave it up to Harriet to make a good sale if there was one to be had but he thought she'd have her work cut out. The farmer's wife was young and probably had no sway with her grotesque husband. There was no spark in her eyes, her hair had no shine and her dress was a deep brown, which did nothing for her sallow complexion. He could see no indication of feminine charm and who could blame her, stuck out there with such a man.

Septimus shifted his gaze to her husband. "Your good wife is probably taking the opportunity to enjoy some female conversation, Mr Bull," he said and went back to testing the wool.

Harriet was proving to be quite an asset. When he recalled the day, almost a year earlier now, he'd returned to camp with the new wagon all loaded up with supplies and found her in a wet and bedraggled heap by the cold fire, he still felt a jolt of dismay. He'd thought she was dead but, like a cat, Harriet seemed to have nine lives. He'd plucked her from the soggy ground, warmed her up and watched over her as she recovered.

When the blue had left her lips and she'd been well enough to talk, he'd asked her why she hadn't looked after herself.

"It must have been something I ate. I took sick," she'd said.

Septimus had given a quick thought to leaving her behind. He had no use for her if she couldn't do her share but she'd recovered quickly and now very profitably spent her time with the women in the isolated huts, farms and even hotels they visited.

Harriet was his wife in every sense but the legal and he was happy for people to accept her as that. He had to admire her tenacity. It had been her suggestion they buy the small table and dainty wooden chairs from a downtrodden squatter. Harriet had taken to setting up under whatever shade she could find close to the wagon. She used a tablecloth and the china tea set and in no time had the lady of the property engaged in conversation as if they were in a tea shop in town.

"If it's of no use, I may as well throw it away."

Septimus gritted his teeth at the grumbling sound of Bull's voice but he pulled his face into a smile and stood tall. How this ridiculous man had come to own this place and run sheep was beyond him. Although he wouldn't own it for long the way he was going. Septimus had already loaned him some money. It was a small amount but the interest was high. Bull's lack of management skills would soon see him owing a lot more. His wool had been sent to the port but there was quite a bit of quality left in the bags of daggy off-cuts if one was prepared to take the time to clean it. If Bull had realised the money to be made he wouldn't have needed to borrow more.

"I can take them off your hands if you like." Septimus watched the piggy eyes opposite him narrow.

"How much?"

So the man wasn't a complete fool. Septimus made a quick calculation. There were several bags and with the new wagon there was plenty of room. They'd been on the road for a couple of weeks. Many of the supplies had been sold, leaving space. If they bought this wool, Harriet could clean it. Then they wouldn't be travelling back to Adelaide with an empty wagon as they'd done in the past. He knew he could sell clean bags of wool for a tidy sum. It made good sense to have a return cargo rather than an empty wagon.

Septimus made his offer. He stepped back quickly as Bull snorted and sprayed him with spittle.

"There's another traveller comes through here pays better than that."

"Very well, sir," Septimus said. He took care to mask his contempt for the man with polite words. A minute ago he was going to throw the wool away. "We won't trouble you any longer. My wife and I must be on our way."

As much as Septimus would love to have punched the vile man on the nose and have nothing more to do with him, there was the future to consider. Bull had purchased several items from the wagon and return trips should be profitable.

"Wait a minute," Bull said. "Don't you want the wool?"

Septimus turned back with his head slightly bowed, his hands clasped loosely in front of him. "It's not my usual fare, Mr Bull.

If you can make better money with your regular buyer I won't interfere."

"I don't know when he'll be back this way." Bull began to huff and tug at his beard. "It would be better for me if it was gone."

"I shouldn't have suggested it. Our wagon doesn't have much space –"

"I want to be rid of it," Bull cut in.

"You didn't like my offer," Septimus said in a low voice.

"Well you can make me a better one."

"I'm sorry, Mr Bull." Septimus put on his most pitiful look. "My dear wife and I are simple merchants. We don't have a lot of money. That was my best offer. I'm sure you understand."

"Well." Bull almost hopped from foot to foot. "Well," he said again then puffed himself up. "There will be more wool soon and I need to clear my shed. If you can take it all I'll accept your offer."

"Very well, Mr Bull." Septimus bowed his head again. "I will see what space we can make."

Harriet saw Septimus striding with purpose down the slope towards her. She couldn't help but let her gaze linger on him. He had recovered well from the broken leg. She only noticed him limp when he was tired. She was careful with their provisions but fed him well. He cut a fine figure now, tall and lean with his dark hair swept to the side. She noticed most of the women they met gave him a second look. Not this poor mouse of a woman she was engaging with tea and conversation, though.

"Well, Mrs Bull," Harriet smiled sweetly at the woman opposite, "it has been very nice to talk with you. So good to have female company, isn't it?"

The woman gave a fleeting smile as Harriet reached across and began collecting the ribbons she had laid out on the table.

"If you're sure you won't want anything I'd best pack up." Once again Harriet smiled. She could see the wistful look in Mrs Bull's eyes but knew from their conversation there'd be no sale there. Mr Bull was aptly named. He bullied his wife and gave her no money for herself. She was lucky she had the rough dress she wore. The fabric was so thick – Harriet didn't know how she coped with the heat. The temperature had been steadily rising for a week. Even though the day was early and they had the shade of the trees, the air was warm.

Septimus stopped beside them. He gave Mrs Bull a charming smile. "Do you favour one of these colours, Mrs Bull?" he asked. He waved his hand over the ribbons Harriet was yet to collect.

Mrs Bull jumped to her feet, making the china cups rattle in their saucers. "They're very beautiful," she said, "but I don't have the means to purchase –"

"I think the emerald," Septimus said. He scooped up the ribbon and held it close to the young woman's hazel eyes. "Don't you think the colour suits, my dear?" He glanced at Harriet and gave a wink, then pushed the ribbon into Mrs Bull's hands. "Your good husband has made several purchases. I think it only fair that you have something: a gift from us for entertaining my wife."

Harriet watched the little glimmer of hope appear on Mrs Bull's flushed face and felt a pang of sorrow for the poor woman. Septimus must have made good sales. He rarely gave anything away and in this case it would do no good. The horrible Mr Bull would probably throw the ribbon out the moment he laid eyes on it.

"Please take it, Mrs Bull," Harriet said. "You've been so kind to keep me company while the men did their business and the colour really does suit you."

"Thank you," the young woman said then jumped as her husband bellowed her name. "I must be off."

Harriet watched her hurry away, pushing the ribbon up her sleeve; perhaps it would be worn when the monster of a man wasn't around.

"Pack up, Harriet." Septimus was already collecting the chairs; the charm he had oozed for Mrs Bull had evaporated. "We have to make space for some wool bags."

Harriet lifted the cups and saucers. She had barely removed the cloth before he took the table to pack with the chairs in the wagon.

"I'll lead the horses and wagon up to Bull's shed, load up, then come back for you."

Harriet still felt a thread of doubt when he said those words but she straightened her spine and nodded.

"Make sure you have everything packed ready. I want to make the creek with the deeper water before dark. We've work to do."

"Yes, Septimus," she said but he was already moving away. Harriet knew there was no point in asking what the job was. He would tell her when he was ready.

She rinsed the delicate cups with their dainty blue flowers in water from the billy and packed them back into the little wooden box he'd found for them. They were enveloped between layers of jute so they didn't rattle against each other. The other things from the big trunk had either been sold or packed somewhere else and the trunk itself had become the storage box for special supplies like bags of sugar, tea and dried fruit.

She'd used a little of the precious dried fruit in the damper and Mrs Bull had eaten three pieces. Harriet wrapped the remaining loaf in calico. Septimus could eat it for his supper. If he had a job planned, she might not have time to prepare anything else. She was packed and ready in time to see him leading the horses and wagon back down the hill. Even from the distance she could see the self-satisfied look on his face. She felt a flutter of anticipation for whatever task he was planning. Life with Septimus was never dull.

Twenty-six

"This second load of wool is bigger than your first, Thomas, and the quality is excellent." AJ gripped his shoulder as they left the wool merchant's office together. "You have certainly been doing well. It was my very good fortune to put you in charge at Penakie."

"A lot has happened in two years." Thomas nodded at the man who'd become his friend as well as his employer. "I'm grateful for the opportunity."

"Let me buy you a meal," AJ said. "We have more to discuss."

They had come to a halt in front of a new building. The solid stone British Hotel with its tiled roof and shuttered windows had not been built the last time Thomas had been in Port Adelaide.

"Thank you," he said and followed AJ through the thick wooden door. Inside, the main room had high ceilings and a bar that ran the length of one wall. Several patrons were already seated at sturdy wooden tables with mugs of ale, even though it was not yet midday.

How much had changed in the two years since his arrival in South Australia. When he'd first stepped ashore here he had no idea of what was in store for him. He still felt the loss of his parents but he'd grown to love the bush and life on Penakie. Working for AJ was a good arrangement, one he hoped his employer would want to continue for some time.

AJ directed him to one of the empty tables and returned from the bar with two mugs of ale.

"I hope you like fish. There's little else on the menu," AJ said as he sat.

"I look forward to it," he said. "No fish in the streams at Penakie."

"You have plenty of water though?" AJ's eyes darkened as he got down to business.

"Yes, we've had rain in the hills and on the property. The streams continue to have some water even during the hottest months."

"And Wick has taken to the life of a shepherd?"

"He's a quick learner."

"Like you."

"Now that he no longer has to fear a beating for every mistake, he's become more relaxed and has taken to the work well." Thomas still detected a hint of edginess in Wick's manner from time to time. Life had been rough for him with the shearers. They'd treated him badly. Thomas suspected something in his past had bound him to them but Thomas found Wick a hard worker and enjoyed his company.

"He was lucky you discovered his plight and let him stay," AJ said.

"He couldn't have without your formal offer of employment."

A pretty barmaid put steaming plates in front of them.

"Thank you," AJ said.

Thomas stared down at the large bowl brimming with pieces of fat fish in a thick white sauce. His mouth watered as the aromatic smell of herbs and onion wafted up from it. The girl returned with a plate of bread and cheese and left them to their meal.

"Eat up," AJ said and immediately took a mouthful.

Thomas did the same and was rewarded with the delicious flavour.

"This is very good," AJ murmured.

Thomas nodded his head in agreement and took another spoonful. The fish was a welcome change from his predominantly meat and damper diet; he was also looking forward to some of the fresh bread and cheese. They spoke little while they enjoyed the food.

"So you would like to keep Wick on as shepherd?" AJ asked once they'd mopped the last of the sauce with a chunk of the bread.

"I would. With Wick and some help from Gulda, I manage quite well."

"Gulda is the native you've spoken of before?"

"Yes." Thomas straightened his shoulders. He didn't mention the extent of Gulda's help in case AJ objected to having the native work for him, like so many others.

"And you pay him with rations and goods?"

Thomas couldn't read from AJ's expression whether he was going to object or accept the native's presence.

"It seems only fair." He spoke firmly. "Gulda has no use for money. Giving him the odd sheep seems to cut our losses to other natives and he makes use of flour, sugar, tea and some clothing."

AJ studied him a moment then reached forward, and cut a piece of cheese.

"I have no objection. You are the man on the property. If it works for you then it works for me." He put the cheese in his mouth and chewed.

"The Smith sons have also helped out when we need extra hands, but on the whole Wick and I manage with Gulda's help."

"It's good to have company and neighbours you can rely on. I seem to remember the Smiths also have a daughter, don't they?"

Thomas felt a prickle of heat course over him at the thought of Lizzie. He was head-over-heels in love with her but he kept that to himself.

"Yes, both Miss Smith and her mother have been most generous in providing food from time to time. Wick and I eat a basic diet. We have learned a few different ways to cook kangaroo and some of the smaller animals are quite tasty. There are also fruits and berries that we can eat. Between us we do well."

"You're a good man, Thomas." AJ sat back in his chair. "I am grateful I have someone as hard working and honest as you to manage Penakie for me."

"Thank you, AJ." Thomas held his employer's steady gaze. "That means a lot to me."

"I understand." AJ let out a long sigh. "My father was a gentleman farmer back in England but I am the youngest of five sons. I had to find work in a shop. I had a good head for figures but I didn't enjoy the confines of being inside all day. One day I read about the opportunities in Australia and from that moment I could think of nothing else." His gaze softened as he spoke. "You and I have much in common, Thomas. When I finally got passage here, I was alone and had very little. I found work on a property in New South Wales. I quickly grew to love the bush, the rich colours and smells, the pelting rain and the pressing sun. I was lucky to have a benevolent employer. He also used convict labour but everyone who worked for him was treated fairly, convict or free man." AJ paused. He looked beyond Thomas as if he wasn't there. "I learned so much from him. He was like a father to me. We talked a lot about the future. He knew I wanted a place of my own. I earned enough to make a start for myself."

"Is that when you came to South Australia?"

AJ turned back to him. "I worked my way here. I was never lucky enough to work for someone as generous and wise as my first employer again but I've remembered what he taught me always. An honest wage for an honest day's work, expect loyalty and trust and reap the rewards." AJ smiled at Thomas. "You'll have your own place one day."

Thomas shifted in his chair. It was his dream but he was nowhere near achieving it. "I enjoy working for you at Penakie."

"And I hope you will continue to do so for a while longer yet." AJ sat forward again, his look businesslike. "We must get on. As we did last year, I am putting up your wage and making funds available to cover extras such as supplies for the native."

"That would be very helpful."

"I am also giving you a bonus."

"You don't have to do that." Thomas was just pleased to receive a raise in his wage.

"I wouldn't be getting the income I am without you, Thomas. You deserve some extra reward for your work and loyalty."

He accepted with a nod. AJ was determined and so it would happen. Thomas already knew what he would do with the money. He had hoped to buy a new horse while in Adelaide. Derriere had done the job but he wasn't good on long trips like the ride to Adelaide and back. He and McKenzie's horse would stay on at Penakie for Wick or Gulda to ride and with his bonus, Thomas would select a new mount for himself. And he hoped there'd be some left over to buy a gift for Lizzie.

"There are no other improvements you would like to see?" AJ took another cut of cheese.

"No. The new yards and shearing shed work well and our living arrangements are comfortable enough."

"I hope to make the journey up to see it all again soon," AJ said.

"I would like you to see what we've achieved."

"I have been kept busy by my other properties and I have to admit I enjoy the cooler climate south of Adelaide. The land there almost reminds me of England."

"Do you think you will go back one day?" Thomas asked.

"No." AJ's reply was firm. "I'm happy here. What about you?"

"I've no wish to return. This is my home now." Thomas felt a warmth inside him that wasn't from the food he'd eaten. It was contentment. Even though Penakie didn't belong to him it was home and he was happy to call it so.

AJ stood. "If you've had sufficient we should get on."

Thomas pushed back his chair. Amazing how he felt so comfortable now with the decisions and the work ahead. He walked out of the hotel into the stiff, salty breeze with a determined stride, looking forward to the day.

Twenty-seven

Harriet lay still and looked at the fruit of their labour as it was slowly revealed in the early morning light. All around their camp clumps of cleaned wool dried in the bushes and trees. Her back and arms ached and her hands were still stained from the dirty wool even though she'd scrubbed them in hot water using some of her carefully preserved soap.

Septimus had found them a camp by a creek not far from the inn. No sooner had he unhitched the horses than he'd begun to pull several bags of wool from the wagon. Then he proceeded to pluck prickles and little black clumps from the wool. It turned out the black clumps were manure from the sheep and it was her job to wash the wool in the creek. The day was still hot so it was no hardship at first. She wore the men's clothes that she kept for camp life when there was no one to see her and, with the trousers rolled up, she bent to her task. It had been a big job. Her back and arms had grown tired and the water had eventually chilled her through, making her old leg injury ache.

Even though they'd both fallen into bed exhausted, Septimus had felt for her body under the blanket. She'd feigned interest, hoping he'd be quick. He had fallen asleep as soon as he'd finished with her. She had done her usual careful ablutions afterwards, emptying her bladder and washing carefully, as the women who worked for Mabel had done. One of them had explained it was no guarantee against pregnancy, but it had worked so far.

Harriet turned her head slightly. Septimus lay close beside her, still asleep. She slipped from under the blanket. Now she felt the need to wash herself all over. The smell of the dirty wool reminded her too much of Pig Boy. Even though nearly two years had passed it was a memory she had not managed to erase.

She dipped quickly in the water, dried herself and pulled on her clothes. She ran her hands down the folds of the dress that Septimus had bought her most recently. It was a much lighter fabric than the previous one and she liked the soft grey colour.

"Well, well, well, what do we have here?"

Harriet gasped. She spun quickly to see a man standing a little further along the creek. He wore a battered hat, a grubby shirt and baggy pants held up with a piece of rope.

"What are you doing out here all alone?" he said. He cast his eyes about and took a step towards her.

Harriet nodded sideways to the path she'd taken through the bush. "I'm not alone," she said. "My husband is just up there."

"Is that so?" the man said. "Well I like to be sociable. The name's Jed Burch. I'm on my way to Burra. See if I can get some work there."

"It's a busy place," Harriet said.

"You been there?" The man had moved closer and his eyes lit up with interest.

"A long time ago." Harriet started to walk and he followed her.

"Maybe your husband can tell me more about it."

Fresh smoke wafted from the fire and swirled around them. Septimus must be up, Harriet thought with relief.

"I've run out of tea," Burch said from behind her. "Don't s'pose you could spare a bit, could ya?"

Septimus was standing beside the wagon. He was dressed and had one arm under the canvas cover. The wool had already been packed in the bags. Harriet saw the purse of his lips as he looked over her shoulder at the man following her.

"Whitby!" Burch uttered. "Is this mongrel your husband?"

Harriet hurried away from both men to stand on the other side of the fire. Septimus neither moved nor spoke but he kept his gaze locked on the man.

"I wondered if I'd ever get the chance to catch up with you again and here you are." There was no mistaking Burch's sinister tone.

"Mr Burch," Septimus said. "This is an unexpected pleasure."

"Pleasure!" Burch spat and pulled his hat from his head to reveal a completely bald scalp dotted with red blotches. "This is not a pleasure, Whitby. I paid you most of my money for those fancy Royal Remedy pills of yours and instead of restoring my hair, I've lost the lot."

"The pills have worked well on others." Septimus moved his arm slightly under the canvas.

"They made me sick. Doctor said if I hadn't stopped taking them I might have died."

"There must have been some other cause. My pills have never –"

"Liar." Burch took a step towards Septimus. "I want my money back."

"I no longer have your money, Mr Burch. I sold you the pills in good faith."

Harriet watched Burch flick his eyes around their camp and saw him take in their big wagon with two horses, the pots and pans of their camp kitchen, the table and chairs they'd taken out in order to rearrange the wool bags and finally the comfortable bedroll with extra its padding and proper pillows.

"Looks like you're doing all right to me." He looked from Septimus to Harriet and she could see the wildness in his eyes.

Suddenly he leaped around the fire and grabbed her. At the same time she heard Septimus shout. She looked up to see him pointing the firearm at Burch.

Burch growled, wrapped his arm tighter around her and pulled her in front of him. The scowl on Septimus's face deepened but he didn't change the direction of the firearm.

"No need to get nasty," Burch said. "This fancy wife of yours is well decked out and she smells so nice." Harriet shuddered as she felt the vile man nuzzle the back of her neck. "Perhaps you could share her and we could call it quits."

To Harriet's horror, Septimus lowered his firearm and shrugged his shoulders.

"She's not my wife. If that's all you want, take her. I've got work to do, but you'd better be done when I get back."

Harriet felt as if a knife had stabbed her heart. Did Septimus really not think her worth saving?

"My mate might like a piece too," Burch said, keeping Harriet between him and Septimus.

"Your mate?" Septimus said as if he was considering it.

Harriet wanted to scream in protest but she made no sound. To try to resist might earn her the same treatment as Pig Boy had dealt.

"He's taken his horse to the inn for food. We've only got the one between us."

"I've got business at the inn myself." Septimus spoke as if he was chatting to a guest over a cup of tea. "I plan to convince the innkeeper to let me cart in some of his supplies."

Burch held Harriet so tightly she could barely breathe. Her head was beginning to spin.

"It will take me some time." Septimus twisted his lips into a smile and he winked.

Harriet couldn't believe he was leaving her to this man's mercies – not to mention his friend's.

Septimus limped away in the direction of the inn. Harriet's mind was so clouded with fear it took her a moment to register the limp. Just before he disappeared into the bush she noticed he still had the firearm held down the length of his body. She relaxed in Burch's arms, hoping her distraction would take his eyes off Septimus.

Burch spun her around. With one hand gripping her arm, he used the other to fumble with her dress. Harriet tried to keep her breathing calm. Septimus had already been to see the innkeeper yesterday. He'd had no luck convincing him to allow them to cart his supplies. There were plenty of teamsters passing through who did the job for a good price. Was it his way of telling her he wasn't really deserting her?

Burch had his full attention on Harriet but he lifted his head at a noise behind him in the bush. He looked around then back at Harriet. His face was twisted in a mixture of lust and suspicion.

"I think we'll go to my camp," he said. "It's not far."

He took her by the wrist and dragged her along with him. Harriet glanced from side to side, hoping Septimus would appear, but he didn't. Perhaps he really had deserted her. She was too frightened to struggle. Burch was strong and she feared a belt from his hand. She would need all her wits about her if she were to escape safely.

They followed the creek for a distance until they came to a small clearing in the bush. Harriet could see the remains of a fire with a few stones around it and some flattened patches of grass.

Burch threw off his hat and shoved her against a tree, pinning her with one hand while he grappled with the rope at his waist. There was no sign of Septimus. Harriet's only hope was to save herself. If she could get away from Burch she could hide in the bush. While he was distracted trying to undo his pants, she brought her knee up swiftly into his groin and shoved with all her strength.

Burch yelled in pain. Harriet gasped as the end of a firearm swung down and hit him on the head. Septimus stepped from the bush beside her. Burch fell to the ground, striking his head on one of the rocks at the edge of his campfire. He sprawled, face down in the dirt. Harriet stared at him. He made no movement or sound.

Septimus poked Burch with his foot. When the man didn't move, Septimus bent over him and gave him a closer inspection.

Harriet put her hands to her face. "Is he dead?" she whispered.

"I wouldn't have thought your shove or my strike would kill him but perhaps the rock."

Harriet stared at the horrid spectacle at her feet. Burch's mottled head lay in the dirt. Beside it was a rock with a smear of vivid red blood on its white surface.

She shivered at the thought of the grotesque man's hands on her.

"What is it about you, Harriet? You seem to attract bad men."

She glared at Septimus. He'd never asked how she'd come to be beaten up when she'd first crawled into his wagon. She'd never spoken of it but now it was as fresh and raw as if it had just happened. "You were going to let him have me."

Septimus grabbed her arm and pulled her close. She winced as his fingers dug into her skin. His face was so close to hers she could see the fine twitch of his taut cheek muscles. His grey eyes were cold with rage.

"No one else will ever have you," he hissed. "If another man ever used you, I would give you to him. You would be nothing to me."

Harriet felt a shudder go through her. Septimus dropped her wrist as quickly as he'd snatched it up. He glanced around then smiled at her. Harriet felt more terror at that smile than at his cold words. "I knew you were safe enough for the moment." He waved an arm to the trees. "I was checking around to see where his friend was. There are signs of a horse so he must have gone to the inn as Burch said. We need to be gone before he gets back."

Harriet continued to stare at him. "A man's dead. We can't leave him like a piece of meat."

She shuddered as Septimus gripped her arm again. He put his face close to hers. "Listen to me, Harriet. He tripped and fell. You can stay if you want but I'm not going back …" Septimus pulled himself up and looked around. "I'm not going to be accused of murder. There's nothing we can do for him now."

Harriet looked down at the body on the ground. The morning was warming up. Flies crawled over his face, already seeking the blood.

"This was an unfortunate accident, Harriet." Septimus put pressure on her arm and propelled her away. "You go and finish packing the wagon. I'll make sure everything is … tidy here."

Harriet hesitated. She had detested Burch for what he'd planned to do but she hadn't wished him dead. However, had he violated her, she might as well have been dead. Septimus would have abandoned her: of that she had no doubt.

"Go, Harriet."

He gave her a shove. She found herself running. She arrived breathless at their camp and began to throw their possessions into the wagon. It wasn't long and Septimus was back hitching the horses. They didn't speak, but once he had scoured the area to make sure they'd left nothing, he urged Harriet inside the wagon. She sank gratefully into the soft bags of wool and gave in to the silent tears, letting them run down her cheeks unchecked.

Twenty-eight

Septimus took extra care with the fire, burying the coals and dispersing the stones. In the flattened area where their bedroll had been he spread leaves and sticks. There was little he could do about the horse and wagon tracks but he hoped that by the time anyone came looking, if they came looking, their camping site would be less obvious.

He'd done his best to disguise signs of disturbance around Burch. The summer sun had already baked the soil hard where he'd chosen his camp, so footprints didn't show. Thankfully the mark left by the firearm handle looked like another blotch on Burch's mottled head. He looked like a man who'd tripped and fallen and hit his head on a rock.

With one last glance around, he urged the horses through the bush to join the road to the inn. He would have preferred not to be seen there but was no way to bypass with a large wagon and two horses.

The inn was busy even though most of the teamsters had already left on their journeys to the mine or south to Adelaide. Septimus hoped nobody would take much notice of a wagon passing by. He'd not planned to stop in there this morning anyway.

He suppressed his impulse to urge the horses on at speed until they were out of sight of the hamlet. Then he shouted at Clover to pick up the pace. Septimus wanted to put as much space between them and the inn as he could before Burch was discovered.

Thomas cracked the whip. The lead bullocks picked up the pace. He was confident with them now. He'd taken Bert's advice and discovered the old bullocky had been right. They were dependable and had learned his voice. Only the odd crack of the whip was necessary when one of them slackened off.

They were making good time. He planned to give the animals a rest and water at the inn further up the track. It was probably too late in the day but he hoped he might see Bert there again, as he had on his way to Adelaide. He enjoyed the older man's company and he always had some words of wisdom. Even though they'd only met on three occasions, Thomas felt as if he knew him well.

The trip to Adelaide had been slow with such a huge load of wool, and fraught with the usual difficulties of overhanging branches and crossing the deep cutaways made by streams. Even though it was the second year he'd made the trip, it had been no easier. The bags of wool had to be piled precariously high. Of course this return journey with a wagonload of provisions taking up much less space was a little easier.

He thought back over the day he'd spent with AJ. His employer was a generous man, and a shrewd businessman with a good heart. It was a relief to know Wick and Gulda were assured of work. Thomas wouldn't like a return to his life in the early days without them. He was also glad he didn't have to rely on the Smiths' generosity so much, although he was always pleased at the opportunity to see Lizzie.

He couldn't help the smile forming on his face when he thought of her. With her golden hair and pretty blue eyes, he found it hard to take his gaze from her when she was visiting. And her sharp wit and quick tongue often made him laugh. He had fallen in love with her and he knew she felt the same way about him, but they had little time together and certainly were rarely alone. Dancing with her at the cut-out parties were the highlights of the year. She was soft and supple under his rough hands, and light on her feet. He loved the glow dancing brought to her cheeks and the opportunity to hold her close.

Unlike the rest of her family, Lizzie accepted Gulda. Not that she saw him, but Thomas had told her about him. Thomas was grateful to the native, who made life on Penakie far easier than it might have been. He could ride a horse well now and round up sheep, and he knew the best places to take them for feed and water. Thomas had grown used to his regular disappearances, especially when other people came, like shearers, or the rare time when the Smiths came as a family.

Edmund was never with them. Thomas hadn't set eyes on him since the terrible day when he'd taken Gulda back to Penakie after his whipping. George had come for the cut-out party after this last shearing but Edmund was always the one to stay home.

The horse shifted and pranced beneath him. Thomas glanced across at the bullocks. They continued their steady forward movement. Attached to the back of the wagon was Derriere. Thomas was now riding a fine strong horse – still a little flighty, but they were already getting used to each other. It riled him still to think how he'd been duped by that Whitby fellow. It had cost him dearly. He'd paid his boss back for a horse he'd never owned, not that Thomas had ever told AJ about what had happened.

Every penny he earned had become very important to Thomas. If he could get land of his own, one day George might allow him to marry Lizzie. Thomas couldn't ask for her hand without prospects, even though the thought of her brought a smile to his face and set his heart thumping in his chest.

The horse pranced again. Thomas became aware of the sound of hooves and wagon wheels up ahead. They were approaching at a fast pace. He called the bullocks to a halt. The advancing wagon raced over the hill and hurtled towards him along the narrow stretch of road.

Thomas pulled his horse sideways as the wagon passed him. The man at the reins barely looked his way but Thomas saw his sweep of dark hair, the pointed nose and the glint of eyes that widened for a moment as they drew level … and then the man was gone, his wagon careering on down the road.

Thomas gripped the reins of his horse but the animal had become so agitated it reared up and he was thrown to the ground. He landed with a jarring thud on his backside. It took a moment to test all parts of his body before he scrambled to his feet. His new horse had disappeared up the road and behind him the bullocks had pulled the wagon dangerously close to a wash-away.

It took him some manoeuvring to get them moving in the right direction. He walked beside the wagon, feeling the aches from his fall with every step. Thankfully his horse had stopped not too far up the road but the animal was still flighty. It took Thomas some effort to calm him and get his little procession moving again.

What had possessed the man to drive his wagon so recklessly? Now that Thomas had time to think, there had been something familiar about him. It had only been a glimpse but the sharp look from those grey eyes reminded him of –

"Whitby," Thomas growled, and twisted in his saddle.

His hair was longer, he had a beard and a thicker moustache, but Thomas was sure. For a brief moment he contemplated leaving his wagon and chasing after Whitby, but at the pace he'd been travelling, the thief would be well gone. In the direction he was headed there was a crossroad and further along closer to Adelaide there were more tiny settlements and roads. Whitby could take any one of them and Thomas would waste precious time trying to find him.

Whitby was a mistake from the past. Thomas knew he wouldn't ever be so easily duped again. He tried to keep his mind on the road ahead and getting back to Penakie with his supplies and the special gift he'd bought for Lizzie, but even though he conjured up her happy face in his mind, the shine had gone from his day. No matter how hard he tried to forget Whitby's trickery, it replayed itself again and again, niggling at him deep down like a festering sore.

Twenty-nine

1849

The waddy was a well-crafted solid piece of wood. It hit the thick stick Thomas held, close to his fingers. The force jarred along his arms. He grimaced and danced backwards then sideways on his toes, never taking his eyes from the man wielding the waddy. The native was smaller than Thomas, with a wiry frame. He was quick on his feet. They circled each other. Thomas could feel the sweat running down his naked back. It stung as it trickled over the burn from the rays of the autumn sun.

He had caught the native taking a sheep. He wasn't known to Thomas but Gulda had spoken angrily, using his hands to make gestures. There was a loose understanding between Thomas, Gulda and the local group of natives who spent some of their time living near his hut that sheep were not to be pilfered. This man circling Thomas with his waddy was not a local, but Gulda obviously knew him and had brought him forth as the ringleader to be dealt with.

Thomas could not bring himself to use whips or firearms like his neighbours. He'd spent enough time with Gulda to learn a little about the way the natives moved about the land. They stored very little, yet could live easily in the often harsh bush conditions. He'd managed to make Gulda understand that the sheep weren't to be used as food unless earned. He had enough trouble with the wild dogs without the natives helping themselves.

The mournful cry of a large black bird wailed through the morning air. Thomas glanced away. From the corner of his eye he caught the movement of the waddy descending towards his exposed shoulder. He side-stepped then spun and swung his weapon. The hefty blow from Thomas's stick and the native's own momentum propelled him forward and onto the ground. He sprawled there, the wind knocked from his body.

Thomas watched the thief closely even though he was sure the man wouldn't get up and keep fighting. He was the loser and would accept that but Thomas had to make sure he understood not to take the sheep. He took the large tuft of wool hooked on the railing close by and waved it in the man's face. "No sheep," he said in a gruff voice.

Gulda appeared from the shadows. He added his piece, speaking in a fierce tone to the man. The only words Thomas understood were "sheep" and "Mr Tom". Gulda waved his hands to the south as he spoke then sent the other native on his way.

"I hope he understands," Thomas said. He took his shirt from the rails and pulled it over his head. "He can't take the sheep."

"No, Mr Tom, sheep," Gulda said solemnly.

Thomas studied the man who'd come to be a great help to him since he'd arrived at Penakie. Gulda had picked up quite a bit of English, enough so that they could communicate, but Thomas knew little about Gulda's language. Except that the word for water seemed to be "wirra". At least that's how Thomas said it, as he couldn't make the same sounds as Gulda.

Water had featured a lot in their conversation of late. They'd had another long hot summer and autumn had produced some cooler conditions but no rain yet. The creek, as Thomas now called the watercourse in front of the hut, was a dry bed except for the few holes deep enough to still retain water. The sheep were struggling, having to walk long distances to find tufts of grass to eat and access the pools left in the other dry creek beds across Penakie. Deeper in the foothills there were what appeared to be permanent pools, but even they were getting low. Thomas prayed they would receive good rains soon.

He turned at the sound of horses approaching. Wick had ridden over to the Smiths' to return some tools they'd borrowed. He had proved a useful addition to Penakie and had grown from gangly lad to a solid man. He had been helping Thomas make some improvements on the hut. They'd extended the back room out and made a door with a low verandah that faced the outside fire.

Thomas was glad it was AJ who paid the annual occupation licence the government demanded for these northerly runs. He knew others were struggling to pay theirs. The current extended dry was a difficult time for everyone around.

Thomas hoped the sound of more than one horse might mean Lizzie had ridden back with Wick. She nearly always found some excuse to come his way. He rarely went to the Smiths' unless he knew the irksome Edmund wouldn't be at home. He was fairly certain she'd accept if he gave in to his desperate heart and proposed, but he had nothing to offer her. Penakie wasn't his. He'd saved quite a lot of money over his time as overseer but with Wick and him sharing the little hut, Thomas couldn't see his way forward to taking a wife.

He hid his disappointment with a smile when he saw the other rider was Jacob. The Smiths always had plenty of workers between George and his four sons, so Jacob was often the one to come and help out.

Jacob jumped from his horse and strode towards Thomas. "I've had enough of this biding time," he said before Thomas could even say hello. "We're all tripping over each other at our place; except Edmund, who keeps going off to visit his lady friend and is never there when there is work to be done."

"Not a lot to do here either I'm afraid," Thomas said.

"Let's explore further north," Jacob said. "Few people have been beyond Penakie and there's talk that the government is going to have leases that will last for several years rather than these punishing one-year licences." Jacob's eyes gleamed and he grabbed Thomas by the elbow. "Just think: we might be able to find better runs in the north. If the leases do come to be, we'll know where to stake a claim."

"I'm only the overseer here." Thomas gently shook his head and eased his arm from Jacob's grip. "I do the job as instructed by my employer."

"AJ has several runs and he's always looking for more. I bet he'd back you."

Thomas could see the fervour burning in Jacob's eyes but he was free to come and go as he pleased.

"Your family owns your lease. You have time to go exploring."

"Only to a point. At the moment Father has us building a new hut for whoever marries first. It's likely to be Edmund, and Samuel won't be far behind." He looked pointedly at Thomas. "Unless Lizzie beats them all."

Thomas gave a little frown. Jacob was often the one to accompany Lizzie on her visits. The three of them and Wick all enjoyed each other's company.

Jacob dug the toe of his boot into the soft red dirt. "Anyway, don't get grand ideas about our place. There're five of us to live off it, and Mother and Lizzie. Our land isn't big enough for us all. Father's talking of finding someone who might back Zac and me if we can find a decent run in the north." He looked over Thomas's shoulder. "I've been a bit of a way past your northern boundary a few years back but I was on my own and couldn't get far. There's a mountain range out there. Bet there's good vegetation and plenty of water. AJ might even give you a bonus if you were to find it. Then you could ask Lizzie to be your wife."

"How ...? I ... It's n-not ..." Thomas stuttered, feeling the heat in his cheeks.

"Look, Thomas," once again Jacob took him by the arm, "this is a great opportunity. I know you want to marry Lizzie. It's only your pride and your belief you haven't got many prospects that's stopping you. She'd marry you tomorrow if you asked her but if you think you need something more substantial than an overseer's life to offer her, then this might well be your opportunity. Neither of you is getting any younger."

Thomas studied Jacob. The eagerness was still there but his eyes also shone with friendship. Jacob had become the brother he'd never had, but the talk about Lizzie and marriage was new. He hadn't been so indiscreet before.

"You think she'd say yes?"

"Of course." Jacob threw his hands in the air. "Thomas, sometimes I wonder what goes on in that head of yours. Lizzie doesn't care about fancy huts or lots of money. We're not rich and her bed is the couch in our kitchen. She and Mother spend all their free time sewing things for the box she has stored under it. Since you arrived, it's filled up and they've had to find another space. She's just waiting for you to ask."

"But Edmund –"

"Who cares what Edmund thinks? Lizzie's old enough to marry without asking anyone's permission. Anyway, I'm sure Father would happily give it to you and that's what counts."

Thomas felt as if a window had opened inside him and sunshine warmed his heart. Perhaps he could ask Lizzie to marry him – but how much better would it be if they could look to somehow owning their own place in the future? Penakie provided a living but ultimately it was hard work for someone else's future. Maybe there *was* something better in these ranges Jacob had seen.

From the hut came the banging of a hammer. Wick had got back to work. Thomas knew he could rely on him to take care of the place. He'd done well each year on his own when Thomas took the load of wool to Adelaide.

"How long would we be gone?" Thomas said.

Jacob's face lit up. "About a week. Maybe a little longer. We'll carry as many supplies as we can. Do you think you could get Gulda to come with us? I bet he knows where the water is."

Before Thomas could express any more doubts, Jacob was organising provisions. Wick was given a list of instructions and Gulda appeared in time for Thomas to explain via a series of words, hand signals and rough scratchings in the dirt what they wanted to do. A short time later the three men set out, Gulda leading the way and the two white men jubilant with anticipation, in search of the elusive heart of the country.

Thirty

Yardu welcomed Gulda and took him to sit in the shade of the huge gum beside the creek. A bit further along, three small children played on the bank, digging in the mud with little sticks, under the watchful eyes of their older siblings and cousins. He smiled as his eyes found Binda. The little boy wobbled forward on unsteady legs: he hadn't been walking long. A few more weeks and he would be running.

"It's good that you have taken another wife, cousin," Gulda said. "Your son is a good strong boy."

"You have come a long way on your own." They had spoken at length when Gulda had first appeared in their camp. Now Yardu had brought his cousin to a space alone, sensing there was something important to be said.

"I am not alone."

Yardu glanced beyond Gulda then back at his cousin and waited. Like the gathering grey clouds above, discomfort stirred in his belly.

"I have brought my friend, Mr Tom," Gulda said, "and another white man."

Yardu felt the tension tighten in his body. He stared at the ground in front of him. "Where are they?"

"A long walk from here. I did not want to cause you trouble, but these men are not like those who came long ago. They are my friends. They won't harm you or your family."

"Why have you brought them?"

"They have animals called sheep. They are much easier to catch than kangaroo. You remember the sheep we shared when you came to our country?"

Yardu nodded. He seldom thought of his first wife. He'd helped her spirit return to her country and avenged her death when he killed the white man. He hadn't thought much of the meat from the animal Gulda had shared with him that night. Kangaroo was better and all Yardu's instincts told him it was best to keep away from the white men and their animals. He had a new family now.

"These sheep need lots of water. This creek is a good one. The springs keep the waterholes full even when there has been no rain for a long time. I want to show my friends this country."

"We all share it. I would not stop you." Yardu said the words and opened his arms wide, but his sense of foreboding was building.

"They are not like us," Gulda said. "They build huts and stay, thinking the land will provide everything they need in one place. I am showing my friends they must move about as the seasons change."

"Do they understand you?"

"Mr Tom tries. I know he is a good man."

"I do not trust them. I don't want my family to see them."

His first wife had been so frightened by the white men appearing that day long ago. Yardu's father had told him all about it when he had returned to the camp. Some of the women had run, terrified by the strangers, the big screaming animals they rode and the noisy sticks that made the huge banging sound. Yardu had seen few white men since the day he'd thrown his spear at the man on the big animal in Gulda's country, and he would prefer not to see any more.

"I don't like these men."

"They are my friends, but we also met others who were travelling further up into the hills. They had one of your northern cousins with them. There will be more white men. You can't stop them."

Yardu thought about that. If what Gulda said was true and the interlopers weren't prepared to share, there were other places he could go. He could take his family and the white men would never find them.

"We will move on," Yardu said. His heart was heavy in his chest but the season was changing and they would have had to move soon anyway. It would be sad not to come back to this waterhole but if the white men had it they might leave the rest of the hills country alone. Gulda had only seen a few of them. Perhaps they would build their huts here and not travel further. "You must teach them to respect the sacred places," he said.

"I will try."

Yardu stood, said goodbye to his cousin and watched as Gulda left their camp. Once more he turned his solemn eyes to the children playing with the digging sticks. The creek was running faster and they had moved further up onto the flat above the bank. He heard the sudden excitement in their voices as one of them found some of the special wild pear roots in the soil.

The light was dimming in the sky even though the sun was still high. The spirits of his ancestors were sad like him. Yardu moved slowly; it was time to meet with his brothers and cousins. They must move on today.

Thirty-one

Jacob stood beside the creek with its deep waterhole. "That Gulda knows his way around. We would never have found our way here without him."

"That's for certain." Thomas looked across at the native, who was a distance away, staring at the hills behind them as if watching for something. "I was ready to give up and turn back two days ago when we came across that William Chace. He made it sound as if there was nothing out this way."

"It's a huge country; perhaps Chace didn't follow this creek," Jacob said.

"I think he was planning to go further north, but he wasn't giving much away."

"I didn't like the look of that black fellow with him," Jacob said. "He had shifty eyes."

"I wish Gulda could tell us about him; he didn't understand what I meant when I asked."

"This area we've ridden through for the last few days would work well with the foliage and this permanent water supply. Do you think we can get Gulda to show us more country? We'd need a run each if we were to make a go of it. Zac wants to come too."

"We've been gone a long time." Thomas looked to the sky. "Those clouds are getting heavier and darker. I think we should turn back."

He could see the reluctance on Jacob's face. "If the pastoral leases are announced you can have this area," Thomas said. "You're more likely to get the finance than me. If AJ wants a run I'm sure the country's big enough to find another."

The low rumble of thunder reverberated off the hills. Jacob looked from Thomas to the sky and nodded his head.

"Gulda," Thomas called, "time to go home."

Gulda was already at the horses. He was muttering something Thomas couldn't understand.

They had no sooner mounted their horses than heavy drops of rain began to fall. Neither Thomas nor Jacob had brought their thick coats and Gulda wore only a shirt and pants. Within minutes they were wet through. The creek they were following, which had been flowing steadily, was now rushing and tumbling with the extra water. They climbed the steep banks when their way south was blocked by the widening torrent of water. The rolling hills behind them were providing a giant catchment, funnelling the flow their way.

Lightning split the sky and thunder rumbled. Gulda turned back and pointed. They all watched through the sheets of rain as giant forks of light split the sky over the hills.

"What's he saying?" Jacob yelled into Thomas's ear.

"I don't know. Sounds like 'garragadoo'."

"What do you suppose it means?"

"I don't know," Thomas said again, "but we're going the wrong way. Gulda," he shouted through the rain at the native, who had turned his horse west. "That way is home."

Gulda shook his head, pointed in the direction he was going and urged his horse on. Thomas knew the way home was across the creek but he had lost all his bearings in the deluge and the afternoon sky was as dark as early evening. They had no choice but to follow. Perhaps Gulda had a safer place to cross.

It was a nightmare journey. The thunder and lightning moved on but the rain continued and above its steady thrum they could hear the sound of water rushing in torrents. Land that had been parched for a long time was soon in flood. Thomas was shivering with cold and had given up taking any notice of his surroundings. They were travelling single file now. He simply directed his horse to follow Jacob's, which followed Gulda's.

Thomas knew by the way he sat in the saddle that the ground was gradually climbing beneath them. He guessed it must be early evening by the time Gulda stopped and tethered his horse. He waved at Jacob and Thomas to do the same and to take their bed-rolls and supplies. The bush that Thomas could see was low and straggly. He couldn't imagine why Gulda would pick this place to camp but he followed wordlessly. His legs were like blocks of wood and his fingers were icy and cramped from gripping the reins, making it difficult to carry his belongings.

Gulda led them over sloping ground covered in slippery shale rock. The sound of a raging creek grew louder. Thomas sensed it was somewhere below them but it was too dark to see. Just ahead a darker patch appeared in the gloom. Gulda disappeared into it. Following him, Thomas lowered his head and stooped into a cave. The instant relief of being out of the rain was overwhelming. He sank to the rocky dirt floor.

Jacob tumbled down beside him. "That was wild," he said and rubbed his hands together. "All that rain – it's a miracle. Let's hope we're getting some at home. The storm looked as if it was travelling south."

Thomas was shuddering with cold. He could barely hold his head up. He registered the excitement in Jacob's voice and some-where behind him, Gulda was rustling something but he was beyond speech. The air in the cave had a rank animal smell, but at least it was dry.

Jacob leaned closer. "Are you all right?"

Thomas tried to nod his head but only managed a stiff jerk. Pain shot down his neck.

Suddenly there was a little flicker of light in the cave. It quickly became a glow.

"Well, would you look at that!"

Thomas spun himself around. Gulda had a small fire going.

"I'd heard blackfellows could make a fire out of nothing and now I've seen it. How did you do that?" Jacob shuffled past Thomas as Gulda stripped himself of his wet clothes. "Good idea," he said. "We should do the same, Thomas. The bedrolls should be dry inside the oilskins. We can wrap ourselves in a blanket."

Thomas watched as Jacob began to pull the wet clothes from his body then he turned his head to the fire. The warmth had penetrated his cheeks. He stretched his hands towards it. There was no way he would strip right down like a native. The fire would surely dry his clothes soon enough. Gulda tended the fire totally naked; Jacob sat beside him in his underwear then, with a grin on his face, stripped off the last of his clothes. Thomas shook his head. Life in this land was beyond anything he could ever have imagined back in England.

Birdcalls woke him, and the strong smell of smoke. He forced his eyes open. It was early but there was enough light for him to make out the lump that was Jacob still wrapped in his bedroll. Beyond their feet the little fire was burning. Perhaps Gulda had just brought it to life again.

Thomas flicked a look around the cave. In the morning light he could see it wasn't very big, but it had served them well. Through the mouth, the soft glow of dawn brushed the rocks and bush with pink hues. Thomas stretched out his legs. Immediately the air was cold on his damp underwear. He was naked from the waist up but he hadn't been able to bring himself to strip totally like Gulda and Jacob. Jacob had no doubt been right. Now Thomas lay in a half-sodden bedroll.

He dragged himself out, pulled on his wet boots, wrapped the dry part of the blanket around his shoulders against the cold and stepped outside. He sucked in a breath of glorious fresh air and lifted his gaze. The dark clouds had gone. The sun was rising on the other side of the hill so that it lit up the valley opposite but left him still in the shade. Further away, their wet clothes were draped over exposed rocks and branches where the first rays of the sun were already reaching them. Gulda had been busy.

The cave was high up on one side of a deep valley. The rushing of water below was a constant background sound as Thomas made his way up and behind the cave. There were no horses but Thomas could see where they'd been tethered overnight. He hoped their absence meant that Gulda had taken them to find food and water. The ground was even rockier beneath his feet and the vegetation low as he made his way to the top. What he saw when he reached it made him pause.

He wished he were an artist who could capture the beauty before him with a paintbrush. This side of the hill dropped away, part of a rocky ridge that jutted out from a higher rise. That in turn fell away more gently to lower slopes, which finally gave way to a wide flat valley. Rocky ridges poked out into the valley like bony fingers. Across the valley, forming a backdrop to the vista before him, was a huge mountain range stretching along the horizon. Even from this distance it looked impassable, a formidable barrier to whatever lay beyond it.

The creek that roared below the cave widened out and met other watercourses. He couldn't see the flow but he discerned where each creek wound its way between the hills and wriggled across the plains: the trees were always much taller wherever there was water. Just along from Thomas was a scattering of rocks, most of them bigger than him. He climbed onto one and sat, letting the blanket fall from his shoulders. The sun warmed his back as he watched its rays change the colours of the landscape before him.

He took a deep breath and slowly exhaled. Even though he knew Jacob and Gulda were somewhere nearby, he felt as if he were the only man on earth. He lifted his head to see a large bird high in the sky. It appeared to hang in the air, a silent sentinel watching over the land.

The hairs on the back of Thomas's neck prickled. A shiver rippled down his spine. He reached down to gather the blanket back and took a closer look at the rocks around him. He'd been so busy looking at the vista before him he'd not taken much notice.

They were toppled together as if by some giant hand and closer inspection showed a protected space like a small cave. It was there, on a section sheltered by the rest of the formation, that he saw the markings. They were dark against the deep browns of the rock and were mostly a series of small straight lines. Some ran parallel to each other and some fanned in circles while others were longer with an angular line topping them so that they looked like an arrow pointing.

"Wildu."

Thomas jumped at the sound of Gulda's voice. He turned to see the native standing some distance away near the point where Thomas had stepped to the top of the ridge.

"Wildu," Gulda said again then pointed to the sky.

Thomas turned his head in the direction Gulda indicated and saw the large bird had come closer; its wingspan must have been several feet. Beyond it two more large birds circled slowly.

"This is magnificent, Gulda." Thomas was reluctant to leave the vision before him. He knew it was the best country they'd seen on their travels.

"Come, Mr Tom." Gulda came no closer but beckoned him urgently. "We go."

Thomas sighed. He wished he could communicate with Gulda more than a few shared words and gestures. He felt there was much he could learn from the native if they could only understand each other better.

"Wildu." He said the word out loud to the valley. He liked the sound of it although he knew it wasn't exactly what Gulda had said. With land like this a man could make some money. Thomas smiled. "One day I'll come back here," he murmured.

He turned to follow Gulda but the native had already gone.

Thirty-two

"I'm glad you didn't camp too close to the creek, Mrs Wiltshire."

Harriet smiled at the two women seated on her chairs under the canvas awning. The morning sun was warm and the rays slanted through the trees, sparkling off the wet leaves. After the overnight rain the earth smelled fresh and the scent of eucalyptus filled the air. It was a beautiful day.

"Please call me, Harriet, Mrs Smith."

"Oh we're all so stiff and starchy, aren't we?" Lizzie Smith put down her cup and smiled at Harriet. "Let's all use our first names, Mother."

"Very well, Lizzie," the older woman said. "Anyway, Harriet, the creek rose the highest we've ever seen it in the night. There must have been a lot more rain in the hills than we had here. I'm glad you weren't washed away."

"We might come from Adelaide but we spend so much time travelling," Harriet said. "Septimus is astute when it comes to surviving in the bush."

"If you don't mind me saying so, your husband is a very fine-looking man," Lizzie said.

Harriet smiled. "I am indeed blessed that he is also a very clever man."

"Perhaps charismatic." Mrs Smith had a questioning look on her face.

"An astute businessman." Harriet cast her hand over the goods she had displayed. "He's always on the lookout for new items that people so far from town might require."

"It's amazing how much you can fit into your wagon," Lizzie said.

"We are well practised now," Harriet said.

"And you seem to have everything you need." Lizzie picked up the tea cup again. "This is the most beautiful tea set, isn't it, Mother."

"Quite delightful." Mrs Smith took another sip.

"I see you've been reading," Lizzie said and nodded at the small pile of books on the little shelf beside the wagon. "We have the bible and four other books. Mother and I are the only keen readers here."

Harriet smiled. The tea set constantly impressed and she always put the little pile of books out to add to the homely touch of her outdoor parlour. "They belonged to my husband's mother. Would you like to look at them?"

Lizzie leaned forward eagerly as Harriet put the pile of books on the table. "Oh," she exclaimed as she opened the first book, "is this his mother's name? Hester Baker?"

"Yes."

"Our neighbour is Thomas Baker," Lizzie said. "Wouldn't it be funny if they were related?"

Harriet paused. Where had she heard that name before? "I never met Septimus's parents," she said and began to restack the bolts of cloth she'd piled on top of the trunk. She had hoped to make a substantial sale here but the women had been very frugal in their purchases. A broom and a tablecloth to be put away for Lizzie had been the extent of their shopping. From the way they spoke, Harriet assumed the younger woman was soon to be married.

"Keep the book for now, Lizzie," she said. "You can return it before we leave."

"How kind," Lizzie said and began turning the pages.

"What about your own parents, Harriet? Where are they?" Mrs Smith's question was one Harriet had been asked many times before by the ladies she met. It was a natural curiosity when so many of them had links to England, but Harriet didn't like to speak of her parents.

"They died when I was young."

"I'm so sorry. You can't be that old now. How sad for you not to have your mother."

Harriet ran her hands over the bolts of cloth as if she were daydreaming. "I do miss her. My parents hadn't long been in Australia so they left me very little other than happy memories." Harriet allowed a soft sigh to escape her lips, then she put a hand to her bosom. "Luckily I met my Septimus and together we have been making a new start. We very much enjoy travelling and bringing supplies to people like yourselves, who are so far from Adelaide."

Harriet lowered her lashes but not before she saw a shared look of concern pass between mother and daughter.

"Lizzie, I think you will need a new dress before long." Mrs Smith stood up and inspected the bolts of fabric she'd only given a cursory look before.

"You were saying as much just the other day." Lizzie joined her mother to look at the fabric.

"What about this blue?" Harriet unrolled a few yards of a deep sapphire-blue cloth and held it towards Lizzie. "Oh, and what a beautiful locket." She admired the tiny gold heart that hung around Lizzie's neck. "Did someone special give you that?"

Lizzie's eyes danced. "The neighbour I mentioned before, Thomas Baker."

"Are you to be married?"

"You have a most beautiful pendant yourself." Lizzie changed the topic and looked wistfully at the locket.

Harriet put her hand to the delicate gold heart. "Yes. My husband gave it to me." Harriet had been touched that Septimus would give her such a beautiful gift with her initial engraved on the front. "I am very lucky to have such a special piece of jewellery of my own. I have nothing of my mother's." She tucked it back inside her bodice and lifted the fabric in her hands close around Lizzie's neck. Harriet knew her pendant was twice the size and quality of the little one around the other woman's neck and she didn't want anything to detract from the sale she hoped she was about to make. If only she could work out what was going on. Was Lizzie to be married or not? "This colour makes your eyes sparkle."

"She's right, Lizzie," Mrs Smith said. "It's perfect for you. Not really the right fabric for working in but … perhaps for a special dress."

"Mother." Lizzie's voice had a warning tone.

"Well, you're not getting any younger, my girl."

"Just ignore my mother, Harriet. Our neighbour is a very good friend but …"

Mrs Smith gave a gentle snort. "He's the only decent man in the district. I think it's time your father pressed him for his intentions."

Harriet saw the faint blush spread across Lizzie's cheeks.

"Mother," Lizzie said again, but much firmer this time. "This is not the place."

"Please don't worry, Lizzie," Harriet said. "I hear lots of stories when I'm travelling around. So many women are without female company. Just think of me as a sister. I never repeat anything I hear in confidence." She swallowed her curiosity and smile reassuringly in the hope she would still make a sale. "Now your mother seems to think this fabric would be lovely for a special dress, even if it's just for dancing, and I have to agree with her. The colour matches your eyes and makes your skin glow."

"We'll make it up together, Lizzie." Mrs Smith patted her daughter's hand. "You can wear it for Edmund's wedding."

"I wouldn't want to outshine the bride."

"Elizabeth." This time Mrs Smith's voice had taken on the warning tone.

Lizzie lowered her voice. "I know one shouldn't blow one's own trumpet, Harriet, but my brother Edmund's bride is the most dour-faced person I've ever met."

"She is a rather serious young woman," Mrs Smith conceded, "but she does enjoy a little joke sometimes."

"And then she has that silly snort."

Lizzie pulled a face and Harriet relaxed as mother and daughter both began to laugh.

Mrs Smith picked up the soft cloth again. "I am sure your father would be happy to allow you a new dress, Lizzie. You do your share of work."

Harriet smiled, assured of a good sale at last.

Septimus nodded his head. He had resigned himself to the fact that he would do no business with George Smith but the man was happy to speak about life so far from civilisation. He had four sons, providing enough manpower to manage the property and release one of them to make trips to Adelaide to sell their wool and buy supplies when necessary.

George had been happy to show him around the improvements they'd made. One new hut just finished in readiness for his oldest son's marriage and another being built next door for the second son, who was also to take a wife. There was a large shearing shed and stockyards, and George's own hut was a good size. It had an enclosed backyard, where his wife and daughter clearly did their best to maintain a small vegetable and fruit garden.

What Septimus was most interested in was George's talk of the land to the north. He hinted that the country could be suitable to expand into. When Septimus had last been in Adelaide there was talk that the government was going to grant longer-term pastoral leases and at each stop he'd made since then the landholders had only added to the speculation. He had quite a bit of money put away and investing in land seemed a good opportunity, but he knew little about farming so he asked questions and listened.

"The land to the north will be taken up next," George said.

"You think so?" Septimus followed the man's gaze.

"I'm sure of it."

"Will you make a claim?"

"It will require some financing. I've got the labour with my big family but this long dry spell has been hard on our savings."

Septimus studied the man's profile. Perhaps there was an opportunity here. "I am a humble merchant, Mr Smith." He pulled his hat from his head and held it in his hands. "I have no desire to work the land, but I have money to invest. Perhaps we could come to a mutually beneficial arrangement."

Septimus felt the gaze of the older man sweep over him. He arranged his face in a small smile and looked up into the dark blue eyes that studied him. Septimus saw a glimmer of curiosity.

"You don't understand farming?" George said but Septimus could see he was truly interested.

"I wouldn't interfere in the running of things, of course. It would be a kind of loan for which I would receive some return once the property made some money."

George lifted his own hat from his head and ran his fingers through his hair. "Perhaps," he said.

Septimus could see the man was proud. He'd made his own way thus far and wasn't one to take help easily. "You've worked this land with no one but you and your sons. It's a fine achievement. If it's only money that's stopping you from expanding, then perhaps we can come to some sort of agreement. One that would help your sons get their own places." He swept his arm towards the north. "The northerly runs are there for the taking."

"You might be right, Mr Wiltshire." George clasped Septimus on the shoulder and walked him towards the hut. "Perhaps we could discuss it further with Edmund. My eldest son is visiting his wife-to-be but he should be home for the evening meal."

Septimus stopped, forcing George to do the same. He turned so that the big hand slid from his shoulder. "I think this arrangement is best made between you and me, George, don't you? The less complicated the better. What will it matter to your sons where the money comes from? You will soon have it paid back, I am sure." Once again Septimus looked at George with a smile.

George held his gaze. Septimus could see the desire in his look.

"Have you seen this land, Mr Smith?" Septimus asked.

"No." George stopped by his front verandah and looked towards the gushing creek. "I am expecting my son Jacob back any day. He's gone exploring with our neighbour, Mr Baker."

Septimus clenched his jaw. There could be many Bakers but he was always wary of running into Thomas again one day. He knew the man was in the bush somewhere. He'd passed him the day he'd despatched Jed Burch. Septimus had been shocked to see Baker sitting atop a horse on the rough road not far beyond the inn. He'd nearly run the fool down.

"Is Baker an older man?" he said.

"No." George chuckled. "Young and wet behind the ears when he first arrived, but he's been a fast learner. You have to be to survive out here. Thomas is his name."

Septimus sucked in a breath.

"Do you know him?" George said.

"No. I once knew another Baker, an older man," Septimus said quickly. "We lost touch."

"Can't be related to Thomas then. He's on his own. Parents both dead and no siblings."

"Poor chap," Septimus said and followed George's gaze as he looked towards the creek again.

"I'm hoping Baker and my son will return safely with good news very soon."

Septimus pushed his hat further onto his head. "It's time for my wife and me to pack up and move on, Mr Smith." He held out a hand. "Thank you for your hospitality."

"But we thought you were staying. I'm sure my wife and daughter were looking forward to company at our table tonight."

"That's very kind of you." Septimus looked around, trying to think of an excuse to leave after saying they would stay another night. The creek was still high with rushing water. "It's that rain, you see. We may have trouble passing the creeks in some places. I am eager to return to Adelaide and find out about these pastoral leases. What do you say, Mr Smith?" He thrust out his hand.

Once again the other man studied him closely then his lips turned up in a smile. "It's George," he said and took the offered hand in a firm grip.

"And you must call me Septimus."

"Then I think our arrangement could be of mutual benefit, Septimus."

"I agree, but I would prefer to keep it between ourselves. There are other hawkers like myself who aren't doing so well, George.

If they got wind that I had money to invest in land it might make life difficult." He clutched his hat to his chest. "I'm concerned for my dear wife of course."

"Of course. I agree," George said. "This will be between you and me."

They shook hands again then Septimus turned on his heel and strode towards the high ground further along the creek, where Harriet was entertaining the ladies.

Thirty-three

The Reverend Jones hoisted himself up from the log he'd been sitting on. He was a young man but already his head was balding. Lizzie could see it was pink on top where the sunlight had reached it through the dappled shade.

"Today has certainly been a most joyous occasion," he proclaimed. "So many able to gather in God's name is always something to be thankful for in this vast new land."

Lizzie returned his smile. She was so glad they'd had warning he was coming. Among the neighbours who had joined them for the service in the shearing shed was Thomas. The others had gone home again but he had stayed for the picnic along with Edmund's fiancé, Eliza. They had all been relaxing after the large meal they'd shared in the shade along the bank of the creek. Thomas sat near Lizzie, his back against the trunk of a tree, his eyes closed. She had been surreptitiously studying his handsome face while the conversation flowed around her.

"Thank you for providing such a wonderful picnic, Anne." Jones pushed his broad-brimmed black hat firmly back on to his head. "We should discuss the upcoming nuptials and then I must take my leave."

"We're so glad you could be with us today and we could have a proper service." Lizzie's mother beamed at the reverend.

"I've a large flock spread far and wide." He turned his flushed face to George. "You would understand the work that takes."

"My flock don't feed me as well as you have been, Reverend."

Lizzie smiled at the serious face her father pulled. He wasn't so fond of the young priest. He thought him far too pious.

Jones mopped his brow. "But you surely enjoy the fruits of your labour. The cold mutton we had for our picnic was most delicious."

George puffed out his chest. Anne put out a restraining hand and Lizzie bit her lip.

"We'll go up to the house," Anne said. "Edmund and Eliza will come of course and George."

"Do you need me?" George asked and gave the reverend a stern look.

"Of course we do," his wife replied. "And you, Samuel. You may as well listen in too. If you are to ask for Sarah's hand you will know all that a wedding entails."

"We might as well all go," George said and raised his eyes to the heavens.

"Goodness, no," Anne said. "There'll be enough of us around our table as it is. The rest of you stay here and enjoy this rare afternoon off." She thrust her arm through George's and almost dragged him up the slope behind the reverend.

Isaac threw a rock across the creek.

"First to hit the large gum," he said. "Jacob, Thomas? Who's up for it? Winner has the other two chop wood for a week."

"Is that your way of making Thomas stay?" Jacob grinned and gave Thomas a gentle shove.

Lizzie could only see the back of her brother's head. He nodded at Thomas, who glanced at her.

"Come on, Zac," Jacob said. "I'll take you on. I'd be more than happy to not chop wood for a week."

"We'll see," Isaac replied.

"Thomas has other things to do."

Once more Jacob nodded his head at Thomas.

Lizzie frowned. What was he up to?

"Would you care to take a walk, Lizzie?" Thomas stood up and brushed off his clothes. "All that food has made me sleepy."

"I'd love to," she said, forgetting all about her brother. "The reverend will have them bailed up for hours at the house."

Thomas offered his hand and helped her to her feet. "It was good to have him here."

They set off along the creek enjoying the shade thrown by the large gums. Lizzie chatted about Edmund and Eliza's upcoming wedding. After a while she realised Thomas had said little more than two words.

"You're very quiet, Thomas." They had rounded a bend and were out of sight of her brothers. Lizzie boldly thrust her arm through his. "Penny for them."

"I've nothing to say." He patted her arm and left his hand resting there. "I'd much rather listen to you."

"Oh, Thomas. You are a funny fellow. I'd love to hear more about the country you and Jacob saw on your travels. You've been back for weeks now and we haven't seen you until today. Jacob has talked of nothing else but I'd like to hear your views. Is the land as good as Jacob says? Do you really think the government will allow people to –"

He stopped, forcing her to do the same. She looked up. The longing in his deep brown eyes made her draw in a breath. He leaned closer. She yearned for the feel of his lips on hers.

"Lizzie." The huskiness in his voice made her knees go weak.

"Yes, Thomas," she whispered.

His head bent closer. She took in the soft lines around his eyes, the brown of his weathered skin, the pink of his lips. He clasped her other hand in his.

"I ... I ..."

"Yes."

"I love you, Lizzie Smith. I know I haven't got much to offer but –"

"Yes."

"It's a lot to ask. Penakie doesn't have the comforts you have here and it's quite a distance from your home. I don't know if George ..."

Lizzie squeezed his hand.

He took a deep breath. "If your father gave his permission, and if you felt so inclined, I wondered if you ... well, if you ..."

"Oh Lord, Thomas what are you trying to say?"

"Would you do me the honour of becoming my wife?"

"Yes."

His eyes widened. "You mean –"

"Yes."

He stared at her with such a perplexed look Lizzie couldn't help the giggle that escaped her lips. "For a man of few words, Thomas Baker, you took the long way round to ask."

He gripped both her hands tightly. "You've made me the happiest man alive. I wasn't sure you'd say yes."

"Oh, Thomas. I've loved you since nearly the first time we met." She studied him closely. "Did Jacob put you up to this?"

"I've wanted to tell you how I feel for a long time." Thomas smiled. "Let's say Jacob encouraged me not to delay any longer."

He glanced around then drew her back with him against the trunk of a tree. His gaze swept over her. She shivered in delight as he wrapped his arms around her and bent his lips to hers. His kiss was soft at first then more urgent. She melted against him then suddenly he stopped. He put his hands on her shoulders and gently moved her back.

"I must ask you father's permission," he said and spun on his heel and strode away.

Lizzie put her fingers to her lips and closed her eyes. She could feel her heart thudding in her chest. She knew in that instant she was the happiest woman alive. When she opened her eyes Thomas was disappearing around the bend.

"Thomas," she called.

He stopped and turned back.

"Please wait for me, dearest."

In a few strides he was back beside her. He studied her with his deep brown eyes. "Dearest," he said. "I like the sound of that."

She smiled up at him and was rewarded with another kiss. Then he took her hand and they walked back together.

Thirty-four

"Three cheers for Lizzie and Thomas."

Voices chorused around them. Thomas felt he would burst with pride as Lizzie slipped her hand into his and squeezed it tight.

"Lucky Edmund and Eliza had booked the priest." Jacob slapped Thomas on the back. "Who knows how many more years it could have been before you married my sister?"

"Jacob, don't tease," Lizzie warned but the smile didn't leave her face.

"He wouldn't have asked you if it wasn't for me," Jacob said. "Or at least not till you were old and grey." He clasped his sister by the shoulders and kissed her cheeks.

Thomas smiled. Every one of the Smiths had been happy to welcome him into their family but Edmund.

Thomas moved closer to Lizzie so their arms were touching. She was as happy as he was, even if they did have to share their wedding day with standoffish Edmund and his sour-faced Eliza. More people joined the line to wish them well and finally it was Isaac's turn.

"I have to say you clean up all right," he said as he shook Thomas's hand. "No doubt about Lizzie's ability with a needle."

Thomas glanced down at the loose white shirt that Lizzie had made for him. It felt so much nicer against his skin than the coarse brown fabric his few shirts were made of. He'd never worn anything like it in his life.

Isaac kissed his sister's cheek and moved on to Edmund and Eliza. For the first time, Thomas stood alone with his new wife.

"It was a very thoughtful gift," he said.

"You were already the most handsome man here." Lizzie beamed up at him. "But that white fabric against your sun-browned skin and dark hair.' She brushed the back of her hand across his cheek. "You take my breath away."

Thomas gazed into her eyes then lowered his lips to hers. He kissed her once and then again. Her lips melted against his. She was so sweet and soft. His arms drew her in close and his heart thumped in his chest at the feel of her body against his. He was surely the luckiest man alive.

Jacob and Isaac whistled and everyone turned to look at them. Thomas dropped his arms and stepped away from Lizzie. She brushed the folds of her dress and he straightened the neck of his shirt. They stood in silence a moment. The rest of the group went back to their conversations. Voices and laugher floated around them. Thomas had never felt so awkward, except the time when Lizzie lanced his boil. His cheeks warmed at the thought.

"Do you like the −?"

"The decorations are −"

They both spoke at once and Lizzie giggled.

"The decorations are very clever," Thomas said. "You've done a fine job."

"Mother did most of it. She has an eye for embellishing."

They looked around the Smiths' shearing shed, which had been turned in to a makeshift church. Branches of blue bush covered the rafters and stems laden with little ball-like yellow flowers stood in buckets around the shed. Eliza's family had lived in New South Wales before moving to South Australia and Eliza's equally sour mother had mentioned several times how the yellow wattle, as she said it was named, was much prettier in the eastern parts of Australia. This primitive variety, as she called it, looking down her nose, was far too strong of scent and made her eyes water.

Thomas cared little about that: the golden flowers would remind him of this special day for the rest of his life. They were in sharp contrast to the beautiful blue of Lizzie's dress, which in its turn highlighted the cornflower colour of her eyes. He prayed they would always be this happy.

"Time to serve the food," Mrs Smith called.

"Come on, Thomas," Lizzie said.

He groaned. His stomach was still in knots from the nervous tension of the wedding vows but he allowed her to drag him towards a splendid feast laid out on a table covered in a crisp white cloth. It was only mid-morning but the spring days were already proving warm and so it had been decided to have the ceremony first thing followed by an early lunch.

Just as when they gathered for the cut out after each year's shearing, the double wedding was a chance for fellowship and celebration. The neighbours came and all the women had been cooking for days. The table was laden with food. Cold sliced mutton, sheep's-brain pie, and potted meats sat beside potato and pumpkin pies, turnip mash, beetroot slices and melon pickle. One of Lizzie's famous wild peach pies was dwarfed by a two-tiered fruitcake. Eliza's mother had made it and brought it with her, and Mrs Smith had decorated it with the pale yellow flowers from another native bush.

Thomas reached for a plate just as Edmund did. His new brother-in-law's dark eyes glared back at him. Thomas held his look but let go the plate. He and Edmund had managed to avoid each other over the years except on family occasions like this. Thomas was happy to concede to the eldest son and keep out of his way this time. He didn't want anything to spoil the day but he worried the time would come when he and Edmund would lock horns again over something. When that time came, Thomas would no longer be prepared to retreat.

John Gibson had of course brought his harmonica and as soon as the food had been eaten the dancing began. Thomas swept Lizzie around the wooden floor, relishing the chance to hold her in his arms again. Edmund did the same with Eliza, although at arm's length and in a much more stilted fashion, and then everyone else joined in. Wick danced with another neighbour's daughter and Thomas was pleased to see the serious young man enjoying himself.

Before long they were all stopping for cups of water or sweet cordial. The older men were patting at their foreheads and necks with handkerchiefs, and the ladies used theirs to fan themselves. Thomas noticed Duffy had his flask as usual and Jacob and Isaac were taking swigs from it. Everyone was red faced from the dancing, regardless of what they were drinking.

Once he'd regained his breath, George called the bridal couples forward to cut the cake together. Lizzie and Eliza stood in the middle between the two men and each couple had a knife. No sooner had they completed the honours than Anne was cutting the cake into slices to hand around.

"I really don't think I could eat any more," Lizzie said. She put a hand to her waist. "Mother has laced me in far too tightly."

"It's perfect," Thomas said. Each time he looked at her it was difficult to drag his eyes from the swell of her breasts above the low neckline. A surge of desire coursed through him. "We should be on our way soon if we are to be home before dark." He was surprised at the throaty tenor in his voice.

"I must go and get changed then," Lizzie said. "This dress is not at all practical for travelling by dray."

Reluctantly, Thomas let go of her hand. Anne went with her, along with Eliza and her mother. The Smith men helped Thomas load the dray. It took them a while to organise Lizzie's assorted goods and chattels so that everything had a place. There was a small chest of drawers her father had made for her, a large trunk, wooden boxes, pots and pans and preserved foods, along with several small gifts from the neighbours. Thomas was beginning to think the Smiths thought him unable to provide for his new wife.

George took him aside. "Anne and Lizzie have been hoarding for this day for a long time. You'll just have to make the best of it. There will be nothing they'll leave behind." He chuckled.

"Wick's going to stay the night here with us," Jacob said with a wink.

Thomas could feel the extra heat in his cheeks yet again. Getting married was certainly a fiery affair.

"We'll send him back tomorrow." Jacob nudged Wick, who broke into a shy smile.

There was a sudden burst of excited female voices and Lizzie appeared from the house, flanked by her mother and Eliza. The younger women carried one more small trunk between them and Anne a basket. Thomas hurried to help, thankful for the distraction. He fitted the trunk and the basket loaded with leftovers from their wedding feast into the dray and tucked the covering in tightly in an attempt to keep the worst of the dust out.

Finally, he lifted Lizzie up and climbed onto the bench beside her.

"One more thing," George called.

They twisted on their seat to see him leading a young cow. There was a blue ribbon around her neck with a bell attached.

"A gift to the young couple from us," he said and tethered the animal to back of the dray.

"You've been very generous," Thomas said as George reached up to shake his hand.

"You look after our Lizzie," George murmured.

"I will," Thomas said and flicked the whip.

Farewells chorused all around them. They were setting off in the hottest part of the day but Lizzie had her umbrella and part of their journey would take them under the giant gums along the creeks. The carthorse set forth, pulling the dray, leaving the shearing shed and Lizzie's family behind them.

They had only gone a little way when Thomas realised she hadn't said a word.

"What is it, Lizzie?" he asked. "Are you sad to be leaving home?"

"No," she said. "My home is with you now and not so far away." She chewed her lip.

"What is it then?"

She kept her face forward and said in a soft voice: "I must confess to feeling a little bit nervous."

Thomas threw back his head and laughed. "That must be a first," he said.

Behind them the cow gave a soft moo and, accompanied by the jangle of its bell, they made their way home.

It hadn't taken long for Lizzie to get over her apprehension. The trip back to Penakie seemed not to take the time it usually did. Thomas enjoyed the sound of her voice and the realisation that he was no longer alone. Lizzie was his wife.

When they finally rattled and clanged their way around the last bend, their laughter echoed back to them along the creek.

Lizzie stopped abruptly as she looked up at the hut they were to share. "There's a man on the verandah," she said.

Thomas followed her gaze. Sure enough, a man leaned against the verandah post in the shadows. At the sound of their approach he stepped out into the bright afternoon sun.

He had a broad-brimmed straw hat, a full beard, a belt at his ample waist and long leather leggings. Thomas grinned and waved. "It's Mr Browne," he said and urged the horse and dray over the last piece of ground to the hut.

"Thomas." AJ held out his hand as Thomas jumped to the ground.

"AJ. I didn't expect to see you. Each year you say you'll visit."

They shook hands then AJ threw his arms out wide. "Here I am at last. I was beginning to think you and Wick were out bush, but I see you've been busy elsewhere." He nodded at Lizzie.

Thomas turned. "Oh, yes … I'm sorry … this is Lizzie Sm—" He stuttered and stumbled over his words. "My wife," he said and hurried around the dray to help her down.

"Well, well," AJ said. "You have been busy. You didn't mention a wife last time we met."

Lizzie stepped forward. "Hello, Mr Browne. Thomas has told me so much about you. It's wonderful to meet you at last. You must be tired from your journey. If you'll just give me a moment to get myself organised, I'll prepare some food."

"Thank you, Mrs Baker."

"Lizzie, please," she said with the beautiful smile that Thomas could see was charming his employer already. "I'll have something for you to eat in two shakes of a lamb's tail."

"And you must call me AJ. Please don't rush on my account. There's much for Thomas and I to look at and talk about."

Thomas glanced from Lizzie to his employer. This was not the homecoming he'd planned, but there was nothing for it. "I'll take the cow around to the yards," he said, and unhitched the animal. "Wick and I have made some additions to the holding pens you'll be interested to see."

"I had a bit of a look while I was waiting," AJ said. "I like the way you've used the bush to make a natural barrier on one side." He strode ahead. Thomas followed with the cow in tow, giving Lizzie an apologetic smile as he left.

By the time they returned, Lizzie was just lighting the lamp. She had set some of the leftover potted meats on the table with some freshly baked damper and a pot of melon pickle. Thomas noticed the small trunk was by the bedroom door, but apart from that and the food, everything else they'd brought was still in the dray.

"Can I make you a cup of tea, AJ?" Lizzie asked.

"I'll just wash up first, if I may."

Thomas snatched a cloth that served him as a towel from beside the door and followed his employer outside.

"How long have you been married?" AJ asked as they washed their hands in the rough bowl by the back door.

Thomas rubbed his hands vigorously on the drying cloth, not looking at AJ. He cleared his throat. "Since this morning," he said.

"Good God, man," AJ bellowed. "Do you mean to tell me I've arrived on your wedding night?"

"You weren't to know."

"Give your wife my apologies. I've set my swag up among the trees. We have much to talk about but not tonight. I'll leave you in peace."

"Please eat with us first." Thomas put a restraining hand on AJ's arm. "Believe me, if I allow you to leave before you've been fed, I will get no peace."

AJ looked at him a moment then slapped him on the back and laughed out loud. "You're a very wise husband already, Thomas. Very wise indeed."

AJ ate with them. He kept up a constant conversation to match Lizzie's but he didn't stay long once the meal was over. He apologised again for interrupting their wedding night. As soon as he was gone Lizzie went into the bedroom and shut the door. Thomas stood in the kitchen totally at a loss. Was he to follow her? Should she have time alone?

He poked at the fire to make sure there would be coals for the morning. He shifted the rough chairs firmly under the table, rattled the front door and then the back to make sure they were securely shut. Finally he extinguished the lantern. The glow of the full moon shone through the small window, more than enough light for him to see by. He pulled the now dusty white shirt over his head and hung it on a chair.

The bedroom door creaked open.

"What are you doing, Thomas?"

"Nothing."

A hand reached around the door. "Please stop doing nothing and come here."

Thomas's heart sped up. He took her hand and stepped into the bedroom. Lizzie stood before him, a tiny smile on her lips. Her hair was loose and flowed over her shoulders where it met the white nightgown that covered her body, hiding all the curves her dress had promised.

"What now?" he asked.

Lizzie giggled. "Don't you know?"

"You have one up on me, Lizzie. You seem to know a lot about the male form but I know nothing of women."

"Tosh," she said. "I've had to mend a few broken bodies but ..." She placed a hand carefully on his bare chest. His skin tingled at her touch. "Well, I've never seen a fully naked man before."

Thomas's self-control was disappearing fast. He put his hand under her chin and tilted her head towards his. "We'll learn together then."

Lizzie's eyes sparkled in the moonlight. He leaned in and covered her lips with his. The sweet softness of her mouth flamed his desire and he let out a small moan.

She pulled back. "Are you hurt?"

He grinned and shook his head slowly. "No." He carefully eased the soft fabric from her shoulders. It slid to the floor. His gaze travelled down over her ample breasts and the rounded curves of her body.

She gave a little shiver. He wrapped his arms around her and drew her to the bed.

Desire made him want to rush but nerves, both his and hers, made him slow down. He nudged aside her hair and caressed her neck with his kisses. Gradually he moved lower to the soft skin of her breasts. She reached around him, drawing him closer, skin to skin. Her hands began to roam over his body, exploring as he was with her. They were gentle with each other, guiding and helping until they came together. The rhythm of her body matched his and they were one.

Afterwards they lay together, arms and legs still entangled. Lizzie traced a finger across his lips and down his neck to his chest. "Dearest Thomas," she whispered. "I love you."

Thomas kissed her again. "And I you, my sweet Lizzie."

He inhaled the sweet scent of her and smiled into the darkness. Finally they were husband and wife. He felt like a man with the world at his feet.

Thirty-five

Wick returned by midmorning the following day and AJ stayed on. Together the three men went off each day to look at the improvements Thomas had made and to check the sheep. AJ was pleased with the number of lambs, and the quality of the wool promised another good return after shearing.

Each night they ate together, but as soon as the meal was over, AJ would go to his swag and Wick to the lean-to they'd built at the side of the shearing shed, leaving Thomas and Lizzie alone.

After their first night together, they quickly got to know each other's bodies, learning together what pleased each other best. Thomas was invariably exhausted from the work of the day yet found renewed energy each night in bed with Lizzie. He had never imagined how wonderful being with her could be. And he knew she was happy too. Each afternoon when he returned he could hear her singing as she worked in and around the house. Already she'd made his simple hut into a home.

The morning of AJ's departure, he asked Thomas to walk with him to the creek. They sat beside the barrel roller. Thomas had made a stronger, improved model and the structure had survived much better than his first attempt.

"You're an innovative man, Thomas," AJ said. "I am thankful for the day we met. Penakie has been in fine hands."

"I enjoy the work," Thomas said with pride.

"And Wick has been a fast learner as well."

AJ paused. The sound of chopping echoed from behind the hut. Wick was already hard at work stockpiling wood for Lizzie's fire.

"Perhaps capable of being in charge?"

Thomas studied AJ, unsure where this conversation was leading.

"You can rely on Wick," he said.

"And this land to the north. They're calling it 'Flinders Ranges'. You have seen it?"

"I did not know its name but the area Jacob and I visited had plentiful water and vegetation suitable for sheep." Thomas pictured the view he'd had from the top of the mountain and the large circling bird. "Magnificent country," he said softly.

"Could you find your way there again?"

"Yes, although …" Thomas frowned. They had taken a circuitous route because of the raging creeks. "I might need Gulda's help to find the exact place again."

"I'd like to meet him."

"His family camps near here from time to time. I haven't seen him for a while but I'm sure he'll return soon. He is wary of strangers. I don't think he'll appear while you're here."

AJ stared at the creek trickling below them. "Managing all these properties, keeping them stocked, is hard work. I love the bush but I'm tiring of the effort. It's made me a wealthy man," he said, "and I'm not getting any younger. I'm going to put overseers on all my properties and move to our house by the sea in Adelaide. My wife is happier there. She's not so fond of the isolation in the bush and I can still visit my properties to the south easily enough."

Thomas stared at AJ. In all the time he'd known his employer, he'd never heard him mention a wife. They sat without speaking, listening to Wick's axe, the rustle of the breeze in the trees and the bubble of the water below them.

Suddenly AJ got to his feet, brushing dirt and twigs from his pants. Thomas did the same.

"I have a proposition for you." AJ looked him square in the eye. "You can take it or leave it. You will always have a job as overseer at Penakie if that is your wish, but you've talked of having your own place."

Thomas held AJ's look but didn't speak. He still wasn't sure where this was leading.

"I am sure the South Australian Government will soon allow pastoral leases for up to fourteen years – it may be announced later next year. You need to be ready. Talk is, to make a claim, you must have an accurately drawn plan that relates to some point laid down by the Surveyor General's map."

A glimmer of anticipation surged inside Thomas. Yet surely a lease was beyond his reach. "I have savings but not the amount that would be needed to stock such a lease."

AJ put up his hand. "Hear me out, Thomas. I owe you more than the wage you've received for the work you've done here. You've seen the northern country. If you think you can make a go of it I'm prepared to back you."

"I couldn't –"

"I am certain your hard work will pay me back some day – less my gift, of course."

"Gift?" Thomas was struggling to take in everything that AJ was saying

"Call it a late wedding present. We can work out the exact details later. Are you interested?"

"Yes," Thomas said softly. This was his dream, to own his own land. He wasn't afraid of hard work and he was sure he could repay AJ. He threw back his shoulders and spoke again with conviction. "Yes, I am."

"What about your wife? It will be a much tougher life than you have here."

Thomas glanced towards their hut. Lizzie would want them to be independent and she was used to hard work. "She'll be pleased," he said.

AJ thrust out his hand. Thomas gripped it in a firm shake. Nearby one of the black and white birds warbled its morning welcome. Thomas looked around at the place that had been his home for the last three years. He'd arrived knowing little about the job in front of him. AJ was right. He had made great improvements, both in himself and to the property.

"What about Penakie?" he asked.

"I want to offer the overseer's job to Wick. If you think he'd be up to it."

"I'm certain he would be."

AJ threw an arm across Thomas's shoulders and they walked back towards the hut. "I am glad to call you a friend, Thomas. Fortune smiled upon us the day we met."

Thomas had a sudden recollection of his first meeting with AJ. He was lucky that meeting started him on this journey. His own hard work had continued it but he was grateful to AJ nonetheless.

"Very fortunate indeed," he said. Beside him he felt AJ's body rumble in a jubilant laugh.

Thirty-six

1850

"You've got the morning to pack your things and leave." Septimus spoke in a low voice but there was no doubting the menace in his words. "If you're not off my property by then I'll throw you off."

"You snide little upstart," Bull blathered. His eyes bulged and spittle trickled from his mouth. "This is my property."

"Not any longer." Septimus pointed at the paper he'd laid carefully on the table in front of Bull. "You have defaulted on your loan. You signed this document that states the property becomes mine if you don't meet the repayments."

"That print was too small." Bull flicked a hand over the paper. "I didn't see that part so I don't agree."

"You signed it." Septimus picked up the paper, folded it and slipped it carefully inside his coat pocket. He smiled at the fat, red-faced man sitting before him. "You should always read the fine print, Mr Bull."

"Look here, Wiltshire." Bull mopped his forehead with a grimy handkerchief and twisted his lips into a smile. "Surely we can come to an arrangement. I'll have the money after the next wool payment."

"I can't wait that long and I've seen your sheep. The few you have left are unfit. You'll be lucky to get enough money to pay the shearers."

"Once upon a time a man's word was all that was needed." Bull lurched to his feet. "I can get the money."

Septimus looked around the hut. Over the years he had gradually fleeced Bull of anything of value. The few furnishings that remained were of no interest to him. He patted his pocket. "The law favours the written word these days."

"You're no gentleman." The red in Bull's face deepened. "You're a blackguard and a thief."

"Call me what you will." Septimus strolled to the door of the neat little hut. At least Mrs Bull, wherever she was hiding, had managed to keep their abode and what remained of their furniture in good condition. "Be gone from here by midday or I shall bring the constable to evict you." He lifted his hat. "Goodbye, Mr Bull."

The man roared all kinds of obscenities as Septimus pulled the door shut on him. From the corner of his eye he saw the end of a skirt disappear around the corner of the hut. Mrs Bull was obviously well used to keeping out of her husband's way.

He looked up at the cloudless autumn sky and grinned. He had just acquired his first piece of land and it wouldn't be the last. He mounted his horse and rode back along the track to the bush where he'd set up camp and left Harriet. She hadn't been her usual self lately. They'd been a long time living in a wagon. Perhaps a house of her own would brighten her up.

Later that afternoon, he drove the wagon back to Bull's property and was pleased to see his threats had worked. The place already had a deserted air. There was no cart beside the house or horses in the yard. He helped Harriet down and led her onto the verandah.

There would be no way Septimus would have drawn attention to himself by involving the law but Bull didn't know that. He'd packed up and gone.

"It doesn't look as if anyone is at home, Septimus." Harriet peered through the small window. "The house is completely empty."

"Except for the new owners."

"Owners?" Harriet turned her pale face to him. "Where are the Bulls?"

"Gone. Mr Bull was not able to meet his financial commitment to me so his property is now mine."

Harriet's mouth fell open.

"Welcome to your new home, Harriet." He pushed open the door to the empty hut.

"Home?"

"Come, Harriet, surely you are as tired as I am of being on the move all the time. This will be our permanent home."

"What about poor Mrs Bull?"

"She's not our concern." Septimus stepped inside, a little annoyed that Harriet wasn't as excited at the prospect of their own home as he was.

She followed him. "This is so far from anywhere."

"There is talk of a town being laid out at the head of Spencer Gulf. It will only be a day's ride down across the plain."

"I had thought perhaps ..." She brushed a loose piece of hair from her face and turned sad eyes in his direction. "Perhaps a town."

"We will have a grand house in town." Septimus took her hand and spun her round. "This is a stepping stone along the way."

Harriet moaned. Her hand slid from his. He just managed to catch her before she collapsed.

"Harriet!" Septimus called as he lowered her to the floor. Her eyes were closed and small beads of perspiration dotted the skin above her lips. He propped her against the rough wood of the wall. "Harriet," he said again and gave her a gentle slap on each cheek.

Her eyes fluttered open. She moaned softly again. "Water," she whispered.

Septimus ran outside to the wagon, where they kept a water pouch hanging in the shade. He hurried back inside and helped her take a sip.

"This is not like you, Harriet," he said. He hoped she wasn't ill. They had much work to do.

"I'll be all right." She tried to get up but he put a hand against her shoulder.

"Sit a little longer," he said. At least the pink was returning to her cheeks.

"Then this is to be our new home. Septimus, can you please sit beside me?" She patted the rough wooden floor. "I have news of my own."

Septimus eyed her a moment then did as she asked. A short rest wouldn't hurt. He was feeling a little weary himself. "We can't sit long," he said.

"You're going to be a father, Septimus." Her gaze locked with his.

He held her look a moment then glanced at the hand she placed across her waist. "You are with child?"

"Our child. The house has come at just the right time."

Septimus scrambled to his feet. "This is why you haven't been well?"

"I've been a little off-colour, but that will pass. Aren't you pleased? You will have a son to carry on the business."

Septimus watched her pull herself up against the wall. A son — that would be something; but it could be a girl and what use would she be to his business? Then again there could be no child at all. He studied Harriet's waistline but could see no change. Many a woman had lost a child before it got the chance to take air in its lungs.

"When are you expecting this child?"

"I saw a doctor when we were last in Adelaide. Six months from now we shall have our baby boy." Harriet's face gleamed in excitement.

"Well, best not to look too far ahead."

"We must find a priest, Septimus. I don't mind for myself but I won't have our son born a bastard."

Septimus paused. He'd never planned to marry Harriet. She'd been goods to be used just like any other possession and yet she had become *very* useful.

"We shall see." He straightened his shoulders and tugged down his jacket. "In the meantime we've got a property to fix up. Mrs Bull has kept this hut neat and tidy but the same can't be said for her husband and the rest of the place. If you're feeling better, there's a wagon to unload. I'm going to inspect our holdings."

"Of course," she said all too quickly. "I'm much improved. I will unpack our provisions first and prepare some food for your return."

He nodded and left her. Somehow her news had dampened the brightness of his day. They'd managed very well with just the two of them. Having a pretty woman like Harriet with him had worked to his advantage on many occasions, but she would be no use to him swollen with child. He could only hope she would lose it.

Harriet watched through the window as Septimus mounted his horse and rode around the hut out of sight. When she could no longer hear the sound of hooves she turned to inspect her new home. The structure was made from sturdy wooden planks and it had a wooden floor, unlike the dirt that covered so many she'd seen on her journeys with Septimus. There were two main rooms. The one she stood in was quite large and it had a fireplace built into the back wall. Shelves ranged down one side of it but apart from that the room was empty. The Bulls had taken everything with them. It would make a spacious living area. She crossed to the only internal door. It opened into a smaller room, which would be their bedroom.

There was not a speck of dust or a cobweb to be seen. Septimus had been right when he said Mrs Bull was a tidy housekeeper. Harriet turned slowly and took in her new home again. She had hoped she would be living in Adelaide when their son was born but she had to agree, this was a start, and a better place to raise a child than in a wagon.

She took another swig from the water pouch then set to the task of unloading their possessions. Several hours passed. She unloaded as much as she could on her own. Septimus didn't return and her hunger made her nauseous. She sat on the verandah and ate a hunk of bread spread with pickle.

Above her, clouds began to gather and the day lost its brightness. The sad cry of a black crow wailed across the valley below. The hut was nestled in the foothills. Behind it was rugged, impassable country and in front, a large plain stretched to the sea. They'd travelled across the plain on several occasions, visiting properties dotted between the hills and the gulf.

The late afternoon breeze strengthened. The noise it made as it passed through the trees sounded like a person moaning. She shivered at the sound. Septimus had been gone a long time.

Perhaps she had been wrong to tell him about the baby so early. She had thought his exuberance at finally owning his own property would extend to a child, but he hadn't seemed pleased. She had managed to keep her nausea hidden from him but her skirts were getting too tight and he would have noticed her growing belly soon enough. Best he knew now. Septimus didn't like surprises.

She pressed her hands gently against her stomach. It was hard for men to understand when there was nothing to see. Once she produced their son she knew Septimus would be pleased. The baby was a boy, she was sure of it. She gave no thought to the possibility of a girl. It was most important this baby was a son for Septimus – a son for him to teach and be proud of.

Harriet had thought a baby would have him looking to make their arrangement official. That was something she would have to work on. There was no way her child would be born a bastard like she had been. Still, it had been a shock to Septimus. There was time enough to organise a marriage.

The sun disappeared behind a cloud, sending a chill over her shoulders. Even though they were only midway through autumn, the warm days gave way to cool nights. She cast one last look in the direction Septimus had taken then went inside in search of her shawl.

Septimus sat back from the table and looked around the room once more. A piece of checked cloth hung in the window to hide the ink-black night beyond the glass. The china tea set adorned the shelves along one wall, and most of their pots and pans, along with their meat safe and chairs, had already been brought inside when he finally returned just before dark. Harriet even had a fire going, which took the chill off the room, and she had boiled the kettle for his cup of tea. On his return he had helped her bring in the table and they had sat down to a meal of mutton and pickles and a piece of her delicious fruit scone.

"You've accomplished so much already, Harriet."

"Is there much to be done outside?"

Septimus snorted. "The fool of a man has let the place go. The shearing shed is sturdy but the yards are in disrepair and there are sheep carcases everywhere. Wild dogs have been having their pick and probably the blacks as well. I will have some work to do before I set off on the road again."

"On the road?"

"I still have my customers, Harriet. This place alone won't get you a fine house in Adelaide." He leaned closer to her across the table. "I've a chance at more land. I need income to be able to expand."

"I had thought we'd stay here a while."

"You will."

"Me?" Harriet's mouth formed a circle of surprise. "I can't stay here alone."

"I need someone to keep an eye on the place and the sheep once I get more."

Harriet's forehead creased. "I can't do it alone."

"Of course you can." Septimus thumped the table with his hand. He felt a small ripple of pleasure that it made her jump. "This is our future."

Harriet sucked in the edge of her lip and chewed it. Septimus watched. He felt the stirrings of desire. He liked it when she did that same thing with his ear.

"I won't be gone long," he said, softening his voice.

There was silence except for the crackle of the fire and the moaning of the wind through the trees outside.

"This is a fine hut," he said brightly. "We should be celebrating."

"There is sherry in the wagon." Harriet started to rise from her seat.

Septimus smiled at her. "That's for our customers, Harriet. We don't need alcohol to enjoy our good fortune."

She sat back.

"The only thing we need is a proper bed," he said thinking it was time for them to retire to it. When Harriet deferred to his every wish like she was doing now she became even more desirable.

"We'll make do as we always have with our simple travelling mattress." She lifted her eyes to his. "I'm sure I can make you comfortable."

She leaned forward a little and her plump breasts bulged from the top of her bodice. How he loved smothering them with his lips, kissing and – he flicked his eyes lower. How had he not noticed she was filling out? For a moment he'd forgotten the baby she carried.

"You're with child, Harriet," he huffed. He shifted on his seat, trying to ease the discomfort of his arousal against his pants.

"I was with child last night and the night before. It made no difference." Harriet moved slowly towards him then lifted her skirts and straddled his lap. "My body is still yours," she said. She cupped his face in her hands and covered his lips with hers.

Septimus groaned. She was right. While there was no sign of the baby he could still have her as often as he wanted. Perhaps he would marry her. It made no difference to him but if it made her happy … Her tongue probed his mouth. He stood up, clasping her buttocks to him as she hooked her legs around his hips. In the meantime there was no point in wasting an opportunity.

Thirty-seven

The last rays of the sun reflected off the thick cloud bank in orange hues. It had been a dry autumn so far and even though the clouds had been thick all day they hadn't opened into rain as the previous year's had. Lizzie could hear the axe. Thomas was determined to make a mountain of wood for her before he went.

She put a hand to her stomach. Since she'd found out she was pregnant he had forbidden her to do any heavy work. She smiled. There were so many jobs that required lifting and shifting – just to get enough water to wash their bedding was a huge task. He really had no idea of how much she did each day, but she loved that he tried to spare her as much as he could.

"Thomas," she called as the sound of the axe paused.

He came down the hill, a dark shape in the dusky light.

"What's the matter?" he asked.

The cold air suddenly made Lizzie shiver.

He was beside her, putting an arm around her.

"There's nothing wrong," she said. "It's almost dark. I want you to come inside. You've chopped enough wood for several families and there will only be me and Wick to use it."

"He can chop more if you need."

Lizzie chuckled. "We'll be fine, Thomas." She prised his sweaty arm from her shoulders. "You wash up. I've made us a nice stew for our last night together."

He took both her hands in his, his rugged face lit by the lantern behind her. She could see the tenderness etched into his eyes.

"I hate leaving you, Lizzie." He dropped one hand and placed it on her stomach. "Both of you."

Lizzie laughed again. "You won't be gone that long. We'll both be perfectly fine. This baby is going to need clothes. I have lots of sewing to keep me busy at night while you're away."

His face pulled into a teasing smile and she noticed the glint in his deep brown eyes before he pulled her close.

"But you'll have no one to keep you warm," he murmured in her ear.

Once more she shivered, though not from the cold. How she loved this man. She would be happy for him to take her to bed right then but there were still things to do before he left early in the morning.

She slipped away from him. "Go and wash up, Thomas," she chided. "Or I might make you sleep on the floor tonight."

He tapped her on the bottom. "No chance of that," he said and did as she bid.

Lizzie sang to herself as she served up two plates of steaming stew. In the mornings she still felt quite unwell but by evening she had an appetite.

Thomas came in and sat opposite her at the rough wooden table.

"Your bedroll is ready and I've almost finished packing your food supplies." She nodded at the mountain of stores stacked in the corner of the room.

"Lizzie, that will be more than enough. Poor old Derriere makes a good packhorse but he's only one beast."

"You need provisions."

"Don't forget your mother will be loading Jacob up in the same way. There are abundant animals where we're going and Gulda will be with us. We won't go hungry."

Lizzie fiddled with her fork. The native hadn't been around for a few days.

"Where is Gulda?" she asked.

"I don't know. Gone to organise his family before he leaves with us to go north, perhaps."

"Does he have family?"

Thomas frowned. "He has cousins. I'm not sure about a wife or children."

"Margaret Gibson called in yesterday while you were out with the stock."

"What did that sourpuss want?"

"Company, I believe. Mr Gibson is away from home a lot."

"I don't blame him. He's such a cheerful chap and she's so glum."

"She wants a child, Thomas, but cannot get far enough along in her confinements for them to survive."

Thomas stopped eating. "I didn't know. No doubt that's the reason for her sadness."

"Yes, but not the reason for her call."

Thomas looked at her across the table, his eyes dark in the soft light of the lantern.

"There's been an increase in sheep pilfering. Evidently Mr Gibson and a few others rounded up several natives and gave them all severe beatings."

Thomas thumped the table with his hand. "When will they learn?" he growled.

"Margaret hinted it was partly our fault."

"What?" Thomas got up from his chair. "How can that be?"

"They know Gulda works for us. They think it encourages him to take what he likes and to get his friends to do the same."

"Gulda earns the sheep he gets."

"I know that." Lizzie went to stand beside her husband. "But –"

"But what, Lizzie? Surely you don't begrudge the few supplies we give Gulda in payment for his work. He has no use for money."

"Of course I don't. Gulda works as hard as you and Wick when he's here. I just wonder whether he might respect you enough not to steal from here but perhaps feel differently about our neighbours. It was him Edmund caught that time taking one of our sheep."

Thomas held her gaze. His dear face was full of concern. "I'd trust Gulda with my life, Lizzie."

"So he wouldn't have been with those they rounded up."

"Dear God, I hope not, but who would know?" Thomas paced the floor. "When they dish out those beatings they've no way of knowing if they've got the real culprits or just any poor native who had the misfortune to be in the vicinity."

"Let's hope he wasn't one of them." Lizzie sat at the table and took another mouthful of the cooling stew. She liked Gulda and admired the way Thomas tried his best to be fair with his treatment of the man, but he was still a native. Just like a wild animal, she wasn't sure he could be truly tamed, but she kept this doubt to herself. "Finish your meal, Thomas," she said. "I'm sure Gulda will be here in the morning."

Thomas sat. "It's a bad business. I don't like leaving you."

"I will be fine."

They ate the remainder of their meal in silence. Finally Thomas used a piece of bread to mop up the juice from the stew and sat back.

"Wick should be back tomorrow afternoon. I would stay but we must get this claim mapped out."

"Stop worrying." Lizzie reached across and patted his hand. "I've been on my own plenty of times before. And Mother and Father have promised to come and visit. Your job is to get this new land mapped out for us. I can't wait to see it."

Once more Thomas's eyes darkened as he gazed into hers. He wrapped his large hands around hers. "You truly are a remarkable woman, Lizzie Baker."

"Yes, well, I'd best clean these dishes," she said. "There is still some packing to do then I might need to remind you just how remarkable, so that you hurry back to me."

He pushed up from the table and was around her side in a couple of strides. Lizzie giggled as he scooped her up. The giggles turned to a sigh as he nuzzled her neck and his warm lips sought hers. She didn't protest as he carried her to their bed. The packing would have to wait.

Thirty-eight

Harriet groaned and put down the water bucket as the pain in her back deepened. She looked up the hill towards the hut. Suddenly the distance seemed so far. She sank awkwardly to the ground, shifted her legs out from the weight of her huge stomach and propped her back against a tree.

She'd felt tired for days and hadn't had the energy to make the trek to the creek for water, but this morning she'd run out. Now that she'd filled the heavy wooden bucket she could barely lift it, and the pain that had come and gone all night was getting stronger.

"Septimus, where are you?" she murmured. He'd been away over a month this time. While she'd managed quite well with his previous absences, her huge bulk had now slowed her to the point of being able to do only small tasks before exhaustion consumed her.

A shadow moved across the creek.

She looked around for something to throw. The native girl was back. Harriet had seen her several times in the last month. At first only from the corner of her eye, a movement in the shadows but enough to be able to make out her black skin against the pale bark of a tree. Then gradually, the girl had become more brazen, until last week, when Harriet had taken her wash in the creek and felt someone watching her. The girl had come right out of the trees, totally naked, and had stared at Harriet as she scrambled to cover herself.

Another wave of pain swept across her back and around her stomach. She gasped at the strength of it and clasped her rounded form with both hands.

"Don't come yet, son," she moaned. "Not yet. Wait for –"

She gasped again. The pain was so strong a wave of nausea engulfed her. She tried to spit into the dirt but her mouth was too dry. She rolled to one side and then the other, trying to find some release. The pain wouldn't let her go.

Just when she thought she would be ripped apart by it, strong hands took her arms, dragging her to her feet. She opened her eyes to see a black woman either side of her. One was the young girl who'd been watching her and the other an old woman with leathery skin. Harriet closed her eyes on the nightmare. Still the pain wracked her body. Hands pulled at her clothes. She heard soothing voices and short giggles and when finally she was stripped naked, the women pushed her down.

"No," she yelled with the last bit of breath she could muster.

A hand took her chin and shook it. She opened her eyes and watched as the girl acted out squatting, gesturing and speaking words Harriet didn't understand. A wave of pain took the strength from her knees. She sagged to a squat, supported by the older woman, while the younger one nodded her head in excitement. Heat coursed through her body. They wanted her to squat in the dirt. This wasn't how her son should be born. She threw back her head. She cried and wailed at the pain and the ignominy of it all. Finally, after uncountable, unfathomable pains, her baby slid from between her legs into the hands of the girl.

The baby gave a lusty squawk as they sat her back on the bundle they'd made of her clothes. Harriet looked from one native to the other then down at her son. She lowered her head over him and her tears dropped onto his skin. "A boy," she murmured. "I knew you were a boy."

The women moved quietly around her, severing the cord, probing and fussing. The sun was low in the sky now and she shivered with cold. Somehow they got her back to the hut. She crawled into bed with her baby safely tucked up in the crook of her arm. He suckled from her breast, making little snuffling sounds. She felt a surge of love for the tiny being and her pain was forgotten. She lay a long time gazing at her son before sleep finally claimed her.

Light flooded through the little bedroom window. Harriet blinked heavy eyes while her brain tried to remember something important. The baby! She sat up. The room moved and she put a hand on the bed to steady herself. On her other side was the baby. She pulled the blanket back. Her son brought up one little arm and stretched. His tiny mouth formed an O. The wrinkles of skin across his forehead gave him the look of a wizened old man. Tears brimmed in her eyes and rolled down her cheeks. He was the most beautiful thing she'd ever seen – her very own son.

She turned at a small bump from the other room. The firearm Septimus had taught her to use hung beside the door in there: no use to her from here. Something scraped across the wooden floor. Perhaps he'd returned.

"Septimus?" she called, then screamed as a black face peered around the door.

The face registered surprise then smiled. It was the girl who had helped her give birth. She came into the room with a cup of water, a piece of the bread Harriet had made two days before and some small orange berries in another cup. Harriet gulped the water greedily then laid back. She let the girl feed her the berries. They had a sharp tangy taste. She left the dry bread untouched.

The baby stirred and began to cry. The girl came around the bed and lifted the squirming baby to Harriet's breast. She gasped at the strength of his suck. The girl smiled and tucked the blanket around mother and baby. Harriet nestled into the pillow. She'd never had anyone look after her before. Not since she was a child.

By the next day she'd had enough of the bed. The room was stuffy and she could smell her sour body. She rose, stripped the grimy sheets, bundled them under her arm then paused over the box where her son slept. He was a strong feeder and slumbered soundly as soon as his little belly was full. She bent over him, trailing a finger across his forehead and down his soft cheek to his chin. His lips made small puckering movements then relaxed. She smiled and kissed his milky cheek.

"You need a name," she murmured. "A fine name." She thought longingly of her father. "Henry James is strong, and goes well with Wiltshire." At least Septimus had agreed to be married when the travelling priest had passed through some months earlier. Their son would not be a bastard.

"No," she said, "you will be strong and handsome and make your way proudly in this world."

Harriet stood back. She had been of little use to Septimus while she'd been confined, but it was time to take up her duties again both as a wife to him and as a support to their business. Their son would not have to sleep by the side of the road and barter for food as they had. She gazed once more at her baby.

"I will make sure of that," she said.

The girl looked up in surprise when Harriet entered the kitchen. She had obviously been preparing something for Harriet to eat as she had done the day before.

"I am going to wash in the creek." Harriet pointed out the window and made rubbing movements across her arms and body. "You make tea."

The fire had gone cold but the bucket of water Harriet had filled was sitting beside it. She transferred some water to the kettle then showed the girl how to stack the fire and light it. "I will have a nice cup of tea when I get back," she said. "And we will make some bread."

The girl smiled. Her big brown eyes were wide, and held no sign of understanding.

Harriet sighed. "You stay here."

She lowered the girl to a chair, careful to barely touch the naked black shoulders.

"I am going to wash."

Harriet took her clean clothes and her precious soap and let herself out into the fresh morning.

When she returned the kettle was boiling over the fire and the girl was nursing the baby. He sucked contently on the black finger in his mouth.

Harriet dropped her things and snatched her son. "No," she said sternly.

The girl looked at her, wide eyed again, but this time with sadness. She lowered her gaze.

"I will look after the baby," Harriet said. "You can help me in the house." Henry began to wail loudly. She put him to her breast again. With all this feeding she wouldn't be able to do as much as she had been. Septimus liked a tidy house and she was supposed to keep an eye on their few sheep, something she hadn't done for more than a week.

Harriet studied the girl, who was now watching her feed. She looked strong and appeared keen to help. Perhaps Harriet had been a little harsh. Other women had servants and nannies. If this girl would wear a dress and learn some jobs she might prove very useful. Septimus was certainly not here to help.

Harriet eased Henry from her breast and lifted him to her shoulder. His little belly rumbled and he let out a belch worthy of someone much older. All the while the girl watched him closely, with longing in her eyes.

Harriet rose to her feet. She still had the dress she'd patched and worn in her early days with Septimus. It would be about the right size. She clutched Henry to her and rummaged in the trunk. Once she had found it, she took it and jiggled it in front of the girl. "Put this on."

The girl looked from the dress to Harriet but didn't move.

"You must wear clothes."

Still the girl didn't move. Her eyes were firmly fixed on the baby in the crook of Harriet's arm.

Harriet offered her son. The girl reached eager arms forward. Harriet quickly shoved the dress between them. "If you want to hold the baby you must wear this," she said firmly.

The girl looked from Harriet to the baby and then at the dress.

Harriet shook the dress at her again. "You must wear a dress."

Slowly the girl reached out and took hold of the fabric.

Harriet smiled. "I'll help you put it on," she said. "Then we must think of a name for you. What about Dulcie? That's a pretty name."

Thirty-nine

Septimus left his wagon secured in the bush and rode his horse the last few miles towards George Smith's hut. He hadn't been this way since he'd found out Thomas Baker occupied the neighbouring property – there were plenty of other farms and settlers for him to call on. Now, however, he had a reason to return.

He'd been held up in Adelaide waiting for a new shipment of clothing and tools, as late September storms had delayed the ship he'd been expecting with his goods. This had worked, in the end, in his favour. While he was there, the *Government Gazette* published Governor Young's Order in Council finally authorising the granting of the much discussed fourteen-year pastoral leases. So, instead of making his way towards home with his wagon, he travelled to the district he'd been avoiding for more than a year. He wanted to renew his acquaintance with George Smith. The man had four sons and a need to expand. George had the labour and Septimus had the money. It should work out beneficially for both of them to begin with. Septimus was already forming a plan to wrestle the property from George, but one step at a time.

He approached with caution. There was a horse tethered in the yard, smoke drifted from the chimney and from somewhere beyond the house he could hear chickens cackling. He had no way of knowing whether George was at home or indeed if Baker had become a regular visitor.

He slowed his horse. It tossed its head and snorted. The door of the hut opened and George Smith strode to the edge of the verandah. Septimus glanced around. He urged his horse a few steps closer.

"Mr Smith," he called. "It is I, Septimus Wiltshire."

"Wiltshire?" George pushed his hat onto his head and stepped out into the sunlight.

"It's some time since my dear wife and I visited you with our wagonload of goods."

"Wiltshire?" George came closer.

"My wife entertained your wife and daughter at our wagon down by the creek."

"Oh, yes. I remember," George said. "That was a while ago. Lizzie has married our neighbour and lives on Penakie now. You'd be better off visiting them if you have things to sell. I am devoid of female company. My wife is with our daughters-in-law visiting the Gibsons."

"I don't have time to set up shop, as it happens. My own wife will be waiting for me. She is due to have her baby soon."

"Well, congratulations." George slapped Septimus on the back as he dismounted. "Our dear Lizzie is expecting a baby in the new year."

"That's good news." Septimus smiled at the older man. Good news indeed, he thought. He could conduct his business and with luck be gone before any of George's family returned.

"Come inside," George urged. "It's quite warm today. Let me offer you a drink."

"Thank you, George."

Septimus took the liberty of using the man's first name and placing his hand on his shoulder as they stepped inside. "I have some news I think you will want to hear."

Septimus turned his wagon off the bullock track and onto the even rougher trail that led to his house. Long shadows enveloped him and the moaning of the wind through the trees brought a gloom to the late afternoon. He whistled softly as his wagon rolled and dipped. He was returning home a tired but happy man. Darkening skies couldn't dampen his mood. Business was certainly good and the deal he'd made with George Smith should bring him great returns.

He'd been gone longer than he'd expected this time but he was glad of it. Harriet had become so swollen with child on his last trip home that he could hardly bear to share her bed, let alone release his sexual needs with her. He hoped she'd given birth by now. He had grown used to having her body whenever he needed it – and he was longing for a comfortable bed too. Since Harriet no longer travelled with him, he'd reverted to the swag when on the road.

A light glowed at the window and smoke drifted from the chimney. At the sound of the wagon the door flew open and there was Harriet, a much thinner Harriet, waving at him from the verandah.

"Welcome home, Septimus," she called.

He nodded in her direction. "I'll see to the animals then come in," he said.

It was dark by the time he came inside. He stooped through the door and stopped to look around. The hut was neat as always. Some bush flowers sat on the trunk Harriet used as a cupboard. Fire glowed beneath the oven and the kettle steamed. Harriet hovered by the table. Her hair shone and she once again wore her dress nipped in at the waist. Septimus sat at the table. All was well.

"Time for you to meet your son, Septimus."

She bent to a box beside the fire he hadn't noticed and lifted a parcel of cloth. She leaned in beside him and slid the bundle into his arms.

Septimus looked down as she gently turned back the cloth. There was a tiny being, dark hair, wrinkled brow, pointy nose and ears – it could have been an elf. He glanced at Harriet, who was watching him expectantly.

"Does it have a name?" he asked.

"Your son was born four weeks ago."

Septimus frowned. Her tone had an accusing edge.

"I was … Well I was quite alone," Harriet said, softly this time. "I couldn't keep calling him Baby. I chose Henry James after my father as I didn't know yours, but we could change the second name if you would rather –"

"No." It was of no concern to him what she called it. "Henry James will do."

The baby stirred in his arms, opened its small brown eyes, then grimaced and let out a wail. Septimus stiffened and Harriet took the screaming bundle from him.

"Let me settle him," she said. She nodded to the food set out on the table. "You eat. I've only got bread and pickles for supper, but I've put some fruit scones in the oven. They'll be ready for you to have with a cup of tea later."

She made shushing noises and carried the baby into the bedroom, where she shut the door.

Septimus picked at the food. He didn't feel like eating, he wanted to bed his wife. By the time she came back and slipped the baby into its bed he was desperate to have her.

"It's been hard work since Henry was born," Harriet said.

He watched her while she removed the scones from the oven. Not even the tempting smell could sway him.

"I've needed help." She paused and tucked a cloth around the hot scones. "There's a local girl … a native."

Septimus didn't want to hear about Harriet's troubles, he just wanted to bed her. He lurched from his chair and in a stride he was beside her. He scooped her up. The surprise on Harriet's face was quickly replaced by her knowing smile. Without a word, he carried her to their bed.

Septimus rolled over without opening his sleep-crusted eyes. He felt the warmth of Harriet's soft body beside him. The night before he'd been too tired for more than a quick coupling with her. With the morning he felt more refreshed. They could take their time. Just the thought of it aroused him. Then he would eat. He had an appetite large enough to consume a horse after the slim pickings she'd set out for him on his arrival.

There was a sucking sound beside him. He opened his eyes and pushed away in horror. There, right beside him, the elf was attached to Harriet's breast, sucking in the way Septimus had just imagined he would be. He looked at Harriet, lying against the pillow, her eyes closed, dark shadows below them in her pale skin. She looked exhausted, but her lips were turned up in a small smile.

Septimus climbed out of the bed and pulled on his pants. He had been the only one to have her body and now he was sharing it with a baby. The thought repulsed him. The brat had taken what was his. He felt sick to his stomach.

In the kitchen he ate some of the cold fruit scones. He couldn't sit for long. Anger burned inside him, along with unfulfilled need. He went outside. Below him the trees that dotted the creek line were perfectly still. No breeze today. He would go and inspect the property. That would take his mind off what ailed him. He would have to make haste to Adelaide again soon to finalise the deal he'd made with Smith. In the meantime he'd check the few sheep left alive after Bull's departure. Hopefully Harriet had managed to keep her eye on things.

Harriet. He shook his head and made his way towards the creek. He would wash away the smell of her from his skin and perhaps the cold water would ease his need for her.

His steps slowed at the sound of a splash. He edged up behind a large tree that grew close to the creek. There was another splash. He peered around the trunk. His eyes opened wide at the sight of a young black woman, totally naked. She was stooped in the water with her back to him and she was filling a water bucket. Septimus stared. It had to be his water bucket but what would this native be doing with it?

Dark wavy hair fell to her shoulders and her black skin gleamed in the sunlight slanting through the trees. As she turned he pressed back behind the tree. He studied the surroundings either side of him. She appeared to be alone.

There was a thud on the other side of the tree. Septimus risked a look. The bucket was on the bank and the girl was squatting in the creek further downstream, splashing water over herself with the carefree abandon of a child. Then he saw a dress hanging over a nearby branch. Harriet's old dress. What had Harriet said the previous night? Something about needing help and a native girl.

Anger rose inside him. How could she allow a savage to …? His mind went numb as the girl rose and turned. She was young, perhaps the age Harriet had been when he'd first taken her. This girl had plump full breasts, and a body ripe for the plucking.

She moved to the edge of the creek then looked up and saw him. Fear filled her face and she stepped back into the creek.

He put up a hand. "Don't be afraid," he soothed and eased himself around the tree. "I am your master." He pointed towards the house. "Mrs Wiltshire's husband."

The girl continued to stare at him wide eyed. She took a tiny step backwards.

Septimus moved carefully forward. "Baby Henry's father."

"Henry," she repeated. He saw the hesitation cross her face.

"That's right, Henry." He moved closer.

She took another step and lost her footing. She tumbled backwards into the water. Septimus pounced on her. As her face surfaced she opened her mouth. He tried to cover it but she didn't scream, she just looked at him with big frightened eyes.

"Don't be afraid." He took her hand and helped her up, barely able to take his eyes from her breasts, supple and glistening as water dripped from them.

He led her to the bank. "I am your master." He pointed to the hut. "You can help Mrs Wiltshire in the house."

"Henry," the girl whispered. She tried to take her hand from his grip.

"Yes." He nodded and gently moved a lock of thick wet hair from her face then traced a finger around her face and under her chin "You can look after Henry in the house."

He backed her towards the tree. He could see her eyes brimming with tears but still she didn't cry out.

"Don't be afraid," he murmured as he pressed her to the tree. He nuzzled at her neck and gently brushed his hand over one breast. He looked up at her gasp and he smiled. "And out here you can look after your master." He used a low, sing-song voice. "It will be our little secret."

He plucked her dress from the branch with one hand and continued to stroke her with the other. Then he tossed the dress at his feet and tenderly lowered her to it. He caressed her with his lips and stroked her with his fingers until she was squirming with desire and then he took her. His delight heightened by the slight resistance and her small gasp as he slid inside her.

Ah yes, if he couldn't have Harriet there was another unsullied body he could enjoy.

Forty

"You can't take a young infant on such a long journey in the heat of summer." Anne Smith looked from Lizzie to the baby she cradled in her arms and back to Thomas. "Can't you wait until everything is finalised and you've built a proper house?"

"We will be fine, Mother. We won't travel in the heat of the day," Lizzie said. "Anyway it will be autumn next week. I'd rather make our way there in heat than in rain. I need to look after our new place while Thomas and my brothers get the stock."

"You'll be there alone." Anne shook her head. "It isn't right."

"Gulda will be with me. There will be little to do until the men return with the sheep." Lizzie smiled at her mother and handed over the baby. "Hold Annie for me while I check I've packed everything."

Thomas groaned. "We can't fit another thing," he called after her as she left the verandah.

She threw a grin over her shoulder then crossed the dirt to where Wick was putting the last of the boxes into the wagon. He looked up as Lizzie began to give him instructions on where best to squeeze the box he held in his hands. He listened then followed her directions. How wise he's become, thought Thomas. He'd be sad to say good-bye but he knew Wick would continue to look after Penakie well.

Behind the wagon was the small dray pulled by Derriere. It was also loaded to the brim. Perched on top was a cage with chickens and containers of carefully dug plants for Lizzie's new vegetable garden. Attached to that was their cow. Thomas had already taken tools and equipment when he went north to map out the property he was calling Wildu Creek. He was moving there with many more worldly goods than he'd arrived on Penakie with – and now he had a wife and daughter as well. It was a pity he no longer had his trunk. Lizzie would have liked some of his mother's things. He frowned. It was a long time since he'd given any thought to Seth Whitby and the items he'd stolen.

"She's still so small," Mrs Smith murmured.

He swung back to the present and smiled at his mother-in-law gazing at the yawning bundle in her arms.

"We have to go now or we'll miss out on the opportunity," he said.

Anne raised her eyes to his. Thomas saw a glimmer of hope as she spoke. "You can't let your wife and baby live in a makeshift hut alone. Lizzie and Annie could stay with us until you get back with the sheep. George and I would be happy to accompany her later. We want to see where you and the boys have taken up your runs."

"We've been over this many times already."

"Annie's still so tiny. It will take her a while to recover from being born too early."

"She's gone three months and thriving." He looked at his baby with pride. She had surprised them by arriving ahead of her time but even though she was small, she was perfect and feeding well. "Lizzie is a wonderful mother."

"You're her husband, Thomas. Tell her she must stay."

He shook his head. "I tried in the beginning but she wants this new land as much as I do and it will indeed be much better if someone is there while we get the stock."

"Leave Thomas alone, Anne." George had rounded the corner of the hut on silent feet. He stepped up onto the verandah and looked over his wife's shoulder at his tiny granddaughter. "The decision has been made," he said gently. "You know our Lizzie. Once she's set her mind on something there's no changing it."

They all looked up at the sound of another wagon and horses. "Here are the boys," George said.

Jacob rode his horse and Isaac drove their bullock wagon. Altogether they were quite a collection of animals and carts.

"Time for you to set off." George shook Thomas's hand. "Good luck."

Thomas turned to Anne. She gave the baby one last kiss and carefully handed her into his arms.

"Look after them, Thomas," she said.

Doubt wormed in his belly but he pushed it away. "I will."

Lizzie rushed across to give her parents final hugs and kisses and took the baby from him. He shook Wick's hand.

"Good luck," Wick said.

Thomas stepped back. He cast one more look at the hut that had been his home for four years. His gaze shifted up the slope beyond the hut, where the shearing shed and yards nestled into the hill. It was Wick's domain now. He turned his back and, with a roll of his shoulders, he climbed aboard the wagon beside Lizzie. He cracked the whip above the bullocks, unleashing a chorus of goodbyes that mingled with the rumble of wheels, the squawk of chickens, the moo of the cow and the jangle of her bell. Beside him, Annie began to cry and Lizzie quickly silenced her with a breast.

Thomas stared ahead and just as he turned to take one more look, his wife patted his leg. He gazed into pretty blue eyes that always shone for him.

"No looking back," she said.

"No looking back," he agreed.

They did have to stop not far along the track once the house was out of sight, when Gulda emerged from the bushes. He grinned at Thomas then climbed onto the cart they'd been leading behind the dray. The native who had become his friend had also accepted Jacob and Isaac could be trusted, though Thomas knew he still wasn't sure of George and his other two sons. Once more Thomas cracked the whip and the dray lurched forward. Now they were truly on their way.

The sun beat down on them, reflecting off leaf and rock. Thomas had no idea if this was usual weather for autumn but their new property was much warmer than Penakie. They'd been rumbling across it for half a day now. Jacob and Isaac had left them that morning to veer further west to the run they were claiming. Full of high spirits, they'd arranged to meet again in a few days to head south for their stock.

For the moment it was just Thomas, Lizzie and the baby. Gulda had hitched the horse and cart to the back of the dray again, and promised to return when they reached the hut. The wheels hit a rut and Lizzie pressed harder against him. Thomas tried to shift his arm. It was stiff and losing feeling after hours of supporting her sleeping weight. The journey had been long and arduous and the last few nights Annie had woken often. Lizzie had only been able to silence her by offering her breast.

He had felt his tired wife's head nod against him not long after they had set out on the last stretch that morning. He'd pulled her in close to stop her sliding from the dray and supported her head in the crook of his shoulder. Annie slept in her little box cradle wedged in the dray behind them.

Now they were following a creek that wound its way through low hills to the site he'd chosen for their home. The small wood-and-canvas hut he'd hastily thrown together on his previous trip was just visible through the trees.

"Lizzie," he said softly.

She stirred under his arm and lifted her sleep-reddened face to his, blinking tired eyes.

"We're nearly there." He nodded ahead. "This is Wildu Creek."

Lizzie peeped behind her at the sleeping baby then sat up straight, staring ahead. He hoped she would see the promise of the future that he had seen on his first journey here. The hut sat on a plateau that stretched across the base of low hills. The hills in turn gave way to steep gullies, and ridges of red and brown rock dotted with the greys and greens of bush and trees. It was somewhere up there that Gulda had taken him, with Jacob, to the cave, and where Thomas had looked out over this valley and the wide plain that would support as many sheep as he could drove there to the next mountain range.

"Oh, Thomas," Lizzie gasped.

He held his breath.

"It's magnificent country," she said.

"I'm glad you think so."

They passed under the shade of some large gums then up the last small rise to the hut perched well back from the creek below. As soon as the cart stopped, Annie began to cry.

Refreshed from her sleep, Lizzie laughed and plucked the baby from her cradle. "We're here, little one." She held Annie up. "This is your new home."

Annie's wails grew stronger.

"There's nothing wrong with her lungs," Thomas said and helped them to the ground.

"She's hungry again," Lizzie said. "You have a big appetite like your father, Annie." She crooned to the screaming bundle as she fumbled with her buttons.

"I'll get a chair from the dray." Thomas hovered. He always felt so helpless when Annie cried. Most times she just wanted to be fed and there was little he could do about that.

"No," Lizzie said. "This will be perfect." She made her way to a large gum overhanging the creek. She nestled herself against its thick trunk and Annie's wails became snuffles as she began to drink. "Come sit beside us, Thomas. Let's spend a few minutes – just our little family together. You will be busy and gone all too soon."

Thomas sank down beside her. He put his arm around her shoulders and watched the little miracle that was his daughter suck strongly at her mother's breast. He still marvelled that they could create something so perfect. Above them a gentle breeze stirred the leaves and below them water trickled over rocks and branches on its way south. He kissed the top of Lizzie's head. "Are you happy?" he asked.

"I could burst. This is the most beautiful place. And those mountains in the distance: they look so rugged yet the colours are so striking."

Thomas followed her gaze. Beside him Annie squirmed in her mother's arms.

"Let me hold her," he said. He lifted his daughter in front of him. She grinned and a small dribble of milk trickled from her mouth. He sat her in the crook of his arm and wiped the milk away with his thumb. "You are the prettiest baby, Annie," he said.

Lizzie put an arm around his shoulder and kissed his cheek.

"Mother said she's never seen a man so besotted with a baby as you." She chuckled.

"Never was a man so lucky as me," he said. "When I think of my life before ..."

Lizzie squeezed him tighter. "Your parents would be so proud of what you've achieved."

Annie gurgled. He lifted her to face the mountains. "This is our new life now."

High in the blue sky, close to the range, he saw two dark shapes gliding in the current. He took a deep breath of the eucalypt-scented air. "Welcome to Wildu Creek," he murmured.

They spent the rest of the day unpacking and stowing supplies. The hut had one room with no floor and canvas was strung out to a tree as its verandah. They couldn't fit everything inside so Thomas and Gulda used stones and wood to make a low shelter beside the fire pit. The conditions were rougher than he'd experienced on his arrival at Penakie and, as he looked around at the crude quarters, Thomas had a pang of doubt. Perhaps Anne had been right. Standing here shadowed by rugged mountains so far from anyone else he questioned the wisdom of bringing Lizzie and the baby here before a proper house could be built.

That night they sat together by the fire under a black sky full of glittering stars. Earlier they'd eaten kangaroo, which Gulda had produced from somewhere. Thomas assumed he must have a fire of his own. The meat had melted in their mouths. They'd followed it with some of Lizzie's fruit damper.

"I've stockpiled enough wood for several weeks but if you need more, Gulda can cut it," Thomas said and tossed a small branch on the fire. Smoke eddied around him then drifted away.

"There's hardly a breeze," Lizzie said, flapping a hand in front of her as a swirl of smoke blew her way. "And look at all those stars." She threw back her head. "What a wonderful display to eat our picnic under."

"Mmm," Thomas murmured. No clouds meant no rain for now, but he'd be gone for over a month. "The hut should be waterproof if the weather turns."

"We can always add more thatch. There's plenty of suitable bush nearby."

Thomas poked the branch with his boot, sending more smoke swirling.

"There's a good flow of water in the creek," he said, "and Gulda will keep the barrels full for you."

"Thomas, stop worrying." Lizzie wrapped an arm around his waist and laid her head on his shoulder. "We will manage just fine."

"I'll be back as soon as I can."

"I know you will."

A shadow appeared at the edge of the firelight, then Gulda stepped forward.

"Mr Tom, Mrs Lizzie, this is my wife," he said. "You call her Daisy."

A native woman stepped out from behind him. Her eyes were lowered. She had a possum skin draped around her shoulders and a string creation hung from her hips. Thomas kept his eyes on Gulda, who at least wore the shirt and trousers he'd been given, though his feet were bare.

"Welcome, Daisy," Lizzie said.

"This her country," Gulda said.

Thomas wasn't sure what Gulda meant by her country – the land in general or this particular part of it?

"You have kept her a secret," Lizzie said. "We didn't know you had a wife, did we, Thomas?" She looked up at him and winked. She had that mischievous sparkle in her eye as she bent her head closer. "We might have to find Daisy some clothes if she's to stay," she murmured, "or you'll be tying yourself in knots not to look at her."

Gulda gave a big grin. "We go home now," he said.

"Good night," Thomas called as they merged back into the shadows.

Home was a small dwelling of sticks and branches Gulda had made further up the hill. Thomas was pleased Daisy was nearby. He hadn't been sure Gulda could be relied upon to stay with Lizzie for the duration of his absence. Having Daisy there might mean he would stay put, and his wife might be company for Lizzie.

The next morning, Thomas left as the pink hue of pre-dawn light crept across the sky. Lizzie stood in front of the hut holding Annie and waving goodbye. Gulda and Daisy were a small distance beyond her. He kept twisting back to look at them until he could see them no longer, then he pressed his horse forward.

They had three months after their application to stock their land and already half of that time was gone – he only had six weeks to make it to Encounter Bay, where the sheep AJ had purchased were waiting, then bring them back to Wildu Creek. Jacob and Isaac must do the same. Edmund and Samuel had already gone south to load a dray with provisions and buy more horses. Five men had to bring over six thousand sheep across three hundred miles to stock their new runs. It would be a difficult job.

It had taken a significant portion of his savings to pay the lease and organise provisions. If he didn't have enough stock or make it back to Wildu Creek in time, someone else could take the lease and all his hard work and investment would be for nothing. The same went for the Smiths.

He hadn't thought George would have had enough money to back his sons but they had stock waiting as he did. Thomas urged his horse into a gallop once he reached open country. The Smiths' finances were none of his business. His job was to get his sheep back in time to secure a property for his family. There was no going back now.

Forty-one

Thomas dragged his leg over the saddle and slithered to the ground. His legs were numb. He leaned against the sweat-soaked horse for support. It snorted and stomped one foot but remained firm against his back. They had been droving the sheep for three weeks now and he was beyond exhausted. When they had started out, the days had been warm but with a cooling breeze. The further north they'd moved, the hotter it got. Over the past few days the heat had been oppressive, with no wind.

Edmund reined his horse in beside him, stirring up the dust and flies. "We should stop here," he said.

Thomas gritted his teeth. He was thankful for the help of Lizzie's two eldest brothers but they were both pompous and demanding. Edmund was by far worse than Samuel, who could at least manage a smile from time to time.

"There's a creek several miles ahead," Thomas said. "We could make that before dark."

"You're driving them too hard."

Edmund's horse pranced around. Thomas pushed himself away from his own horse and took Edmund's by the reins. He squared his shoulders and looked up at his brother-in-law.

"We could even cross it if we make good time," he said.

"Don't forget Jacob and Isaac," Edmund persisted. "They're a day behind us. They will get further behind."

Thomas looked back in the direction they had come. His stock had been ready to move out as soon as he'd arrived in Encounter Bay. AJ was there to meet him and wish him luck. There had been some delay, however, with paperwork over the Smiths' sheep. He had set out with his stock and Edmund to help him. Samuel followed with the bullock wagon and the spare horses. Each day two of them would move the sheep forward. Before dark they took it in turns to drop back to the wagon and eat the mutton and damper Samuel prepared. Then one of the three of them would stay with the sheep for the night while the other two got some sleep. It had been Thomas's turn to keep watch the previous night.

Nearly a week had passed before Jacob caught up to the wagon. Thomas had dropped back and was taking some food when his friend rode in. From then on, Jacob and Isaac rotated the nights in the same fashion as Edmund and Thomas, with Samuel sometimes doing a night for them. Their sheep were following much the same route. Jacob had said they were zigzagging east and west as there was little vegetation where Thomas's stock had been, but in some cases they had no choice. Thomas knew it would be harder on the second flock. They would have to walk further foraging for food and water.

"Jacob will have the good sense to keep moving them as long as he can," Thomas said.

"Jacob! Jacob and good sense are often parted. This is where we're staying. We need to give them time to catch up and rest all the stock"

"Have it your way," Thomas growled. He was tired and in no mood to fight.

Edmund pulled his horse around. "I'll go and eat first."

Without another word, he urged his horse away. Once more Thomas was surrounded by clouds of dust. He batted the air and stirred up the small black flies that clung all over him. He glanced up at the murky sky and then to the north and the purple haze of the mountains. Not much longer and he wouldn't have to put up with the officious Edmund.

He took some gulps from his water pouch and dragged himself back onto the horse. AJ had advised he purchase leather leggings and he was grateful for the suggestion. They certainly made full-time life on a horse bearable.

Thomas began to move around the sheep, stopping their amble, encouraging them to stay together in a group and so make Edmund's night watch easier. The bush was low and thick here and the ground rose and fell in small undulations. It was as good a place as any to hold them for the night.

They'd had breakaways only twice during the journey so far: both times had been after a long stretch without water. Once the sheep sensed it ahead there had been no stopping them. He suspected they'd missed a few in the round up that followed and knew they'd lost a few more to broken legs and wild dogs but he was happy with their condition and progress.

He had six days to make the deadline and by his reckoning he'd only need three to reach the edge of the property he'd marked out as his own. He wondered again how Lizzie was managing. Long days on the horse and even longer nights gave him plenty of thinking time. He ranged from excitement at the prospect of the future they were building to terror at the thought of her alone at Wildu Creek. Almost alone. He hoped Gulda had stayed.

Thomas thought of the presents he had packed in the wagon. When he'd bought the leggings for himself he'd noticed a straw bonnet with a flower and pretty blue ribbons and straight away imagined it on Lizzie. He'd purchased a dress for Annie too. It would be big for her yet but by the summer he was sure she'd wear the soft white fabric. He knew what Lizzie would say about white and spending money, but he didn't care. He wanted to see his little girl dressed like a princess. He bought a small axe for Gulda and a mirror for Daisy. Thomas knew how much Lizzie valued the mirror she had. He hoped Daisy would like hers just as much.

The sun was low in the sky before Edmund returned to take the watch. His mood was no better. The heaviness in the air added to the tension. Thomas was grateful to leave him and ride back to the wagon.

"Edmund says you wanted to cross the next creek before we stopped."

Samuel hurled the words at Thomas as soon as he stepped down from his horse.

"We could have," Thomas said not wanting to argue with Samuel either.

"You'll kill more sheep with your pushing."

The sound of sheep bleating close by drew their attention to the bush behind them. There was a whistle and the sound of horse's hooves, then Jacob rode into view.

"Food," he groaned as he came to a stop beside them. "What a dreadful day."

"You've brought your sheep right up to the wagon?" Thomas said. He could hear more bleating now and glimpses of sheep in the nearby bushes.

"Edmund rode down and suggested we move up closer."

Damn Edmund, thought Thomas. That would explain his longer absence.

"We've split our mob in two," Jacob said, accepting the mug of tea Samuel offered him. "I've pushed up the weaker ones and Zac's back with the rest."

"They'll be looking for water," Thomas said.

"Samuel says there's a waterhole to the west that you didn't use."

Thomas frowned. He'd done wide sweeps of the country in front of the advancing mob and had seen no evidence of other waterholes nearby.

"I rode out for a while this afternoon." Samuel offered Thomas a mug of tea. "I told Edmund about it. That's why he suggested Jacob bring the less able animals forward. They can rest near the good water. They'll be ready to tackle that creek crossing after you tomorrow."

"Going so far out of our way might scatter the mob," Thomas said.

"Don't worry." Jacob grinned and slapped him on the shoulder. "They'll be fine."

"I just want us both to have enough stock to meet the quota." The Smiths' sheep had started out in poorer condition than his and Jacob had suffered larger losses on the journey already: they were required to have one hundred sheep per square mile or lose their leases.

"We won't have any if they die from exhaustion," Samuel said. He held Thomas's look.

"Any chance of some food?" Jacob stepped between them towards the fire. "A man's starving."

"Zac's not coming?" Samuel followed his brother and gave him a plate of freshly baked damper and cold mutton.

"Not now we've split the mob. He's going to stay back till morning. He'll move the leftovers forward at first light." Jacob's words were distorted by his mouthful of food. "You and I have to move this lot to that waterhole you found."

"In the dark?" Thomas said. Both men turned to look at him. He couldn't believe Jacob would do something so foolish. "You'd be best to wait till morning and bring them forward after we've moved out. There's plenty of water ahead."

"Edmund didn't think there would be much left by the time your mob has finished," Samuel said, "and there's little feed. The place I found hasn't been touched by stock. It will be just what Jacob's cut need before they cross the next creek. Zac will bring the rest of the mob straight through. They're stronger and can manage with the pickings left from yours."

"You're more likely to lose them out there." Thomas waved his hand at the bush, where the last rays of the setting sun cast long shadows.

Jacob shovelled another hunk of meat into his mouth, looking from Samuel to Thomas. Thomas watched the lump in his throat go up and down as he swallowed, then Jacob's grimy face split in a grin.

"We'll be right, Thomas. Don't worry so much." He strode to his horse, calling Samuel as he went.

"I'll come with you," Thomas said. He wished he didn't have to, but what they were proposing was madness.

"No." Jacob's response was determined. "You stay with the wagon. Once we've moved the sheep one of us will come back."

Thomas watched as the two of them rode off. He sat by the fire and pulled the plate of food Samuel had prepared from under its calico cover. Immediately a cloud of black flies appeared. He batted them away and pushed meat into his mouth, trying to get some food before the little black pests carried it away. It was the same fare he'd eaten every night since Lizzie's picnic under the stars, but it was strangely comforting.

Around him in the bush he could hear the sounds of Jacob and Samuel moving their sheep until finally the ink black of night fell and all was quiet. No stars tonight, not even a moon. With a final burst of energy he checked the horses and the fire. He dragged a bigger log onto it so that it would give some light to lead Jacob or Samuel back. Then it was all he could do to pull off his boots and his leggings. He gave one last brief thought to the Smiths then crawled into his swag, where sleep claimed him immediately.

Forty-two

Lizzie stumbled. She put the heavy bucket down, put her hands to her hips and bent backwards in a stretch. Perspiration trickled from her brow down the sides of her cheeks. She turned her gaze west along the creek. Thomas had been gone so long. She'd been marking the weeks off and hoped it would be only two more before she saw him again. Lizzie knew if anyone could get their stock home in time, Thomas could – and he had the help of her brothers.

She had been so full of excitement to arrive at Wildu Creek. Thomas had told her so much about it and his descriptions had been right. It was rugged country but beautiful. Already she was getting used to the changing colours and hues of the days, though the terrible heat of the previous week had surprised her. She could find no relief from it. A wind had come up, bringing with it such fine dust it crept into everything. And when there was no wind there were flies, little black creatures that crawled into every nook and cranny. Lizzie tried to keep everything clean but even in their hut the dust and flies settled on everything. And Annie was of an age to pull everything into her mouth.

Lizzie lifted her head. Just the thought of her baby had conjured up a cry. She listened, but only the long plaintive call of a black bird could be heard over the gentle rustle of leaves ruffled by the breeze.

She wondered when Gulda and Daisy would return. Everything had gone well for the first few weeks. The two natives had been constant companions: they'd shared both work and meals. The night before, Gulda had said they were going hunting first thing in the morning. He said they would be back by dark. Lizzie glanced in the direction of the sun beating down from the sky. It wasn't even noon yet.

From the hut behind her came a pathetic cry. She had only just put the child down before making her trek to the creek. Surely she didn't want to be fed again. Lizzie picked up the bucket. Annie had been irritable for days. Daisy was a wonder at calming the baby, who'd become increasingly demanding with her feeding. Lizzie felt her breasts were like empty bags with nothing left to give. She was going to boil some water to trickle into her daughter's mouth. The poor little mite was probably as thirsty as she was hungry.

Lizzie set the bucket by the fire in a swirl of ash: the breeze had picked up. She covered it with the calico bag to keep out the dust and tied down the sides so it wouldn't blow off.

Inside the hut the air was cooler. Annie gave a sharp cry; her arms flailed against the side of the cradle then flopped. Lizzie stretched a hand to the baby's forehead then tugged back the blanket. Annie was burning up. Her clothes were soaked.

"No, no," Lizzie muttered. There was something very wrong.

She scooped Annie from the cradle, laid her on the bed and stripped her. Her soiled napkin was streaked with blood.

"Dear Lord, help us," Lizzie said.

She ran outside for fresh water and bathed the listless baby before wrapping her again. Lizzie put Annie to her breast. She prayed there would be some sustenance for her child. Annie made several feeble attempts to suck then fell back, limp in her arms.

Lizzie closed her eyes and said a silent prayer over her daughter. She wanted to hold her close but the baby was so hot in her arms. Lizzie thought of Thomas, but he wasn't here to help her. She had to face this fight alone.

The sun beat down on the little hut, raising the temperature inside, but it was still better than being out where the only respite was the shade of the gums. Out there Lizzie would have to battle the dust and the flies. She kept Annie as cool as she could, bathing her arms and legs and trying to trickle the cold boiled water down her throat. In spite of her efforts, Annie burned with fever and the vile liquid kept coursing from her little body. Lizzie was running out of garments and linen.

By evening, Annie finally drifted into a deeper sleep. Lizzie was exhausted. She gathered up the soiled garments and linen. If she could get them washed she would have supplies for the next day. She couldn't bear the thought of her precious baby lying in filth.

Outside the air was fresh and cool. She placed her hands on her grumbling stomach. How long since she'd eaten? She wasn't sure but she felt too tired now to care. She built up the fire and boiled more water. While she was at it she made herself some tea and cut a slab of the bread she'd made the day before. She didn't feel hungry but she knew she had to keep up her strength to be able to look after Annie.

The next morning dawned with the promise of another hot day. Lizzie had barely slept. She staggered outside to gather some of the things she'd strung on the clothesline. Pains gripped her stomach. She scrabbled to reach the hole Thomas had dug away from the hut. Waves of heat coursed through her. To her horror, like Annie, she passed vile liquid threaded with blood. Lizzie knew she too had whatever ailed her baby.

She dragged herself to a tree and propped herself against its cool thick trunk. If she could just shut her eyes for a short time she thought she'd feel better, but doubt niggled.

Lizzie woke to gentle hands shaking her.

"Thomas?" she moaned.

"Mrs Lizzie?"

Through bleary eyes Lizzie took in the concerned face of Gulda. She turned her head at Annie's feeble cry close by. Daisy was rocking the baby in her arms, trying to calm her.

"How long have I been here?" Lizzie pushed herself forward and immediately the pains gripped her. She remembered the bouts of diarrhoea. She hadn't been able to crawl far.

Daisy put Annie to her breast. Lizzie flopped back in agony: even though Annie's sucking was pathetic it felt like claws pulling at her burning breasts. She knew there was little there to give her baby.

Daisy lifted Annie away. Immediately she began to cry again. The two natives exchanged words then Gulda was lifting Lizzie and carrying her to the creek well downstream where the water flowed quickly past deep pools. Daisy handed Annie to him. The baby's wails slowly retreated as Gulda moved away. Daisy began to remove Lizzie's clothes. The cold of the water was a shock and a relief all at the same time.

Lizzie remembered little about the next few days. Every time she woke she felt hot and her stomach would be gripped with pains. Daisy or Gulda were always nearby. They put cool cloths on her brow and sometimes gave her a vile-tasting liquid to drink. One of them always held Annie. Lizzie could only slip back into the sleep that was her release.

Sounds of movement outside woke Lizzie from a deep sleep. It took a moment for her to remember where she was. She rolled over to look at the cradle beside her bed. It was empty. She struggled to her feet then sat a moment waiting for the room to stop spinning. A fire crackled and she could hear the soft murmuring of voices. Thank goodness for Gulda and Daisy. They would have Annie with them. She moved outside and squinted in the daylight. How many days had she been sick? At least the sun was hidden behind a thick bank of clouds. Lizzie sucked in the fresh morning air. Even though she felt so weak it was good to be out of the hut.

Gulda was bent over the fire, where the big pot they used for water was steaming.

Lizzie knew she must try again to get some fluid into Annie.

"Mrs Lizzie." The native stood and studied her, his face full of concern.

"Where's Annie?"

As she asked, Lizzie saw Daisy coming from the direction of the creek. She held a tiny bundle in her arms. Daisy's dark face was shining with tears.

Lizzie's heart thumped in her chest. She took two stumbling steps towards Daisy and then her world went black.

Forty-three

The sound of a wagon rumbling woke Thomas from a deep sleep. He sat up and peered around, stretching cramped arms and legs. The light was hazy and the birds were silent and yet he knew it was morning. The wagon was still beside him. Perhaps the rumbling noise had been in his dreams.

There was no sign of Jacob or Samuel and the fire had burned down to a few coals. Normally, Samuel would have porridge cooking for breakfast by now. Another rumble echoed across the sky. That was the noise that had woken him. He looked to the north and a flash of light briefly lit the dull early morning sky. Thomas pulled on his leggings and boots and strode to his horse. It wasn't the thunder and lightning that worried him, it was the creek crossing ahead. If rain was falling on the hills he had seen for himself that it didn't take long for it to turn trickling creeks into raging torrents.

He saddled his horse. Hobbled nearby, the other horses shifted restlessly. He hoped Samuel would make it back swiftly to deal with them and the wagon but Thomas didn't have time. He had to reach Edmund and get the sheep across that creek.

By the time he got to the edge of the mob, the thunder was louder and the lightning flashes much closer.

Edmund didn't waste words on greetings. "Where are the others?"

"No sign of any of them."

"Zac should have had his mob up to the wagon by now."

"I know but I couldn't risk going back. If we don't get this mob across the creek we might have to wait days."

Edmund opened his mouth but Thomas didn't wait to hear. He urged his horse on. Edmund could blather all he liked but for now they must move the sheep forward.

Just as the lead animals reached the creek, thunder boomed overhead and lightning forked at a nearby gum. Thomas could see the creek was already running faster. They drove the sheep across in any way they could. In between rolls of thunder, the air was full of bleating, whistling, shouting and cracking whips. There was no time for gentle persuasion. His mob would probably scatter in all directions on the other side but Thomas would deal with that later.

Finally the last one was across. Edmund brought his horse to a stop beside Thomas. "You follow them over. I'm going back to help my brothers."

Thomas looked to where the last of his sheep were scrabbling up the bank on the other side. The water was steadily rising. He flinched as another deafening roll of thunder sounded overhead and then large drops began to fall.

He turned his horse back. "I'll come with you," he yelled.

Edmund nodded and rode ahead.

They hadn't gone far when they came across Isaac's leading sheep. He was pushing them and the driverless bullock dray forward – doing the job of two men with fearless determination.

"Where are the others?" Edmund yelled to be heard over the pounding rain.

"I don't know," Isaac shouted. "When I reached the wagon, Samuel had it ready to move, then he went back to help Jacob. He said their sheep had scattered in the night."

"You help Isaac get this lot across." Edmund's voice reached them in snatches. "I'll go and help Jacob and Samuel." He rode on and soon disappeared behind a curtain of rain.

Isaac and Thomas herded the sheep to the creek. To his dismay, Thomas could see the water was flowing even faster and already carrying pieces of vegetation and debris in its brown wake.

"You take the wagon across," he said to Isaac. "I'll round up the stragglers."

Isaac didn't argue. He set about getting the wagon to the other side.

By the time Thomas got the sheep across, he thought it too late for the rest to attempt it. He and Isaac watched from the inadequate shelter of a tree as Jacob's lead sheep reached the torrent.

"It's too late," Thomas yelled, but his words were lost in the pounding of the rain and the roar of the creek. The three men on horses on the other side drove the mob harder. He watched for a moment as the first sheep plunged into the water. They were quickly swept along but managed to find a foothold and, to his amazement, scrabbled to safety. More came but some were too weak to swim against the force and were swept away. Thomas leaped from his horse and waded out to a tree trunk. He clung to it and caught some of the sodden creatures as they lost their footing. Isaac joined him and together they managed to pull a few more out of the water.

The three horsemen plunged into the torrent after the last sheep. It was hard to make out who was who. Thomas saw the lead horse falter halfway across. The other two came up beside it and together they surged forward. They were almost to the other side when a large log tumbled past, clipping one of the horses and sending the rider into the water. The terrified horses scrambled onto the bank.

As the rider came towards him, Thomas stretched out and grasped a handful of fabric. He slipped and then steadied as Isaac grabbed him by the back of his pants. Together they heaved a bedraggled and spluttering Edmund to the bank. He rolled to his knees and staggered to his feet. Isaac put out a steadying hand but he shook it off.

"You should have found a safer place to cross," Edmund snarled when he finally gained his breath.

Thomas clenched his jaw. He obviously wasn't going to get any thanks for dragging his brother-in-law from the creek.

"We should have crossed yesterday," he said.

"The sheep were too tired." Edmund rounded on Thomas, thrusting out his chest. "They'd spread too far."

Thomas held his ground. "I wasn't the one who told Jacob to cut some sheep and take them miles out of the way. They would have been at the creek well before if you'd just let them follow mine."

"They needed water and your stock hadn't left enough."

Edmund jabbed again. Thomas slapped his hand away, conscious that Samuel had come to stand beside his older brother.

"Stop it," Jacob yelled. "Stop blaming each other. What's done is done. There's plenty of water to be had now." Rain ran down his face and dripped off his chin. They were all wet through and near exhaustion.

"We can do nothing more today," Isaac said. "Help me rig up a shelter, Edmund." He pulled his brother behind him back to the wagon.

"I've got tinder to get a fire started if you can find some dry wood," Samuel said.

Jacob immediately set off. Thomas turned in the other direction. He pulled his oilskin collar higher and poked about beneath the trees, looking for any wood that might have been sheltered from the deluge. Damn Edmund. Everything he did only strengthened Thomas's dislike of him. He'd made things worse with his meddling. Jacob had lost a lot more sheep to the raging water. Thomas could only hope there'd be enough left for the Smiths to reach their quota once they rounded them up again.

When he got back, Isaac and Edmund had dragged a canvas from the wagon and strung it to a tree. The ground was wet underneath but at least it kept more rain from falling on their heads. Samuel had managed to coax his tinder alight. Thomas produced the driest of the wood he'd found and finally the fire gave out a little heat. Jacob returned with more wood and they each managed to find a spot under the canvas. With their smoking fire and some cold damper, all they could do was huddle together and wait for the storm to pass.

The next morning, weak sunlight shafted through a patchy sky. The dark clouds of the day before were rolling away to the south. Still wet and miserable, the five men took in their surroundings. The bleats of sheep told them there were some nearby.

"The sheep are most likely scattered to the four corners of the earth," Edmund said.

"They may not have gone far," Thomas said. "In a storm they're more likely to bunch together."

In spite of this optimism it took the five of them the best part of the day to round up all the sheep. He knew his animals had been far healthier from the outset but now they had one big mob. They'd made a narrow gap to drive the sheep through aided by a fallen log and some thick bush, and Jacob and Thomas did the count. There was no way to say definitely which beasts were whose and they had lost more stock since the last count. To add to Thomas's worries, some of the sheep didn't look as if they'd survive the rest of the journey.

Edmund was suddenly keen to press on, but by late afternoon the rest of his brothers agreed with Thomas: they should rest the stock and move in the morning.

As he rode back to where Samuel still had the wagon set up high above the creek, Thomas noticed Jacob sitting atop his horse, further along the bank. Thomas rode to him.

"We must have left some back there when we lost them in the night." Jacob nodded to the other side. Below them the creek was still running fast, the banks filled to the top.

"There's no way you can go back unless you wait for the water to drop," Thomas said.

"I've lost a lot of stock, Thomas. I don't think I'll have enough for my quota."

"There's still over five thousand head between us."

"But not enough of them are mine."

Thomas studied the side of his brother-in-law's face as he continued to gaze across the creek. He was likely to do something stupid like try to cross back. Then they'd all be held up and probably for no good result.

"I had plenty of extras when I left," Thomas said. "We'll share them between us to get the numbers. Besides, who's to say which sheep belong to who?"

Jacob slowly turned desperate eyes in his direction. "That's very generous."

"We're family now."

"Let's hope our final count will get us across the line then."

For a moment they held each other's gaze.

A whistle pierced the silence between them, followed by Samuel's bellow. "Tucker time!"

Jacob's face split in a small grin. Some sparkle returned to eyes that reminded Thomas so much of Lizzie's.

"Let me guess," he said. "Mutton and damper or *maybe* damper and mutton?"

Thomas reached across and grasped his shoulder. They turned their horses to the wagon.

Two days later they reached the watercourse with the large rocky outcrop that marked the beginning of Wildu Creek. Water was flowing steadily but here the creek bed opened out wide; Thomas would be able to get his sheep across with no difficulty.

Jacob turned his mob west. They counted just over two thousand head, which was enough for the smaller run they were calling Smith's Ridge. The rest, which numbered more than three thousand, were for Wildu Creek. Jacob waved and kept moving. Samuel followed with the wagon.

Edmund glared at Thomas. They had barely spoken since the storm. "You don't need me any longer." He wheeled his horse around and rode up beside the wagon.

"I'll come with you," Isaac said to Thomas. "Get them across the creek."

Thomas watched his sheep streaming through the shallow water and spreading out among the blue bush on the other side.

"Thanks, Zac, but there's no need. They're home now."

Isaac pulled his horse in next to Thomas. Together they watched the last of the sheep cross onto Wildu Creek land.

"Say hello to Lizzie for us," Zac said. "We'll come for a visit once we've set things straight at the Ridge. We'll be hoping for one of her pies." He grinned and shook hands with Thomas then turned to follow his brothers.

Thomas trailed his sheep across the creek. Once on the other side he remembered the gifts, still packed in the wagon. No matter, he thought. All he wanted was to hold his wife and daughter in his arms. Presents could come later.

Forty-four

Thomas looked eagerly ahead, scanning the trees for the first glimpse of his hut. A small waft of smoke appeared and then he could see the roof. He encouraged his poor horse on. He'd only taken little more than a day to cover a distance that normally took two. He was desperate to see his women.

The sound of the hooves must have alerted Lizzie. He saw her stop part way to the creek. She put down the basket she was carrying and put her hand up to shade her eyes.

"Lizzie," he called. He slid from his horse before it had come to a stop.

He threw his arms around her and pulled her close. "We made it," he said. "We've got enough stock and with two days to spare. Your brothers have too." He nestled his face into her hair. "It's so good to be home."

She pulled back from him. It was then he noticed her pale face and the dark shadows under her eyes.

"Thomas," she murmured. Tears brimmed and began to trickle down both cheeks. She batted them away.

Instead of joy in her eyes he could only see sorrow. His chest tightened. He looked past her towards the hut. "Where's Annie?"

"Thomas," she said again.

He gripped both her arms. His robust Lizzie felt so thin beneath her sleeves.

"Where is she?" he whispered.

"She's … she's left us –"

"No." Thomas shook his head and looked around. A lump formed in his chest. His body felt clumsy, heavy with dread. He gave Lizzie a little shake. "No," he said again but the look in her eyes told him it was true. "Not Annie."

Lizzie's face creased in sorrow. "She's with the angels now."

"She was born too soon and yet she survived."

"She wasn't strong enough for this."

"What happened?" he asked, needing to know the answer but not wanting to hear it.

"It was so hot." Lizzie swayed slightly.

He guided her to a tree and sat her in the shade. She looked steadily ahead past his shoulder; he knew she was gazing at the distant mountain range.

"Lizzie?" he pressed gently.

She brought her eyes back to his. "The heat and the flies and the dust were so bad. I couldn't keep anything clean. She took sick." Lizzie shook her head. "We both got diarrhoea and then nothing would stay in her. Daisy and Gulda helped me but there was nothing we could do. I think I would have died as well if it hadn't been for them."

Thomas felt his mouth fall open but no sound came out. Lizzie put her hand on his.

"We only buried her a week ago. Up on the hill. There'd been a big storm the night before. The air was fresh and the sun shone gently instead of the pounding heat we'd been having. She's rest-ing now, looking at that magnificent view." Once more, tears rolled down Lizzie's cheeks.

He pulled her into his arms and held her tight. Pain surged through him as if a knife were cutting out his heart. His baby girl was dead and he'd nearly lost his wife. His mother-in-law had been right.

"I shouldn't have brought you here," he said. "I must take you back to your parents."

Lizzie pulled back. There was anger in her eyes. "Don't say that," she snapped. "If you say that, it's as if Annie's life was for nothing."

"But what will we do, Lizzie?" Thomas slumped forward and put his head in his hands.

"We will go on as we'd planned."

"How can we?" He rubbed at the tears he could no longer hold back.

"We'll do it for Annie," she said gently. "And for the children we haven't had yet and for their children." She slid a hand under his chin. "Look up, Thomas."

Slowly he raised his head. Through the trees he could see the valley. There were sheep there now and beyond the wide plain were the mountains, appearing brown and green in the afternoon light.

"This is our home now," Lizzie said.

Thomas felt as if his shoulders would collapse under the weight of his sorrow and yet her words roused something deep within him. The dream that he'd kindled with Lizzie to have their own place was still alive, just.

"We mustn't look back," she said.

Once more he wrapped his arm around his wife and held her close. How precious his Lizzie was and how brave. If she could lose her firstborn and keep going then he must too.

"Thomas?" She was frowning up at him. Her cornflower-blue eyes had lost a little of their spark but none of their determination.

"No looking back," he murmured.

*

Gulda and Daisy welcomed him home later that day. The sadness brimming in their deep brown eyes told him of their sorrow without a need for words. That evening, as the sun set in a glorious array of orange and pink, Lizzie took him up the hill behind their hut. He held her tight as she cried over the pathetic pile of rocks that marked the spot where their daughter was buried. His own grief was raw pain, burning in his chest.

The next day he fashioned a cross out of some native pine and carved Annie's name on it. Each evening he made the trip up the hill alone to keep watch over her until Lizzie called him to eat. She moved like a shadow around their camp and between them they ate little. One day rolled into the next. Somehow they got through the first few weeks after his return, all of them bumbling along together in their grief.

When the government man arrived to take the count, Thomas could barely speak to him.

"You've done very well, Mr Baker. This is a fine place you've claimed and you've ample stock."

Thomas heard the words, acknowledged them somehow, but he found no joy in them. It was Lizzie who made sure the man had all the details correct and fed him. Thomas marvelled at her strength. She had lost a lot of weight but she worked as hard as he did and always had clean clothes and linen and order in the yard around the hut, and water on hand and something for them to eat. He fell into bed each night thankful that sleep consumed him easily.

One morning, in that small space between night and the first light of the new day, he woke to the sound of muffled sobs. He lay perfectly still, listening as Lizzie gave in to her grief. He felt so helpless.

Finally, unable to bear her tears any longer, he moved a hand to touch hers. He heard her suck in a breath.

"I'm here, Lizzie," he whispered and reached out his arm.

She rolled into him. He held her until the shudders from her tears stopped, then he kissed her hair, her wet cheeks and finally her lips.

She slid her arms around his neck. He ran his hands under her nightgown and across her back. He felt her shiver.

"I've missed you," she whispered.

He kissed her again with an urgency welling from deep within him.

Slowly they came together, discovering each other all over again, as if it were their wedding night. They found solace in each other's touch and their lovemaking brought some peace to their broken hearts.

When Lizzie finally slid from his arms, sunlight was streaming around the gaps in the door of the hut. The sheet was a bundle on the floor with her nightclothes and his. He watched her as she took the two steps to the door. She was so thin. He reached out a hand, not wanting her to leave.

"Come on, husband," she chided. "We can't stay in bed all day."

He propped himself up on one elbow. "Unless you put some clothes on I might drag you back."

She threw him a cheeky look. It reminded him of happier times. "I'm going to wash in the creek." She took her dress from the hook. "You can join me if you want."

"In the creek? Someone might see us."

"Oh, Thomas." She giggled and let herself out the door.

He sighed and lay back on the bed, listening as Lizzie's laugh mingled with the calls of the morning birds. Just for a moment they'd forgotten the pain of their loss.

Forty-five

Lizzie sat on one of the outdoor chairs Thomas had made, an open book on her lap. He had four chairs and a rough table set up in the shade of the trees closer to the creek. In the evenings they sometimes got a breeze, which helped keep the flies away. She was so grateful to have Thomas back and safe. She had worried he might blame her for not looking after Annie well enough. She questioned her care of her baby but Thomas hadn't, not once. He hadn't turned away from her, hadn't blamed her.

A figure approached her from along the creek. She recognised Thomas's long gait. Gulda had been with him when they'd gone to investigate a waterhole further along the creek. Now her husband was alone. She stood up as he came closer.

"I just had to sit for a while," she said. "I find reading helps me take my mind off … things. Would you like tea? There's still some cake –"

"You should rest more," he said. "You were very sick and you work too hard."

"So do you," she said.

"It helps …"

They shared the same grief. There was no need for explanation.

"*Coo-ee!*"

They looked around. A rider was making his way towards them. He lifted a hand in a brief wave.

Lizzie sucked in a sharp breath. "It's Jacob."

"I should have ridden over to tell them about Annie, and sent word to your parents."

Lizzie took his hand as they stood side by side, watching her brother's approach. She hadn't wanted to spread the word either. It was bad enough dealing with their own grief.

"This won't be easy," Thomas said as Jacob drew closer.

"I'll tell him," Lizzie said. She could tell by the droop of Jacob's shoulders that something was wrong.

"Hello, sister dearest," he said as he got down from his horse.

Thomas took the reins. Lizzie hugged her brother. When he lifted his head, his customary grin was missing.

"I've bad news," Jacob said.

Lizzie linked an arm through his. "So have we, I'm afraid."

Thomas took the horse to water while Lizzie led Jacob to the chairs overlooking the creek. He looked up at Jacob's cry. Brother and sister clung together. Thomas gave them a few minutes then he joined them.

"I'm so sorry." Jacob pulled him close. Thomas stiffened. He couldn't bear to go over Annie's death again.

"Is Zac well?" he asked when Jacob finally let him go. "What's your news?"

"We are all well as far as I know. Once we reached Smith's Ridge, Samuel and Edmund only took a night's rest then they headed for home. I can only assume they arrived safely. It's probably just as well they left when they did."

"Why?" Lizzie asked. "For pity's sake tell us what's happened."

"Two days after we arrived, the government man came."

"Yes, he came to us later," Lizzie said and lowered herself to a chair.

"We lost a few sheep by the time we made Smith's Ridge," Jacob said. "And more in the days that followed."

"You arrived with the right quota," Thomas said. "That's all that counts."

"That's true, but he said we'd got there too late. Showed us the lease, signed a week earlier than we thought. Then another man turned up." Jacob clenched his hat in his hands. "He said he was our financial backer. Said he paid for most of the sheep for our place and that we hadn't made it in time so he was taking up the lease."

"What?" Lizzie jumped up.

"That can't be," Thomas said at the same time.

"That's what Zac and I said, but he showed us the papers."

"The lease for Smith's Ridge was signed the same time as Wildu Creek," Thomas said.

"I thought so too but the man who backed us got Father to sign it and then *he* took it to Adelaide." Jacob's shoulders slumped even lower. "Our date was a week before yours. The government man looked over it and agreed we hadn't filled our quota by the due date. He may have let it go if it hadn't been for the backer standing beside him, demanding we forfeit the lease."

"I thought Father was paying for everything," Lizzie said.

"He didn't have the money," Jacob replied.

Thomas recalled his concerns that George Smith was stretching his finances to help his sons.

"Surely a decent man would give you some grace," Thomas said. "Who is this backer that he can turn up so quickly, the same day as the government man, and take what should be yours?"

"His name is Septimus Wiltshire."

"Wiltshire?" Lizzie frowned. "Is he the same man who used to come around the district hawking goods?"

"I don't know. Father was the one to do the deal. After I leave you, I'm going home to find out more."

The late afternoon sky had turned grey and the gully breeze stirred the trees with a rush of cool air. Unease wormed its way into Thomas's chest.

"What did this Wiltshire look like?"

"Tall and quite handsome in an angular way," Lizzie said. "Mother called him charismatic, as I recall."

"Piercing grey eyes?"

"Why, yes. How did you know?

"He sounds remarkably like the man that sold me the stolen horse. His name was Seth Whitby, very similar, don't you think?"

"Could they be the same man?" Jacob asked.

"Possibly," Lizzie said.

Jacob scratched his head. "Why would Father take up with a horse thief?"

"Mr Wiltshire the hawker didn't act like a thief." Lizzie plucked a book from behind her. "And his wife was very kind. She loaned me this book. I've never seen her since to give it back. It feels special because of the name inside. It belonged to a lady called Hester Baker."

Thomas stared at the little book in Lizzie's hand. He'd never taken much notice of it before but now he could see it was like the set of books that had belonged to his mother. The books that had been in the stolen trunk. "Let me see it." He traced his finger carefully over the neat letters of the handwritten name.

"Is Hester Baker a relation?" Lizzie asked. "I didn't think you had any other family."

"She was my mother."

"Surely not." Lizzie frowned at him. "Mrs Wiltshire said it had belonged to her mother-in-law."

"I don't care what story she spun." Thomas tapped the book against the palm of his hand. "This book was my mother's. I left it in the trunk that Seth Whitby stole. If he is this Septimus Wiltshire, your father has been swindled by a seasoned liar and thief."

"Surely Father would have seen through him?" Jacob said.

"Father did spend time alone with him," Lizzie said. "They could have been discussing all manner of things, although that was a few years ago now."

"So, this Wiltshire man has taken over Smith's Ridge?" Thomas said.

"In a way," Jacob said. "He doesn't want to stay on the property. He offered Zac and me work as shepherds."

"Shepherds!" Thomas exclaimed. "What kind of man takes your land and then rubs salt into the wound, offering you scraps?"

"I turned him down," Jacob said. "But Zac decided to stay. He says there's nothing for him back home."

"I want to meet this man and look at these papers myself," Thomas growled. "You'll stay here with Lizzie, won't you, Jacob?"

Lizzie put a hand on his arm. "It's too late to go today, Thomas."

"And there's no purpose," Jacob said. "He left before I did. He'd be long gone now."

"Where does he live?"

"I don't know."

"And Zac is there alone?" Lizzie said.

"Wiltshire says he's sending another man to be overseer."

Thomas slapped the side of his leg.

"It's not your worry, Thomas," Jacob said. "You've got your own place to manage. We'll get by."

"What will you do?" Lizzie asked.

"I am going home to give Father the news and then I don't know." Jacob turned his poor crumpled hat in his hands once more. "I'll find something somewhere else. South Australia has other opportunities. There's plenty of work at the copper mines."

"You must stay with us tonight." Lizzie stood to place a hand on her brother's arm. "We all need each other's company now."

"Lizzie's right, Jacob. You must stay the night. Who knows when we will see you again?" Thomas gripped Jacob's hand firmly.

"I'll prepare some food," Lizzie said. "It will be ready in two shakes of a lamb's tail."

They both watched her stride off to her camp kitchen.

"I've brought your bag."

"Bag?"

Thomas watched as Jacob went to his horse and unhooked a bag from the saddle. Then he remembered the gifts he had purchased.

"I don't know what you have in here but I hope it's tough." Jacob held up the dirty calico package. "It was jammed in the wagon under everything else."

Thomas looked at the bag in Jacob's outstretched hand as if it were a snake about to strike him. He shuddered.

"Didn't you have something in here for Lizzie?" Jacob jiggled the bag.

Thomas took it and lowered himself to a chair. He tugged the drawstring. The axe with its head wrapped in leather slid to the ground between his feet. He reached in and felt for the small mirror. It too was wrapped. He set it beside the axe.

"For Gulda and Daisy," he said.

Next he took out the small flat package wrapped in brown paper. He laid it across his lap. Inside his chest, a vice gripped his heart – the little dress that Annie would never wear.

"This … this was for Annie." The words stuck in his mouth, coming out in a hollow whisper.

Jacob shifted closer and put a gentle hand on Thomas's shoulder.

Thomas pulled the last thing from the bag. Lizzie's bonnet was now bent out of shape, the flower had fallen off and there was a hole in the crown.

Thomas grunted as the air left his lungs.

Jacob gripped his shoulder tightly. "She's a strong woman, my sister."

"It's been too tough." Thomas turned the ruined bonnet around and around in his fingers. "Losing Annie and living like this –"

"She's never been one to want fancy things."

They both stared at the hat.

"Which is just as well –" Jacob's words were cut short by the laugh that gurgled from his throat.

Thomas was surprised to feel the lump in his own throat dissolve in laughter. Jacob sank to the chair beside him and they both wiped tears from their eyes.

"What were you thinking, putting something so delicate in a bag in a wagon?" Jacob chuckled again.

Thomas stuffed the hat and the little parcel back in the bag. He'd deal with them later, when he was alone. He glanced around their camp. Jacob was right. Lizzie had never complained about the rudimentary makings of their settlement, but she deserved better. Once again he pondered the difference it might have made for Annie if only he'd waited and built a proper hut before moving them here.

"You and Lizzie together is what matters," Jacob said. "You'll make Wildu Creek prosper."

Thomas looked at his brother-in-law as an idea began to form. "Are you in a hurry to start your new life?"

Jacob put his head to one side. "That depends."

"Would you stay with us for the winter? Help me build a home for Lizzie. I can't pay much, but you'll be well fed."

Jacob's shoulders rose from the droop they'd had since he arrived. "I don't have anything else to do," he said. "And I have missed my sister's cooking."

"What are you two grinning about?" Lizzie was back with mugs of hot tea.

"Jacob is staying a while to give us a hand." Thomas pushed the calico bag into the bush behind his chair.

"Well that's some good news at least," Lizzie said. "And you can begin by setting a fire here. It's coming in cooler."

Jacob groaned. "I'd forgotten how good you were at giving orders."

Thomas listened as the two of them chatted back and forth. He was glad Jacob was staying but he couldn't shake his earlier unease. He didn't like the sound of this rogue, Septimus Wiltshire, who was now to be his neighbour – in name, at least. Something just didn't feel right.

Forty-six

1855

"Septimus, it's perfect." Harriet threw her arms around his neck and kissed his cheek. They stood in the bigger front room of the stone cottage Septimus had acquired.

"I've a good room at last, separate from the kitchen. And the windows have proper curtains." She brushed her fingers over the soft white fabric draped in front of the glass. "And padded chairs." She laughed with delight.

She stood behind one of the two armchairs before the fireplace and brushed the top of it with her hands. "How did you find such a place?"

"I bought the house, complete with furniture, from a sea captain whose wife had died." Septimus smiled. The man had been in a hurry to return to England and had been too distraught to haggle. He had readily accepted the pittance Septimus had offered. "I promised you a home, my dear," he said. "For you and Henry."

At the sound of his name the child dropped the little wooden train he'd been holding and rushed to his mother's side. He grasped her hand and put the thumb of his other hand to his mouth.

"For all of us," Harriet corrected. "It's our home."

She picked Henry up and twirled around. He giggled.

"Yes, for all of us. Now put Henry down. He's getting too big for that. I've something else to show you."

"He's only five," Harriet retorted, but put the child back on his feet.

Immediately Henry's eyes lost their sparkle. The thumb went back in his mouth.

Septimus wrinkled his brow. Harriet had been too soft with the boy. Henry was wary of him. He jumped when Septimus spoke to him and cried for Harriet in the night. Septimus knew she still secretly fed him like a baby from her breast.

Septimus had coupled with her when he'd been desperate for release but he no longer touched her breasts. He would not share her. Thank goodness for Dulcie. Now that he'd moved Harriet and Henry to Port Augusta, he could have Dulcie whenever he spent time at the little hut in the hills, without the need for secrecy. And when Harriet finally weaned that brat, he'd have her to himself again too.

He was definitely coming up in the world – a new house, two properties and the wool income lining his pockets. He was kept busy managing his investments but he still took his hawking wagon on the road to some of his regular customers. There was no better way to find out who was doing well and who might be in need of financial support. There was always someone who could be hoodwinked and Septimus was always the one to benefit.

"What is it you want to show me, Septimus?"

He came back to Harriet and their new house. "Something very special," he said and crossed the room to the bedroom door. He turned the latch and let it swing open.

Harriet gasped from behind him. "Oh, Septimus, a four-poster bed."

She stepped around him into the room and ran her hands over the floral quilt.

"It's beautiful. And proper white pillow cases."

She drew back the soft netting and sat on the bed. She gave a little bounce up and down.

"And so soft." She tipped her head back and laughed. "Oh, how different from our first bed."

The hair fell back from her neck, revealing her pale skin and the locket hanging from the delicate chain. He had a sudden vision of the smooth black of Dulcie's skin against the creamy white of Harriet's. He imagined them together, the three of them in this bed. A shudder went through him.

"Are you all right, Septimus?" Harriet jumped up. "I should light the fire. There's a chill in the air."

"There are other ways to warm us, Harriet." He pushed the door shut with his boot.

"Not now, Septimus." Harriet gave him one of her coy looks. "Tonight."

He grabbed her arms and pulled her against him. "I've bought you a new bed, wife," he growled, "and I want to test it out."

"Mama?" Henry whined from beyond the door.

Harriet twisted in his grasp. "Septimus, you're hurting me."

"Mama!"

"Septimus." Harriet struggled.

He let go one hand and slapped her face.

She gasped.

"Shut him up," he hissed, "or I'll do it."

Harriet stared at him, then her eyes lowered in compliance. "Mama's all right, Henry," she called. "Play with your train. I'll be out in a minute."

There was a whimper then silence.

Septimus smiled and pushed her back onto the bed. Her body was still his for the taking. He leaned over her.

"Unbutton me, Harriet," he commanded.

Harriet listened to the steady breaths that told her Septimus was asleep. She eased out of bed, made herself decent then let herself quietly out the door.

Henry was asleep on the floor, his head resting on his outstretched arm, the train still clutched in his hand. She bent down to pick him up. Her heart ached at the sight of his face, damp with tears. She kissed his pale cheek. He stirred in her arms but didn't wake.

He became withdrawn and nervy only when Septimus was at home. The rest of the time he was such a good little boy and so happy. She carried him to the small room off the kitchen and laid him on one of the two matching single beds. Even this room was well furnished and had its own small window overlooking the backyard.

She brushed a lock of dark hair from Henry's forehead and kissed him again. She almost wished Septimus would stay away forever. He hardly ever took her to bed any more and today, quite suddenly, he'd forced her. That had never happened before. Or perhaps it was that she'd always complied easily whenever he'd wanted her.

Whatever the case, she didn't want it to happen again while Henry was about. He must have been so frightened. She would have to do her best to satisfy Septimus again at night so that he wouldn't be wanting more during the day.

She sighed and shut the door on her sleeping child. Just for a moment she had her body and her house to herself. She wandered between the two main rooms, checking every corner.

The kitchen had a proper wood oven and griddle top with a separate grate to heat the kettle. Running across the wall above it was a mantel crafted from wood and polished to a shine. The best part of the house, however, was the solid wood of the floors. Harriet closed her eyes and drew in a breath. She couldn't smell dirt. After years of living in a wagon and then in the little hut up in the hills with its rough wooden floor, she was happy to have a house that she could keep free of dirt.

She gave a brief thought to the captain who had built this for his wife. How sad she never got to see it. It was so beautiful and fresh there must have been people lined up to buy it. She wondered how Septimus had come to purchase it. Harriet turned slowly in the middle of the room and banished sad thoughts from her mind. She busied herself setting the fires, one in the kitchen and one in the front room. She had a delightful new house and she knew better than to ask how it had come to be theirs.

By the time Septimus and Henry woke from their afternoon naps she had a mutton stew simmering over the fire – Septimus had brought the meat from their hills property – and she'd prepared a roly-poly to cook in her new oven.

Septimus came into the kitchen. He stepped around Henry, who was once again on the floor with his train. "Can't he play outside?"

"He likes the new house too." She shuffled Henry to a corner out of the way.

"Hmph!" Septimus snorted. He lifted the lid on the stew. "That smells good, at least."

"We can have a celebratory dinner." Harriet smiled at him. "Then an even better celebration later." She fluttered her eyelashes.

He pounced on her in a flash and pushed her up against the table. Harriet braced herself. Her hands gripped the wooden top.

"You want me to take you again," he snarled in her ear, "right here in front of the boy?"

She gasped.

"Might do him good to learn what a man does," Septimus said.

"Mama?" Henry's voice wavered from the corner.

"Mama," Septimus mimicked and screwed up his face.

He let her go and stepped away from her. Harriet pushed herself upright then moved forward as Septimus lowered his hand towards Henry. She stopped as he roughed up his son's hair.

Henry cowered away from his father.

"Pfff!" Septimus exhaled. "The day will come when I have to take the boy in hand. Can't have him at your apron strings forever, Harriet."

He strode away from Henry. "Get the food ready," he snapped as he passed Harriet. "I have to go out later."

Henry opened his mouth but she put a finger to her lips and he closed it again, watching her intently.

She listened as Septimus settled himself in a chair in the front room. Then she heard the rustle of the newspaper. Finally she kneeled down and Henry fell into her outstretched arms.

Septimus made his way down the alley behind one of the new sheds at the wharf. There was barely a moon, so little light shone to mark his progress and he was glad of it. He had a contact who was going to be his eyes and ears at the port. He didn't want anyone else observing their meeting.

Septimus had learned over the years to keep his business within the law. If, on the odd occasion, something unlawful needed to be done, he'd found others to do the work for him. He'd killed two men and got away with it. He didn't want to risk his luck further.

A shadow emerged from the gloom at the end of the alley. Septimus stopped as a second figure joined the first.

"It's me, Mr Wiltshire, Rix. I've got me friend Pavey with me."

Septimus let out a breath, hissing over his teeth. He'd come across Rix and Pavey at a roadside inn a few months prior. They were heading to Port Augusta in search of work. He'd picked them as a pair of ex-convicts still willing to cross the line for some extra money. He'd kept in touch and was pleased to find they had secured jobs loading and unloading ships.

"I told you to come alone," Septimus growled.

"Pavey has seen something," Rix said. "I thought he should come and tell you himself what he saw. I think you'll be interested."

Septimus stepped closer. "What is it, man?" He put his sleeve to his nose. There was a rank, fishy smell surrounding the pair.

"There's a load of wool," Pavey said. "Just been delivered today. I had to help get it off the wagon."

"That's your job, you fool," Septimus snapped.

"Yeah, but some of it was unmarked."

Septimus stared into the eyes of the man opposite him. Pavey shuffled his feet and looked from side to side.

"In what way, unmarked?" Septimus asked.

"There's no name on them. Don't know how it happened but the bales are free of any markings."

Septimus lowered his arm and rubbed his hands together against the damp chill of the air. "Where are they now?"

"With all the other bales that come in from the property. I thought maybe the owner might pay a reward for having it pointed out to him."

Pavey yelped as Rix gave him a swift slap over the head.

"Be quiet, man," Septimus hissed.

"I told Pavey we work for you now, Mr Wiltshire, and that *you* would be rewarding us for this information."

"Possibly." Septimus was wary. "How would bales leave a property unmarked?"

"There's a few shearers we've met that does the rounds," Rix said. "If they were to have a connection with a port ..."

Septimus frowned at the man. "But what if the owner notices unmarked bales being loaded on the wagon?"

"If he does then it's a mistake, ain't it? The mark is applied and the deal on the side is lost. For this time."

"So are you saying you've intercepted someone else's cut?"

"Were only Pavey and the driver unloading this lot," Rix said.

"He was drunk on slops." Pavey spat and Septimus took a step back.

Rix hit him again but Pavey stood his ground. "Was barely any help to me at all. I was doing all the hard work." His eyes glinted in the weak light.

"Where are these unmarked bales now?" Septimus said.

"They're still with the rest from the property, waiting to be loaded on the ship due in tomorrow. I faced all the bales in so no one would notice the unmarked ones."

"You fool," Rix said. "How will you find them again without turning them all over?"

"I counted along the row." Pavey grinned. "There's four of them on the top at the back."

"Whose property has this load come from?" Septimus knew the shearers had recently been at Smith's Ridge. This fool could have him robbing himself.

"Wildu Creek."

Septimus blew out a breath that hissed between his teeth. His reluctant and arrogant neighbour had been careless with his wool. It would be a pleasure to fleece Thomas Baker again. He sniggered at his own cunning.

Pavey fidgeted at the sound.

Septimus wondered who'd been fool enough to try to steal from Mr High and Mighty Baker. Not that it mattered: Septimus Wiltshire had intercepted the job. No doubt the drunk in charge of the wagon was Baker's brother-in-law, Isaac Smith. Septimus had kept him on at Smith's Ridge but he'd become a thorn in his side, asking too many questions, always watching. Septimus had paid his other shepherd, Terrett, to rough the lad up, remind him who he worked for. Terrett had done that but the idiot had also filled Isaac with grog and made it a habit. Septimus couldn't abide drinking on the job. He'd kicked Isaac off the property on his last visit there. No doubt his sister had talked her husband into giving him work.

"We'll get a good cut for this information?" Rix broke into his thoughts.

"Yes, yes," Septimus said. "You'll be paid once the Smith's Ridge stamp is on those bales. See to it and I'll be back in town next week to pay you."

Rix nodded and Septimus turned, happy to get away from the foul stench of rotten fish.

Forty-seven

1856

"What is it, Thomas?"

He looked up from the paper he was holding into Lizzie's eyes. The cornflower blue was as pretty as ever in spite of years of hardship and loss.

"Nothing," he said.

"Why are you frowning over nothing?"

She came over to the little desk where he sat in the corner of their good room. Times had been tough but at least he'd been able to build a house with Jacob's help, and the structure kept out most of the dust and flies. They'd used solid pine trunks and filled the gaps with plaster made from mud. The paling roof kept out the rain. There was no ceiling but the house had glass windows and wooden floors. The two main rooms were large enough for them to move in without bumping into each other and there was a third room right across the back for cooking and stores.

"I'm doing my sums."

"That would explain it," she teased.

"The wool cheque should be in when I get to Port Augusta."

He put the paper back on the desk and stood up.

"Do you have to go?" she asked.

"You know I'd rather not but we need another shepherd."

"You wouldn't if Zac –"

"It's a much bigger job now," he said quickly. He didn't want to go over Zac's shortcomings again. He'd hoped his youngest brother-in-law would have settled with time. He smiled at Lizzie, not wanting to add to her worries. "And I want to pick out a new ram myself. I hear there are some for sale at the port." Thomas wouldn't add he didn't trust Zac to do that job either. "I'm going to bring back another horse and cart too."

"Don't you go getting too grand, Thomas Baker."

"I'm not, Lizzie. But if we're to lower our sheep losses we need another shepherd; and the cart we brought with us from Penakie is not ours."

"You're a proud man. You know my father won't ever want it back."

"I know. But I want everything to be our own. To come from the work of our hands."

"You'll be gone a month or more."

"I'm sorry, Lizzie."

Since that first trip away when Annie had died, Thomas hated leaving her, and now his two-year-old son, Joseph, behind. The year before he'd sent Zac to the port with their wool but he hadn't returned. Thomas had had to go looking and bring his drunken brother-in-law home.

"Don't be sorry," she said. "I can manage fine without you." She gave him a wink and lifted her head to kiss his lips. "It's Joseph who misses his father."

"And you won't miss me – just a little bit?"

He pulled her close in his arms and smothered her lips with his. Lizzie still made him feel like he was the luckiest man alive, in spite of everything they'd suffered.

"Who will keep you warm at night when I'm not here?" he whispered in her ear.

"The nights are warm enough without your –"

"Give it a break you two."

They pulled apart and turned to the figure swaying in the open doorway.

"Zac, have you been drinking again?" Lizzie moved towards her brother.

He held up his hand. "No." He wobbled against the doorframe. "Well maybe a little." He chuckled and staggered away from the door.

Lizzie turned to Thomas in exasperation. "Where does he get it?" she muttered.

"He must have another still going."

Zac's curse was something neither of them could understand. He would spend weeks as sober as a judge then something would set him off. When he was sober he was a good worker, and Joseph doted on his merry uncle.

Thomas squinted into the bright sunshine beyond Zac. "Where's Joseph?"

Zac put his head to one side as if he was thinking.

"You were looking after him," Lizzie said. "Where is he?" She pushed past her brother and Thomas came around his other side.

They stopped at the sight of Daisy leading two giggling toddlers up the hill. They were both naked and streaked with mud. One little boy had black skin and dark curls like Daisy's and the other was white skinned with fair hair like Lizzie's.

"The boys been in the creek, Mrs Lizzie. I been telling them off."

"Thank you," Lizzie said.

Thomas reached down and picked up his son. Daisy swept her boy to her hip and carried him away.

Lizzie rounded on Zac. "You said you'd look after him."

"There's hardly any water there."

"He could have drowned."

"Lizzie, I'm sorry."

"You keep saying that, Zac." Lizzie glowered at him. "But it makes no difference. You're sober for a while and you work hard, then in no time at all you're back drinking again."

Thomas put a steadying hand on his wife's shoulder. "Joseph's all right." He put the squirming boy into her arms. Joseph giggled at his mother and clasped her cheeks in his dirty hands. She kissed the top of his head and, with a final glare at Zac, carried him inside.

"He's a good boy." Zac's words slurred over his lips.

Thomas swallowed his frustration. "Go and sleep it off, Zac. You can't leave all the shepherding to Gulda and Tarka."

Zac tipped his head to one side and tried to look at Thomas but his eyes kept shutting. He wobbled to the end of the verandah and staggered in the direction of the original little wooden hut that had become his quarters.

Thomas leaned against the verandah post and looked down the slope towards the creek. Zac was right. There was barely any water. During their first three summers at Wildu Creek there had always been pools fed by occasional cloudbursts in the hills behind them. This last summer had been long and hot and even though they were well into autumn they'd still had no rain to feed the creek. It was the same all over the property. His sheep were spreading further in their search for water, making it harder to look after them. They had lost a lot more to wild dogs in the past few months than ever before.

At least he didn't suffer many losses to the natives. Gulda's presence seemed to make the difference. Not that he or Tarka stayed permanently – Gulda was sometimes away for weeks. He always returned and spent time at Wildu Creek, though. He and Daisy were camped with their son, Tommie, in their usual spot further up the hill. Thomas desperately needed another shepherd. With the natives' occasional disappearances and Zac's lack of reliability, he was often doing the work of three men alone.

The sound of hooves approaching fast made him step down from the verandah. Gulda emerged from the bushes, bouncing on the back of Derriere. "Mr Tom, bad thing." He was yelling before his horse had come to a stop.

Thomas took the reins as Gulda slid from the horse's back, waving his arms and pointing behind him.

"What's happened?"

"Bad thing, bad thing," he said and shook his head vigorously.

Thomas put a tentative hand on his friend's heaving shoulder. "What bad thing?" He had learned over the years that Gulda could exaggerate the importance of some events.

"Terrett."

Thomas frowned and looked past him in the direction of Smith's Ridge. He'd met Wiltshire's overseer, Terrett, on a few occasions and had found nothing to like in the man. He'd also recognised fear in Zac's eyes at any mention of the overseer's name.

Thomas looked back at Gulda. His chest had stopped heaving. Thomas pointed to the shade of the verandah and called Lizzie to bring some water. The April sun wasn't as intense as in summer but the heat was still oppressive.

Lizzie brought a drink for both of them. She raised an enquiring eyebrow at Thomas as Gulda drained the cup but she didn't speak. Joseph was at her side, clean and wearing clothes.

"Now," Thomas said. "Tell me about Terrett."

Gulda gave the empty cup back to Lizzie with a nod of thanks and immediately began waving his arms about. "He said black men stole your sheep. They didn't, Mr Tom. I saw signs around the waterhole. Many sheep came there and horses herd them away."

"Are you saying we have sheep missing?"

Gulda nodded. "Young ones. Not marked yet. They were at the waterhole close to Smith's Ridge."

Thomas knew the waterhole Gulda was talking about. It had to be a spring: there was always water in it. It was on his land, a few miles from the boundary he shared with Smith's Ridge. Once more he cast his eyes in that direction. Terrett let his animals use it and there was little Thomas could do about it, but if the overseer was stealing his sheep that was another matter.

"What will you do, Thomas?" Lizzie asked.

"I'll have to go and see for myself."

"Bad thing." Gulda began to get agitated again.

"You should let it go."

They all turned to see Zac standing in the dirt at the end of the verandah. His face was blotchy and his eyes red.

"I can't let him get away with stealing my sheep and blaming it on the natives."

"You won't get the truth from Terrett," Zac said.

"I don't like that man," Lizzie said. "He looks at me as if he can see right through my clothes."

"He's evil," Zac rasped and he shuddered. Then he turned and walked back to his hut.

Thomas and Lizzie looked at each other. They both knew something bad had happened while Zac had been working with Terrett but he'd never talked about it.

Thomas clenched his jaw. "I've got to go," he said. "If he has taken some sheep and he thinks he can get away with it, he'll do it again."

He stepped inside and took the firearm from its hook on the wall.

Lizzie put a restraining hand on his arm as he passed her. "Be careful, Thomas," she said, her face creased in concern.

He kissed her and ruffled Joseph's fluffy hair. "I'll be home by tomorrow evening."

Thomas didn't look back but he could feel their eyes watching him as he rode away. It took him a couple of hours to reach the waterhole. There were prints everywhere, made by sheep and horses, and no way of working out how many or who they belonged to. He turned his horse west towards the ridge that gave the neighbouring property its name. The afternoon sun bounced off the red and brown rocks. Sweat trickled down his back under his shirt and yet he knew when the sun went down, the night would be very cold.

He crossed one dry creek and then another. There were plenty of hoof prints but nothing for their owners to drink. Terrett would have trouble keeping his own stock watered let alone stealing someone else's. When they'd mapped out their runs the creeks had been flowing through Smith's Ridge but there'd been little rain since Wiltshire had taken over.

The sun was low in the sky when he heard the bleating of sheep and saw the smoke of a fire up ahead.

Terrett turned from the sheep he'd been holding at the sound of Thomas's approach. Thomas didn't recognise the man with him, though he knew Wiltshire had employed a shepherd to replace Zac. He watched the man push the sheep away. Blood dripped from the ear clippers he held in his hand.

"Well, well, Neales, we've got a visitor." Terrett put his hands to his hips. His bare arms were thick as tree branches and covered in black hair. "I don't believe you've met our neighbour, Thomas Baker."

Neales nodded. Thomas responded then cast a look around the makeshift camp. The only sheep visible was the one Neales had just pushed away, but he could hear the occasional bleats of others nearby.

"What brings you here?"

Thomas turned slowly back to Terrett. "I'm missing some sheep."

"Blacks, the thieving bastards." Terrett spat to the side. "We've lost some too. That's why me and Neales here thought we'd best do a check. Make sure our stock's got their ears marked."

"That won't stop natives stealing your sheep," Thomas said.

"No, but when I catch 'em with 'em I'll know they belong to Smith's Ridge and the bastards will be dealt with." His face split in an ugly grin. "Speaking of Smiths, how's that lovely wife of yours and her young brother?"

"My family are well and no concern of yours, Mr Terrett."

Terrett dropped his arms to his sides and took a step towards Thomas. "No need for that tone, Baker. I'm just being neighbourly."

"Neighbours return what's not theirs," Thomas said. Once more he cast his eyes around but there was nothing to suggest they had tagged his sheep. When he looked back, Neales had moved closer to Terrett.

"Are you saying we have something of yours?" The grin had left Terrett's face.

"No," Thomas replied. "I'm saying keep to your side of the boundary and make sure the sheep you tag are Wiltshire's and not mine."

Terrett glowered at him. He opened his mouth to speak then apparently changed his mind about what to say. "Mr Wiltshire was only here yesterday." His lips twisted into a grin. "He was checking up on things. Says I'm doing a mighty fine job."

"Does he?" Thomas said carefully. He'd never managed to pin down the elusive Septimus Wiltshire but he thought it time he met his unwelcome neighbour. He was also keen to find out how

Wiltshire's wife had come to be in possession of his mother's book. "I'm sorry I missed him again. I'd like to talk to him myself."

"You'll have to go to Port Augusta." Neales grinned.

"Shut ya stupid face," Terrett snarled at him.

Thomas's horse shifted under him. So Wiltshire was in Port Augusta. Maybe even lived there. It would make sense. Far enough away and yet close enough to pay a visit to his property once or twice a year.

"He asked after you too." The sneering grin was back on Terrett's face. "Asked if I'd seen your drunk of a brother-in-law. Wanted to make sure he hadn't come snivelling back here."

Thomas stiffened. He locked eyes with Terrett.

"He liked the grog, young Zac. Used to beg me for it." He threw back his head and laughed. "I told Mr Wiltshire the good-for-nothing wouldn't come back here again. Not after the beating the boss ordered for him and I dished out."

"You bastard!" Thomas roared. His horse reared. Terrett sprang at Thomas and Neales grabbed at the reins.

Thomas wheeled his horse away and both men lost their hold. He took the whip from his saddle and cracked it.

They both stopped where they were, half stooped, their hands hanging at their sides, watching him closely.

"I'll have this out with Wiltshire when I find him in Port Augusta. In the meantime you keep your sheep and yourselves off my land," Thomas growled. "And Terrett, if ever I find you've taken a Wildu Creek sheep, I'll make sure the law finds you."

Terrett glowered at him then slowly put his hands to his hips. "I'm not frightened of you, Baker, or the law," he said.

Thomas turned his horse and rode away. Behind him Terrett began to laugh. The awful sound echoed around him in the gloom of the late afternoon shadows. He hoped he'd delivered a strong message but he had the uneasy feeling he'd only stirred up more trouble.

*

The sound of a horse nickering woke him. There was just the hint of light to the east; it was too early for most people to be about. Thomas sat up and reached for the firearm he'd kept at his side. The fire was out and his fingers were stiff with cold.

He'd camped just inside the boundary of his property, not far from the waterhole he'd checked yesterday. Dark had fallen not long after he'd left Terrett and he'd been keen to put distance between them, but it had been a moonless night and eventually he'd had to stop. He couldn't be sure Terrett wouldn't follow him but at least the darkness that made travel difficult for him would do the same for Terrett.

A bush rustled. Thomas raised the firearm.

A figure loomed.

"Mr Tom?"

Thomas blew out a breath. "Gulda. What are you doing creeping around in the dark?"

"Mrs Lizzie worry."

Thomas groaned. Then he thought about his trip to Port Augusta. He had planned to go home to see Lizzie then head straight off again. Wiltshire might be only a few days ahead of him and Thomas wanted to get on the road.

"It might be a good thing you've found me, Gulda. You can ride back and tell Mrs Lizzie I am well and I have gone straight to the port."

"No, Mr Tom." Gulda squatted down beside him. "Mrs Lizzie needs you."

"Why?" Thomas jumped to his feet. "Is it Joseph?" Please God; he'd lost one child. He couldn't bear to lose another.

"Joseph is well, Mr Tom. It's Mr Zac. He's bad." Gulda shook his head. "Very bad."

Forty-eight

Lizzie was waiting on the verandah as Thomas rode up. He was pleased to see Joseph and Tommie were both safe and playing under a tree beside Daisy while she worked on a possum skin.

"What's happened?" he asked. He could see the exhausted lines of Lizzie's face now that he was closer.

"It's Zac. After you left he kept drinking." She gripped both his arms as he reached her. "Oh Thomas," she whispered. "I think he tried to kill himself."

"Tell me," Thomas said gently.

"He was in such a bad way he could barely walk. I found two empty flasks in his hut and another half full. I emptied it all out then I put him to bed to sleep it off but … Well, last night I went to check on him and he wasn't there. Gulda and Daisy and I all set out looking for him. Gulda found him in the waterhole further along the creek. The only part with any decent water left in it."

"Perhaps he was going to wash. Try to sober himself up."

Lizzie looked up at him with tired, sad eyes. "He had his boots on and … his pockets were full of stones. When Gulda tried to pull him out, he started to scream." Her lip trembled. "It was such a horrible sound, Thomas. Daisy and I both came running. It took all three of us to drag him from the water." She stopped and sucked in a breath. "He pleaded with me to let him die." The last words came out in a gush as tears began to roll down her cheeks.

Thomas pulled her into his arms and pressed his lips to her hair. She sobbed into his chest. It hurt to see Zac turning into this person they didn't know and yet he felt powerless to stop it.

He felt Lizzie relax in his arms. "Where is he now?" he asked.

"In our back room. On the bed you made for Joseph. He's sleeping but I didn't want to let him out of my sight. I sent Gulda to find you because I didn't know what to do."

He stood back from her and saw the tears begin to brim in her eyes again. Thomas sighed. He knew Zac was a troubled man but he hadn't thought him a danger to himself. "I don't know what I can do," he said.

"Can't you talk to him? Make him see we love him and he's got a home here."

"I know that."

They both spun at Zac's voice. He was standing just inside the house, squinting out at them. Thomas was shocked to see how much thinner and more gaunt he looked just since the previous day.

Lizzie moved towards her brother but Thomas held her back. There was something else about Zac. He looked like a man who'd been through hell and yet – it was his eyes. There was something in his look that Thomas hadn't seen since their droving days: determination, perhaps.

"I'm thirsty," Thomas said. "Let's take some water and go sit under the trees."

Once more Lizzie made to move.

"It's all right, Lizzie," he said and kissed her forehead. "Just Zac and me this time."

Over the top of her head, Zac gave a slight nod.

"You go ahead," Thomas said. "I'll bring the water pouch."

He took a moment to reassure Lizzie then made his way down the slope to the trees that had become their outdoor room. Zac was sitting in one of the rough chairs, staring across the creek.

Thomas offered him the pouch and watched while he drank deeply. Then he took a few mouthfuls for himself and hung the pouch between them on a jutting branch. He looked out at the scene that held Zac's attention. The valley stretched before them, changing to rolling hills covered in the green of eucalypt and bluebush stretching up to the brown haze of Smith's Ridge. Beyond that the rugged mountain range towered into a grey sky.

Zac broke the silence between them. "I'm sorry I've caused you and Lizzie trouble," he said.

Thomas kept his eyes on the view. He hoped Zac would be able to talk about what bothered him. "Trouble usually has a reason."

He heard Zac take in a deep breath then slowly let it out. "Jacob and I were never so happy as those first days at Smith's Ridge. We lost a few more sheep after we got back but we still managed to make the quota. The sun was shining, there was plenty of feed and water in the creeks. We even thought about building a proper hut." He paused. "We didn't know about Annie, of course."

Thomas lifted his shoulders. "There was no way you could."

"When the government man came, we were as happy as larks. We showed him the count but when he checked his papers he said we were a week late. Jacob and I were having it out with him. We said we'd been there two days before but he said that made us five days late. Then, out of the blue, this Wiltshire bloke turns up. He had another paper that said the lease was his too. It had Father's signature and the date was a week earlier than we thought. Because we hadn't stocked by the due date, Wiltshire took over the lease. He acted all concerned and offered Jacob and me work as shepherds. Said he had his own man who would arrive later and be overseer. Jacob blew his stack there and then but I believed Wiltshire when he said it was all unfortunate and he would do his best to see us back on our feet."

Thomas nodded. He'd heard the same story from Jacob when he'd left Smith's Ridge and lived at Wildu Creek for that first winter.

"It wasn't too bad there for another week or so. I was on my own and imagined it was still our lease even if it wasn't. Then Terrett turned up."

From the corner of his eye, Thomas saw Zac grip his hands together. "He's a mean bastard." He pulled his hands apart and formed them into fists. "Treated animals bad; treated the blacks even worse; and if I spoke up he laid into me. He made a still. Wiltshire didn't permit drinking but Terrett said what we did in our own time was our own business. I had a swig or two at night. Made working with that animal a little easier."

"Why didn't you leave?" Thomas asked. "We'd have welcomed you here."

Zac glanced at Thomas then looked away again. "I know, but I thought I could somehow get Smith's Ridge back. Terrett was so terrible I thought the soft-looking Wiltshire would send him packing and decide it was all too hard to manage." Zac let out a snort. "How wrong I was. Wiltshire might dress like a gentleman but he's out of the gutter. He was no better than Terrett. I tried to tell him about Terrett on his next visit but he just laughed at me. Told me to toughen up or move on."

"But you stayed." Thomas was more puzzled than ever.

"Yes. I heard them talking when they thought I was away with the sheep, but I snuck back to get a bit of Terrett's grog. He had a stash near the shelter he slept in. He and Wiltshire were sitting by the fire laughing. Then I heard Father's name mentioned and I stopped to listen. Wiltshire was bragging about how he'd duped the old man."

Thomas sat forward and studied Zac. He'd often wondered what had happened. George and Anne had visited after Joseph was born but his father-in-law had clammed up when Thomas broached the topic of Smith's Ridge. Said he'd been a fool, and lost his money, and that's all there was to it.

"Wiltshire got Father to sign the papers," Zac said. "Then he rode hell for leather to make Adelaide as quickly as he could. He lodged the lease application then held up the paperwork to purchase the sheep. It was nearly all his money going into the stock. We were a week late leaving Encounter Bay but what we didn't know was we were already two weeks into the time we had to get the stock back to the Ridge. Wiltshire set it up so that we wouldn't make the deadline and he was waiting to take over the lease. No doubt it had been his intention all along. We did all the hard work, finding the place, marking it out and stocking it, then he took it away from us."

Thomas shook his head.

"Anyway, they heard me," Zac continued. "Wiltshire told Terrett to rough me up so I knew to keep my trap shut."

"You still didn't leave."

"No. I thought I could make them think I didn't care. All along I was trying to find a way to get the lease back, but it was useless. I drank Terrett's grog and listened to his stories. That was bad enough. Then one day we were out checking waterholes and we came across this young native woman. Terrett leaped on her. I thought he was just trying to frighten her but then he tied her to a tree and ..."

Zac spat then took another long drink from the water pouch. He continued in a low voice. Thomas had to strain to hear.

"I tried to get him off her but he clobbered me so hard I didn't feel my head hit the ground. When I came to he was still at her."

Zac's chest began to heave and he tipped his head to the side and brought up some water. Thomas felt his own stomach clench. Terrett was an animal.

"Sorry," Zac mumbled. "I still have nightmares about what he did to that poor girl. But that wasn't the worst of it. He came and pulled me to my feet by my hair. He dragged me over and made me look at her and then he said … He told me if I spoke a word of it he'd do my sister the same."

Thomas leaped to his feet. "Bastard!" His roar echoed across the creek.

Zac continued to talk. Fury burned inside Thomas. He didn't want to hear any more but he knew he must.

"From then on I couldn't get enough of his grog. Anything to drown out that poor girl's cries, her big eyes pleading with me to help her, and I couldn't. Every time I closed my eyes I saw her. I thought of Lizzie. The grog knocked me out so I couldn't think any more. And then I didn't want to leave. I was frightened if I came here, he might think I'd tell you and then he'd take it out on Lizzie. I had nowhere else to go and he had the grog. I was desperate for it."

Thomas turned back to Zac, who was still sitting in the chair.

"But you did leave eventually."

"Wiltshire turned up about a week later. I was drunk and he lost his temper. He bellowed at Terrett to give me a lesson I wouldn't forget and to send me packing."

Thomas breathed deeply. Anger burned within him. That was what Terrett had bragged about.

"I still couldn't leave," Zac said. "I couldn't even walk let alone ride a horse after Terrett had finished with me. He dumped me on the edge of our boundary. I lived there for nearly a month. Gulda found me but I begged him not to tell you. He brought me food and kept an eye on me until my wounds had healed and the bruises had faded. Then I came here. I hadn't intended to stay but it was so good to be with my family again. All I had to do was keep my mouth shut. But I couldn't escape the dreams." Zac clutched his head in his hands. "Those terrible dreams."

Thomas put a gentle hand on Zac's shoulder but inside he was consumed with his own terrible rage. This was Daisy's country. The woman could be her sister or cousin. Whoever the poor girl was, it made him sick to the stomach to think about Terrett and what he'd done. Septimus Wiltshire was an underhanded crook but surely even he wouldn't condone Terrett's actions.

Thomas squatted down in front of Zac and pulled his hands from his face.

"You didn't carry out the vile act, Zac, and you did your best to prevent it. You must stop blaming yourself."

Zac slowly raised his head. He met Thomas's gaze and Thomas knew he'd been right earlier. He could see a purpose in Zac's eyes that had been missing for months.

"Lizzie pulled me out of that waterhole and then last night she sat with me. She was there whenever I woke. I found myself thinking of her instead of myself. She would walk over hot coals for me. I know I have to do more than that in return."

Thomas gripped Zac's hands and shook them. "You'll be all right, Zac, and so will Lizzie." He stood up. "I'm going to have it out with this Wiltshire."

Zac stood too. "But he could be anywhere. I heard enough of his talk to know he's got his greedy fingers in many pies."

"I'm going to start in Port Augusta. I think he might have a house there."

"He does. I've seen it. A small whitewashed cottage not far from the wharf." Zac's eyes flared with excitement. "I'll come with you."

"No." Thomas put up a hand. "I want you to stay here with Lizzie and Joseph."

Zac held his gaze. "Do you trust me?"

Thomas saw the doubt cross his brother-in-law's face. He clapped a hand on Zac's shoulder. "With their lives."

Zac nodded and they moved up the slope towards the house.

"No a word of any of this to Lizzie," Thomas said. "She will still think I'm going to the port on business as planned."

"I'll look out for her."

"Gulda will help. And Zac –"

They each paused mid stride.

"I'm leaving you the firearm."

Forty-nine

Septimus nestled his head into Dulcie's soft breasts. He sighed. It was so peaceful here in his little hut in the hills. His halfway house, just a few days by horse from his property in the north and a day from his house at Port Augusta. He smiled to himself. A secret hideaway complete with his obliging Dulcie. It didn't matter to her what time of day it was.

She had quickly learned discretion in the early days but as soon as Harriet had moved to Port Augusta she had taken over the little house, seeing to his every need whenever he visited. Dulcie had become his second wife. He enjoyed the thought of being master of two women.

He shifted his head to see the glow of dawn lighting the sky through the window. Dulcie stirred beneath him and began to stroke his hair.

"Ahh. My sweet," he murmured and rested his head again.

After breakfast he would go and inspect his latest investment. He was having a small stone inn built a mile or so away on the edge of the track that the bullockies had forged through the rugged hills. Not only did the new track shorten his journey north, it also brought a lot more traffic along the road. His inn would be a day's ride from Port Augusta and close to permanent water, the perfect place for bullock teams to break their journey.

Septimus sucked in a breath as Dulcie's hands left his head and slithered down his back and then lower. He rolled over and pulled her on top of him. There was plenty of time before he met with the builder. He smiled up at Dulcie and cupped her beautiful full breasts in his hands. Right now he didn't want to think of anything but the pleasure she brought to his body.

Several hours later, Septimus walked through the building that was to be his inn. From the front door he could see along the track in both directions and down the valley to the creek. It was perfectly positioned to be seen by traffic approaching from either direction. Only problem was it had no roof.

"One more week," he said to the man he'd put in charge of the building. He'd taken Burrows on because he'd been able to get him cheap. To Septimus's surprise, the construction had initially developed well; but since his last visit, little had been done.

"More like two or three, Mr Wiltshire."

Septimus stepped down from the verandah that ran right around the building. It was only the builder and him. No workers to be seen.

"Where are your men?" he asked.

Burrows's eyes shifted back and forth. "I gave them the day off. They've hardly stopped in a month."

Septimus pulled himself up tall. It was hopeless trying to hold the fool's gaze the way his eyes moved. "We had an agreement," he said. "You signed on it. The inn was to be ready for use by the last day of April."

"There were some difficulties getting the –"

"Don't give me excuses, Burrows." Septimus scowled. "You will get your money only when the job is complete – and only what we agreed."

"But –"

"If it takes longer you work for nothing." Septimus didn't raise his voice. "I will be back in a week with the supplies and my inn-keeper. I expect to be open for business on the first day of May."

"Yes, Mr Wiltshire."

"Good. If that's clear, I won't hold you up any longer."

Burrows nodded and scurried away in the direction of the trees, where his tools were set out in a makeshift work area. Before long, Septimus heard the sound of sawing. If the fool gave his workers a day off, he'd have to do their share and his. It was of no consequence to Septimus. Even if the building wasn't ready as stated, it would cost him no more. He could serve peo-ple from the verandah if he had to. One way or another, he expected to be profiting from the passing teamsters by the start of next month.

He turned back to survey the building again. Harriet hadn't been to see it but she had looked at the plan with him. It had been her suggestion to make the verandah wide and have it go all the way around the building. No matter which direction the sun shone or where the wind blew, there would be a place to take shade and either enjoy the breeze or be protected from it.

He had to concede Harriet had a brain for things like that. Strange that he'd tried so hard to get rid of her in those early days on the road together. She had proved to have all kinds of assets that were of use to him. She was never idle. Now that she lived in the town and had more time on her hands, she had begun sewing again. She had offered to make curtains for the inn. He thought that too much expense but she had convinced him that comfort-able patrons would take more time – and spend more coin.

He'd been away for a month but the thought of Harriet didn't tempt him as it had. Her body was an asset he no longer desired so much. When he was with her he thought of Dulcie. She was more to his liking – and he didn't have to share her with a lily-livered child.

Septimus cast one last look over the inn then mounted his horse and turned it back towards the farm. Yes, he'd have one more night with the delectable Dulcie before he made the journey to Port Augusta and all the duties that awaited him there.

Harriet put down her sewing and listened. The steady crunch of boots on the gravel path had to be male. She jumped as the door flung open.

"Septimus!" she cried. "I expected you days ago." The words were out before she could stop them.

"I was delayed in the hills." He glared at her. "I've been busy looking after my investments."

"Of course." Harriet was quick to soften her tone. "I was just concerned for you, that's all."

"You know my work keeps me on the road."

"Yes, Septimus." She hurried to help him out of his jacket. Perhaps something had happened with his new building. "Is everything all right? The inn?"

"The inn is coming along fine."

She was surprised by his harsh tone. Once she had easily judged his moods but his last few visits home had been short and he'd been hard to read.

Septimus poked his head into the kitchen. "Where's the boy?"

"Henry's outside."

"Has he been practising his letters and numbers?"

"Yes, Septimus, but you mustn't forget he's still young." She pulled her face into a smile.

"If he's to take over my business one day," Septimus thumped the back of his armchair, "he needs to know how to read and count."

"And he will." Harriet glanced towards the kitchen. She hoped Henry would stay outside a little longer. She tried to get him to practise every day as Septimus had commanded on his last visit home, but the child much preferred to play.

"He must practise." Septimus thumped the chair again.

"He does." Thankfully Henry was a quick learner, but she knew he'd stutter if his father pressed him and that made Septimus angry. "Can I make you a cup of tea? I have some currant buns fresh from the oven."

"Don't fuss, Harriet," he snapped.

She looked around for something else to distract him. Her sewing lay on the small table beside her chair.

"I've nearly finished the curtains for the inn." She picked up the blue and white checked fabric. "Perhaps I could come with you next time you visit. I can hang –"

"No!"

Harriet jumped.

He snatched up his jacket. "I've got business at the port. Save me some supper. I'll eat later. And Harriet …"

He stopped at the door and turned back to her. She looked into his cold grey eyes.

"Don't wait up for me."

She listened as the crunch of his boots faded. When she was sure he was gone she slid into his armchair. Life was much simpler when Septimus wasn't at home. Henry was happier; she had far less to worry over. She enjoyed having the time to sew and she'd had several new clients just in the last week.

When they'd first moved to Port Augusta she'd been one of the few white women there. Now there were more families and other men were making money too. That meant their wives were spending it on dresses, pretty bonnets, curtains for windows and tablecloths. Harriet particularly enjoyed embroidering delicate flowers on table linen and she was getting a name for it. She was also careful to stash a good portion of the money it brought her. Septimus thought it a small sideline and had never questioned how much she earned. Everything they had, including the house, had been provided by him. She led a simple life but wanted for nothing. He left her money for food and household items. Even so, Harriet never felt entirely safe. Septimus was away more than he was home and she could never fully shake the fear that one day he might not return.

She bent forward and reached under the chair, feeling for the pouch she'd slid into the webbing. It was her nest egg. After all, she was no longer responsible for only herself. Henry would learn to read and write, Septimus expected that as did she, but Henry would also be cultured and refined. None of the rough and dirty beginnings she and Septimus had lived through would touch her son. Harriet would make sure of that.

She looked at the clock as it chimed the hour from the mantelpiece. It had been another of Septimus's acquisitions, and she had to wind it every day. Four o'clock. She was expecting Mrs Forbes, wife of Captain Forbes the harbourmaster, at any moment. She opened the glass cabinet beside the fireplace and lifted out her china tea set. The dainty blue flowers were as pretty as ever in her eyes and she always impressed her customers by offering tea in the delicate china cups. She'd embroidered napkins with flowers to match. Harriet hummed as she prepared for her visitor, Septimus's bad mood gone from her thoughts.

Only a few days later, she was preparing for his departure. It was a grey day. The wind had sprung up from the north, blowing dust and unsettling the horses. Septimus loaded his old bullock wagon with supplies for his new inn. In a horse-drawn cart sat the man he'd employed as a publican and his loud, buxom wife.

Harriet noticed Septimus wince every time the woman let out one of her raucous laughs, which was quite often. In spite of the disagreeable weather, Ethel was in good spirits and apparently looking forward to their new life in the hills.

"Don't you worry about a thing at the inn, Mrs Wiltshire." Ethel's voice was as bellicose as her laugh. "Ned and me will have it shipshape in no time. Perhaps you'll come up and visit one day."

"Mrs Wiltshire has plenty to keep her occupied here," Septimus barked. "She has no need to make the tedious journey to the hills."

"Ahh, but when she gets there she'll be able to have a little holiday from all her chores. Ned and me will look after her, won't we, Ned?" She dug her husband in the ribs. His serious expression did not so much as twitch but he nodded at Harriet. Ethel let forth another of her laughs.

Septimus stalked off around the wagon, checking again that it was tied down properly, before mounting his horse. Harriet liked Ethel. Most people wilted after one look from Septimus, but not her.

Harriet beamed. "You'll make sure the curtains are hung properly."

"Course I will, lovey."

Harriet leaned closer. "And I just might take you up on that holiday," she said, "if I'm ever not so busy here."

Ethel winked at her, but Septimus rode up and Harriet was forced to step back from the cart.

"I could be gone for a month or more," he said.

"I have plenty to keep me busy in your absence." She put on her sweetest smile.

"Make sure the boy keeps working on those letters. He can't seem to say them properly yet."

Harriet glanced back at where Henry stood on the verandah, clutching a pole with one hand, thumb in his mouth.

"Of course," she said and lifted a hand to protect her eyes as a gust of wind drove more dirt through the air. Henry wouldn't miss his father and Harriet realised she wouldn't either. Septimus hadn't looked for the comforts of her body at all on that visit. She had used to enjoy his attentions, but since Henry had been born, Septimus had become less attentive. Their coupling was rougher and over quickly: she was just as happy without. She pulled her shawl more tightly around her shoulders.

"Take what time you need," she said. "Henry and I will be well until your return."

He raised his hat and stared down at her with his icy eyes, then he tugged the reins and moved away, urging the bullocks forward. The cart with the jovial Ethel and the sombre-faced Ned followed behind.

Harriet watched a moment until Henry let out a whine behind her. She turned away from the procession and hurried him inside out of the dirty day.

Fifty

Night had fallen when Thomas reached Port Augusta. He'd ridden hard for several days and both he and his horse were exhausted. He stayed in one of the new hotels and stabled his horse out the back. The wool cheque he was expecting meant he could spend a little money.

The bed proved harder than the several nights he'd spent in his swag. Thomas was restless and couldn't fall asleep. Zac's story was never far from his thoughts: what was he to do about Terrett? He prayed that Wiltshire would get rid of the man, but in truth Thomas wasn't sure how he'd react. Plenty of settlers, even honourable men such as his father-in-law, would consider the molestation of a black woman a matter of no great import. Wiltshire had already proven himself less than honourable in his dealings with the Smiths, so Thomas had little hope the incident would sway him.

Pleased to see the first light of dawn, Thomas ate a simple breakfast and decided to approach Wiltshire's house on foot. He came across a cottage just as Zac had described. There was no sign of horse or people. The house was quiet. He assumed Wiltshire still had a wife and possibly children. It would be very rash of him to batter on their door at this early hour.

He hesitated at the gate then turned and walked back along the rough path towards the port, where he would conduct his chief business. The commission agent began his day early, he knew. Along the jetty men worked to load a ketch already sitting low in the water. Further out to sea the sails of a large ocean-going clipper filled with the breeze. Port Augusta had been barely a village when he'd first taken his wool there. The journey was much shorter than the trek to Adelaide but there had been no other reason to visit. Now there were two hotels, a couple of wool stores, offices and shops, along with the more permanent dwellings of the people who had moved there.

Thomas stepped through the door of the small wooden office. He planned to collect his wool cheque, pay his debt and make some purchases with the little money that would be left over. Then he would tackle Wiltshire. Once that was done, he would ride for home as quickly as he could. Even though he'd meant it when he said he trusted Zac to look out for his family, he felt uneasy. Terrett was a monster and he was far too close to Wildu Creek and everything that was precious to Thomas.

"Is something wrong, Mr Baker?"

Thomas looked from the paper to the commission agent, Mr Grant. He was an officious little man wearing, as he always did, a starched white shirt and thin black tie. A pair of glasses perched on the end of his nose above a slightly curled moustache. Thomas had dealt with him on several occasions and, while he found the man aloof, he'd had no reason to doubt his business ability.

"My count says I've been paid for four fewer bales than I delivered."

"That can't be." Grant peered at him over the top of his glasses. "Let me check my file."

He leafed through a folder and pulled out another paper, then held out his hand for Thomas's copy. He studied both without speaking then opened a large ledger and leafed back through the pages.

"Here it is." Grant tapped a line of writing in the middle of a page. "The same number as recorded on your paper. The date they were loaded on the ship, and my signature." He folded his hands at the base of the page and stared at Thomas. "I count every bale as it is loaded. I hope you do not doubt my word, Mr Baker."

Thomas met his look. "I've never had reason to before, Mr Grant, but the number I've been paid for does not match the number that left my property. I counted them onto the wagon myself."

"But you didn't travel with them last time, as I recall."

"No, my brother-in-law drove the wagon." Thomas frowned.

Mr Grant closed his ledger with a thud. "I am sure you trust your brother-in-law, Mr Baker, but perhaps you need to take it up with him."

Thomas frowned. Even though the money he'd been paid for his wool this year had risen, the loss of those bales had a big impact on his plans for Wildu Creek. A year earlier, without telling Lizzie, he'd borrowed money from Grant against this wool cheque. It was a gamble that had paid off, in spite of the poor weather conditions. Not as well as it would have with those extra four bales, of course.

Grant clasped his hands over the ledger. "Is there anything else I can do for you today, Mr Baker?"

"I wish to pay the debt I owe."

"That's good to hear, Mr Baker, but I no longer hold your note."

Thomas leaned forward. "What do you mean?"

"I held notes for several pastoralists and was concerned I had over-stretched myself. I sold some off, yours included."

"Who to?"

"I sold to a few different backers." Grant stood up. "I'll have to look it up."

Thomas watched as the man pulled a wooden box from a drawer and began to look through the papers it contained. The morning was not going to plan at all.

Thomas did trust Zac, but he had been in a bad way when he'd driven those loaded wagons to Port Augusta. Thomas hadn't realised how bad. Perhaps he'd sold some bales on the side to buy his grog and the makings of his still. No – if he had, he'd have money left over. After his recent unburdening, Thomas felt sure Zac would have told him if he had stolen the bales.

Thomas had had no idea back then just how much Zac had been drinking. He'd found Zac baled up by a Port Augusta constable for drunken behaviour. Thomas had managed to talk the constable into releasing Zac into his care, and they'd gone back to where Zac had been sleeping under the wagon on the edge of town. The bullocks had hardly been fed. Zac had been a pitiful mess, having drunk his meagre earnings. There had certainly been no sign that he'd had extra money to spend.

It was a puzzle that led Thomas in circles. He could do nothing until he spoke to Zac.

"Mr Septimus Wiltshire."

Grant's voice cut into his thoughts. Thomas glared at the agent. "Septimus Wiltshire?" he repeated.

"That's correct."

The name hammered in Thomas's head. The very man who had fleeced the Smiths of their lease and who Thomas suspected had also gone by the name Seth Whitby, held a note of debt over Wildu Creek.

"He has a house here in the port."

"I know where he lives." Thomas pushed back his chair and lurched to his feet.

"You have the money, of course, so it shouldn't be a problem."

Thomas gave the hand Grant offered a quick shake and left the office deep in thought. Outside the sun was a ball of yellow in a brilliant blue sky. He pushed his hat onto his head and stopped on the edge of the road as a bullock dray loaded with bales of wool rumbled past. He gripped a hitching rail with both hands. Somehow this Wiltshire seemed to keep taking possession of things he shouldn't have.

Thomas now had two reasons to visit the man. The problem of Terrett must be dealt with and now the debt repaid. He had a busy day ahead. Lizzie had given him a list and he had his own idea for something special for her, but there was also equipment and livestock to be purchased, and far less money than expected with which to do it.

As well as all that he had to find a new shepherd. He hoped he would find someone as easily as AJ had found him all those years back.

None of those errands, however, held his interest. His debt and the person who covered it occupied his thoughts. It was time to meet Septimus Wiltshire face to face.

Fifty-one

Harriet was surprised to see a man hesitate at her front gate then step in. She rarely got gentleman callers. Septimus conducted all his business at the wharf and her customers were always ladies, except on the odd occasion when one of their husbands came to pay for their purchases.

She leaned back from her window. The man was tall and wore the clothes of a bushman. Perhaps he wanted to spend money on something for his wife. He knocked on her door. Even though she expected it, she jumped at the sharpness of the sound.

She turned to the little boy playing on the floor. "Henry, the oatmeal biscuits will be cool enough to eat now," she said. "Take your train into the kitchen and you may have one biscuit."

He obeyed instantly. He was used to his mother having callers. Harriet slid her old shawl from her shoulders. She had a much nicer one now but she wore the green on cool days about the house. She laid the shawl over a dining chair and straightened her dress.

The knock came again. Harriet opened the door and looked up at her visitor. She paused briefly. There was something vaguely familiar about him. He removed his hat to reveal thick dark hair. It was neatly groomed in spite of the rugged look of his attire.

"Good morning," he said. "Mrs Wiltshire?"

"I am. Have you come on business, Mr …?"

"Baker, Thomas Baker."

Harriet hesitated a moment. Had she heard the name some-where before?

"Please come in, Mr Baker." She stepped back and cast her mind over the items she might be able to show him ready for immediate purchase. She sold most of her needlework for a decent price. His jacket was the thick brown variety favoured by men of the bush. His shirt was flannel and his trousers well worn. He didn't look like a man with money to spare.

Thomas stepped into the front room and glanced around. "I was hoping to speak with your husband," he said.

"Oh." It didn't look as though she was going to get a sale after all. "My husband isn't here, Mr Baker. His work takes him away from home a lot."

"When do you expect him back?"

"Not for a month or more. You've only just missed him. He's been gone but a few days."

Baker stopped in front of her. A frown creased his brow. He reached a hand towards her neck.

Harriet gasped and took a small step back.

"Where did you get that locket?" he asked.

Harriet put her fingers to the gold heart. "It was a gift from my husband."

Baker glanced around the room as if he thought Septimus might suddenly appear.

Harriet set her jaw. She was beginning to wish she hadn't let this stranger in. His eyes searched everywhere. Perhaps he was planning to rob her.

"My wife said you loaned her a book."

"Your wife?" Harriet had no idea what Baker was talking about.

"You visited her family property a few years ago, before we were married. Her name was Lizzie Smith."

"Oh! I remember her –"

"You gave her a book. Just like these." Thomas plucked a book from the shelf beside the door and leafed through it. "With my mother's name in it." He thrust the open book under her nose. "The page seems to be gone."

Harriet didn't look down. She knew Septimus had ripped the page with the name from each book long ago.

Baker's eyes narrowed. He snapped the book shut. "Very strange, isn't it, Mrs Wiltshire? The page that bore my mother's name is missing. And you wear a locket exactly like the one my father gave my mother on their wedding day."

"I cannot explain it, Mr Baker, but I would like you to leave now," she said. "I am expecting Captain Harrison's wife to call." The lady wasn't coming until the afternoon but Harriet hoped the imminent arrival of an important caller might encourage her unwelcome visitor to leave.

He ignored her. Instead, he strode across the room to her little glass cabinet. "Where did you get this?"

Harriet stared at her precious china tea set, the one Septimus had let her keep from the big trunk. The trunk that she assumed hadn't been his but hadn't asked any questions about. Baker turned to her but before she could speak he snatched up her old shawl from the chair.

"And this?"

Harriet's heart began to beat faster. Baker's eyes were fierce.

"These are all gifts from my husband, Mr Baker. He …" Harriet was suddenly back under the wagon the day Pig Boy had raped her.

This was the man Septimus had bumped into that day. Even though the man glowering at her across the room was more solid, and had an air of strength about him that he'd lacked back then, she recognised him now – Thomas Baker. That had been the name he'd said.

Thomas stepped across the room towards her. Harriet stood her ground. "Where did your husband acquire all these things?"

Once again she put her hand to her locket as his gaze swept down to it then back to meet her eyes. "That is none of your business, I'm sure."

"It is most certainly my business, Mrs Wiltshire. These things –" He swung his arm out in a wide arc. "The books, the china, the shawl." He waved it under her nose. "These items were all my mother's, all stored in a trunk that was stolen from me by a man named Seth Whitby. A name very like Septimus Wiltshire." His deep brown eyes glowered at her.

She swallowed. "My husband is not Seth Whitby and I know nothing about your trunk," she said. The very trunk now stood in the corner of the room full of fabric and threads for her sewing. She glanced in that direction. It was almost completely covered by a long cushion so that it could also be used as a seat. She moved towards the door, drawing Baker's attention away. "As my husband is not home I think you should leave, Mr Baker."

Harriet spoke with a firmness she didn't feel. She could see Baker was struggling to keep his emotion in check.

"Your husband runs a lease in the Flinders Ranges, Mrs Wiltshire."

"I know little about my husband's business."

"So it seems." Baker gave a soft snort. "Nevertheless, the property is called Smith's Ridge and borders mine." The man's eyes blazed but his voice was low. "He has an overseer called Terrett, who has done some terrible things. Tell your husband he must remove the man or I will call in the law."

"I really don't know how soon –"

"Just tell him," Baker cut her off. "And when he next visits Smith's Ridge, he can call on me. It seems, in yet another unlikely coincidence, I owe him a debt and I'd like to repay it as soon as possible."

He looked briefly at her fingers fiddling with the locket, glanced again around the room then turned for the door.

Harriet moved swiftly to shut it behind him and draw the bolt. Thomas Baker hadn't threatened her and yet she felt uneasy. She put her back to the door, closed her eyes and leaned against it. "Septimus, what have you got us tangled up in?" she murmured.

A small sound made her eyes flick open. Standing in the kitchen doorway was Henry, his train hanging at his side, one thumb in his mouth, watching her with big round eyes.

Fifty-two

"Ready, Timothy?" Thomas lifted his hat and raised his eyebrows at the young man driving his new cart.

The lad gave a nod and encouraged the horse forward. Thomas took his horse to the front, leading the way as he'd done each day since they'd departed Port Augusta. His visit to Wiltshire's house had answered none of his questions. He'd stalked back into town with frustration gnawing in his chest. Unable to have it out with the man, he'd thrown his energy into completing his business in the port and left that same afternoon.

He had selected Timothy Castles as the best of a motley group of young men eager to work as a shepherd. He was the youngest of a family of seven boys and his parents were happy for him to find work away from the port. He was confident with horses, and went with Thomas to select a gelding to pull the new cart. Thomas hoped that understanding would also transfer to the sheep that Timothy would be working with.

The cart was partitioned with a wooden gate. The ram Thomas had bought was tethered in the back section and the front was piled high with provisions, including a small mulberry tree wobbling along on the side where the ram couldn't reach it. It wasn't ideal but he wanted to travel quickly and get home as soon as possible.

They had made good time. Timothy had been efficient and eager to please. He was up and ready to go first thing each morning. Thomas hoped they'd make Wildu Creek before nightfall.

The thought of Terrett, what he'd done and the threats he'd made, still troubled Thomas. He'd called in to see the constable and explained what Zac had told him about Terrett's treatment of the native girl. The constable hadn't been too interested and even less so when he remembered Zac as a drunkard. He'd told Thomas that without a reliable witness there was little he could do. Thomas had been enraged: something had to be done about the girl's fate. Thomas just hadn't worked out what yet. After that he hadn't bothered to mention the theft of his mother's possessions. He had no way to identify the items. It was this Septimus Wiltshire he needed to meet. Every troubled thought led back to him.

Between Wiltshire, Terrett and the loss of the income from four bales of wool, Thomas had plenty to occupy his mind on the journey home. They made the dry creek that marked the beginning of Wildu Creek just after midday. Thomas resisted the urge to gallop ahead and instead reined his horse in under the shade of some trees.

"This is where Wildu Creek begins," he said.

Timothy climbed down from the cart and rubbed his behind. "I'm glad to be here at last," he said. "It looks like good country."

"It's much drier than it was when we first arrived, but there are permanent waterholes for the sheep and plenty of bluebush for them to eat when the grass is low. This creek marks our southern boundary. To the east and north we're hemmed in by mountains and vegetation; to the west our boundary lines up with a small ridge. That's the start of our neighbour's lease – Smith's Ridge."

Thomas cast his eyes in the direction of the hazy brown outcrop above Wiltshire's run. With the help of another shepherd,

Thomas planned to spend more of his own time along that boundary. He didn't trust Terrett. He looked in the direction of his home. Now that he was on his own land again he was anxious to see Lizzie and Joseph.

His horse turned in a circle, stirring up the dust. Thomas could wait no longer. "I'm going to ride ahead," he said. "Once you've rested, work your way across the plain. You'll see the tracks made by our wagon. You'll come to a creek. Follow it up through the low hills and our little settlement will be visible through the trees."

Timothy nodded.

"If you tether the ram to the back of the cart it can walk the rest of the way."

"Good idea, Mr Baker. I might do the same. My behind's still numb from the seat of that cart." He gave Thomas a wry grin.

"Mrs Baker will have a meal ready for you when you arrive."

Thomas gave Timothy one last look then turned his horse for home. Unease had built in his chest. He wouldn't be happy until he saw his family again, safe and sound.

The small relief he felt at the first sign of smoke above the trees turned to suspicion at the sight of a strange horse tethered in the bush well before the house. Whose was it, and why would someone leave their horse such a distance away?

Thomas moved his own horse at walking pace. There was no sign of the rider. He rode on, searching the bush and trees as he went. It was very quiet: too quiet. Just before he reached the place where his house would come into view, he dismounted and tethered his own horse. He slid his whip from its holder and made his way on foot. He rounded the last of the thicker bushes and looked up the slope. There was no sign of Lizzie or Zac or Gulda. He shook off his fear. The men were most likely off with the sheep and Lizzie out the back in her garden.

Thomas reached the clear ground in front of his house. There was no one at the seats by the creek where Lizzie often worked in the fresh air. The silence was unsettling. The door to the house was open. His heart gave an extra thump at the sight of a basket of washing tipped over on the verandah with its contents spilled out onto the dirt. Then he heard a laugh that made his blood go cold.

Terrett's goading voice came from somewhere beyond the house.

"Come on, you weak excuse for a man."

Thomas edged along the side of the house, his whip firmly gripped in his hand. He peered around the corner. Fear flooded through him. Lizzie was sprawled on the ground, not moving. Zac stood just beyond her. His back was to Thomas but he held the firearm pointing off to the side. Thomas couldn't see what he was aiming at but he assumed it was Terrett.

Lizzie's head was twisted back towards Thomas. He scanned her again. The bodice of her dress was ripped and there was blood on her cheek, but he saw her eyelids flutter then the small movement of one hand. Thank the Lord she wasn't dead. Thomas cast another look over his wife then eased his way back around the house to come at Terrett from the other side.

Zac had the gun but Thomas wasn't sure of his state of mind. Terrett was goading the younger man, calling him all kinds of names. The noise he was making, he wouldn't hear Thomas coming. Thomas reached the other side of his house and once more peered around the corner. Terrett was just in front of him and further to the right was Zac, side on.

"You'd trade your sister for some booze, wouldn't you, Zaccy boy?" Terrett said.

Thomas saw the muscles in Zac's arms stiffen, as did his own.

Terrett howled in surprise and fell to his knees as the whip wrapped around his body.

Thomas stepped up in front of him, gripping the handle of the whip as Terrett twisted back and forth. "If you've harmed my wife, you mongrel, I'll horsewhip you from here to Port Augusta."

"She'll be all right." Zac's voice was low but edged with steel.

Thomas flicked a glance at his brother-in-law. He had stepped closer, his finger rested on the firing pin of the weapon he aimed at Terrett's head. Beyond him Lizzie was struggling to sit up.

"The same can't be said for the poor native woman you brutalised, Terrett," Zac growled. "You'll die for that and for coming here, wanting to do the same to my sister."

Thomas felt a small ripple of relief. It sounded as if Zac had stopped Terrett from harming Lizzie.

"You haven't got the guts," Terrett spat.

Thomas looked back to Zac. Terrett was wrong. He'd only ever known him as half the man he was capable of being.

"Don't do it, Zac," Thomas said quietly. "We'll hand him over and let the law deal with him."

Zac snorted but he didn't shift his look from Terrett. "The law doesn't care about the natives," he said. "You know that. The only justice she'll get is whatever I dish out."

"You're not man enough," Terrett sneered. "If your brother-in-law hadn't come along, I'd have done you by now and then had your sister."

Zac's finger moved slightly on the firing pin.

"It takes a bigger man to hold off, Zac." Thomas spoke again. "I'll make sure they listen."

His brother-in-law kept his steely glare on Terrett then he lowered the firearm a little.

"I told you you were too weak." Terrett began to laugh a terrible laugh that was cut short as Thomas's fist connected with the side of his face. He fell to the ground, where Zac kicked him in the stomach. They stood over him together. His piggy eyes rolled in his head, then shut.

"Stop."

Thomas and Zac both turned at the sound of Lizzie's voice. She had made it to her feet. Thomas groaned at the sight of her ripped blouse and bloodied cheek. He crossed the space between them and wrapped her in his arms.

In the brief silence, Joseph's sleepy cry came from the direction of the house.

"We'll let the law deal with Mr Terrett," Lizzie said.

Joseph's wail grew louder. She eased from his embrace and limped inside.

Thomas watched the door close behind her before he turned back to the vile man spread eagled at his feet. He poked Terrett with his boot. He didn't move but Thomas could see the rise and fall of his chest.

Zac broke the silence. "I'm sorry. I wasn't gone long, but he must have been biding his time, watching the place. He knew you were away and must have seen that Gulda and Daisy are working the east side."

"What happened?" Every muscle in Thomas's body tensed. Anger continued to simmer inside him.

"I came back from checking the sheep down by the house creek." Zac paused and gripped the firearm so tightly his knuckles went white. "I was just in time to see him dragging Lizzie around the house."

"Dear God." The thought of Terrett even laying a finger on Lizzie had Thomas's hands curling into fists again.

"He didn't see me." Zac's lips turned up. "She bit him and he gave her a backhander just as I got there with the firearm."

"He'll pay for that," Thomas snarled.

"A few bruises and scratches. I'll live." Lizzie was back with a fresh shirt, the blood gone from the cut on her cheek and a bleary-eyed Joseph in her arms.

"What about your head? You were knocked out." Thomas put a finger to the cut on her cheek.

"I must have hit my head on the wall when he shoved me away. Caught my cheek on a rock. I feel fine, Thomas, really."

They stood in a circle, all looking down upon the motionless form of Terrett.

"What'll we do with him?" Zac asked.

"Hello?" a voice called. Thomas's new shepherd walked around the hut. He stopped, his face full of alarm.

"You found your way then, Timothy." Thomas grinned. The tension eased out of him. "This is our new shepherd, Timothy Castles." Thomas put an arm around Lizzie. "This is my wife, Lizzie, my son, Joseph, and the fellow with the firearm is my brother-in-law, Zac."

Timothy looked at each of them then gaped down at Terrett. "And who's that?" he asked.

They all stared at Terrett, who was beginning to moan.

"Our neighbour."

"An animal."

Lizzie and Thomas both spoke at once.

"He's lower than an animal." Zac growled and pushed Terrett back as he tried to sit himself up.

"Bring me that rope by the back door, Timothy," Thomas said.

They bound Terrett's feet. Thomas removed the whip and then used the rest of the rope to tie his hands.

"He can stay out here under the tree for now," Thomas said once they had the groaning Terrett securely tethered. Thomas rolled his shoulders and looked around. The last of the light was quickly leaving the sky. "I'll take him in the new cart to the constable in Port Augusta tomorrow."

"You've just got home." Lizzie looked at him, her face full of concern.

"I'll go," Zac said.

"I know you would." Thomas shook his head. "I'm sorry, Zac, but after your last trip to Port Augusta, the constable won't take your word very easily." He turned to his new shepherd. "Timothy, it will have to be you and me. You can ride ahead. I'll write a letter for you to give the constable. Get him to come and meet me along the way."

Timothy beamed. "Sure thing, Mr Baker. A horse will be better than that wooden cart seat. My backside's still numb." He paused and looked at Lizzie. "Beg your pardon, Mrs Baker."

Lizzie laughed. How Thomas loved that sound and how relieved he was, she appeared unharmed.

"I think we'll all need a decent meal tonight," she said.

Joseph was happier now, and squirming to get out of her arms. Thomas saw her wince. He took the child from her but before he could speak, she cut him off.

"I'll go and prepare the meal while you men show Timothy where he's to sleep, and get yourselves cleaned up."

Thomas watched her walk away. She wasn't moving at her usual quick pace. Joseph began to wriggle, trying to get to the ground. Thomas let him slide down his body then took him by the hand. Zac took his nephew's other hand. The little boy swung between them all the way to the original hut, where Zac now slept. The men had added a second room for the new shepherd.

"It's nothing fancy, I'm afraid," Thomas said as the lad stepped inside.

Timothy turned full circle then looked back at Thomas, his mouth open. "But it's my own room," he gasped. "I've never had a room all to myself before."

Thomas laughed at the joy on the lad's face. "Welcome to Wildu Creek," he said.

Fifty-three

After the meal, Timothy, happy to entertain Joseph, quickly made a friend of him. The little boy eventually fell asleep in his arms.

"Time for us to turn in," Zac said. "It was a wonderful meal as usual, Lizzie."

"Yes, thank you, Mrs Baker," Timothy said.

Thomas took the sleeping child from his arms.

"I'll check Terrett is still secure on my way," Zac said.

Thomas nodded. He'd already taken some bread and water to the man and checked him then. Terrett had roared abuse for quite a while after that but he'd quietened down again now. Joseph curled into a ball as Thomas tucked him into his cot. He ran a hand over his son's fair head, the same colour as his mother's. How different this homecoming might have been, had he taken longer, or had Zac been occupied elsewhere. Thomas pushed the terrible thoughts from his mind.

"I think you've chosen well with your new shepherd," Lizzie said when he went back to the kitchen. "Timothy's a bright young man."

"Keen to learn."

"He reminds me a little of you when we first met." Lizzie chuckled and collected the plates from the table.

"Was I that green?"

"Yes, and look at you now. You have your own run and sheep from here to beyond."

"I don't know, Lizzie. I hope I'm not chasing something that will always be outside our reach."

"Why do you say that?" She came and sat beside him again.

"Our wool cheque was a few bales short." Since George's loss to Wiltshire, Lizzie had been dead against borrowing money, and now Thomas had all the more reason not to tell her about his loan.

"How could that happen?"

"I don't know. I want to talk to Zac about it."

"You don't think he –"

"No." Thomas had been over and over it in his head and he couldn't believe Zac had anything to do with it. "He might be able to fill in some gaps between leaving here and unloading at the port, that's all. Anyway, it means I've perhaps spent too much in taking on Timothy and buying the new ram."

"Losing a few wool bales won't be the end of us."

"The provisions will have to stretch further."

"We never go without, Thomas."

"I know, but I wanted to get something for you and Joseph. The last time I bought you a gift it didn't turn out so well."

Lizzie laughed. "Nothing wrong with my straw bonnet."

Thomas glanced at the fraying hat on the hook by the door. She had discovered the grubby calico bag he'd brought home on that first trek with the sheep before he'd been able to get rid of it. She'd packed the dress for Annie in a trunk, hoping there'd be another little girl one day and wore the hat often. The ribbon that secured it in place made it the best thing for windy days, she said.

"I'm happy with my new mulberry tree. I'm going to plant it among the vegetables."

Thomas shook his head slowly. "You have to work so hard, Lizzie. I want better for you and for Joseph," he said.

"We've both got everything we need right here," she said and leaned close to kiss him.

Thomas kissed her back, then thought of the lovely things he'd seen at Wiltshire's house: his mother's things.

Terrett began to call out he was cold.

"Damn Wiltshire for employing such a vile man," Thomas said and gave the table a thump with his fist. "You know I missed seeing him in Port Augusta, but I went to his house. It's full of things that belonged to my mother and I'm still no wiser as to how he came to possess them."

"You spoke to his wife? Harriet?"

"Yes. There were several things in her house that were my mother's, including the heart locket Mrs Wiltshire wore around her neck. It has the letter H etched in it in a filigree pattern. The H was for Hester."

"Or for Harriet. I remember her wearing it," Lizzie said and put her fingers to the locket she still wore around her own neck. "He may have said they were his mother's to explain the name in the books. Lucky for him his new wife had a name beginning with H."

"Damn the man." Thomas rubbed at the thick stubble on his chin. "First he sells me a stolen horse then he takes my trunk load of family possessions." He frowned. And now a man he didn't trust held their note of debt. "I must have been a fool."

"Just a bit green." Lizzie laughed and gave him a gentle poke. "It's in the past."

Terrett bellowed loudly.

The smile left her face and she shivered.

Thomas stood up. "I should just leave him, but we'll get no peace tonight if I do."

"I'll get a blanket."

"No. We've got little enough for ourselves. I'll drag the canvas from the wagon over him."

When he came back inside, Lizzie was sitting on the edge of the bed. Only a candle lit the room. Her cheek was purple around the cut and wet with tears.

"Lizzie," he said. "What is it? Are you sure Terrett didn't … harm you."

She shook her head. "Gave me a fright. Knocked me about a bit. That's all."

He sat beside her and pulled her close. "My dear sweet brave Lizzie. I'd like to kill him myself. Part of me wishes I'd let Zac do it."

"Then you'd both be as bad," Lizzie whispered. "Neither of you are that kind of man."

He stroked her hair. Rage simmered within him as it had when he'd found her sprawled on the ground and Terrett baled up by Zac. He'd kept it in check until Terrett had let forth with his goading laugh. Thomas had hit him and had wanted to keep hitting him and he knew Zac had felt the same. Perhaps they were barely better than the man they detested.

"I'll be all right," she said and eased from his arms.

He watched her pull herself carefully upright. Then she turned her smile on him. "We'd better get to bed. You have another early start in the morning."

Thomas unbuttoned his shirt, turning as she shrugged out of her dress. There was a deep bruise on her arm. He went to her and gently removed her shift. She shivered before him. Thomas let out a groan at the sight of several other bruises on her body.

"That bastard," he muttered and helped her slide under the covers. He lay beside her and gently held her.

"I'll be glad once you've taken Mr Terrett away," Lizzie whispered. "Promise me you'll take care, Thomas. He is an evil man."

Thomas felt her shiver again. Carefully he held her tighter and kissed the top of her head.

"I will, my darling Lizzie. I will."

Fifty-four

"This is getting worse and worse." Rix spat a fly from his mouth. "How much further?" he called.

Septimus drew in a breath, stopped his horse and waited for the wagon to roll to a stop beside him. "We've been on Smith's Ridge country since we came through that last stand of tall gum trees above the creek. You're nearly home, Mr Rix."

"Home." Rix went to spit again but with Septimus right beside him he thought better of it. "I told you Pavey and me preferred town life to being out here."

"Had you minded *my* business and kept *your* mouths shut you could still be in Port Augusta, but the constable somehow got wind of our last cargo."

Rix flung a look at Pavey, who was on another horse droving the sheep Septimus had purchased.

"You'll be out of sight up here," Septimus said. "We'll all have to keep our noses clean for a while."

He was still angry over the constable's discovery of the extra exports in the last two ships to dock at the port. Rix had become too brash and Pavey too slack. Septimus had lost a lot of money in the confiscation of those goods but he couldn't step up and claim them. They hadn't been his in the first place and the owners might recognise them. No, it was best they let their port dealings go for a while until things cooled down.

Fortunately for him, his new inn had done well in its first few months of trading, despite the dry winter, and he still had Smith's Ridge and the potential it offered. Terrett had done a good job of managing the place but the fool had mistreated a native. Septimus thought of the sweet delights offered by his own dear Dulcie. There was no need for violence. The pompous Baker had trussed Terrett, tied him in a sheep pen and delivered him to the constable.

"Lucky for you I need a new overseer and with the extra stock I've bought, there will be more than enough work for two shepherds. Neales will be glad to see you."

The frown was still firmly stuck on Rix's face. "We've no experience with sheep."

"I am confident you'll learn." Septimus leaned forward in the saddle. "If you want to keep working for me."

Rix scowled but didn't say any more.

"Onward," Septimus commanded. "We want to make the homestead before dark." At least he wouldn't have to listen to Rix's complaints for much longer. He rode off to the other side of the mob of sheep. He'd used his inn money to purchase them at a good price from yet another farmer who'd fallen on hard times. Septimus smiled. How often had he made money over the years from someone else's misfortune or mismanagement? There were many fools to be fleeced in this country. He patted his saddlebag. It contained several notes of debt he held over properties. One in particular was his prize possession.

The smile left his face a few miles further on when he got down from his horse to check the bodies of two sheep. Flies buzzed all over them and maggots crawled out of their eye sockets. The stench from their swollen bellies was sickening. He moved a few feet away and surveyed the rough country around him. There was not a blade of grass to be seen. There were more carcasses off in the distance. Neales would have some explaining to do.

The late-afternoon sun pounded down and reflected back at them from the rocky ridge above as they reached the hut.

The wagon rolled to a stop. Rix groaned. "You call this a homestead?"

Septimus watched him try to spit with no result. "There's another job for you." Septimus climbed down from his horse. "You can build a new hut."

He looked around. There was debris of human habitation everywhere but no sign of Neales. The carcass of a sheep hung from a tree in the shade with one leg missing. Only one of the water barrels remained upright with a lid on it. Bones were scattered by the fire with tin plates and upturned wooden boxes. Away to one side was a stinking mound of wool crawling with maggots.

Septimus stepped up to the rough, one-roomed dwelling and kicked the door with his boot. The smell of stale sweat and rotten food wafted around him. He put his sleeve to his nose. The hut had two raised wooden boards that served as beds, and was carpeted with a jumble of clothing, dirty plates and food scraps, but Neales wasn't among it. Septimus stepped around Rix, who was trying to see inside.

"You might need to live under the canvas until you can build a new hut," he called over his shoulder.

Rix growled in response. For the next few hours, Septimus sat in the shade of a tree, taking sips of water and watching Rix clean out the hut. Pavey kept out of his way, busy unloading the wagon and stacking the provisions in the rough lean-to behind the hut. By the time the sun was a low orange ball in the sky, he'd set a fire going. The smell of roasting meat had Septimus's stomach rumbling. One thing about Rix: he might grumble but Septimus had discovered he was reliable and kept the idiot Pavey in check most of the time. Rix was the brains and Pavey was the brawn. Up until the recent upset at the port it had worked well for all of them.

They'd just made themselves at home by the fire, sitting on the upturned boxes, plates of meat and potato on their knees, when Neales rode in.

He slithered from his horse and struggled to stand upright. He was filthy, with a temper to match.

"You've brought more sheep," he yelled.

Septimus glared at the man. When Terrett had been there he'd hardly spoken, let alone in such a manner.

"Lucky I have, Mr Neales," Septimus said in a steady tone. "You seem to have let quite a few of my other sheep die."

"There's no water and little for them to eat. Didn't you see the bodies along the way here, you fool?"

Rix gave a low growl, put down his plate and rose slowly to his feet. "You don't speak to your employer like that." His thick body was twice the bulk of Neales's, who looked much thinner than the last time Septimus had seen him.

"Who are you?" Neales pulled the hat from his head and looked from Rix to Pavey. His hair was plastered flat with sweat and a dirty brown line ran across his forehead.

"I am the new overseer. Mr Rix to you."

"That's all I need, another bloke with no brains telling me what to do."

Quick as a flash Rix crossed the space between them. He twisted Neales in a headlock.

Septimus could hear the fool gasping for breath as Rix put pressure on his neck. "Don't harm him too much, Rix," he said. "You will need him."

Rix held Neales a moment longer then let him go. Neales fell to the ground, gasping for breath. Rix put a boot on his hand and twisted it. The other man let out a guttural cry. "You ready to do what you're told, Mr Neales?"

"Yes." Neales's reply came out in a whisper.

"Good, because my friend Pavey has used some of that sheep you've helped yourself to and cooked us a fine meal." He crossed back and picked up his plate. "You got enough for this fellow, Pavey?"

"Plenty."

"There you are, Neales. You go and get cleaned up and you can come back and eat with us."

Neales struggled to his feet. The filthy clothes he was wearing were even dirtier now. He threw a cautious look at Rix then began to hobble towards the hut.

"And Neales." Rix spoke through a mouthful of food. "You can sleep under the stars tonight. Pavey and me are having the hut."

Neales disappeared into the gloom beyond the firelight. Septimus cut off another piece of meat. He placed it carefully in his mouth and began to chew. He was quite confident he could leave Smith's Ridge in the care of Rix. The next morning he'd be on his way again. He was finally going to come face to face with Thomas Baker again after all these years.

Septimus arose the next morning in a bad humour. A gusting wind had come up in the night, stirring the ash of the fire and dousing the camp in the stench from the rotting wool pile. It had infiltrated his nostrils so that he could smell nothing else and he had slept restlessly. He'd be glad to get on his horse and move on. Smith's Ridge was a money-making venture, but he found no joy in it. He certainly couldn't imagine why men would work their own leases, let alone bring wives and families to live in such desolate conditions.

Neales was boiling the billy over the fire by the time Septimus was dressed. There was no sign of Rix or Pavey.

"You've let my property run down," Septimus said as he took the mug offered by the sour-faced Neales. "Lucky I got here when I did."

"There's too many sheep for one person to manage," Neales whined. "The blacks and wild dogs help themselves and now there's little water and feed."

"I thought Terrett found some permanent water."

"Not on your land," Neales said. "It's across the boundary on Wildu Creek. Mr Baker keeps a close eye on it these days."

"You're making excuses for your lazy work. Mr Rix will soon have things back in order."

Neales gave a small snort into his tea. He squatted and stared into the fire.

His disdain irritated Septimus. "This camp was disgusting when we arrived and there's more cleaning up to be done." Septimus waved a hand towards the wool. "You can get rid of that stinking pile."

Neales continued to stare at the fire. "That wool might just save your bacon, Mr Wiltshire."

"In what way?" Septimus studied the sideways profile of his shepherd and remembered a time, years earlier, when he and Harriet had bought dirty wool from farmers, cleaned it and made a pretty penny.

"I've been cutting it from the dead sheep."

No wonder it smells so bad, Septimus thought.

"I wouldn't have thought you'd be one to throw good money after bad," Neales said. "There's not enough feed and water for the stock that's here now and you've brought more – which are already on their last legs by the look of them."

"It's your job to look after them, Neales. Make sure they improve."

Neales turned and studied him through eyes narrowed against the swirling smoke. It gave him a disturbing look.

"With no feed?"

Septimus glowered. He'd made a profit off Smith's Ridge until Terrett had been carted away. He tossed the bitter tea at the fire. Obviously this lazy scum knew nothing. Septimus couldn't stand the man or the place. "Mr Rix is in charge now," he said. "You will follow his instructions."

As Septimus spoke, his new overseer staggered from the hut. When he saw Septimus, he straightened up and strode over. "You're off then?"

Septimus nodded and Rix walked beside him to his horse.

"I'm relying on you to keep your eye on things here, Rix. The place has gone downhill since Terrett left. You will report to me when you bring the wool after shearing. I will visit you to check on things mid-year after that."

Rix scowled back at him. "You're not going to leave us here to rot, are you, Mr Wiltshire?"

"You need a place to lay low for a while. I'm offering you another chance, Rix. Bring Smith's Ridge back to scratch and we'll see how things are in Port Augusta. There's no reason we can't eventually resume our business ventures there." He leaned down. "I encouraged Terrett to make the best of the opportunities these isolated ranges provide. You've seen how wild dogs take their toll, and the blacks. My neighbour puts his unexplained stock losses down to these, if you get my meaning. Between you and me, I expect you to do what you must to turn a profit, Mr Rix."

Rix nodded slowly and Septimus noted the glint in his dark eyes. He lifted a hand in farewell. Perhaps it was fortuitous that his business had taken a turn for the worse in the port. Rix might have come to Smith's Ridge reluctantly but he would make a go of the job he'd been given, Septimus was sure of that. He squared his shoulders and turned his horse in the direction of Wildu Creek.

His nosy neighbour, Thomas Baker, had visited Harriet. She had been quite rattled by it. Worried he was going to come back and take away her precious china. Septimus had forgotten the bits and pieces she still liked to use, like that tea set and the old shawl, had come from Baker's trunk. He cared little. It was long ago and Baker could prove nothing. Septimus had torn the inscribed pages from the books. Let Baker make his allegations if that's what he wanted – get it over and done with. Septimus knew the note of debt he had safely in his bag gave him the upper hand now.

Baker had been busy during his trip to the port. Septimus had heard he'd also made enquiries about missing wool bales. There was no way he'd be able to trace them. That was the one part of his port business still under way. He had another means, unknown to Rix and Pavey.

Septimus had discovered he knew the man sneaking unmarked bales of wool to the port, so he cornered him and made him a deal he couldn't refuse. Fowler had worked alongside him in the road gangs in New South Wales. Only thing was, Septimus had done his time and had a ticket of leave, but Fowler had escaped before his time was up. He'd made it to South Australia, where he was making a living shifting gangs of shearers around the countryside, well away from the eyes of the New South Wales police.

It had therefore been easy to get Fowler to send the bales his way. Between them they had a nice little sideline slipping the odd unmarked wool bale away from under a farmer's nose and putting the Smith's Ridge mark on it once it reached the port or simply passing it off as off-cut wool.

There was no way Baker would find out where his missing wool had gone or be able to pin any of his losses on Septimus. It was high time they came face to face. Why, he was even planning to apologise for Terrett's attack on Baker's wife. They would see Septimus as a caring neighbour and be grateful for his concern. He would extract a nice extra sum of interest from their debt. The thought gave him reason to smile as he made his way to Wildu Creek.

Fifty-five

Septimus reined in his horse as he rounded the last of the thick bush in front of Thomas Baker's home. He blew out a long, slow breath. Two huts sat on the hill above the creek. One was hardly more than a lean-to, but the other was solid, well constructed and much bigger than the first, with a wide verandah across the front. He could see water barrels lined up along one wall and a fenced area nearby, with a fruit tree reaching above it. He moved his horse forward. On the small cliff above the creek, a set of chairs and a table nestled in the shade thrown from the trees, and a canvas canopy stretched between two boughs.

Now that he was closer he could hear the sound of sheep, many sheep, and he could smell them. Shouts and whistles pierced the bleating. He passed under a group of larger trees closer to the house and had a clear view up the slope to a plateaued area. A shed had been built in the middle of the flat, and it was surrounded by yards full of sheep, some with wool and some without. Baker was shearing.

That would explain why he'd seen no animals on his journey across country from his own lease. He'd stopped to water the horse and take a break at the permanent waterhole a few miles inside Wildu Creek land. There was a large wooden bucket hanging from a nearby tree. He'd made use of it to gather some water for his morning ablutions. It had been a relief to wash away the smell of the Smith's Ridge camp and don a fresh set of clothes. Baker was lucky to have such a place. There appeared to be no permanent water on Smith's Ridge. However, the long dry year must have taken its toll on Baker's stock as well. There were several carcasses piled to the side of the last yard, probably animals not strong enough to make the trek to the shed and then be shorn.

From where he sat in the saddle he could see vegetables growing inside the fenced area in neat rows around the fruit tree. At the back of the main house a third room ran its length and a small lean-to was attached to that. Baker had been very busy. Septimus thought of the rough camp he'd left at Smith's Ridge. His property should be established like Baker's by now. Of course, Septimus didn't have to live there, so what did it matter, as long as it made money.

He looked around the neatly laid out house area and thought of the note of debt he carried in his coat pocket. Now that he'd seen the property he wasn't so keen for Baker to pay him in a timely fashion. Baker probably had no other income and he'd endured the dry the same as Smith's Ridge. Septimus smiled. Perhaps there was a way he could acquire Wildu Creek too. There was more than one way to fleece a sheep.

"Hello?"

Septimus looked up from his musing to see a woman coming down the slope. She carried a wide, flat basket empty except for the blue and white checked cloth that covered its base. A small bare-footed boy trotted at her side. This woman was George Smith's daughter and she'd married Baker. She was a lot more solid than he remembered, but he could still see evidence of her fair hair under the ridiculous straw bonnet tied to her head. Her shirt and skirt bore several patches. Either times were indeed difficult for Baker or he didn't waste money on his wife.

"Hello, Mrs Baker," he said.

She hesitated and Septimus performed his best smile. "I am your neighbour, Septimus Wiltshire."

"Mr Wiltshire?" she said and stepped closer as he climbed from his horse.

"I am glad to find you looking so well, Mrs Baker."

Septimus saw a look of recognition cross her face and then a small frown. She threw a quick glance over her shoulder. The little boy beside her stared up at him with large blue eyes.

"I'm sorry, Mr Wiltshire, but you won't find a warm welcome here," she said.

Septimus removed his hat and lowered his gaze to the ground. "I've come to apologise, Mrs Baker, for my previous overseer Mr Terrett's terrible actions." He looked up with a smile that he imagined oozed charm. "I am most relieved to see you looking so well. I hope he caused you no permanent harm."

"I didn't suffer too much, Mr Wiltshire, and I thank you for your concern but I do think it best if you continue on your way."

"It's my dearest wish not to cause you any further distress but I've come at your husband's request."

"Thomas?" Her expression was one of complete puzzlement.

"When he was last in Port Augusta he called on me, but sadly I was away on other business. He left a message with my wife to seek him out at Wildu Creek when next I came to Smith's Ridge."

"I do recall …" Lizzie shifted the basket to her hip. "My husband is very busy with the last of the shearing but he was hopeful cut out would be this afternoon."

"Perhaps I can go up there. Take a look around and let him know I'm here."

"I think it best you wait here." Lizzie glanced over her shoulder again. "Would you care for a cup of tea? They've just had their afternoon break in the shed but the kettle won't take long to boil again."

"Thank you. I would appreciate that. I've been riding all day."

"Why don't you sit over by the creek? It's nicely shaded at this time of day." She nodded towards the seats he'd seen on his arrival. "I'll bring you something to eat as well."

"That's very kind of you."

She bent to take the hand of the child and hurried to the back door of the house. Septimus tethered his horse and strolled across to the seats in the shade. He was slightly amused at her attempts to get rid of him. Lizzie Baker wasn't keen for him to stay. No doubt she carried a grudge for her brothers over his taking Smith's Ridge away from them, but he'd done nothing illegal. It was hardly his fault if George hadn't read carefully what he'd signed. Surely that was all behind them now.

He sat on the rough wooden seat. From here he could see along the dry creek bed in both directions and out across the plains to the foothills, the distant rugged terrain of his property and the mountains beyond. It was quite a view. Septimus settled back in the chair. Now that he'd seen Wildu Creek's improvements he was more interested than ever to chat with Thomas Baker.

Fifty-six

The clicking of the blades fell silent. Thomas turned around to see the last man stand up, put his hands to his hips and arch himself backwards.

"That's it," Fowler said. He strode along the boards, collecting the shears from each man. "Go and get yourselves washed up and be back here for rations before dark." The snarl of his voice echoed through the shed.

Thomas hadn't liked the boss of the boards the first time they'd met over a year earlier. Nothing he'd seen since had changed his opinion. Fowler was a big man. His shoulders were as wide as an axe handle and he was a good head taller than Thomas. He had a thick black beard and dark brooding eyes that missed nothing. He goaded his men with language far worse than anything Thomas had heard before. He never let Lizzie or Joseph hang around once the food had been consumed.

The men tugged off their soft moccasin shoes and sat around pulling on their boots. They were a different crew, bar one, from the men Fowler had brought the previous year, but just as rough. Shearers were hard to come by this far north, so Thomas had been thankful to see them arrive. Now he'd be thankful to see them go. He understood most of these men were ex-convicts from Van Diemen's Land. Nearly four thousand sheep they'd shorn, almost a thousand more than last year. Some of them were very rough with the blades – a few of the sheep were so badly injured he'd had to slaughter them – but the wool was off. He moved among them, thanking them for their work.

"Thomas."

He looked up at Zac's call.

"A word outside," he said.

Thomas followed him to a pen of sheep, where Zac selected one and made a show of inspecting its mouth. "I found two unmarked bales," he said. His voice carried to Thomas but was lost beyond that in the shuffle and bleats of the sheep.

"So, it has to be Fowler or the man he has doing jobs for him."

"Or both. They're the only two who were here last year."

"I'll get to the bottom of it right now," Thomas said but Zac grabbed his arm.

"Why don't we let it go?" he said.

"What?" Thomas looked at Zac. "Have you lost your senses? They got four bales last year. I'm not letting them have two more."

"Think about it, Thomas." Zac kept his voice low. "If we accuse anyone now it will be a mistake. After all, we're the ones branding the bales. We would only be laughed at for not doing a thorough job."

"How are they getting unbranded bales?" Thomas scratched at the hair under his chin. He was looking forward to a shave once shearing was finished.

"I don't know: I've branded each one myself. At any rate, I think we can put a small mark on the two I've found so it won't be noticed."

"How?"

"With some of Lizzie's thread."

Thomas smiled at Zac's ingenuity.

"The trick will be to catch them at the port when our bales are unloaded," Zac said. "That's when they must slip the unmarked ones away. Before the agent counts them."

"How will we be able to watch? Once our bales are unloaded that's that."

"I think you and I both need to go with the wool this time. Somehow we'll work it out when we get there."

"I'm not leaving Lizzie and Joseph with just a boy to look out for them. Gulda has gone bush again. I don't know when he'll be back."

"Bring them with us. It's a long time since she's been near a town."

"Thomas." They both lifted their heads to see Lizzie beckoning from beyond the yards.

"I'll think on it," Thomas said and climbed over the wooden railing to meet his wife.

"Are you finished?" she asked.

"Yes, thank the Lord."

"You've got a visitor waiting for you by the creek."

"Who is it?"

Lizzie grasped his hand. "Septimus Wiltshire."

Thomas raised his eyes towards the house, which blocked his view. "Well, well," he murmured. "We get to meet at last."

Lizzie gripped his hand tighter. "Keep calm, Thomas. We don't want any trouble."

"I'll be calm. I am curious to meet him." He slid his hand from hers. "You go back to the house, Lizzie. I'll take care of Mr Wiltshire."

He kissed her firmly on the lips and strode down the hill. He'd placated Lizzie with his words but beneath the surface his curiosity mingled with anger. As he approached the seat where Wiltshire sat, he had a moment to observe the tidy clothes of his visitor. Even though he sat in the shade he still had his hat on his head.

Wiltshire rose to his feet at the sound of Thomas's tread and held out his hand.

"Mr Baker, we meet at last."

Thomas shook the hand briefly. Cool, grey eyes glittered beneath Wiltshire's hat and the scent of spice lingered in the air.

"Oh, we've met before," Thomas said. "Only then you went by the name, Seth Whitby."

"I did have that name once." Septimus straightened his shoulders. "You asked me to call on you and here I am. Septimus Wiltshire at your service."

The sight of the man pretending as if nothing had happened unleashed a fury Thomas had kept at bay for years. "I don't care what your name is, you blackguard," he roared, and swung his fist at Wiltshire's head.

The man ducked. Thomas only clipped him a glancing blow across his ear, knocking his hat from his head.

"Thomas, what's got in to you?" Lizzie called as she came running.

"Your husband tried to strike me, madam."

Lizzie tugged at Thomas's arm. They both watched Wiltshire bend to pick up his hat.

"This blackguard sold me a horse that wasn't his to sell."

"I found the horse and sold it to you in good faith."

Thomas snorted. "And my trunk? I suppose that happened to walk away with you."

Septimus pushed the hat back onto his head. "The trunk was gone when I returned; I assumed you'd found somewhere else to store it."

"Yet much of its contents are in your house and my mother's gold locket hangs around your wife's neck." Thomas jabbed his finger at Wiltshire's chest. The man took a small step back.

"I have been a hawker for many years. All kinds of items come into my possession." Septimus's lips turned up in a sly grin. "People will trade anything if their need is great enough."

Thomas felt his hand clench into a fist again but Lizzie kept a firm hold of his arm.

"And what about the rotten deal you did with my father-in-law?"

"It was all perfectly legal."

"You are a liar." Zac stepped up level with Wiltshire.

"Ah, the drunken brother-in-law."

Zac lurched at Wiltshire but Lizzie grabbed him with her spare hand. Septimus took another small step backwards.

"Now of course there is the matter of the debt on Wildu Creek."

Thomas pulled himself from Lizzie's grasp. He took a step towards Wiltshire. "Not for long," he growled.

"Ah." Septimus smiled. "You think you have the money to pay." He ran a finger over his moustache. "Since I have held the debt the interest has been growing."

"What's he talking about, Thomas?"

"Nothing to worry about," he said but he didn't take his eyes from the loathsome man gloating in front of him. "Hand over the paper, Wiltshire. You'll have your money."

"Thomas?" He could hear the hurt in Lizzie's voice.

"Surely you didn't go into debt to this man," Zac said.

"Not intentionally," Thomas snapped. "I will explain later. Hand over the paper, Wiltshire."

Thomas watched as the man extracted a paper from his pocket.

"I understand times have been tough." Wiltshire's voice was smooth. "If you need longer to pay –"

Thomas snatched the paper from his hands, cutting off his words. He wanted this man off his property for good. The figure on the paper was a ridiculous amount; far more than he would have paid back to Grant. It would take him to the brink again but Thomas had no choice. He crushed the note in his hand and locked his gaze with Wiltshire's.

"You'll have your money as soon as I can get to Port Augusta."

Zac stepped up beside Thomas. "You'll not steal Wildu Creek like you did Smith's Ridge."

"Smith's Ridge is mine through a legal document, signed by your father." Wiltshire smiled. "I can't help it if his sons didn't do their job properly."

Zac lunged. He threw a punch, which Wiltshire sidestepped. It took him to the edge of the bank. With a small cry of surprise, the odious man disappeared over the edge.

"Mr Wiltshire," Lizzie called in alarm.

They all stepped up to the edge of the bank to see Wiltshire getting to his feet. There was no water in this part of the creek, just sand and leaves and sticks.

"I'll go and deal with him," Zac said.

"We will have no more violence here." Lizzie stood hands on hips. "Zac!" She turned back to Thomas, eyes blazing. "I mean it."

They all watched as Wiltshire brushed off his jacket and tugged at his sleeves. He walked along the edge of the creek and back to the bank where the slope was less steep. From that distance he glared from Thomas to Zac.

"I came as a neighbour to talk like gentlemen but I see there are no gentlemen here. Don't call at my home again, Baker. If there are any matters regarding Smith's Ridge to be brought to my attention you may do so through my new overseer, Mr Rix, and his assistant Mr Pavey. And your debt had best be paid before the end of the month or there will be the next round of interest to add."

Thomas uttered a low growl. Zac punched his fist into his hand. Wiltshire turned on his heel and scurried away to his horse.

"Thomas?" Lizzie's quiet voice broke the silence

He glanced from Lizzie to Zac then back at the questioning look from his wife.

"I borrowed a small amount –"

"Oh, Thomas."

"From Wiltshire?" Zac stared at him with sadness in his eyes.

"Let me finish," Thomas said. "I borrowed from Mr Grant against our next wool cheque."

"Why?" Lizzie shook her head slowly.

"We've had some tough years but our stock numbers were growing. I knew it would be all right, and Grant is an honest man."

Zac snorted.

"Seems he overstretched himself and sold off some of the debts he held. That's how Wiltshire got our note."

"Now we are in debt to that man." Lizzie's hand went to her stomach.

"Not for much longer. I will pay what he asks as soon as I make the trip to Port Augusta."

"Why did you do it?" Lizzie asked softly.

"We had to keep this place running; there were things we needed."

"You gambled with Wildu Creek."

Her words stabbed at him. Thomas knew he shouldn't have taken such a risk.

"It's all right, Lizzie. I'll pay him and we'll be back on our feet in no time. We've got all this wool to deliver. It's been a good year for us in spite of the stock losses.

"You should have told me."

He looked down into the sad eyes of his wife. "I know."

He reached out. He was hurt by the hesitation in her eyes.

"I'm sorry," he said. "I promise I'll never take such a risk again. Not without talking it over with you, at least."

She gave a small nod then took the step into his arms. Over her head he looked out across the plains and ridges of Wildu Creek. He'd had a lucky escape.

"Have you met Rix?" Zac had been standing silently beside them.

Thomas looked at his brother-in-law. "No but let us hope he's a better man than Terrett."

"Oh." Lizzie shivered in spite of the heat still in the air.

Thomas kept an arm around her.

"Why did you stop us from thumping the man, Lizzie?" Zac complained. "Wiltshire's a thief and a liar."

"It's all in the past," Lizzie said. "What's done is done. Beating Mr Wiltshire black and blue won't change anything."

"Perhaps not, but I would have felt better." Zac grinned.

"Anyway, he'll have a few bruises and scratches to remind him of his visit," Thomas said, and was surprised by the urge to smile.

"Oh, Thomas." Lizzie began to giggle.

They laughed together. It was Lizzie who drew breath first.

"I have better news to brighten our day," she said. "I've been waiting for shearing to be finished to tell you."

Thomas looked into her dancing blue eyes.

"I'm going to have a baby."

"That's wonderful news, Lizzie," Zac said. "We've cause for a grand celebration tonight."

She frowned at her brother.

"Don't give me that look." He laughed. "I'm going to break out the cordial."

He shook Thomas's hand, kissed his sister on the cheek and walked away, chuckling to himself.

"Aren't you happy, Thomas?" Lizzie gazed up at him.

He pulled her close and hugged her tight. "Of course I am."

"Joseph needs a brother or sister," she said. "He's far too spoiled."

Thomas looked over her head to the verandah where Zac had found his nephew and hoisted him aloft. Joseph's delighted squeals echoed back to them.

"I must get on," Lizzie said. "There's still so much food to prepare for tonight's cut-out feast." She stretched up and kissed him. Her eyes sparkled. "Come on, husband," she said. "We've all got work to do."

Thomas followed her up the slope. Alongside his joy at the prospect of a new baby there also simmered a little fear, but he would never say as much to Lizzie.

A few days later he stood with Lizzie and Joseph, waving goodbye to Zac and Timothy. Gulda was there as well with Tommie and Daisy, who had a new baby in her arms. They'd returned as soon as the shearers had moved on in the direction of Smith's Ridge. Lizzie had been so excited to see Daisy's new daughter. She'd suggested the name Rose, another floral tribute for Gulda's bunch. They weren't sure Daisy and Gulda understood the joke but they liked the name. It had made Thomas's heart ache to see the joy on Lizzie's face. Once again he'd felt fear for the fragility of her happiness.

Zac cracked the whip. Thomas cast his eyes over the wagon as it lurched forward, followed by the dray and the new cart. They were all loaded high with wool bales, two of which had had the tiny initials *WC* sewn into their seams in blue thread by the nimble-fingered Lizzie.

Thomas had been torn between going with the wool and staying with his family. The trip would be too strenuous for Lizzie in her condition, so it was decided Zac and Timothy would take the wool to Port Augusta. Zac had reassured Thomas he was up to the job and they all knew he'd been sober for several months. Thomas had written a letter to Mr Grant, the commission agent, outlining the situation and entreating him to assist Zac in finding the culprit. Zac also had his authority to pay the debt owed to Wiltshire.

In spite of the sour taste Thomas still got when he thought of Septimus Wiltshire and his unease about an unknown overseer on Smith's Ridge, he felt a surge of optimism as the little convoy set off. The price of wool had gone up again since his last delivery although he would have to wait several months to collect his cheque. In spite of the dry winter he was hopeful the rains would come again in the new year.

"We're doing well, Thomas." Lizzie sighed. She leaned her head against his shoulder.

"It's hard work," he said, lifting a hand to wave as Zac turned back one last time before disappearing into the trees.

"No one's complaining about that. We're very lucky."

Joseph pulled on his hands and Thomas lifted his son to his shoulders and wrapped an arm around his wife.

"Very lucky indeed," he said as the last wagon rolled out of sight.

Fifty-seven

Septimus watched Fowler inspect the shed.

"You've made no improvements since last year." The shearer crossed the rough wooden floor and came to a stop barely a foot away from Septimus, forcing him to look up.

Septimus stood his ground. He wasn't going to back away. They had a partnership but he carried the trump card. Fowler knew it, for all his bravado.

"My overseer was carted off by that pompous neighbour of mine," Septimus said. "Neales has been little more than useless in Terrett's absence. It took me a while to find a replacement. Now that Rix is here, I expect the situation to improve. Besides, my money's gone into stocking the place, not making it look fancy."

Fowler lifted his huge head and looked again at the basic structure Septimus called a shearing shed. "It'll have to do," he snarled. "But rougher conditions means rougher work."

"I hope these shearers are better than the mongrels you brought last year. We had to kill a lot of stock, from what I remember."

"My men will do the best they can with what they've got. I've taken a look at some of those miserable excuses for sheep you've got in the yard. They're lucky to grow wool, let alone survive having it cut off."

"It's been dry," Septimus snapped. "There's been hardly a drop of moisture fallen in a year. Some of those sheep I got cheap from another farmer because he couldn't feed and water them."

"Your neighbour seems to have done all right, and he's had no rain either."

"Luck," Septimus said. "Baker's got permanent water on his property and more bush growth in his hills. Smith's Ridge is aptly named. Nothing much grows in the rocks."

The reminder of his neighbour rankled yet again. It had been a few days since he was pushed into the creek, but his arm was still sore and bruised. He could have broken a limb. They all but drove him off their property. Baker would be sorry. Septimus had ridden straight back to Smith's Ridge to give Rix full encouragement to do what he could to undermine Baker's apparent good fortune at Wildu Creek. Rix would be a thorn in Baker's side, one not easily discovered or extracted.

"If our luck holds he'll have two fewer bales of wool to feather his nest with." Fowler's voice was a loud rumble.

Septimus glanced around. The rough-looking group of men Fowler had brought with him were resting, talking among themselves; no one was paying much attention to their boss. They'd have plenty to do soon enough.

Septimus kept his own voice low. "You managed to swap a couple of bales then?" He needed the extra money Fowler brought him with the unmarked wool.

"Just two this time: don't want to arouse suspicion."

"And you're sure they didn't notice."

"They would have spoken up but nothing was said. I was surprised. That brother-in-law of Baker's stamped every bale and kept checking them. I was sure he'd notice the two we swapped but I got 'em loaded while he was busy elsewhere. He'll be delivering them to the port for us by now." Fowler laughed. It was a deep guttural sound.

"Just one of many little discrepancies that Baker won't notice but that will bring him down." Septimus smacked a fist into the palm of his hand. "Thomas Baker doesn't know it, but one day Wildu Creek will be mine. I will enjoy sending him and his pathetic family packing."

"All of the bales from here will be marked."

Septimus opened his mouth then closed it again as he saw the smirk on Fowler's face. He glared at Fowler. "Don't forget who pays you. And I need at least half of these sheep to survive to get my money back. Make sure your men take care."

Fowler gave a snort then strode away, barking orders at his men.

Just outside the shed, Septimus caught a glimpse of Neales moving some sheep. He wondered how long his pathetic shepherd had been lurking by the door. Septimus's eyes narrowed. He must be sure to remind Rix to keep an eye on the man, make sure he knew who he was working for.

The heat in the shed was already overpowering in spite of the early hour, but Septimus resisted the urge to remove his jacket. He planned to have one last talk to Rix and then be on his way. He'd been on the road a long time, organising Rix and Pavey, purchasing stock and provisions. He was looking forward to a treat, a short holiday with Dulcie in the hills. He had to check on Ned at the inn of course, but that wouldn't take long.

He'd brought a tin tub to the hut and, in spite of the dry, Dulcie always managed to find water to fill it and massage away what ailed him. Septimus smiled. He might even stay a week.

"What do you mean business has dropped off?" Septimus had taken longer than expected to reach the inn near the pass through the hills. His horse had gone lame and he'd had to purchase another. The farmer had driven a hard bargain, not wanting to part with one of his horses. Septimus had paid him far more than the horse was worth and left the lame one in the deal. Now here he was, sitting at the bar of his inn, the only customer.

"The long heat has affected everyone," Ned said. "There's no feed for the bullocks so we've had fewer teamsters through, and those that do pass by camp over near the creek. Not many of them have called in lately. Saving their money, most likely. We've had few other customers. No one wants to travel in the heat."

"Let me see the ledger."

"I can get it if you like but it won't show any different."

"Let me see it." Septimus thumped his hand on the bar.

"Who's doing all this hollering?" Ethel came bustling out of the kitchen. "Well, well," she said as she laid eyes on Septimus. "It's the boss. Why didn't you tell me, Mr Wiltshire was here, Ned? I bet you're hungry after your travels. I've got a nice possum pie just out of the oven. Sit down at a table." Ethel tugged at his arm.

"Don't fuss, woman," Septimus said, but she manoeuvred him to a seat before he knew it.

"It's not fussing." Ethel laughed loudly. "Nothing's too good for the boss. Get him some of that ale we've had cooling in the cellar, Ned."

Septimus hadn't planned to eat at the inn and he didn't often drink ale, but before he knew it Ethel had a plate of delicious-smelling pie in front of him and Ned had produced a mug of beer.

"Once you've got that inside you, I've a nice steamed apple pudding and some clotted cream." Ethel appraised him as if he was a child. "The dear old cow has been giving us a nice lot of milk, hasn't she Ned?"

Septimus's mouth watered. Pavey was a capable cook but he had been travelling a long time and living on dry mutton and black tea for most of it. He settled back and enjoyed the feast Ethel provided.

It was almost dark by the time Septimus mounted his horse and made the journey over the hills behind the inn to his hut. After the meal Ethel had made a pot of tea and they'd all sat out on the verandah, enjoying the gully breeze and the changing colours of the sky. They'd offered him a bed but he'd said he'd prefer to camp out, as he always told them when he visited.

He tethered his horse at the front of his hut and pushed open the door. The main room was empty, as was the bedroom. There was no sign of Dulcie and no coals in the grate. His longed-for bath was not happening tonight by the look of the empty tub. He went out the back towards the shed, through the bush either side of the hut, where she sometimes sat and made an open fire, then out the front. There was no sound except for the evening breeze moaning through the trees. It was the one thing he'd never liked about this place – it sounded like a woman crying.

He walked down to the creek and under the large gums, with their roots reaching down to the creek bed. It was here he'd first taken Dulcie as his own. There was no water in the creek now, but the memory of that encounter had blood pounding through him, kindling the desire that had been building all day.

"Damn!" He thumped his fist against the tree and returned to the hut.

He slept the night alone in the bed. His sleep was restless and he arose early the next morning. Birds were busy carolling in the new day but there was still no sign of Dulcie. Once more he walked around the hut, the now-empty shed and dilapidated sheep yards. He had no use for this place any more. It was only

Dulcie who brought him back here and she had always been waiting for him or appeared not long after he'd arrived. It had been two months since he'd seen her last. He needed her badly.

Blast it. He decided to continue on to Port Augusta. At least he knew Harriet would always be home. He'd grown used to the flies but that morning they were particularly thick, crawling all over his face and hands with no breeze to carry them away. They added to his irritation as he batted at them only to have them return as soon as his hand was still. It was barely spring and the heat was wearing. For the first time since he'd arrived in this rugged country, he didn't look forward to the heat of summer.

He made his way through the hills below the inn and joined the road that wound down through the valley and then across the plain to the port. He overtook several bullock drays loaded with copper ore trundling in the same direction as he was taking. The men driving them acknowledged him as he passed but kept their heads lowered beneath their floppy hats.

He urged his new horse into a gallop, keen to escape the dust cloud created by so many hooves and the discomfort of being in the saddle as soon as he could. It wasn't until he was halfway to Port Augusta that he remembered he'd not gone back to look at the inn ledger. Still, Ned was probably right. It had been a difficult twelve months for everyone, with the prospect of continued dry.

Luckily for Septimus, his investments were spread about. He didn't think Baker would have the common sense or the funds to make such arrangements. Septimus got the impression that paying off the debt would clean the fool out. The thought gave him some cause to smile as he traversed the dusty road towards the port.

Fifty-eight

1857

Thomas shielded his eyes against the heat haze: something moved on the ground ahead. He moved his horse cautiously forward. The creature paused, twisted its head then spread its huge wings and launched itself skywards, the insignificant form of a lamb clutched in its talons. Thomas looked back to the ground where the eagle had been. The carcass of a ewe was split open in a pool of dark blood, buzzing with flies. Wild dogs would have taken it down and the eagle had come to claim the lamb they had somehow overlooked.

It was late afternoon on another long, hot January day. The sun beat down from a cloudless blue sky. Further off to his right along the dry creek bed was a waterhole, one of the last of his permanent supplies to still hold water. The vegetation had been stripped for miles around it, leaving a desolate landscape.

Thomas slithered from his horse; his legs began to crumple beneath him. He gripped the saddle with one hand and thumped his backside with the other, trying to get the circulation moving again. Every day he rode out to keep his sheep from straying too far. The summer had been relentless in its ferocity, but his drive to keep his stock safe was just as ferocious. He was so tired he'd been nearly asleep on the horse when he'd noticed the movement of the eagle. Under such conditions the sheep struggled to find enough food and then make it back to the waterhole. They were easy pickings for dogs, eagles and even the natives.

Gulda did his best to discourage his people but Thomas knew from the prints he'd learned to read around the muddy edges of the waterhole that barefoot men took his sheep as well as the wild creatures of the bush.

Timothy rode in from the other direction. He brought his horse to a stop beside the dead animal and slid to the ground with ease. Thomas envied his energy.

"What a mess," the shepherd said as he bent over the poor creature. "Those blackbirds have got its eyes."

"At least it was dead," Thomas said. "I've found them pecking at the eyes of living sheep too weak to move."

"This is the tenth carcass I've found today along the boundary."

Thomas felt his spirits sink lower. He couldn't afford to lose so many sheep. He squinted skywards but saw not a glimmer of a cloud to give him any hope.

"Only one was ours though." Timothy brushed the flies and ants from the dead animal's ears.

It was then Thomas noticed the two notches he'd missed before. This poor creature was from Smith's Ridge. He gazed in the direction of his boundary.

"Those shepherds don't do much of a job," Timothy said.

Thomas knew Rix brought sheep to the Wildu Creek waterhole. There were other permanent sources of water on Thomas's property but they were all low as well. He would happily have shared if Smith's Ridge still belonged to Jacob and Zac but he had no interest in being neighbourly with the likes of Rix and his employer.

"It doesn't matter what we do," Thomas said. "We've got too much land and too many sheep to be in one place all the time. Zac and Gulda have got their work cut out." He wiped a trickle of sweat from his cheek. "No matter how much time we put in to shepherding, this boundary is a problem."

"That Mr Rix knows we've got water and bluebush. They don't have much of either on Smith's Ridge," Timothy said.

"You've been there?"

"A few times. Just to get a bit of a look. I didn't neglect my duties here," he said quickly. "First time I found myself there by accident. I was following the trail of some sheep. They've got too much stock for the kind of country it is."

Thomas studied the young man. He had adapted to life on Wildu Creek after less than a year. His knowledge of sheep and their management grew every day. He worked hard and he listened and watched. Joseph adored him and Lizzie had him calling her Mrs Lizzie like Gulda did.

"You're right," Thomas said. "I hear Wiltshire bought poor stock just before shearing last year. He might have got the wool off their backs but there'd be few of them left now."

"They keep staggering around looking for feed and water. There's not a blade of grass or a low-hanging leaf between this waterhole and way beyond their boundary."

"If only there was some way to keep him out." Once more Thomas looked to the east.

"I built a fence for Ma back in Port Augusta. The goats kept getting into her vegetables. Pity we can't do the same thing here." Timothy chuckled. "That'd keep those Smith's Ridge sheep out."

Thomas lifted his hat and rubbed at his hair, which was plastered to his scalp. He looked north along the invisible boundary between his property and Wiltshire's. He knew several miles away it was marked by a rocky outcrop pointing south like a huge bony finger.

At the southern end it met a wide dry creek bed dotted with large gums and occasional cliffs and cutaways. If he ran a fence between those two natural barriers, few stock would find their way around it.

He shoved his hat back on his head and grasped Timothy by the shoulders. "That's it," he said. A surge of excitement swept through him. "We'll build a fence."

Timothy gaped at him. Thomas let go the lad's shoulders and strode back to his horse with an energy he hadn't felt in weeks. When he climbed on his horse and looked back, Timothy was still standing there watching him. "Come on," Thomas called. "Time to go home. Mrs Lizzie will have food on the table by the time we get there and we've a lot to work out."

"What will you make it from?" Lizzie asked as they sat out under the stars. They had eaten their meals on the creek bank all summer. As soon as the sun went down they had some relief from the flies and sometimes, like that night, there was a soft breath of a breeze along the gully. They had a small fire on the sandy bank to boil the billy and a lantern hanging in a tree. Their outside room, Joseph called it.

"Further south of us there's thick bush," Thomas said. "We'll make a brush fence."

"It would be a huge job," Zac said.

"I know," he replied. "But we've little else to do but watch our stock die."

"More your neighbour's stock, really," Timothy said.

They all looked at him.

He sank lower in his chair. "It's just that Wildu Creek is a much better property," he said. "Better stock, better management –"

"Better people," Zac said and they all laughed.

"Perhaps Jacob would help," Lizzie said. "He went home for Christmas and wasn't going back to the mines. Mother's letter said he planned to visit us next."

"Won't your father need him?" Thomas asked. He knew George suffered more and more from rheumatism across his shoulders.

"He's still got Edmund and Samuel," Lizzie said. "Anyway, I doubt Jacob would stay here with us. It will just be a visit."

"Well," Zac said, lifting his mug of tea, "it looks like we're building a fence."

They all lifted their mugs to touch his.

"When will we start?" Timothy asked, his eyes aglow with enthusiasm.

"Before dawn tomorrow morning," Thomas said. They turned to look at him. "We take the wagon and the dray and head south. Cut as much brush as we can before it gets too hot and bring it back. We can take it in turns to do our rounds and build the fence. I'm hoping Gulda will help us. He's an expert at making those huts of his from bush. And we have the fine fence builder, Mr Timothy Castles, with us as well." Thomas grinned at his young shepherd. "Isn't that right?"

Timothy's face beamed back. "Sure thing, Mr Baker," he said.

There was more laughter. Thomas tilted his head back and looked at the stars. It felt good to have a project, something more productive than waiting for rain.

The next morning they were cutting the first of the brush as the sun rose, a golden orange ball in a pale, lifeless sky. They were all there, the men cutting, Lizzie and Daisy making bundles and Joseph and Tommie running wild, excited by this totally new experience. Thomas marvelled at Daisy's ability to keep working with baby Rose nestled to her chest in some kind of sling.

By mid-morning the wagon and the dray were both piled high with brush. Thomas asked Gulda to take the women and children home in the cart while he went with Zac and Timothy to make a start on the fence. Lizzie gave Thomas a cheery wave but he could see the work had tired her. She insisted on working as hard as ever and she never complained, but he knew the heat bothered her as her body began to swell with the baby. He worried, but she would have none of it.

"Let's go build a fence," Zac called and cracked the whip over the bullocks.

Thomas put his concern to one side at the prospect of the task ahead.

For all their enthusiasm they got little built that first day. Zac wanted to start at the southern end and Thomas the northern. Timothy suggested they start in the middle. In the end it was decided they would have a team working at either end, finishing wherever they met. Each morning they would cut the brush and then build during the day between looking after the sheep.

They got into a routine. The women came with them each morning to help cut and stack the brush, then they went home and the men continued to build the fence when they could. That the structure had strength was due to Gulda. He was an expert at stacking and winding the brush so it held together. They learned from him. It was slow going but Thomas could see progress was being made.

February arrived with a week of extremely high temperatures, then suddenly clouds appeared and they had their first reprieve from the incessant heat in weeks. Everyone cut and stacked brush as usual but when it was time to go to the boundary, Lizzie insisted the women come to inspect the fence.

"We want to see what our work is going towards," Lizzie said. "I've packed a picnic."

Thomas took a seat on the cart beside her and led the way to the southern end of the fence, where the large gums along the creek would give them some shade. They must have looked a strange procession: Thomas in the cart with Lizzie and Daisy, baby Rose in her arms; Gulda on horseback; Timothy and Zac with the wagon and dray; and Joseph and Tommie bouncing along on top of the bundles of brush.

"Oh, look at it," Lizzie exclaimed as the start of the fence came in sight. Beginning at a high point above the creek, it continued on up the hill and disappeared over the rise.

Thomas felt a small burst of pride. Their hard work was paying off. "It's just as long at the northern end," he said. "A few more weeks and we should meet in the middle."

Thomas took the cart across the creek bed. They'd formed quite a track after the many crossings they'd made. He'd thought about making some kind of sign to hang from a nearby tree, something to announce the start of Wildu Creek. How quickly time had gone since he'd driven the first mob of sheep over this very spot.

"You've achieved a lot in five years," Lizzie said as if reading his mind.

There was a small cry behind them. They turned to look at Daisy. She had climbed down from the slow-moving cart and strode past them towards the fence. Gulda slid from his horse and followed her. Daisy turned on him, speaking loudly in a language none of the others understood.

"I've never heard Daisy sound so upset before," Lizzie said

Gulda put a hand on Daisy's shoulder but she shrugged it off and spoke to him again, waving an arm at the fence.

"It's the fence," Thomas said. He handed the reins to Lizzie and climbed down from the cart.

"What's the matter?" Zac asked as his wagon rolled up next to Thomas.

"I don't know," he said. "Everything was fine until we got here."

He walked towards the natives. He couldn't understand what they were saying but he recognised the tenor of Gulda's voice. At first it had been sharp but now he spoke in soothing low tones, trying to placate the agitated Daisy.

"What is it, Gulda?" Thomas asked.

Daisy stopped her diatribe. Her shoulders sagged and she kept her eyes averted from Thomas. She turned away, called Tommie to her side and walked around the group to the creek.

"Where is she going?" Lizzie called. "We must give them a ride, Thomas."

He turned back to Gulda.

"Daisy not happy, Mr Tom," Gulda said with sadness in his eyes.

"I can see that," Thomas said. "Why is Daisy unhappy?"

"She didn't know this was what we were doing with the brush." Gulda pointed to the fence.

"We've talked about it many times."

"Daisy didn't understand what a fence was. This is her country, Mr Tom. Her people move around it all the time. They won't like this fence you are making." Gulda shook his head and turned his sad eyes in the direction Daisy had gone.

Thomas wasn't going to argue, he knew neither Gulda or Daisy would understand the lease he had for this land. He followed Gulda's gaze. Already Daisy and her children had disappeared from sight. Flat grey clouds covered the sun, deepening the shadows along the creek. Thomas stared but he could see no movement.

"You must go with her, my friend," he said.

Once more Gulda slowly shook his head. "I will stay."

Thomas gripped Gulda's shoulder. "Thank you," he said. He felt uneasy at the disagreement. He knew he wouldn't have survived so well out here without Gulda and Daisy's help. It didn't sit well to see his friends upset.

"Are we unloading?" Zac called.

"Yes," Thomas said. "But we'll have our picnic here in the shade first, then Lizzie and Joseph can go home."

Lizzie gave him a little smile and turned her bulging frame to reach the basket in the cart. Timothy was faster than Thomas, down from his dray in seconds and helping her lift the food.

Gulda made his way to the creek and disappeared among the trees.

"That was a bit of a to-do," Zac said, through a mouthful of bread and pickles.

"Never mind," Lizzie said. "She's had a bit of a shock. I'm sure she'll be the same happy Daisy again before long."

"I hope so," Thomas said, then clutched his hat as a sudden gust of wind threatened to tug it from his head. Lizzie covered the food as the wind strengthened, picking up dust and leaves. The grey clouds spread across the sky but they did little to stop the heat, flies or dust, so the picnic was soon abandoned. With Lizzie and Joseph aboard, Thomas turned the cart in the direction of home.

"Such a shame," Lizzie said. "My little picnic was meant to be a celebration."

"Never mind," Thomas replied.

Lizzie put a hand on his. "It's a wonderful fence, Thomas. Daisy will get over it in two shakes of a lamb's tail. Don't worry about it."

Thomas hoped she was right but that day changed the fence building. Daisy stayed back at the camp with her children and Thomas insisted Lizzie do the same as the temperature began to climb again.

Gulda worked as one of them but Daisy kept away from the house. The men took it in turns: two to cut and build while the other two shepherded sheep. Some days Thomas took Joseph with him. The little boy was wearing Lizzie down without his friend Tommie to occupy his time.

Riding up the last little rise to the house late one afternoon, Joseph asleep against him, Thomas was surprised to see Daisy on the front verandah. He hoped it meant she was willing to be friends again. Lizzie missed her company and her help. The bulk of the baby had slowed his darling down and in spite of the big grey clouds that kept building on the horizon, the days were no cooler. Lizzie was as exhausted as he was.

He smiled in what he hoped was a welcoming way but gave up as he brought his horse to a stop in front of Daisy. Her big round eyes brimmed with tears. His heart thumped in his chest.

"Daisy? Are you all right? Where's Mrs Lizzie?" he called.

Daisy came to the horse and slid Joseph from his arms. "She had the baby."

Thomas jumped down and made the verandah in two strides. It was too early. The baby wasn't due for another month.

"Lizzie," he called.

"Thomas." Her feeble reply came from the bedroom.

He rushed in. The bed was stripped of all but a sheet. Lizzie was lying on top of it in a loose nightgown, soaked in sweat. Her hair was dark with moisture and beads of it dribbled down her forehead.

His hopes lifted at the sight of a small bundle beside her on the bed.

Lizzie turned her eyes to his and he knew.

"Our little girl came too soon." Lizzie's voice was a harsh whisper. "She only breathed a short time."

Thomas rolled back the wrapping to look at the tiny face of his daughter. His heart thumped and then ached as if it had shattered to a thousand pieces.

He kneeled at Lizzie's side. A bowl of water and a cloth sat on the little table beside her. He dipped the cloth into the cool water and wiped her brow. Large tears began to roll down her cheeks and then she shuddered with heartrending sobs. Thomas sat on the edge of the bed. He gently drew his wife into his arms: his dear sweet Lizzie who was being tested beyond endurance. He wiped her face, held her and rocked her, all the time watching the longed-for bundle that would never see life with them. His own grief burning deeply in his chest.

It was dark when Zac came in. Thomas felt his arms would break from holding Lizzie so long, but she was asleep at last and he wasn't going to leave her.

"I'm so sorry, Thomas." Zac stood in the doorway looking as helpless as Thomas felt.

"I'm here too."

Thomas raised his head at the sound of Jacob's voice. The last time he came they had just lost Annie. Now there was another child to return to the earth. His brother-in-law stared at him with eyes full of compassion.

"I'm glad you've come," Thomas said but his words were hollow.

"Is Lizzie …?" Jacob tried to see his sister.

"She's sleeping," Thomas said.

"Is there something we can do?" Zac flicked his eyes to the tiny shape on the bed.

Thomas knew he was going to have to make the trip up the hill to bury his daughter. It was a job he wanted to do alone.

"Can you get Joseph?" he said. "He's with Daisy. Perhaps he can sleep with you two tonight."

"Of course."

They backed out. Thomas pushed the door shut with the toe of his boot. He heard movement in the kitchen, soft voices and the sound of a meal being prepared, but he had no interest in any of it.

Finally the house was silent. Lizzie stirred in his arms, and he eased her back onto the bed. There was little light from the moon tonight but he could see enough to know she was in a deep sleep. Only then did he reach across and pick up his daughter. He carried her outside, took up the shovel and pick and made the journey up the hill.

A breeze ruffled the bushes. After the closeness of the bedroom he felt a chill across his shoulders; finally some relief from the heat. He set the lifeless baby down and began to chip away at the soil, each thrust sending another stab into his grieving heart. He struck at the earth, taking his rage out on the land that had given him so much and yet taken so much away. The ground was baked hard and it took him a long time to make a hollow deep enough. He kissed the tiny head, laid his daughter down and replaced the earth. He gathered rocks from the surrounding ridge to pile on top, then, totally drained, he sat on the rock, as he'd done so many times before, to watch over Annie's grave.

Small taps hit his shoulders. He hunched forward, unable to do more than stare at the two tiny mounds in front of him. The taps splattered all over him and onto the earth and rocks around him. A sweet scent filled the air. The drops got heavier until they stung his arms. His chest constricted, his body began to shudder and he let out a cry of despair. It was lost in the dashing of the rain. Thomas turned his face heavenwards. Tears coursed down his cheeks and mingled with the rain soaking his clothes. He gave in to his grief while the ridges and gullies around him began to flow with water, beginning the process of renewal.

Fifty-nine

"I don't know who I got 'em from." Pell's voice was calm.

"You'd better start remembering."

"I travel all over, constable. People will sell all sorts. During that last dry spell some of 'em would have sold their own mothers."

Septimus pressed himself deeper into the corner of the wooden shed. He'd been waiting to meet with Pell when the constable had shown up. Thankfully the early hour meant the shed was all but dark. The constable hadn't noticed Septimus, who'd managed to squeeze behind some boxes in the back corner.

"Two of those bales you delivered to Mr Grant came from Wildu Creek."

Septimus sucked in a breath. Pell had delivered five assorted bales to the agent the previous day. Months had passed since they had been gathered from several properties. How could Grant know two of them were Baker's?

"I don't keep a tally of where they come from," Pell said. "I don't recall Wildu Creek but I may have been there. Who is the owner?"

"Mr Thomas Baker."

"One bale of wool looks like another unless it bears a brand. How does Mr Baker know two of my bales came from his place?"

"He's got some ..." The constable paused. "Never you mind. Perhaps I'd better take a look at the rest of this shed. Conduct a proper search."

Septimus pressed himself into the corner. His heart thumped hard in his chest. There was no way for him to escape.

"There's no more wool here," Pell said. "I'll come with you if you like but there's nothing more I can tell you."

Septimus marvelled at the man's composure. Still, that was why he'd chosen Pell as his middle man. He had an unreadable face and wasn't one for idle talk. He'd never done time but he'd been involved in smuggling back in England. The law had come too close for comfort there and he'd decided on a new start in Australia. It had worked to their advantage until now.

A boot scraped across the wooden floor and a shadow loomed closer. Septimus could feel sweat wet under his collar. There was no way in hell he could be found here. He would launch an attack if he had to. The constable wasn't a big man and wouldn't be expecting it.

"Perhaps not."

The voice was so close. Septimus braced ready to strike.

"But you can come with me and explain again where you got those bales of wool from. They were part of Mr Baker's last wool delivery. They never made it to the commissioning agent and now they've turned up with your delivery. You've got some explaining to do, Mr Pell."

Septimus jumped as the shed door shut. He eased out from his corner, listening until he was sure the men had gone.

"Damned Baker," he muttered.

Pell could be relied upon to keep quiet but there could be more evidence. They might catch up with Fowler, and Septimus wasn't as assured of his silence. There was nothing for it but to lie low for a while. He stayed where he was for several minutes before easing out of the shed and slipping down an alley away from the wharf.

*

Harriet inspected her sewing shop, a fine room added to the front of their cottage. Everything was as it should be. She wasn't expecting any customers today but she liked to be ready just in case. She stood in the centre and slowly turned a full circle. It wasn't a large room but it did the job well. The wall that faced the street had a six-paned window, which let in a much better light than her parlour boasted.

In the corner was a small fireplace, which would give ample heat in winter. Not that she'd need it for a while. The March weather had remained warm after a summer that had been so hot it was as if a fire burned over their heads each day. Even though they lived close to the sea, the little port was at the top of the gulf and surrounded by red sand. Hot winds like the one that had blown the day before were a common occurrence, and they blasted the fine grains into every nook and cranny. At least a house was easier to manage than the perpetual moving life of their hawking days, but Harriet still dreamed of a home in Adelaide.

She glanced around once more. Her eyes stopped at the bolt of fabric Septimus had brought her. He always managed to find her something that was quite different from her normal purchases. Many of her customers wanted her to make the huge skirts that went over their crinolines. She knew Mrs Forbes would like the broad stripes on this fabric: they would set her gown apart from any other in town. Harriet patted the bolt. The whole fourteen yards would be needed and she anticipated the tidy return it would bring her.

With one more glance around the room, she closed the door and retreated back along the verandah to the cooler air of the house. She should be thankful Septimus had agreed to fund the building of her sewing room. He was hardly ever at home any more but last October, he'd turned up unannounced. That wasn't unusual.

What had surprised her was his taking her to bed and wanting her body. It was the first time in a long time and he hadn't done it since, but Harriet was never one to turn him away. Septimus had at least left with a smile on his face and she had his agreement to fund the small extension at the end of the front verandah. It was most beneficial to have a place where she met with her clients and left her work permanently on display.

Back in the front room of the house, she picked up his vest from the back of a chair, brushed it off and hung it on a hook. This visit, apart from presenting the fabric, he had shown little interest in her at all. Once again, home was just a place to lay his head when he came in late at night. He'd risen before her that morning and gone out. No doubt he would be off again soon, and she and Henry could return to the cosy little life she had made for them. It always unsettled the boy when Septimus was around.

Henry looked up at her now with his examining eyes; the blocks he'd been playing with formed a small castle. She worried sometimes his facial expressions and probing looks were so like his father's. He began to put his thumb towards his mouth, but she gave a small shake of her head. Septimus berated the child for still sucking his thumb, not understanding that Henry only did it when he was anxious. She gave her son a reassuring smile, lowered herself to a chair and held out her arms. He snuggled in to her and she breathed in the sweet smell of soap. He was tall for his age and had mastered his letters and numbers. He only stammered when Septimus pressed him to answer quickly.

Septimus pushed open the front door. He paused at the sight of Harriet fussing over Henry on the floor. He glowered at them and thought he saw the flash of a frown cross Harriet's face before she ducked her head.

"Take your blocks to your room, Henry," she said as she handed over the calico bag they'd just filled.

The boy scurried away like a mouse.

Septimus stomped across the room and flung himself into his chair. He began to tug at his boots but Harriet was there in an instant, easing them off for him.

"Can I get you anything?" she asked in her meek tone.

Usually he liked it when she spoke that way but today it irritated him. He preferred Dulcie, who barely spoke at all. Harriet was far more demanding these days. He still couldn't believe she'd talked him into agreeing to build that extra room. She'd struck him at a weak moment. With his travels to Adelaide to search out goods and his visits to the inn and then time spent with Dulcie it was his first trip home in a long while. He hadn't seen the room finished. The pittance she made from her sewing would never pay for it and now another of his business ventures had gone sour. Everywhere he turned, money was disappearing faster than he could make it.

"I've got a headache," he said. He laid his head back and closed his eyes.

He heard the rustle of her skirts as she left the room. Another thing to irritate him. Dulcie wore nothing except possum skins to warm her shoulders in the winter. She made no sound when she moved about.

The rustle returned and a cool cloth was pressed to his forehead. The sweet smell of lavender wafted around him. Harriet wriggled her fingers through his hair and massaged his scalp, then slowly moved down to his shoulders. Her fingers probed and pushed, unknotting his muscles. Septimus sighed and felt the tension ease from his neck and shoulders.

"You must relax more, Septimus," she murmured in his ear.

"I have too much to do," he said.

"Is there something I can help with?"

His eyes snapped open. "You know nothing about the things that trouble me."

Harriet continued to manipulate the knots and tensions in his muscles. "The inn should be doing well."

"The inn has been barely making enough to cover expenses."

His irritation began to resurface but she replaced the cool cloth with another and her fingers kept working. He gave an exasperated sigh.

"That is surprising," she said softly.

"I agree, but Ned says passing traffic is much decreased and those that stop to access the water don't all make use of the facilities at the inn."

"Have you checked his ledger?"

"Of course, Harriet. There is little money coming in. That's if what he's recorded is correct."

She made soothing sounds and kept massaging. Septimus felt as if every movement of her fingers was leeching his worries from his body.

"Perhaps it will be better with all the rain we've had this last winter," Harriet said. "There will be grass for the bullocks to eat."

Septimus drew in a breath and let it slowly pass out again over his teeth. "That could be so," he said.

It gave him some hope too for Smith's Ridge, which had also been losing money. The rain should certainly make a difference there. He hadn't been back since last shearing and his run in with Baker and his useless brother-in-law.

Rix had reported to Septimus several times at the inn since then. They'd lost huge amounts of stock during the dry year and Baker had built a fence between their properties. Rix did his best to knock it down in places but the wretch kept fixing it. A fence made it much easier for him and his shepherds to patrol the boundary. But Harriet was right, the good rains that had fallen would see a return of the grasses that had covered the lower plains and gullies of Smith's Ridge when he'd first taken it over.

"Papa."

Harriet's fingers stopped working and Septimus opened his eyes. Henry stood before him holding the small slate Septimus had brought him. It was a birthday present although a month late.

Septimus peered at the wobbly writing on the board. "What have you written, boy?"

Henry turned to the slate and spoke slowly and clearly.

"Henry Wiltshire, six years old."

"Very good, Henry," Septimus said and lifted his shoulders under Harriet's stilled fingers. She began to massage again.

"Now tell me," Septimus said. "What is one plus one?"

"Two."

"Two plus two?

"Four."

"Very good. It must be nearly time for you to join Papa on his journeys to learn more about his business. It will be yours one day."

Harriet's fingers left his shoulder altogether. "The boy is only six, Septimus. He's too young to be travelling away for so long."

"You no longer accompany me."

"I have my customers – my shop."

Septimus snorted.

"It all helps feed us when you are short on money," she said.

Septimus swivelled his head and glared at her. "Are you saying I don't provide for you, madam?"

Harriet looked away. "Of course not," she said. "It's just that sometimes you are gone for long periods of time."

"Looking after business," he snapped.

"I know that," she said gently, her fingers back on his shoulders. "Henry, go and clean your slate and make sure there is wood in the box by the kitchen fire."

Henry looked from his mother to his father with eyes that slid quickly from side to side. Harriet gave his head a quick pat. He turned and slipped from the room on silent feet.

Septimus noticed the door to the kitchen swung shut behind him but didn't latch. The boy was always creeping about, listening at doors, peering around corners. Above all, he was never far from Harriet's hand. Septimus found it hard to believe he'd sired such a pussy-footed child. The stupid woman made far too much fuss of him, of course. It was time Septimus took him in hand – and yet he held back.

If he took Henry with him he wouldn't be able to spend time with Dulcie, and he was planning to ride to her that very day. He always made sure his travels took him via his hut in the hills. Except for that one time last year, Dulcie was always waiting for him and happy to accommodate his needs. Septimus didn't want Henry peering about at the hut, nor Harriet. He'd leave off a little longer before he took the boy with him. In a few more years he could go without his mother.

Besides, Septimus wasn't sure how long he'd be gone this time. He might have to stay away longer if things took a turn for the worse with Pell. Perhaps he would divide his time between Smith's Ridge and the inn and keep a closer eye on his investments.

Sixty

"This outside room of yours is most certainly a wonderful innovation." Anne sat under the shade on the bank above the creek, nursing her new granddaughter. "If only we had a similar outlook at home."

"We spend most evenings here in the summer. We sometimes get a gully breeze and the flies leave us alone as the sun goes down." Lizzie patted her husband on the shoulder. "Thomas has rigged the canvas so we can move it to suit the season."

Thomas sat just in front of her on the bank, looking down at the creek. There was still a good amount of water trickling past, even though it was late October. Below him Jacob and Zac were building a castle out of sand, rocks and sticks with Joseph. The structure was so well built he imagined it would stay there until the next big rain sent water roaring past. George Smith was stretched out beside Thomas on the bank, his hat over his face; his gentle snores were the only noise he'd made for an hour or so.

"Well, you've all worked hard. I think a day off has been a very good thing," Anne said.

"A day off," Lizzie scoffed. "I've hardly done a minute's work since you arrived, Mother."

"And neither you should, with this dear babe to look after."

Thomas twisted his head to see his mother-in-law gazing at baby Ellen. Touches of grey wove through her faded blonde hair and wrinkles creased the corners of her eyes but she was as capable as ever. He was so grateful to her for making the journey to stay with them. Lizzie carried the baby full term, but she was born just before shearing. The Smiths had finished ahead of them, so the team George had employed came on to Wildu Creek, bringing Anne with them. Lizzie had still worked but not the long hours she would have had her mother not been there.

"Look at those fat little cheeks," Anne said. "You're doing a good job, Lizzie."

"I'm so glad you're here," Lizzie said. "We haven't been together for such a long time. It reminds me of Christmas. Especially with you bringing us all new hats. I love this straw with the wide brim." She turned a cheeky smile to Thomas. "The bonnet you brought me was lovely but I think I've worn it out."

"I'd be happy for you to burn it." Thomas wished she'd never found the battered bonnet. It always reminded him of losing Annie. "I think your mother's choice is far more practical." He adjusted his own new broad-brimmed felt hat. Anne had been very generous.

"It would be lovely to spend a Christmas together, wouldn't it?" Anne said.

"Perhaps one day," Lizzie said.

Both women fell silent. Travel in December was so hot, and entirely out of the question while Ellen was small. Thomas would not allow anything to jeopardise his children. And there was a growing number of stock to attend to.

He was thankful the Smiths had made the journey to visit their daughter. Thomas and Lizzie had travelled south on several occasions but this was only George and Anne's second visit to Wildu Creek. He knew George had struggled to recover both financially and emotionally from the deal he'd done with Wiltshire. Lizzie had agreed never to mention the close call they'd had escaping the blackguard's clutches. Given Wildu Creek's proximity to Smith's Ridge, it was a reminder of something they all had good reason to forget. However, George had shown no regret and had ridden out with them every day, looking over the property and checking sheep.

Just at that moment the old man lifted his hat from his face and sat up. "We have to return home soon," he said. "There's much to do on our own property."

Thomas felt a little guilty that Zac and Jacob preferred to work with him. Jacob went home from time to time to lend a hand, and he kept saying he was going to move on, but then he'd return to work at Wildu Creek. Thomas was grateful for their support.

"Edmund and Samuel can manage," Anne said.

"If one of them hasn't murdered the other by now," George said. "They both think they're in charge. One's as stubborn as the other." He turned to Thomas. "You were happy with the shearing crew I sent this way?"

"Yes, and thank you," Thomas said. "Of course I refuse to have Fowler and his men back here. It was getting so late and I was having trouble finding another team."

George met his gaze and nodded. Thomas was pleased to see some spark in his eyes again.

"We didn't find any unmarked bales this year either," he went on.

"Nor last, and we had Fowler then," Lizzie said. She was very fair-minded, his Lizzie.

"He would have had word that our specially marked bales had been discovered in that shed at the port. He would have been cautious. He'd only need to steal a bale or two from different sheds each year to turn himself a pretty penny."

"Whatever happened to the man the police caught with it?" George asked.

"He disappeared before they could get any information out of him. They found all sorts in that shed, from wool to tools to bolts of fabric, but they never found out who was responsible."

"Surely it was the man that got away," George said.

"The constable I spoke to said they were sure he was only the go-between."

"Well, at least all of this cut should make it to the commissioning agent," George said. "And it should fetch a good price."

The sound of hoofbeats drew Thomas's attention to the track leading to the house. Timothy had offered to check the boundary fence and he'd been gone most of the day. Now he was pounding towards them on his horse. Thomas could see the young shepherd's customary smile had been replaced by a deep frown. As the horse slowed, Thomas went to meet him. Timothy slid from the saddle.

"Sorry, Mr Baker. I did what I could." Timothy was puffing and his horse was in a lather.

"What's happened?" Thomas took the reins.

Timothy glanced around and Thomas became aware the whole family had come to stand beside them.

"The fence is on fire."

"Fire?" Thomas squinted his eyes against the bright blue of an almost cloudless sky. Past Timothy, above the distant ridge, dark smoke smudged the air. How had he not noticed it before?

"How could it catch fire?" Jacob asked.

"I can guess," Zac growled.

"I was at the waterhole and I saw the smoke." Timothy lifted his new hat from his head and tugged at his matted hair. "I couldn't stop it."

"The whole damn thing will burn," George said.

"I think I've saved a bit," Timothy said. The young shepherd had black smudges on his hands and face. "I got in front of it," he said. "I knocked down a piece. The wind's blowing the fire towards the creek end. The northern end is moving slowly."

Thomas left the horse and strode away to his own.

"What will you do?" Lizzie called after him.

"I've got to try to save the rest."

"We'll all come," Jacob said and Zac was right beside him. George was moving to his horse as well, although not as quickly.

"I'll get a fresh horse," Timothy called.

Thomas stopped. "You stay here," he said. "You've done a good job but you're as exhausted as your horse. If we four can't save the remaining fence then it won't be saved."

He didn't wait to see if the others were ready. He mounted his horse and urged it away at a gallop.

By the time they reached the fence it was a smouldering heap but Thomas was thankful for Timothy's quick thinking. He had dragged away a large piece of fence ahead of the fire. Everything between there and as far as Thomas could see was still standing. They rode north along the blackened fence line to the point where the fire was still spreading slowly against the wind.

As Timothy had done at the other end of the fire, they broke down the fence then followed the smouldering line south again. They dismounted where the fire ended. There were no longer any flames to jump the break Timothy had made. There was nothing else they could do.

"All that work," Zac lamented.

"Do you think natives did this?" George asked.

"No," Thomas, Jacob and Zac chorused.

They stared over the smouldering ruin of the fence towards Smith Ridge.

"Rix would have done it," Thomas said.

"On Wiltshire's orders," Zac said.

George kicked a rock with his boot. "That man continues to thwart us," he said.

"There must be something we can do about him," Jacob said.

Thomas punched his fist into the palm of his other hand. "He never gets his hands dirty. There's always someone to do the job for him."

"Neales isn't happy working there," Zac said.

Thomas turned to his brother-in-law. "You've spoken with him?"

"A few times in the last year. We sometimes end up checking the same boundary. He's not like those others, I don't think."

"Perhaps he's worth cultivating," George said. "You might get information out of him about what's going on over there."

"I doubt he'd say much. He's as frightened of Rix as I was Terrett. I just know he's not happy."

"George is right," Thomas said. "It may be worth having him as a friend if we want to catch Rix out."

"Good job, Rix." From high up on the ridge, Septimus cast his gaze along the blackened remains of the fence. They'd arrived in time to see four men from Wildu Creek ride away. "It will take them a long time to fix that. You should get a good go at the waterhole this summer and any of their strays that wander this way."

"We'll have to be careful a while," Rix said. "Black ash will coat any animal that walks that way. Hopefully we'll get some more rain and the wind will disperse the rest. Then we can cross back and forth as we like."

They stared out over the plain to the black line that was Baker's fence.

"You know Fowler didn't get the shearing job at Wildu Creek this year?"

"I heard," Septimus said. Not that it would have mattered as far as syphoning off some wool went. After the police raid and Pell's disappearance, that little sideline had dried up.

"He allowed his men to be a lot rougher there," Rix said. "Baker was always down some extras by the time Fowler's crew had finished."

The thought gave Septimus some small satisfaction. He did what he could to line his own pockets with the money from the wool he'd been able to steal and then the stock that made its way to his land. He also encouraged Rix to do whatever he could to undermine their neighbour but still Baker seemed to prosper.

"Your profits will be up this year," Rix said. "We've had few stock losses and a lot of wool sent to the port."

Septimus eyed his overseer. He was angling for something. "You already get a bonus for every sheep that's shorn." It was only small but it encouraged Rix to keep stock levels up. Neales was always complaining they were overstocking but even he had been silenced by the returns of the past year.

"I was going to suggest some improvements," Rix said. "If we're going to carry this many sheep, the shearing shed and yards need expanding."

"Isn't that what I pay you for?"

"The three of us are busy enough with the stock. Neales isn't much help with building. I suppose Pavey and I could tackle it, only …"

"Only what, Rix?" Septimus snapped. "Spit it out man."

"Well I've heard there are some hut builders in the area and we could do with some decent lodgings. A place for Neales and somewhere big enough so you could have your own room when you stay."

Septimus opened his mouth to squash the idea then closed it. He rarely returned to Port Augusta these days; he spent most of his time on the road. The inn was still not returning the profits he'd hoped for. He'd gone back to hawking in the district well south of Port Augusta and travelling to Adelaide to stock his wagon. When he needed a break from that, he stayed with Dulcie or came north to Smith's Ridge. He was always comfortable with Dulcie, but the basic hut on the Ridge was barely big enough for two to sleep in, and there was no proper kitchen. Baker had built a decent hut but perhaps Smith's Ridge could do better.

"I'll think on it, Rix," he said. "A few more Wildu Creek sheep should help your cause along." Septimus gave a mirthless laugh and walked his horse down from the ridge.

Sixty-one

1860

"This might take a few years," Jacob said as he looked back along the wire fence.

Thomas stopped hammering the post he'd been driving into the ground and followed the direction of Jacob's gaze. From this vantage point up on the ridge, they could see the new fence stretching away below them, disappearing into the valleys and reappearing on the next hilltop.

"This is the last of the Smith's Ridge boundary," he said with a sigh of satisfaction. The old brush fence they'd been patching since the fire two years earlier was no more.

"Rix will find it difficult to breach."

"In that case it should pay for itself very quickly."

Thomas had invested a lot of money in this fence. If it stopped Smith's Ridge stock grazing his land and Rix pilfering his sheep it would be worth every penny.

"You know it's nearly twelve years since you and I first came to look at this country with Gulda?"

Thomas lifted his hat, rubbed his hair and pushed the hat back in place. What had happened to those two bright-eyed young men who'd wanted to claim this land as their own?

"It seems only yesterday and yet such a long time ago," he said.

"You're sure doing well, Thomas. Plenty of stock, a new stone house being built and all these wire fences."

"Lizzie has earned a decent home after all these years. She works as hard as we do." Thomas gestured, taking in the land below them. "And as for fences, we've only done one boundary. We'll begin the southern section next."

"You never stop working."

"There's always work to be done." Thomas lifted his hammer again. "Like this fence."

"You know people think you're crazy, don't you?" Jacob grinned.

"I don't care what they think. Sheep find their way to water and feed. If they're bound by fences there'll be less shepherding work for us."

"Then you won't need me any longer."

Thomas paused his hammering and studied the man who, along with Zac, was not only family but his close friend. "There will always be work for you here, Jacob," he said.

Jacob leaned against a post and looked to the west. "Things could have been so different," he murmured.

"You know you're welcome to stay as long as you want." Thomas gripped his brother-in-law's shoulder.

"I'll see this job out." He turned back to Thomas. "Then I'll see what Lady Luck has in store for me next."

Thomas was pleased to see the grin back on his face. Like Lizzie, Jacob could always manage to see the silver lining in a bad situation. He'd done all sorts since the loss of Smith's Ridge, from mine work to carting loads with bullock teams, but he'd never stayed at any one job for long. Thomas was grateful he had remained on at Wildu Creek this time as long as he had.

"I hear Wiltshire is back at the Ridge."

Thomas swung the hammer hard. "What that man does is of no concern to me."

Jacob flicked a look at Thomas then set to his own work.

Thomas pounded the post with his hammer. In this vast country, of all the people to have as a neighbour, he had the one man who tested his patience beyond endurance. No matter what the bible said about turning the other cheek, Thomas found each time he did, Wiltshire was there, slapping him again.

Thomas knew he had difficulty seeing reason when Wiltshire was mentioned. Perhaps living out here all these years had made him a little crazy: the hard work, the isolation, the heat, the loss of two babies. He paused the relentless pounding. Even though Ellen was now well past two years, Thomas still watched over her and, according to Lizzie, indulged her far too much. He couldn't help himself. If he lost another little girl he truly thought he would take leave of his senses.

"Father!"

Thomas fought to keep the panic from rising. Why would Lizzie allow Joseph to come all this way alone? He looked up and was relieved to see there were two horses approaching, the pony carrying Joseph and the larger horse with an older man, a stranger. Even though Joseph had turned eight and rode well, he wasn't allowed to head out alone.

"Who's that?" Jacob asked.

"I don't know."

Thomas ignored the stranger. He was intent on his son, who was smiling broadly. At least it couldn't be bad news.

"Father," Joseph said as he got closer. "I've brought Mr Browne to visit you."

Thomas shifted his gaze to the solidly built man now dismounting his horse. The brown jacket and the leather leggings were familiar. The man wearing them had become more portly and the hair visible under his broad hat had greyed but the quickness of his eyes and the smile on his face was the same.

Thomas strode forward, his hand outstretched. "AJ! What are you doing all the way out here?"

His old employer shook his hand firmly and gripped his shoulder. "I've grown a little soft, sitting around in town. I came to spend some time with Wick at Penakie and then I felt the urge to visit you. I wanted to see for myself this country of yours and what my investment has produced."

"It's good to see you," Thomas said. He'd paid back his original debt to AJ, and they corresponded, but he hadn't seen him in a long time.

AJ shook Jacob's hand, then gave the wire fence a look. "This is an interesting idea," he said. "Wick and I have spoken about fences at Penakie."

"It won't stop the wild dogs." Thomas tested the strain on the top wire.

"Or the natives," Jacob added.

"But it will make it easier to manage our stock," Thomas said.

"Look at me," Joseph called.

They all turned to see the boy balancing on the fence further up the hill. His arms were flung wide and his feet were either side of the wire on the steps Thomas had built. They were a kind of stile, a concession to Daisy. Their friendship had never been the same since the first fence was built. He hoped she would approve of a place for her people to cross the new one.

Joseph swung his leg and jumped to the ground on the Smith's Ridge side. He spun around in a circle, and the breeze he made flipped his hat from his head.

Thomas stiffened. Dread coursed through him. "Get back over here."

Joseph froze and stared at his father.

"Now, Joseph."

Thomas wanted nothing to do with Smith's Ridge. In his mind that land had tainted any of his family who had touched it. The fence was a symbol of the safety to be found on the Wildu Creek side.

"Well, we know your crazy contraption works at least." Jacob chuckled, breaking the tension as he walked along the fence towards the steps.

Joseph bent to retrieve his hat, the smile wiped from his face. As he dropped to the ground on Wildu Creek side, Jacob ruffled his hair and pushed his hat firmly on his head.

"Problems?" AJ asked.

"Smith's Ridge has always caused us grief," Thomas said, turning his back on the fence.

"Smith's Ridge?" AJ murmured.

"But you don't want to hear about our troubles," Thomas said. "How are things at Penakie? And Wick, how is he?"

"You'll be able to see for yourself."

Thomas gave AJ a sideways look.

"He came with me. He's back at the house with Lizzie."

"Truly?" Thomas smiled. He had only seen Wick a couple of times since he'd left Penakie. "I will enjoy meeting up with him again."

"And Mother's made cake and wild peach pie." Joseph's natural good humour had returned.

Thomas put a hand on his son's shoulder and gave it a squeeze. He rarely raised his voice to the boy. "In that case I think we should call it a day. Time to go home," he said.

*

Later that evening, after they'd all eaten too much of Lizzie's wonderful roasted mutton and pie, Thomas, AJ and Wick remained in the outside room after everyone else had retired for the night. Thomas kept a small fire going – the days were warm but the last few nights the temperature had dropped quickly after sunset.

"This stone house you're building is a fine construction, Thomas." AJ was settled back in his chair, his hands resting on his rounded stomach. "We should do the same at Penakie, Wick."

"I don't know nothing about building with stone, Mr Browne."

"You're a damn good overseer," AJ said. "You deserve some better lodgings."

Thomas studied Wick. The firelight flickered off his rugged features. His fair hair was thick and nearly to his shoulders and his arms bulged inside his shirt. The terrified shearer's boy had grown into a fine man.

"We had builders help us with the walls and windows," Thomas said. "Part of the supplies Zac will bring from Port Augusta is a load of tin for the roof. We'll finish that ourselves."

"I've seen tin being used. Cheaper and quicker than wood," AJ said. "I think we need to look into a building you a better home, Wick. Then perhaps you can ask that young lady to marry you." He gave a low chuckle that made his stomach wobble.

Wick stretched his hands out to the fire but kept his head lowered. Lizzie had teased him earlier about his good looks and being chased by the girls. His face had coloured then. Evidently there was a local shepherd's daughter he was smitten with. Thomas remembered his own awkwardness when it came to women.

"A new house will make life a little easier for all of us," he said quietly. "Wooden floors, ceilings and good strong windows and a kitchen and wash house. We've got a wide verandah front and back and high walls and roof to help keep it cool. We've even put a new roof and door on the toilet." Thomas could feel the pride inflate his chest as he went on. "The best part will be the tank dug into the hill to store rainwater from the roof. Lizzie won't have to struggle with the barrels any more; and we've dug a small cellar to store food." He lowered his voice again. "But a roof and tank will be little use if it doesn't rain."

"This country looks good even though it's autumn," Wick said.

"We've had some good years." Thomas threw another branch on the fire. Sparks crackled up into the air in a short display of glittery light. "But if we get another long dry like we did in '54, I won't be able to feed the stock I've got."

"Do you think that's likely?" AJ asked.

"Likely? Yes," Thomas said. "When, I don't know. The country's different up here, not like Penakie. We haven't had rain since late last year and there's no sign we're getting any shortly. I'll have too many sheep to maintain if it doesn't come down soon."

"How many sheep do you have now?" AJ asked.

"Six thousand."

"The Gwynns back home are looking to buy more stock," Wick said. "I was talking to their new shepherd just before we came up here."

"How's Duffy?" Thomas asked. "Is he still working for the Gwynns?"

"No," Wick said. "Turned up his toes. Overseer found him dead in his swag a few weeks back. Not sure what killed him but more'n likely the grog, they reckon."

Thomas stared into the fire. He'd never been a good friend of Duffy's but the man had certainly livened up his days at Penakie. It was sad to hear of his passing.

"Anyway," Wick went on, "the new bloke reckons they're down on stock and looking to buy."

"Might be worth thinking about, Thomas," AJ said.

"Yes." Thomas had been pondering what to do as a dry March had dragged into a dry April. He still had feed, but if he kept so much stock, it wouldn't last until next summer without rain.

"I've still got property south of Adelaide. If you ever need to, you could shift a mob down there."

"That's very generous, AJ, though I hope it won't come to that."

"Sounds like this neighbour of yours is causing you some trouble as well," AJ said.

"Irritating. He's overstocked and brings his sheep onto Wildu. We've got better water supplies and more grass country than he has. I'm sure he takes sheep from time to time too."

"Surely they're marked?" AJ leaned closer.

"They're adept at finding ways to disguise markings. I'm hopeful the new fence will slow him down."

"What's his name?"

"Rix is the overseer but Wiltshire is the owner."

"Septimus Wiltshire?" Wick sat straight in his chair.

"Do you know him?"

"He used to travel around our area hawking," Wick said. "Rarely comes Penakie way any more but I've heard he's still plying his trade in other parts."

"He wouldn't go near George Smith and his sons," Thomas said. "It was George he swindled to get his hands on Smith's Ridge."

"Ah. I wondered at the reason for the property name." AJ nodded. "How did he get away with it? I wouldn't have thought George easily duped."

"Neither he is," Thomas said. "But Wiltshire is a cunning devil. I've discovered he's the same man who swindled me when I first began working for you."

"Really?" AJ cast a sharp look at Thomas.

"It's a long story."

"He's the man I told you about, Mr Browne," Wick said. "Remember when I discovered those unmarked wool bales after Fowler's team had been through several years back?"

"We had unmarked bales when Fowler was here," Thomas said.

"I noticed the Penakie bales before they made it onto the wagon and branded them myself," Wick said. "I thought it had been a mistake."

"We lost bales twice while we were using Fowler," Thomas said. "The first time we didn't know until it was too late but the second time we marked them with thread and let them go to the port. The police in Port Augusta tracked them but the man who was found with them escaped custody. From his description I'm sure he wasn't Wiltshire."

"Wiltshire happened to turn up at Penakie before Fowler left," Wick said. "They appeared not to know each other but later I overhead them arguing. It wouldn't surprise me if Fowler supplied Wiltshire somehow."

"He's slippery," Thomas said. "I've never been able to catch him out, but I've suspected him of many things."

"He'll get caught one day, Thomas," AJ said. "It must be difficult having such a neighbour but your hard work has paid off for you here. Don't lose sleep over him. You have enough to battle with the elements."

"You're right about that." Thomas stared out across the creek into the darkness. His mind saw the view even though his eyes couldn't. "If I've learned one thing about living here it's that it's not predictable. Several good years could just as easily lead to several bad."

"Do you want me to speak to Gwynn about buying some of your sheep?" AJ gave him a steady look.

Thomas nodded. "Yes," he said. "I think that's a good idea."

Sixty-two

1864

Septimus pushed open the door of his inn. The hot wind at his back propelled him inside.

"Shut the door!"

He looked up at Ethel's bellow.

"Oh, for gawd's sake, it's you, Mr Wiltshire."

He heaved the door shut behind him. The dust that had blown in settled around the room, but the flies took a little longer. He flung his hand in the air to disperse them. It was barely cooler inside than out.

Ethel bustled around the bar, lifting her apron to fan herself as she moved. "What on earth brings you here in the middle of summer?" She pulled out a chair for him.

"Checking my investment. I've had little income from this inn for months." Septimus cast his eyes about the empty bar. "Where is your husband, madam?"

"Down in the cellar. We're down to our last bag of flour."

Septimus disliked Ethel. She was much too forward and he didn't trust her … but he did like her food. "I've just made the journey from Adelaide."

"In this weather?"

"I would appreciate some food and a cool drink."

"We've no beer."

Septimus squinted through the dusty air at the woman. He didn't care for beer but his customers expected it. "What do you mean you've no beer?"

"We haven't had a wagon through here for over a month."

Septimus rested his elbows on the table and gripped his head in his hands. This damned country was beginning to get the better of him. Everyone was suffering from lack of water. No one wanted to buy the goods he was peddling. He hadn't seen Rix for several months but his most recent trip to Smith's Ridge hadn't been a good one. Feed had been low and stock struggled to make it to what water they had. Baker's wire fence had put paid to grazing his land. Rix had complained he would have few sheep left to shear if things didn't improve. It was now well after shearing time and Septimus hadn't heard from him.

There was a bang from the back of the inn and slow footsteps crossed the wooden floor.

Septimus looked up as Ned entered the room.

"Look who's here, Ned," Ethel said as she put a jug of cordial and a mug on the table. She put her hands to her hips and studied Septimus. "I've some mutton and pickles and bread I can bring you."

Septimus had lived on little else for weeks. "That'll do," he snapped.

Ethel retreated to the kitchen, flapping as she went. Ned watched him with brooding eyes from the other side of the bar.

"Ethel tells me you've had no custom," Septimus said.

"Times are tough." Ned shrugged his shoulders. He picked up a cloth and began wiping the bar. Dust rose around him and settled where he'd been. "There's no feed for bullock or horse for miles and little water. Few are venturing this way unless they've room to cart the feed for their animals with them."

"Damn!" Septimus thumped the table with both fists. The dust rose around him again and he began to cough. He poured himself some of the cordial. It was cool at least.

"Times are tough," Ned said again and continued his wiping.

Septimus glowered at him. Tough times or no, this inn should have done much better that it had. He didn't trust the man or his bumptious wife.

"I'll see the ledger while I'm here," Septimus said.

Ned stopped his wiping as Ethel bustled back into the room.

"Are you planning on staying here long?" she asked as she placed a plate of food next to the cordial.

Septimus shovelled some mutton and pickle into his mouth. At least the meat wasn't dried. "No," he said once he'd swallowed the mouthful. "I've got more business to attend to."

"In this heat." Ethel flapped her apron again.

Septimus ignored her until she left him to his meal.

He was planning to go to the hut before dusk. It was difficult enough managing the rough track on a horse, let alone one pulling a wagon. He hoped Dulcie would be there. She hadn't been several months earlier, when he'd stopped on his way back from Smith's Ridge. He had tried to govern his rage: it was, after all, only the second time that had happened. His wagon was loaded with supplies he couldn't sell. He planned to settle in the hut with Dulcie and wait out this terrible weather. Surely rain had to fall eventually.

"Won't be much of a Christmas for people this year," Ethel said.

"Christmas?" Septimus looked up. She leaned against the front of the bar. Ned was watching from his side.

"It's only a few weeks away," Ethel said. "We were hoping you'd let us stay on here."

Septimus frowned. "Where else would you be going?"

"We thought perhaps you'd close the place up since times were so bad."

Septimus looked around the gloomy interior. Usually Ethel had the place spick and span but after weeks of dust storms and on a day like today, it was a losing battle. If the place were left empty he knew it would soon go to ruin. Good times must surely return and with them would come the teamsters and the business, even if it hadn't previously met his expectations. He needed someone prepared to look after the place, but not cost him money.

"I had planned to," he said.

"Such a shame," Ethel said.

"Yes." Septimus took another sip of the cordial, watching them over the top of the mug. "But if there's no trade I can't afford to pay wages."

"We've nowhere else to go," Ned said.

"That's right, Mr Wiltshire." Ethel flapped again. "If you could see your way clear to letting us stay on, we'd fend for ourselves, wouldn't we, Ned?"

Her husband nodded. "We could keep the place in good repair until it opened for business again."

Septimus leaned back in his chair. His stomach was full and he felt somewhat refreshed now that he was out of the ferocious wind. "It could be a long time," he said. "How will you manage?"

"People are giving away sheep," Ned said. "And there's plenty of animals come to the permanent water down in the creek. I'm having no trouble getting meat."

"We could do with some flour and sugar and tea," Ethel said. "In return for looking after the place, perhaps." She raised her eyebrows expectantly but she wasn't as confident as she had been. She rubbed her hands together. "If you'd be so kind as to leave some with us, that is."

"I've got others to deliver to," Septimus said making a show of his deliberating. "But perhaps there's enough to provide you with some basics." He pushed away his empty plate. "Now let's look at these books and close them off."

"Just until things get better," Ned said.

Septimus put his elbows on the table and tapped his fingers together. "We'll see what the new year brings."

It was almost dark by the time the wagon crested the last rise. The hut, at least in his mind, glowed in the light of the setting sun. There was no smoke from the chimney but it had been so hot Dulcie would surely not have kept the fire going.

Septimus searched the hut and the area around it for signs of life. His heart sank as he found none. Perhaps Dulcie had left for good. He urged the horse on along the track. The wind that had blown for nearly two days had finally abated just as he left the inn. The air was still and thick with dust raised by the horse's hooves and the wheels of the wagon.

A sudden movement near the creek drew his eye. Dulcie stood in her elegant nakedness, and his heart raced. She was there after all and as beautiful as ever. He hadn't been with her for so long he felt he would burst.

He brought the wagon to a halt and jumped down. She took a hesitant few steps towards him.

He paused, puzzled by her reluctance to approach him.

"It's me, Dulcie," he crooned. "Your Septimus, home at last."

Behind her there was a small wail. She turned and hurried back to the creek. He followed her and stopped in surprise. Dulcie sat on the large root of a tree, a baby in one arm and the other around a little boy. Her eyes were round and fearful as she glanced at Septimus then down at her baby.

Septimus stood open mouthed. These must be Dulcie's children. Rage bubbled inside him. She had been with another man. He had thought her faithful only to him and he'd been duped.

He spun on his heel.

"Papa," a small voice said.

Septimus stopped. He turned slowly back.

The boy stood up and took a step away from his mother. She murmured something to him.

"Papa," the boy said again softly.

Septimus stared. The last light of the dying day was filtering through the trees, turning everything red and gold. In the shadow of the tree Septimus could see that Dulcie's skin, a deep velvet black, was much darker than the children's.

Dulcie rose and offered him the chubby baby in her arms.

"Septimus," she said in her funny English. "Papa, Septimus."

"Are you saying these children are mine?"

She put the baby in his arms. "Papa," she said.

Henry, whom he'd not seen for nearly two years, would be fourteen now. Septimus tried to gauge the age of these children. This native boy calling him Papa was perhaps nine or ten and the baby, who was also a boy, not yet one.

He looked back at Dulcie. She looked thinner than when he'd last seen her and ill at ease. She was no doubt anxious about his reaction. Perhaps they were someone else's and she was trying to pass them off as his. But if that were the case why would she wait until now?

Was it possible these two were his? Septimus felt a glow of pride he'd never felt for Henry.

"I am papa?" He pointed to himself and then tentatively to each child.

Dulcie nodded. "Papa."

"You are sure?"

Dulcie nodded again. He had taught her some English over their time together. Quite often she didn't understand but he believed she knew what he was asking now.

The baby clutched his finger and pulled it to his mouth. Before Septimus could react he felt a sharp pressure on his finger.

"Ow!" he yelped.

The older boy gave a soft laugh.

"He bites," Septimus said and tried to hand him back to Dulcie.

Her face lit in a smile. "Papa carry," she said. She spoke quickly to the boy and he went back to collect a bowl of food. Dulcie picked up a bucket full of water.

"Hut," she said and led the way up the hill.

Septimus followed like a puppy. Not only did he have a beautiful wife, but she had raised two strong sons. After all the hardships of the year he felt as if he had come home. What had Ethel said about some people not having much of a Christmas? Septimus didn't care for the occasion but this year he knew it would be very special.

Sixty-three

1865

Harriet drew the rug tighter across her knees and flicked the reins. Her horse picked up speed, making the chilly wind rush past faster. She gritted her teeth, anxious to make the inn before dark. She had spent one night camped out on her way from Port Augusta but it was a long time since her hawking days with Septimus. She didn't like being in the bush alone any more.

She pursed her lips as she thought of her husband. Henry had wanted to come with her to look for him but she had insisted he stay home. They had a nice neighbour who would look out for him and provide his meals. Harriet had always made Septimus out to be a good father who must travel a lot to provide for them. She wasn't sure what she would find out on this journey or how long it would take her and she wanted Henry safe at home, his delusions unshattered.

It had been three years since they'd last seen Septimus. In that time, Harriet had not heard a word from him or received any money. Thankfully her sewing business had done well, although it was a little quiet now with the hard times of dry years. She was getting by but becoming increasingly frustrated with her situation. She was at the mercy of the few people with money at the port. Henry was of an age where he should be taking up a vocation soon and once again there was little on offer. She knew Septimus was hawking again and getting his supplies from Adelaide: there was no reason for his family to live anywhere else.

She didn't care for herself but Henry watched for his father. Septimus had suggested Henry go with him on his travels a few times in the past. Harriet had always been secretly pleased when Septimus reneged but she knew Henry was disappointed.

So she had set off on this journey to find her husband. Discreet enquiries around the port had confirmed he no longer visited, so she had decided to trace him through the businesses she knew he had. The inn was the closest and she needed no directions. If he was not there, she thought she'd try Smith's Ridge, the property Mr Baker had mentioned years back when he frightened her with his visit.

Harriet shivered in spite of her gloves and coat. The wind was cold in a cloudless sky. Dust rose around her and the foothills she travelled through were bare of vegetation except for the bushes and trees. The land had suffered through three years with barely a drop of rain. All vegetation around the port had been stripped by animals or people needing wood and building materials. She hadn't realised the barren land extended up into the hills.

She was thankful to see a light at the window and smoke pouring from the chimney of the inn. It would be pleasant to have company. She had only passed two wagons going in the opposite direction. Their drivers were hunched into the wind like her and had barely given her a wave.

She came to a stop at the front of the inn, climbed down and tethered her horse. She felt stiff and sore. She reached around and patted feeling back into her bottom. "You've grown soft, Harriet," she murmured.

A raucous laugh issued from the inn, and the murmur of voices.

Harriet stepped up onto the verandah. She was looking forward to meeting Ethel again. How lovely! The check curtains she'd made were still hanging in the windows. They were drawn, no doubt to keep out the chilly air.

Harriet pushed open the door. Several men stopped talking and turned to stare at her. They were seated around tables with bowls of steaming food and mugs of drink. From the look of their cheeks there was something warmer in the mugs than hot tea. Ned and Ethel both gaped at her from across the bar.

Ethel was the first to speak. "Mrs Wiltshire!" She came from behind the bar, arms outstretched. "What are you doing here?" She peered past Harriet, a small flick of concern crossing her face. "Where's Mr Wiltshire?"

"I'm travelling alone," Harriet said. She felt a pang of disappointment. She had hoped to find Septimus there, or at least that Ethel and Ned might know where he was, but from their reaction she could see that wasn't the case. "That smells good," she said nodding towards the closest bowl.

"Kangaroo stew's all it is, but you're welcome to it." Ethel closed the door and drew Harriet to a table by herself near the fire. "Warm yourself up, lovey," she said. "You look blue with cold."

"The wind is icy."

"Have you travelled up here all the way from Port Augusta by yourself?"

Harriet nodded, pulled off her gloves and held her hands towards the fire.

"Ned!"

Harriet jumped as Ethel bellowed her husband's name.

"Bring Mrs Wiltshire some of your brew. She needs warming up. I'll go and get you some stew."

"Can someone see to the horse?" Harriet asked.

"Course, lovey." Ethel gave her a grin. "Ned'll see to it soon as he's got you a drink."

Harriet had taken to having the odd glass of sherry but she rarely drank anything else. She wondered what Ned's brew would be.

"You men mind your manners," Ethel said to the room in general then she bustled out to the kitchen. Ned placed a mug in front of Harriet with a glimmer of a smile and a nod, then let himself out the door.

One by one the men went back to their meals and their talking. Harriet sat quietly, studying each one. They were weary-looking men with weathered skin and well-worn clothes. From the snatches of conversation she heard and their appearance, she was guessing they were teamsters. She didn't recall seeing any sign of bullock, horse or wagon near the inn, and the last time she'd seen Septimus he'd said there was little trade. Perhaps that had been a different time of year, because there were five men enjoying the food and drink at the inn tonight.

She reached for the mug and the smell of the liquid nearly took her breath away. Ned was probably making his own grog.

Ethel came back with two bowls of stew.

"I hoped you might feel like company," she said. "I don't see too many women around these parts."

"Of course," Harriet said.

Ned came back inside and Ethel plied Harriet with questions about the port and what was happening there.

Finally Harriet put down the rough spoon and knife. Her bowl was empty.

"That was delicious, Ethel, thank you."

"You're very welcome, Mrs Wiltshire. I'm glad you've finally had the opportunity to visit. You happened to strike us on a rare busy night. That's the first lot we've had here for a good while."

Harriet looked around the room. The other tables were now empty. The men had left while she and Ethel were eating. Ned had disappeared also.

"I didn't see any sign of animals or wagons," Harriet said. "Where do they camp?"

"Further away, I expect. I don't go looking for them. With the permanent water being so low they only bring their animals to drink. They camp elsewhere."

"My husband said trade had been poor the last time I saw him."

"The long dry has affected everyone." Ethel collected the bowls.

"Even before that." Harriet tried to watch Ethel's face but she was bent over the table. "He's never made the return from the inn he expected."

Ethel stood up and looked at Harriet. "I don't understand the way of it, Mrs Wiltshire, but we've stayed on, Ned and me, even though the inn is actually closed. We do the best we can. We've nowhere else to go."

"Closed?"

"The last time your husband was here, he closed the books off. Ned and me don't get a wage but we can stay on and look after the place until things get better."

"When was that, Ethel? When was my husband last here?"

"Oh, now you're testing me." Ethel held the bowls in one hand and put the other to her cheek. "Just before Christmas, that's right. We talked about folks having a tough time of it for Christmas."

"That's five months ago." Harriet slumped in her chair. Septimus could be anywhere by now.

"Something wrong?"

"No, thank you, Ethel. I was hoping to catch up with him here. It's quite a while since he was home last and we've things to discuss."

"Lawd sakes, you don't think something's happened to him?"

"No. It's not unusual for him to be gone for long periods of time." Harriet didn't say it had been three years since she'd last seen her husband. "He's back hawking again, which takes him many places."

"Yes, I remember he had his wagon loaded with supplies to deliver."

Harriet stared at the fire. What would she do now? Had he gone on to the property he had in the north?

"He didn't say which direction he was headed?" she asked.

"No, lovey. He never tells us what he's up to. Sometimes we see him a couple of times in a month and other times not for several months."

Harriet gave a little shiver.

"Would you like me to put more wood on the fire?" Ethel asked.

"No, thank you." Harriet suddenly felt very weary. "Do you have a spare bed where I can stay the night? I'll be off again in the morning."

"Course we do. There's the little room at the end of the verandah. Rarely have visitors who want a bed for the night. I'll go and make it up for you."

Ethel bustled out to the kitchen. Harriet held her hands towards the dying fire.

"Where are you, Septimus?" she murmured.

He had evidently called at the inn more often than he ever did at his home in the port. Why would he call back in a couple of weeks after a visit? Perhaps on his way to and from another place nearby? But there was little in these hills. She remembered how glad she'd felt to move to Port Augusta after the isolation of the little hut.

Harriet stiffened. The hut – perhaps Septimus still used it as a resting place or even storage for some of his goods. Her spirits lifted. She was sure she could find her way there. She'd go tomorrow. Perhaps there'd be a clue to his whereabouts. She rose to find Ethel and the room she was to sleep in. A good sleep was what she needed. She planned an early start in the morning to have a good look around the inn in daylight before she set off. Ethel and Ned were very cosy here for people with little income.

Sixty-four

Septimus scratched at his bushy beard. He really should shave it off. He'd never abided thick facial hair since his convict days but he was in no hurry. In fact he was in no hurry to do anything. He was the happiest he'd ever been here at the hut with Dulcie and the children. He almost felt as if he could stay here forever, to hell with the rest of the world, but deep down he knew that couldn't happen. The wagonload of supplies he'd arrived with in December was nearly all gone. Dulcie was adept at gathering food from the bush but she didn't like to go far from the hut these days. The time was coming when he'd have to face the world again … but not just yet.

Dulcie's sharp tone drew him from the bedroom into the kitchen, where she was standing at the back door with Jack. Septimus had used some of his time to make a door through the back of the hut where he'd added a verandah for the boys to sleep. Jack had grown taller: he was nearly the same height as Dulcie. Neither mother nor son looked pleased.

"What's the matter?"

"I want to hunt, Papa." Jack turned his big pleading eyes to his father.

"What are you hunting?" He smiled at the boy, who was so different from his half-brother, Henry.

Jack's face split in a grin. "Kangaroo, wallaby, possum."

"Whoa." Septimus put up his hand. "One animal will be enough."

"Not hunt today," Dulcie said, her face full of worry. She had been watchful since Septimus's return, but the last few days she'd been even more on edge.

"Why not?" Septimus asked.

She just shook her head.

Septimus looked at the boy. He was tense with anticipation. Jack often went hunting and he was good at it; he saved Septimus supplying meat for the table. It was a sunny day with less chill in the air than they'd been having, a good day to be outside.

Septimus wrapped his arms around Dulcie and tucked her naked back to his bare chest.

"The boy will be fine," he murmured in her ear. "Off you go," he said to Jack. "Don't be too long."

The boy went before his mother could say any more. Septimus looked down at Eddie, who had wobbled across the floor on his pudgy legs and now grasped a handful of his trousers.

The baby on the other hand was still a nuisance, demanding Dulcie's time. Septimus shook his leg to escape the dirty fingers. Eddie plopped to the floor.

Dulcie bent to pick up the child, but a cry from Jack made her rush for the door.

Dulcie cried out in her language. Septimus stepped up behind her and frowned. Two black men had Jack grasped between them. One of the men carried a waddy at his side and the other a spear. They spoke quickly. From their tone, Septimus could tell they weren't happy. He hesitated. Perhaps Jack had encroached on their hunt.

One of the men pointed at him and began to shout. Septimus turned to Dulcie. "What is it? What do they want?"

She shook her head at him, tears brimming in her eyes.

"They not happy," she said, "I am your woman."

"I'll set them straight." Septimus turned back to the men. He pointed to Dulcie. "My woman," he said then he pointed to Jack and Eddie. "My sons."

The men fell silent. Jack pulled away from their grip.

That's all they need, Septimus thought, someone to show them who's boss. He stepped through the door and across the verandah. Even though the sun shone from a cloudless sky, the crisp air made the skin on his bare chest prickle.

"Go," he shouted and pointed away. "Leave my family alone."

One man spoke, then the other. Instead of turning away as Septimus had expected, they rushed forward and grabbed him by the arms. He struggled but their grip was strong. Septimus dug his bare feet into the ground as the men pulled him away from the hut.

"Let me go," he yelled.

Behind him he could hear Dulcie crying out. Septimus twisted and struggled but they only gripped him harder, dragging him towards the bush beyond the hut.

Harriet tethered her horse and cart just off the track before she reached the last rise that led to the hut. She could smell smoke in the fresh morning air, so she expected someone was at home. She just couldn't be sure it would be Septimus.

She followed the track, keeping close to the bush. The hut came into view and she could see the smoke puffing from the chimney. A wagon – Septimus's, she thought with relief – was parked close to one wall of the hut, and there was a chair on the verandah. As she got closer she heard voices and then a woman's cry. She paused at the edge of the verandah then cautiously tapped on the door. No one answered. She heard another shout. It sounded like Septimus, but it wasn't close. She pushed open the door. The hut was well lived in and she recognised a hat and coat hanging on the wall as her husband's. There was a door in the back wall that hadn't been there before.

"Let me go."

Even though Septimus's voice was distant she could hear the fear in it. She stepped quietly to the open back door and peered through. Her heart thumped at the sight of two fierce-looking native men with Septimus held between them.

Harriet spun and took in the room that had been her home, looking for something she could use as a weapon. The firearm was still above the front door. She lifted it down and checked it. Septimus had taught her to use it and she had managed to shoot a few animals during her long stretches alone at the hut.

She moved back to the door, stepped through it and lifted the rifle. "Stop," she yelled in the strongest tone she could create. She looked down the barrel of the firearm at the tallest man.

The natives ceased their struggle with Septimus and turned to look at her. She could see Septimus lift his head, trying to see who it was. She was appalled at how unkempt his appearance was and how thin he had become.

"Missus!"

Harriet shifted her head slightly at the call.

A native woman stood off to her left. Harriet had been so intent on Septimus and his attackers she hadn't noticed her. She was totally naked and yet familiar.

"Dulcie?"

As Dulcie turned towards her, Harriet could see she held a toddler in her arms and that a boy stood at her side.

"What's going on here?" Harriet asked. One of the natives moved and she pointed the firearm at him. "Septimus?" she called.

"Harriet? Harriet, is that you? Thank God. I should have brought the firearm myself."

One of the natives began to speak to Dulcie. His tone was aggressive.

Dulcie answered in a pleading tone. The man yanked Septimus another step towards the bush.

Septimus cried out.

"Papa!" the boy yelled.

Harriet looked at the boy in shock. "Papa?" she said softly. Then she noticed his skin was paler than his mother's, and so was the toddler's.

"It's all a misunderstanding," Septimus called. "Shoot one of them, Harriet, please, before they do me any harm."

Harriet ignored him, her gaze locked on the children. The boy was quite tall. "What's your name?" she asked him.

"Jack."

"And who is your papa, Jack?"

The boy pointed. He could have been waving his finger at any of the three men but he rushed forward and flung his arms around Septimus.

One of the native men pushed the boy away and raised his waddy.

Dulcie screamed and the boy scampered back to her.

Harriet suddenly realised what had been happening all these years. "That's why we've hardly seen you," she said. "All these years you've had another family, another wife, a black one." She spat the words. "You've lied and you've cheated many people, Septimus, but how could you do this to your own son, to Henry?"

"We can sort it out," Septimus said. He twisted in the natives' grip but they dragged him another step. "Harriet," he whined. "Please, Harriet, help me."

Harriet continued to watch the men over the top of the firearm. The natives glared back at her; Septimus had become a whimpering lump in their hands. He was her husband and yet she realised she no longer needed him. She and Henry were better off without him. Slowly she lowered the firearm.

"Harriet!" Septimus screamed.

She glanced at Dulcie and her two boys then turned and walked back inside the hut and out the other door. The sound of Septimus's pleading screams faded as she kept walking back up the track to her cart. She tucked the firearm under the canvas and turned the horse. The wind had sprung up. She shivered from its chill and the soft moaning sound it made through the trees. She pulled her coat tighter, flicked the reins and straightened her shoulders. Her horse picked up speed and she left the hut in the hills without a backwards glance.

Sixty-five

A miserable cold wind blew across the land, stirring up dust and leaving Thomas chilled to the bone. A few sheep staggered around the barren landscape as he entered the last group of trees along the track that led to the house. He would come back and check on them later. For now he would be pleased to get home. Ever since his first trip away from Wildu Creek when Annie had died, he was never happy going on long journeys without Lizzie and the children.

He'd been gone for months, droving the last of the sheep that were strong enough to walk south to AJ's property, where there was still plenty of feed. Jacob and Timothy had gone with him on the slow journey. Jacob had stayed on to help look after the sheep while Thomas and Timothy had made the return trip via Adelaide and Port Augusta. Thomas had left Timothy and the wagon after their last overnight stop, anxious to ride the last leg home as quickly as he could.

Smoke poured from the chimney. No doubt Lizzie and Ellen were inside on such a cold day but Thomas could see Joseph bending over something down near the creek. He lifted his head at the sound of Thomas's horse.

"Father," he called and ran towards the house, where they met.

Thomas slid from his horse, every muscle aching and weary. The strength of Joseph's embrace nearly knocked him over.

"Steady up, young man," he said. "You're getting too strong for your old father."

"I'm nearly fourteen, you know."

"Didn't you have your thirteenth birthday while I was away?"

"Yes, so I'm on my way to fourteen." Joseph pulled himself up straight.

"He'll be there before we know it," Lizzie said.

Thomas looked up at his wife smiling at him from the verandah. He ruffled his son's hair.

"Find something for the horse to eat and drink, son," he said, and in spite of his weariness he made the three steps up the verandah in quick time and wrapped his arms around Lizzie.

"Where's Ellen?" he asked.

"Sulking up a tree somewhere because I asked her to feed the chickens." Lizzie leaned back and looked up at him. "You really have indulged her too much, Thomas. She's the most wilful child."

"Father."

Ellen came running from the direction Joseph had just gone.

"Look at her," Lizzie said. "She's wild like the natives."

Thomas watched his little girl run barefoot up the steps. Her patched skirt was much shorter than he remembered and her dark wavy hair blew loose around her face. He let go of Lizzie and swept Ellen up. He kissed her pink cheeks.

Ellen giggled then grasped his three-month-old beard in her fingers. "You look like a wild man, Father."

"That's the pot calling the kettle black," Lizzie said.

Thomas laughed and threw an arm around his wife's shoulders. He kissed her cheek. "It's good to be home," he said.

"Where's Timothy?" Ellen asked. Thomas raised an eyebrow. The child had learned from an early age she had Timothy entirely at her beck and call.

"He's following in the wagon."

"Is there a present for me?"

"That's enough from you, miss," Lizzie chided. "There'd better be food in that wagon or you'll go hungry."

Thomas lowered Ellen to the ground. "Go and help Joseph bring the bags from my saddle. There may be something in there."

Ellen squealed in delight, jumped down the steps and disappeared around the corner of the house before either of her parents could issue more instructions.

"You shouldn't be wasting money on gifts," Lizzie said.

"It's nothing much. Just a few sweets and a knife for Joseph."

Lizzie opened her mouth.

"For his birthday," Thomas said quickly and kissed her again. "You taste so good."

"And you, dear husband, smell rather bad. I think we'll all have a bath tonight. Sit down and I'll help you get those boots off."

He did as she asked and then struggled back to his feet. He'd like to fall into bed and sleep for a week. She led him inside and through the front room to the kitchen, where the fire gave a warm glow and something smelling most delicious bubbled over it.

"Is there enough water for baths?"

"We had some rain while you were away. Not enough to soak the ground but it helped add to the tank. Besides, I've got no water to keep my vegetables alive unless we wash once a week."

Thomas watched while she fussed over the fire.

"You're looking thin, Lizzie. Have you had enough to eat?"

"We're getting by, but I am looking forward to what you've brought back with you."

"There's food, although not much flour. That's in short supply everywhere." Thomas frowned.

"What is it?" Lizzie asked.

"The wagon is loaded but it's all thanks to AJ. I had little money and he insisted. I've paid back our first debt and now I owe another. I promised you I'd never owe anyone again after the business with Wiltshire."

"Mr Browne wouldn't try to swindle us."

"He's already taking on a large number of our stock."

"You're a proud man, Thomas, but we have to be practical. I'm sure Mr Browne knows we will pay him back when we can. As you say, we've done it once before." Lizzie took a bowl from the shelf and carried it to the fire. "Now, speaking of food, I've a nice soup here. I've no bread to go with it, mind."

"I *don't* mind," Thomas said and clutched his stomach as it growled in anticipation.

Lizzie laughed and he couldn't help but chuckle. He was home.

Timothy reached Wildu Creek with the wagon later in the day. Everyone helped unload the supplies and Lizzie supervised their arrangement in the cellar. Even Ellen did as she was bade, happy to have her chief admirers back. That night they sat down to a meal of boiled mutton, pumpkin and potatoes. Lizzie had used some of the precious flour to make bread. It was quite a feast after the rough food Thomas and Timothy had scrounged on the road.

"Are you expecting Zac in tonight?" Thomas asked.

"I never know when he'll be in," Lizzie said. "While you've been gone he's been spending all his time looking after the remaining stock."

"I've been helping," Joseph said.

"And me," Ellen said, jutting out her chin.

"Everyone has," Lizzie said. "Zac has been staying out a few nights at a time. He's shifted most of the remaining stock to the higher country, where there's still some permanent water."

"I saw a few sheep out beyond the trees on the plain."

"They're nearly dead," Lizzie said. "Joseph has been taking them whatever he can scrounge. We've put a bucket under the trees and we fill it each day." Her brow was creased in concern.

"There's little else you can do," Thomas said.

They all jumped as the door flung open.

"Zac!" Lizzie cried and leapt up to welcome her brother inside.

Thomas stood up to shake his hand.

"We got most of the stock south," he said taking in Zac's appearance. If Thomas thought he felt tired, Zac was his mirror. His face and hands were dark with dirt, his eyes red with dust and lack of sleep, and his hair stuck out in all directions

"I've got the last few sheep up in the hills," he said. "There's a little water but they have to compete with the natives camped nearby. Gulda and Daisy have moved up there with them. Gulda will keep an eye on things."

"They may as well eat what they want," Thomas said. "I'd rather the sheep were food for someone else than see them taken by wild dogs or die and rot."

Lizzie set some food on the table for Zac and he ate hungrily.

"We're not the only ones doing it tough," Thomas said. "We came home through Port Augusta. I wanted to talk to Mr Grant about our options and Timothy visited his family. You should see the land around the port. It's barren for miles. Everywhere north and west of there is little better."

"People are just walking off their properties," Timothy said. "Their animals are dead and they've nothing to eat."

"We had a rough trip back." Thomas raked his fingers through his hair. "I was hard pressed to get feed for the horses."

"The police at Port Augusta brought in a body while we were there," Timothy said. "Some poor man probably lost his way in the hills."

Thomas noticed Ellen's and Joseph's eyes grow wider.

"Aren't you two the voices of doom and gloom?" Lizzie said and began to stack their empty plates.

"Not all." Thomas aided her attempt to change the subject. "Talk in Adelaide is the government may give us a remission on our rent for a time."

"That's good of them," Zac said. "Now that they've finally realised we've nothing to pay them with."

"There's also talk that when they issue the new leases next year," Thomas said, "they will be for twenty-one years."

"Nearly fifteen years we've been here and for what? We won't last another twenty-one." Zac pushed back his chair and stood up. "Well it's too late for me."

There was silence in the room but for the crackle of the fire.

"What do you mean too late, Uncle Zac?" Joseph asked.

Thomas could see both children watching Zac, their faces full of concern.

"You've all been good to me," Zac said, "but there's nothing more I can do for you, Thomas, and I'm just another mouth to feed."

"You know as soon as I get some money I'll pay you," Thomas said. He understood the frustration Zac felt. There'd been no money for Timothy either, but the young shepherd had asked to stay on.

"It's not that. I'm fed up with the struggle. There must be something else."

"You heard what Thomas said, Zac." Lizzie extended a hand to her brother. "The whole of South Australia is doing it tough."

"Not in Adelaide," Zac said, "or the mines or the country around Adelaide. There are other opportunities."

"You don't have to leave," Lizzie said. "Things will get better."

"You're always the optimist, Lizzie girl." Zac's eyes softened as he looked at his sister. "I've got to go. I don't want to end up like I ... like I was before. I have to try something else."

"When will you go?" Thomas asked.

"Soon," Zac said. "While there's still a horse alive to carry me."

"Are the horses going to die too?" Ellen's worried voice drew their attention.

"Not with you and me here to look after them," Timothy said brightly and winked at the little girl.

"I think it's time for bed," Lizzie said. "We can talk more tomorrow."

She ushered the children out of the room and Timothy said good night, leaving Zac and Thomas alone in the kitchen.

"You know I'm grateful to you for all you've done for us, Zac?" Thomas said.

"It's me who's grateful," Zac said. "You and Lizzie saved my life, turned me around, but I can't take this desolation any longer. We're so helpless. It's not just the sheep but all the wild animals that are dying – and even the natives are struggling to survive. I feel so useless. I can't go down that path again, Thomas, you understand. I have to go."

Thomas stood up and gripped Zac in a firm embrace. "I do," he said.

There was a scuffling noise from the front of the house and then a thump on the door.

"Mr Baker?" Timothy called.

Thomas and Zac both hurried through the front room. Thomas opened the door. Timothy was stooped on the verandah with a man draped over his shoulders.

"What's happened?" Thomas asked.

"I found him by the horse trough," Timothy said. "I think it's Mr Neales."

"Is he …?" Zac's voice croaked to a halt.

Thomas reached to help Timothy and Neales groaned.

"Water," he rasped.

All three carried him to the kitchen and propped him on a chair. Thomas offered Neales a mug of water and helped him put it to his lips. Neales sipped at first then gulped down the rest.

"How did he get here?" Thomas asked Timothy.

"I don't know. I didn't see any sign of a horse."

"I walked," Neales croaked.

"From Smith's Ridge?" Zac asked.

"There's only two horses left there and Rix watches them like a hawk."

Zac offered him a piece of Lizzie's bread and refilled his mug. They watched as Neales wolfed everything down.

He wiped a grimy hand across his mouth. "Rix and Pavey and a couple of horses," he said. "That's about all that's left alive at Smith's Ridge. Even the wild dogs don't bother us any more. I thought if I came this way I might be able to get a ride south with someone. My water ran out yesterday. I was worried I wouldn't make it here."

"You're welcome to stay with us, Neales," Thomas said. "As for heading south, we've just returned –"

"He can come with me."

Thomas looked at Zac.

"You haven't got horses to spare, Thomas, and I'm in no hurry to get anywhere. When Neales is feeling better we can share my horse."

"If you're sure," Thomas said.

Zac held his gaze. "I am."

Sixty-six

Yardu sat in the shade of a scrubby tree. The heat from the rock beneath him radiated up through his body. The air was warm around him and yet he wore his possum-skin coat, as he did whenever there were important decisions to be made. From his vantage point high on a ridge of the mountain he could see a vast distance over the country of his people. He liked to sit there and think. Close to the spirits of his elders.

To one side of him was a pile of huge rocks. On them were painted stories of times past. He knew there were some telling of times without water from the sky and yet his people had survived. Now his country was dry but stripped of all goodness by the white invaders and their animals. Not only that, but some had constructed long fences to block the movement of his people and keep them away from the water that kept them alive.

Gulda, who had married his cousin's sister, had tried to tell Yardu about the ways of the white men, but Yardu could not understand their need to possess and not share. Many lives had been lost during the long dry. There was a big rain coming and the land would once again flow with water but he feared it would not change things. Life for his people would never be the same. He knew it was only a matter of time before the ever-searching men on horses discovered the country beyond this mountain; the last of the places he had been able to live safely with his family.

Across the valleys and plains he could see thick grey clouds gathering along the top of the mountain range. Yardu closed his eyes and softly sang a song of mourning.

"How much further?"

Thomas paused his stride at Joseph's question.

"Just up over the ridge," he said. "It's worth it, you'll see."

Joseph turned back. Already the horses they'd tethered at the start of the ridge were lost from sight. He looked forward again. "It's a long way up."

"Up here is where I got my first look at Wildu Creek. It was after a huge rain and every creek ran with water and it flooded the valley below, where our house is now."

"That's a lot of water." Joseph sounded sceptical.

Thomas glanced at the dark clouds hugging the distant mountain range. There had been reports of big rains to the east a few months earlier. Clouds kept building on the horizon and then nothing came of it. He prayed it would, and sooner rather than later. He'd brought Joseph on this journey in the hope it would inspire his son to keep going. They had all lost heart when the lack of rain killed off the last of their stock and drove many of their nearest neighbours from their land. Even Rix and Pavey had left Smith's Ridge. There were only a few families like the Bakers clinging to their properties.

"It will fall like that again one day," he said. "You'll see." Thomas said it with a conviction he sometimes lacked. That was another reason to make this climb today. He wanted to cast his eye over the land from high up once more.

Thomas climbed on. He hadn't been back to this sacred place since the first time he'd seen it, all those years earlier with Jacob when Gulda had found them shelter from the rain. It was a half-day's ride from the house and then hours of climbing. He could understand why Joseph was complaining. Lucky they hadn't brought Ellen. She had pestered to be brought on the adventure, as she called it, but he'd said no and stuck to it, with Lizzie's help.

He looked ahead at the strips of rocks jutting out at all angles and wondered if he'd even be able to find the cave. He picked his way around and over the rocks, through the straggling bushes that managed to survive on the ledges, until finally he saw a deep shadow on the edge of a rock ahead.

"Here it is," he said. He waited for Joseph to catch up to him. "This is the place Gulda found to shelter us on our first visit here."

"Phew!" Joseph gasped as he peered closer to the opening. "It smells as if something's died in there."

"It may well have," Thomas said.

It wasn't a particularly warm day for November but they were both puffing and the flies were a plague. Thomas turned his back on the cave, opened his water pouch and took a drink. Joseph did the same. The vegetation was thicker there and gave only a glimpse of the creek below.

"That's the start of the creek that runs past our house." Thomas pointed through the gap in the trees.

"It must go a long way."

"You can see it better from the top." Thomas set off again. "It's an easier climb around this side of the ridge."

A few more minutes and they were at the top.

Joseph took off his hat and whistled. "It's like looking at a map. Everything's laid out before us."

Thomas felt a surge of pride. He could see on his son's face the same awe he had felt when he'd taken his first look at the land they now called Wildu Creek.

"You can see where the creek goes right across the valley and the other creeks that run into it."

"Where's our house?" Joseph asked, going closer to the edge.

Thomas stood beside him. "You can't see it. It's hidden by the hills and vegetation."

Joseph climbed onto one of the large boulders beside them. He held out his arms like he had the day on the fence. "This is all ours," he shouted.

"Not quite all," Thomas said. "You can see well beyond our boundary."

"Does that land belong to Gulda's family?"

"Why would you think that?"

"You said Gulda brought you and Uncle Jacob here. He knew the best country and where the water was. Does that mean it was his country first?"

Thomas frowned. He'd never thought about it like that. "The government own the country." In his mind he heard Gulda's words the day Daisy had been upset by the fence. This is her country, he'd said.

Thomas stared at the mountain range. He owned the rights to this country now. One day Gulda and Daisy would understand.

"What kind of bird is that?"

Thomas followed Joseph's pointing finger. The clouds were dark beyond the mountains and the sky merged to grey above. A tiny movement caught his eye.

"An eagle," he said. "'Wildu' is what Gulda calls them."

"Is that why you named our place Wildu Creek?" Joseph laughed and slithered down from the rock. "I always thought it was a funny way of saying 'will do'."

Thomas looked at his son in puzzlement.

"You know," Joseph said. "Like, 'this will do'."

Thomas laughed. "Well, you weren't far wrong. When I first saw this place I did think, This will do."

Joseph turned to look at the large rocks toppled beside the one he'd just stood on. "These kind of look like a cave," he said and moved through one of the gaps.

Off to Thomas's other side, in the bush, he sensed a movement. He swivelled his eyes without turning his head. It was difficult to see from that angle but it appeared that a man sat there.

"Father."

Thomas looked in his son's direction.

"Father, look at this."

A shiver ran down Thomas's spine. He couldn't resist the urge to turn back to where he thought he'd seen the man. He stared into the bush and even moved a little closer but there was no one there.

"Father." Joseph stepped out from behind a rock. "Natives have been here. There are paintings on the rocks."

"I know, son," he said. "I saw them the first time I came." He lifted his hand to his eyes and glanced towards the sun. Perhaps this was one part of his property he should leave alone. "It's time for us to go," he said. "We won't make it home before dark."

"Wait till I tell Ellen about the paintings," Joseph said. "She'll be mad she couldn't come."

Thomas put a hand on Joseph's shoulder. "Let's not tell her," he said. "I've never told your mother about the things I saw up here."

"Really?"

"I told her of the country I saw and Wildu Creek laid out before me, but not about the rocks and the paintings."

"Why?"

"I don't know," Thomas said. "It's ... it's as if I've been to someone else's house without asking."

"They're only paintings on a rock." Joseph flung his arms in the air. "Besides there's no one here to ask."

"I know." Thomas glanced at the trees beside him again.

"Come on," he said. "Time to go home."

Sixty-seven

Thomas kneeled down and felt the feeble pulse in the sheep's neck. When he had seen it lying on the ground he had thought at least he wouldn't need to slit its throat but now he would.

There were only ten sheep left alive on Wildu Creek, soon to be nine. He kept them in the yard at the shearing shed and every few days he or Joseph would ride further south to cut some blue-bush or up into the hills to find some other vegetation. They gave the sheep water from their meagre supply in the tank.

The few sheep they'd had in their northern country had been taken by natives or wild dogs. Thomas couldn't believe it had come to this. He knew he was much luckier than some. He'd sold some off early and had moved nearly three thousand sheep south to AJ's property. When the rains came he had the means to start again. If that didn't happen soon, though, he would have to take his family and join the sheep in the south.

Even Lizzie's vegetable patch was no more, although somehow the mulberry tree struggled on. Baths only happened if they made the trek up the hill to the last of the permanent waterholes and even then it was a wash in a bucket. He was very careful with that precious waterhole. The natives who camped nearby relied on it.

Gulda and Tarka had an almost daily task of clearing away dead animals.

Thomas set to his miserable duty, not made any easier by the oppressive heat of the murky grey day. He lifted the feeble animal over the fence and behind the shed where he slit the throat and let the blood drain. There wasn't much meat on the poor sheep, but it would keep them going for a while.

"I'll help you hang it."

Thomas lifted his head. Joseph had rounded the shed and found him.

"Timothy's back from Port Augusta," Joseph said. Their shepherd had gone to the port to visit his family and pick up some supplies with the money Thomas had made by cutting the wool from his dead sheep. There was little work for Timothy at Wildu Creek but he was determined to stay. Each time he went to visit his family, Thomas wondered if he would return. "Mother wants you to come inside. He's brought a letter."

"A letter?"

Thomas was puzzled. It was very rare for them to receive letters. Lizzie and her mother corresponded but they received little other mail.

Joseph helped him hang the sheep in the relative cool of the shearing shed. They walked back to the house, washing in the small basin of water they kept at the back door before they went inside.

Timothy was sitting at the table with a mug of tea.

"What news of the port?" Thomas asked.

"Not a lot. They got a bit of rain. Not as much as has been reported from Leigh Creek. They've been flooded."

"If only it would come this way," Lizzie said as she poured tea into the mugs she'd placed around the table.

"There are dark clouds beyond the hills," Joseph said. "The air feels heavy outside."

"Heavy air," Ellen said. "How can air be heavy? And those clouds have been there for weeks." She poked her tongue out at Joseph.

Thomas saw that an envelope sat in the centre of the table, propped against the sugar pot. No sooner had he sat down than Ellen whipped the letter up and thrust it into his hands.

"Open it, Father," she said.

He flapped the envelope, addressed neatly to him, against his other hand.

"It makes a better fan," he said.

"Father," Ellen groaned.

"How dull our lives have become that a letter can be the cause of such anticipation." Lizzie ran her hand across her brow. "Please open it, Thomas, before we all expire from curiosity."

Thomas took a knife from the table, slit the envelope open and drew out the paper from inside. He was curious himself to know the contents but he could not guess who had sent it. When he opened it he looked immediately to the name at the bottom, and gasped.

"What is it?"

"Who's it from?"

Ellen and Lizzie spoke at once.

"The letter is signed by a Mrs Septimus Wiltshire."

"What does she want?" Lizzie asked.

There was silence as Thomas skimmed down the page. He couldn't believe what he was reading. He put the paper on the table and looked up into the eyes of his family and Timothy, all waiting for him to speak.

"Is it bad news, Father?" Ellen asked more gently this time. "You've gone quite pale."

Thomas picked the paper up again. "Not bad news exactly," he said.

"Read it, Thomas," Lizzie urged from across the table.

Thomas took a deep breath and let it out slowly. Then he began.

"Dear Mr Baker,

I trust this finds you well in these difficult times.

I am writing to tell you the sad news of my husband's passing, although I am well aware now that he has done you several disservices in the past and you may not react unhappily to the news of his death. Septimus had been finding it difficult to make a living like so many at this time and had taken up his hawking trade again. His body was found in a dry creek bed some miles from an inn he owned in the hills across the plain from Port Augusta. His body had been in the elements for some time before he was found and the police can only assume he took ill and became disoriented. They think he died from exposure to the elements.

By the time this letter reaches you I will have left Port Augusta with my son to take up residence in Adelaide. Without Septimus to look out for us I feel we will fare better in a larger town. I have sold my house and the inn and a small farm nearby, but I do not intend to renew the lease my husband held on the property near yours called Smith's Ridge."

Lizzie gasped and Thomas looked up from the page.

"What's the matter, Mother?" Ellen asked.

"That's the man that stole Smith's Ridge from Uncle Zac and Uncle Jacob," Joseph said.

"Finish it," Lizzie said.

Thomas cleared his throat, knowing already what the next lines contained.

"I have left the paperwork with Mr Grant the commission agent in Port Augusta, whom I believe you know. It was Mr Grant who

told me where to address this letter. I want you to have the option of renewing the lease in the hope it may go some way towards righting a wrong that my husband has caused you in the past.

I don't imagine we will ever meet again. It is not my intention. Should there be some need to correspond, Mr Grant will know where to forward the letter. He also holds a box for you containing a china tea seat and some books.

I remain yours faithfully
Harriet Wiltshire."

Silence followed Thomas's folding of the letter.

It was Ellen who broke it.

"I don't understand. What wrong did the man do to you, Father?"

Lizzie held his gaze across the table. Tears brimmed in her eyes and her lip trembled. Thomas turned to his daughter.

"Mr Wiltshire did some unkind things in the past, Ellen. They are best forgotten. But Smith's Ridge was supposed to belong to your uncles. Mr Wiltshire was underhanded in the way he managed the lease, and they lost their money."

"Much more than money," Lizzie murmured.

"Does that mean Uncle Zac and Uncle Jacob will come back?" Ellen asked.

"I don't know, Ellen," Thomas said. "There's more to it than the land. They have no stock or equipment. They might not want to start again."

"Perhaps we could take up the lease," Joseph said. "Manage it for them."

Thomas looked at the anticipation on his son's face. He couldn't help the chuckle that gurgled from his throat. "You've raised an optimist, Lizzie, I'll give you that. Who else would want to take on more land in a drought?"

"Listen," Ellen said. "What's that?"

They all looked up as something made a clattering sound across the tin roof.

"It's *rain*." Joseph jumped up and poked his sister. "I told you it would rain."

The clatter was accompanied by the rumble of thunder. By the time they all got outside, rain was thrumming down beyond the verandah. They could see nothing but grey and the occasional flash of lightning.

The young ones jumped around in excitement and Thomas grabbed Lizzie and pulled her close.

"We've survived, Thomas," she said and he kissed her.

"One shower of rain isn't enough, Lizzie."

She looked at the downpour and back to Thomas and tweaked his nose. "I think it's more than a shower."

They held each other and watched as Joseph and Timothy took turns to dash out into the rain, shout at the sky and run back onto the verandah. Ellen squealed in delight as they splashed her with their wet clothes.

"You're still not smiling, Thomas," Lizzie said.

"I was pondering the letter. Mrs Wiltshire didn't mention the locket. If she was returning Mother's things, I had hoped to recover it to give to you."

Lizzie lifted her own locket from her neck. "You've already given me a locket, dearest. I don't need any more."

"You're a wonder to keep smiling through everything, Lizzie Baker."

"Why wouldn't I smile? It's raining. We can get Smith's Ridge back. Our troubles are over. We'll be back on our feet in two shakes of a lamb's tail. You'll see."

Thomas gazed into Lizzie's cornflower-blue eyes. Even after all their hardships those eyes still sparkled. "If I've learned anything from living here, Lizzie, it's that nothing is predictable. In this country we will always be at the mercy of the land."

Thomas paused and turned his head. Over the noise of the rain he heard another roar, a sound he hadn't heard in a long time.

"Watch," he said and pointed to the creek.

They all craned over the verandah as water began to flow down the dry bed and then build until it was a raging torrent carrying years of debris in its muddy waters.

He put a hand on Joseph's shoulder and pulled Lizzie close. "That's Wildu Creek," he said. "Our life blood."

"It flows through Smith's Ridge as well," Joseph said. "We're much better at managing this land than anyone else. We can improve it can't we, Father?"

Thomas looked into his son's searching gaze and remembered his own youthful enthusiasm. He wasn't an old man yet, even though he'd felt ancient of late. He tugged Joseph into his embrace.

"Together, son, the Bakers will do it together."

"And Gulda and Timothy." Ellen glared at him with her hands on her hips.

Thomas smiled. She was the image of her mother. "There will be work for everyone." He hoisted her onto his shoulders. "Including you, miss."

"I know, Father, I know," she said in a voice much older than her nine years.

Lizzie raised her eyebrows at him; her lips turned up in a smile then she leaned her head on his shoulder.

"Life will be better now, Thomas," she murmured as they looked out over the muddy waters of Wildu Creek. "We've been tested and this is our reward."

"I hope you're right, sweet Lizzie." He couldn't imagine what his life would have been without her by his side. "Whatever the future brings, we'll face it together.'

Time would tell but as Lizzie had said, they had survived this far. He looked forward to restocking, not only Wildu Creek but Smith's Ridge. He'd often thought the neighbouring property cursed. However Joseph was right: better management would improve it.

"Look at that," Ellen squealed.

A huge branch floated past as if it was nothing more than a twig. It rolled with the force of the water, rammed into the bank opposite then broke free and continued down the creek.

Thomas wondered if he wasn't so different to the log, propelled along by the forces of nature with very little power to change course.

Beside him Lizzie shivered. "It's getting cold out here. Everyone inside. We'll eat early tonight."

Thomas slid Ellen from his shoulders.

"Tomorrow everyone can have a proper bath," Lizzie said as she ushered the children and Timothy inside.

Joseph and Ellen protested.

Thomas stared at the creek a little longer. Thunder rumbled close overhead. A shiver ran down his back. He hunched his shoulders. Thank goodness they now had a stone house with a tin roof. He followed the others inside and shut the door on the storm. Tonight they could have a small celebration. Tomorrow would come soon enough.

Author's Note

The people and places in this story are all fictitious except in the case of place names and well-known or documented people of the era, such as the governor of the day, which help set the scene. The dates of real events, such as the naming of a town, may not be completely accurate; this is to permit flexibility within the story.

This is a work of fiction but it became obvious to me early in my writing that one could not tell a story about early European pastoralists and leave out any mention of indigenous Australians. My research revealed much documentation of early encounters between Aboriginal and European people. I have used this research to try to give some sense of realism to my story.

While I read widely on the life and times of the era and have tried to bring it to life with authenticity, any mistakes are my own.

Acknowledgments

This story has been a long time coming. I fell in love with the Flinders Ranges in the north of South Australia on my first visit there in 1989 and I have been going back ever since. After so much time spent exploring the beautiful yet rugged country of the region it didn't surprise me that a story would develop. What did surprise me was *Heart of the Country* was not where my tale originally began. I gave some early chapters to my husband to read and he encouraged me to write Thomas's story. So thank you Daryl, without your encouragement this tale would not have been told.

Research has played a huge part and as I love history, I lost myself in books about the early days of South Australia at the time of European settlement. The biographies and diaries were my favourites. What hardships those early settlers lived through. I spent a lot of time in libraries and I want to particularly thank the delightful Rosie at Hawker library, who pointed me in the right direction with several great books and also allowed me extensions when my reading got held up. Also heartfelt thanks to Andrew and Joy Hilder, who have a great personal local history collection and for providing accommodation and guided tours over the years.

Writing historical fiction is quite a different experience and I am grateful to Kate O'Donnell whose initial editorial skills and attention to the detail of the era were much appreciated.

Once again I am indebted to the fantastic team at Harlequin. Sue Brockhoff believed in the early manuscript, and Annabel Blay, Kylie Mason and Jo Mckay cast their clever editorial eyes over it and were so helpful in tidying things up. Alongside them there is a wonderful band who have helped me in various ways, Adam, Caroline, Louise and many more. Thank you all for embracing this new genre of writing for me.

Margie Arnold champions my books around South Australia. Margie has taken me on tour many times to meet readers and I'm so grateful for her support and encouragement.

Writing can be a solitary profession but I am thankful to the many writers I've met who have become a supportive network over the years. They're all over Australia so it's great when we can meet face to face over a coffee or a wine and share our writing highs and lows.

I am so lucky to have the backing and love of my dear family, close and extended, and wonderful friends who encourage me to follow my dream and cheer me on. My thanks and love to you all.

Here is a sneak peek of

Dust *on the* HORIZON

by

TRICIA STRINGER

AVAILABLE NOW

harlequinbooks.com.au

Prologue

1868

In the bottom of the dry creek bed, the heat pressed like a weight on the motionless figure sprawled beneath the branches of the massive red gum. The sun had burned his pale skin to red and sucked the moisture from his body. Black dots swirled in front of his eyes when he tried to sit up, but the boy was still alive. He had crawled to the shade to gain some respite from the relentless rays and to conserve his energy for one last look. There was a mouthful of precious water in the bag on his hip and he was taking a gamble. At stake was his life.

He had been following the meandering creeks through the hills for three days. Each time he thought he'd found a way through, he had been confronted by steeper, impassable hills and he had been forced to retrace his steps and take another course. The land that stretched out behind him was parched. There was little water for the few sheep that had managed to survive the blistering hot winds and evade the wild dogs.

The remaining hardy stock had become impossible to shepherd and he had given up all hope of saving any of them when, somehow, they'd ended up higher into the ranges than he'd been before. He'd been about to turn back and leave the sheep altogether when he'd found a small waterhole that hadn't dried up and his spirits had lifted.

Then, in the late afternoon, he had seen several kangaroos and a flock of screeching birds. They had to be getting water nearby. He'd left his horse to try to climb a rocky outcrop for a better view of his surroundings. A startled kangaroo had bounded away and scared his untethered horse off, with his swag, food and extra water tied to its saddle. All he had was his water flask. He'd fallen to the ground in despair, thinking it was the end. Just in front of him something sparkled. His hand curled around the rock and his eyes closed.

The sun lowered in the sky as he gathered his strength for one last attempt. He would probably never be found anyway. If he was going to die he wanted to do it looking out over this ruthless land he'd been born in and loved. He staggered to his feet and drained the last precious drop of water into his parched mouth.

Ahead of him the tall sides of the narrow gorge glowed red. The creek bed in front of him was choked with old gums, young saplings and an assortment of timber debris, washed there in some previous time of flowing water. Above him a flock of screeching birds flew in and disappeared inside the gorge.

The boy stumbled on towards the impeding bush. He clasped the rock in one hand and rubbed at his eyes with the other. The black dots still swirled in front of him. He peered closer. There was a gap, a path though the saplings. He pushed on through the overhanging leaves and his tattered boots sunk into the ground. Cold registered in his seared brain. He looked down. Damp grit encased his boots. Several sets of animal tracks indented the sand.

Up ahead he glimpsed a glint but he didn't dare hope. He sucked in a feeble breath and, with a final push, surged forward.

Beneath his feet the soft sand gave way and he fell headfirst into the pool. The flock of large white birds rose from the surrounding trees screaming their protest.

On the ridge above, a shadow moved and took the shape of a man. Binda had been motionless for some time. And even though he no longer feared the figure sprawled below him, the young Aborigine had thought it best to be cautious.

Hunting alone, Binda had been terrified the day before when a huge four-legged animal had crashed through the trees like a wild monster. Once the bush around him had settled, Binda had resumed his hunt for kangaroo, only to be startled again by strange footsteps crunching on the ridge above him. Binda had followed the young white boy ever since, watching him become more and more helpless. Stories were told around the campfire about the pale-skinned men who trampled the bush and spoiled food and water with their animals and the large loads they carried but Binda had never seen one until now.

He took small silent steps down the ridge. Now that life had finally left the intruder, Binda couldn't walk away. He was curious to get a better look and he knew if he didn't move the body the rotting flesh would spoil the waterhole.

The setting sun glowed on his glossy skin as he made his way down the ridge. Once he was in the creek bed he knew he could blend with ease into the shadows if he needed to but he was no longer afraid. Binda was thinking about the elaborate story he would have to tell around the campfire. He would be able to describe in great detail what a white man looked like. He pushed through the last clinging branches at the side of the waterhole and froze. His eyes opened wide in surprise and then fear surged once again through his veins. At the edge of the pool, the sand showed the signs of the intruder but the body was gone.

talk about it

Let's talk about books.

Join the conversation:

 on facebook.com/harlequinaustralia

 on Twitter @harlequinaus

www.harlequinbooks.com.au

If you love reading and want to know about our
authors and titles, then let's talk about it.